A ROBERT CURTIS MYSTERY

FOR GOD AND KING

THE DEADLY PAMPHLETEER

David Martyn

BLUE FORGE PRESS
Port Orchard, Washington

Blue Forge Press is the print division of the volunteer-run, federal 501(c)3 nonprofit company, Blue Legacy, founded in 1989 and dedicated to bringing light to the shadows and voice to the silence. We strive to empower storytellers across all walks of life with our four divisions: Blue Forge Press, Blue Forge Films, Blue Forge Gaming, and Blue Forge Records. Find out more at www.MyBlueLegacy.com

Blue Forge Press
7419 Ebbert Drive Southeast
Port Orchard, Washington 98367
blueforgepress@gmail.com
360-550-2071 ph.txt

dedicated to
Vincent Martyn

"When God wants to judge a nation, he gives them wicked rulers."

—John Calvin

Acknowledgments

I thank my fellow writer, Pauli Pedersen, whose skill with language and discerning review makes me a better writer. I also thank Brianne DiMarco for her patient editing and creative cover designs. The creative force behind Blue Forge Press is Jennifer DiMarco, whose support and encouragement keep me writing.

ALSO BY DAVID MARTYN

THE HALL OF FAITH

The Praise Singer:
A Disciple of Melchizedek

The Oak of Weeping:
The Story of Isaac, Rebekah, and Deborah

The Epistle:
A Story of the Early Church

ROBERT CURTIS MYSTERIES

Called Into Service
Soldiers of the King: The Bramshill Affair
Lords and Ladies: The Banqueting House Plot
For God and King: The Deadly Pamphleteer

NOVELLAS &
SHORT STORY COLLECTIONS

Huldah and the Last Righteous King
A Light in the Darkest Night

www.BlueForgePress.com

FOR GOD AND KING

THE DEADLY PAMPHLETEER

David Martyn

CHAPTER 1
THE HULL TO BARTON FERRY

The waning moon crept on cat's paws, prowling and pouncing behind cloud after cloud as it silently stalked the travelers below. The night air was cool and restful after the warm early spring day. Unnoticed lullabies of peaceful night sounds hummed sweetly in meters measured by the steady cadence of horse hooves on a packed dirt road. Nature's evensong was interrupted by a soft voice, little more than a whisper that trailed off and succumbed to the still darkness of deep woods encompassing them. The voice of Robert Curtis, the Earl of Montclair, carried across the darkness to his companion and friend, Mister Black, riding silently beside him. "What kind of man floods the land with a pamphlet that promises a reward for killing the King? Why it would bring down both crown and church in civil war!"

Ever methodical and analytical, Mister Black

replied, "You ask, man? Cannot a woman be as determined? We surmise it is someone seeking revenge or gain—a coward hiding behind anonymity."

"A coward for certain, but one with wealth, resources, and ability. The treasonous reward is posted everywhere 'Security and income for life to the family of the successful patriot.' Patriot? He calls an assassin a patriot?"

Black answered. "Many are tempted to take the offer. Only a few families close to King Charles are not outraged by his contempt for parliament, disdain for his subjects, and his burdensome new taxes."

"Yes. Someone of wealth and influence. But as for a woman, England has no ruthless Marie de Medici, Queen Mother to King Louis. No, not since Mary Tudor of Scotland. I know of but two great women of influence with motive. Lady Frances Howard, now working hard to recover what she has lost in reputation, and Lady Eleanor, my wife, once confidante to Queen Henrietta Maria, most rudely dismissed. And she is now happily at home with our children. No, it is a man or men we seek."

Black concurred, "Likely it is so, but with such great anger, I rule out no one. Motive—"

Robert cut him off, his voice now urgent. "Motive? We all have motives! First, there is widespread hatred fostered by new taxes. I am troubled that it is the commoner whom the King hurts most. Good people, displaced from the land by enclosure. Families who farmed on the royal forests for generations–good tenants they were. They paid their rent and shared the harvest with the King. Now chased off with nothing. And craftsmen–the smith, the cooper, the miller, and the harness maker–all of them chased off from their homes. Their gardens and rich fields are given over to the King's sheep—worse, torn open for new mines. His Majesty looks for new wealth everywhere. The unfair Ship Tax, of old, only from the port cities to fund a navy for protection against piracy. It is now applied in every market town. Merchants have no choice but to pass the tax on to the most burdened. And now the King sells most of his grain and wool on the starving continent—starving from war! Our king profits on misery! The marches in protest, even riots, over food—grain prices doubled and tripled above the past year. Hunger and desperation of these times try the loyalty of good people ignored by our King. And here we are bound to…."

Robert's voice trailed off to silence.

Black felt his friend's frustration. "You struggle with the injustice of our duty. Is it not right to prevent murder? Perhaps the King will listen to wise counsel. Perhaps the men we stop will find mercy with justice. Perhaps their families will not be dishonored. God is their true judge. Perhaps their very souls will find grace and everlasting peace."

The dim light of a lantern appeared in the distance, and the soft night breeze carrying the smell of the Humber's brackish water alerted them. Robert whispered, "Dismount. We will walk from here."

Both men dismounted and led their horses off the road and tied them to a tree. Three men following behind silently did the same.

Black instructed his men. "Wait here." He turned to Robert and whispered, "Do we take their man now or wait for the boat?"

Robert crept slowly towards the lantern. When he could make out the man seated on the end of a crude pier jutting into the Humber estuary, he stopped, turned away from the light, and whispered to Black. "I have some time before I must return to Kingston-upon-Hull. Let's be certain no signal is missed. We wait for their boat."

Fifteen minutes later, a dim light could be seen on the water in the direction of Barton. Soon after, the white sails of a boat or ship reflected the light of a swinging lantern. The man on the pier stood up and swung his lantern in reply.

Robert studied the ship as it approached. It was a small ketch, maybe fifty feet long. The mainsail was gaff-rigged; the mizzen mast carried a small lugsail, still furled. A long bowsprit carried two small jibs. The tidy little ship was decked over fore and aft, and a small boat hung over its transom.

The small sailing ship doused its light, but the mainsail was still visible in the pale moonlight. The boat lowered its last sail, swung its bow into the wind, and slowly and silently came alongside the rough-hewn planks of the pier. Lines were passed to the man on the dock, and he wordlessly tied the ship to trees along the bank.

Robert whispered, "A dogger—small fishing boat—but certainly capable of a sea crossing. I count three in the crew."

Black replied softly, "Aye, three and the man on the pier."

"We'll move in close, but let them settle in. Perhaps we'll hear something of use. If only we knew if there is to be a signal."

Black whispered his reply, "There will be a guard watching the pier."

After ten minutes, not a sound came from the boat, but a man sat on the gunwale, his feet on the pier. Robert turned away from the boat and whispered, "They've settled in. No use waiting any longer. Take the boat."

Black nodded, and both carefully made their way back to their men. Black told the men what to expect and gave his orders.

Robert untied his horse. "Black, I leave you to your

work. I must return to Kingston-upon-Hull and join the King's entourage. I pray all goes well, but be prepared for treachery. Godspeed, my friend."

Robert mounted his horse. "A red pennant."

"Aye. Red pennant," Black replied, and Robert rode into the still ebony night.

A mile north, Robert rode through the village of Hessle, its good citizens still asleep, and took the road to the right towards Kingston-upon-Hull. The sun was well up when Robert crossed the bridge in Kingston and arrived at the ferry dock. Robert boarded the ferry with his horse and waited another hour before the royal carriages arrived. The curtains in the King's coach remained closed as it rolled onto the ferry, and the wheels chocked against movement. The coachman tended the horses on foot, calming them and holding the reins. Few words were spoken as the ferry's crew went about their work. Only the captain spoke, giving crisp orders as he directed the loading. The three ferrymen slipped the mooring lines and raised sail. Soon the ferry, little more than a wide sailing barge, was making its way out the Hull River into the wide Humber.

The captain set a course southwest for Barton-upon-Humber, and the crew secured the sheets. The ferry settled on a slight starboard list as she came to an easy motion with the wind on the port quarter. The royal party remained in their coaches, content to chat softly among themselves. Robert walked to the windward side and scanned the horizon. He watched the distant sails for several minutes and was satisfied that none was approaching the ferry. Robert made his way to the leeward rail. His eyes soon focused on familiar sails. A small fishing ketch was close-hauled on a starboard tack. Unless the boat tacked, the two would cross far apart. Robert watched and waited. If it was the dogger he ordered Black to seize, it would need to tack soon if the two craft were to meet. Robert stood and watched. A few moments later, the ketch tacked, and the two small ships were closing. They would meet well offshore in the middle of the wide Humber.

Robert smiled at a ferryman that walked by. "Fine day! Seems a different land when viewed from the water," Robert said as he scanned the western horizon. *Where is that blasted red pennant? I should be able to see it by now.* Robert kept his thoughts private.

Robert noticed another crewman standing near the King's Coach. Robert smiled at him, then walked around the other side, slapped the door, and called out, "Not too much longer, your Majesty." Confident he was out of sight, he opened the door and slipped inside. He said nothing to the occupants, sat down, and slid to the other side of the coach. He pulled out his pistol and slid the curtain just enough to glance at the ketch-rigged dogger now closing. *Still no red pennant!* One more glance towards the loitering ferryman, and Robert waited.

Seated in the coach, Robert could feel the ferry's list abruptly end, and the inertia of a change in course made him slide in his seat. He heard the luff of the sails as they spilled their wind. The ferry had turned into the wind and come to a stop. Robert slipped the curtain enough to see the dogger coming alongside. As the dogger's mainsail was luffing, Robert saw a red pennant caught in the gaff spar throat at the mainmast.

A slap on the side of the coach caught him by surprise. "A change in plans, your Majesty. You'll be leaving us here." The door opened, and Robert aimed his pistol at the surprised ferryman.

"Drop your weapon if you wish to live," Robert replied.

The would-be assassin stood stunned and silent. The ferryman's eyes widened as he felt another pistol against the back of his head. "Well, do you wish to die here or pray for mercy?" One of the coachmen spoke as he took the man's pistol.

Two palace guards, pistols at the ready, jumped from the coach. "The captain?" Robert called to another coachman and guard. Two more jumped from the second coach.

A guard was now at the helm. He reported, "The Captain came under gunpoint of a crewman as the fishing boat came near. Claims not to be a part of it."

"I want all three ferrymen bound. Tell all the passengers they are safe but must remain in their coach. We will be on our way soon."

Robert stepped out on the deck and waved to Mister Black on the deck of the dogger. "No problems taking the boat, but your crew—you couldn't raise the pennant without fouling it? If it doesn't try their seamanship, follow us to Barton-upon-Humber."

Black glanced up at the pennant. "It's there—a red pennant as ordered."

Robert shook his head. "Mister Black, is that an attempt at humor? Tell me about your prisoners."

"All four bound and held below. Hired in Shetland–Shetland! Do you believe it? Our man gets around."

"See what you can learn from them before they are sent to the tower. Men will say anything facing the rack. Now, we must get across the Humber."

Robert handled the sails as the captain turned the ferry towards Barton. With the sails set, Robert questioned each of the prisoners. The small dogger followed obediently, and not an hour later, both boats moored at the Barton-upon-Humber ferry dock. The royal coaches were carefully rolled ashore. Black took charge of the prisoners, and Robert ordered the sheriff to hold the seized dogger as crown property. As the small fishing boat was being moved, one of Black's men came to Robert and said, "A word, my Lord."

Robert nodded. "I will always hear from my men. Speak freely."

The man lowered his eyes. "It was my fault. I fouled the pennant. I started to drop the gaff to free it, but Mister Black stopped me. If we lowered the sail, we risked being too late to intercept the ferry. Mister Black took the blame for my mistake."

Robert smiled. "Mister Black knows you to be a good and trusted man. He did right to say nothing. You did well. Tell the others they—we all did well, very well indeed. But allow me some fun at his expense."

Once everything was secure, Robert climbed into the King's coach, called to Black, and said, "Find lodgings at the inn. Stay with the men. I will send word. I'm off to Tyrwhitt Hall. And Black, don't forget my red pennant."

Tyrwhitt Hall, home of the wealthy Philip, Baron Tyrwhitt, was a short carriage ride from the Barton ferry dock. The Royal baggage coaches were lined up beside the house. Viscount Conway, President of the Privy Council, received Robert. "Is all well, Lord Inquirer? His Majesty wishes to hear your report himself."

Robert replied, "The information we received was accurate. We captured three aboard the ferry and four more aboard a fishing boat meant to make their escape. We seized the boat in His Majesty's name."

Robert paused. "Does Lord Weston still travel with the King?"

Conway replied, "Yes, the Lord High Treasurer is with His Majesty now."

Robert replied, "He will want to hear my report as well."

Robert was led into a room where King Charles was seated at a table, his hands tearing the leg from a roasted game bird. Robert bowed and waited to be acknowledged. After a large bite, the King set down the fowl and took a long drink of wine. He belched and placed the goblet in front of him. Looking up, King Charles wiped his mouth with a napkin in his cuff sleeve before speaking. "Lord Inquirer, it is good for you that you have found success. I will not be humiliated again–traveling with the baggage. Most indignant. Now tell me all."

Robert straightened up. "My most sincere apologies, your Majesty, but the information proved true, and our ruse worked perfectly. Three would-be assassins on the ferry and four men on an escape boat were captured. The fishing boat, a dogger from Shetland, has been seized. We have learned the rogues' names and will question them thoroughly, but I doubt they know the man behind the treasonous plot. Your Majesty, we have watchers and secret men going before us searching out plots. Now is not a good time for travel. Give my men time to…."

King Charles interrupted, "Not a good time for travel? Not a good time? Am I to hide in a castle while you lumber about the countryside? No! If need be, I will send for more guards–perhaps a new Lord Inquirer who assures my safety."

Viscount Conway spoke up. "If I may, your Majesty, the Earl of Montclair has found success. He is both trustworthy and capable."

The King reached for the bird. "Yes, there is that. But I will suffer no more humiliation in my travels. Is there anything else, Montclair?"

Robert bowed. "Yes, Your Majesty, I questioned their leader on the ferry and will do so again in depth. I am confident of his motive. He is a merchant, a grain dealer, from Kingston-upon-Hull. He confesses he was driven mad by bankruptcy and was facing debtor's prison. He borrowed to pay the penalty for distraint of knighthood and then could not raise a loan to pay the higher price of grain. He said he was lost to his family already. Perhaps he could provide for them with the promised reward."

The King did not look up. "I am not moved. What

about me? Shall I starve? I cannot rule without money. Parliament grants me nothing. The traitor's bankruptcy is on his own head. He owed the penalty, and the loans were his business."

Lord Weston, Baron of Nayland, had been listening. "Your Majesty, have I not told you the Hull Company of Kingston is all men of no account? Sir Henry Constable and his confederates fail you, my King! They protest paying the ship tax with claims of an exemption–contributions to finish a city wall. An exemption they have claimed for years, and yet the wall is not built. You are right to demand the full amount. And now, with this insult, they shall be required even more."

Viscount Conway spoke, "If you have nothing further to report, Lord Montclair...."

King Charles said, "Yes. If that is all, you may take your leave."

Robert bowed. "Thank you, Your Majesty. I offer only this. Guard your travel plans well. Please, your Majesty, no word to the courtiers beforehand."

Robert bowed and began to back out of the room.

The King laughed. "No word to my courtiers beforehand? Is such a thing even possible? Good day, Lord Inquirer!"

The Black Bull Inn was busy with travelers and locals alike. Robert found Mister Black at a table with his men. Black stood when Robert approached. "I would not wait long to eat, Lord Robert. The inn is filled, and the food is becoming less in portion and taste."

Robert smiled. "Then, by all means, something to fill an empty stomach after a long day."

Black turned to one of the men. "Ask the innkeeper for the game bird and stew I had him set aside."

Robert nodded. "I would say something to you all—Splendid work! I can imagine no finer men in England. Now, where is my blasted red pennant? From hereafter, when I raise the red pennant, the ale is on me!"

Black called out, "You heard the Lord Inquirer, more ale!" Black stood and waved the pennant.

After a round of huzzahs, Robert said to Black, "I would speak with the prisoners. I will start with the leader, Tom Gibbs."

Black replied, "Finish your supper. I will take you to them."

CHAPTER 2
BARTON-UPON-HUMBER

Black escorted Robert to the gaol and brought him to Thomas Gibbs, shackled to the stone wall. Gibbs looked up and said, "My Lord, what is to become of me?"

Robert answered, "You will be taken to the prison at Lincoln Castle." Robert pulled a chair from outside the cell and sat down.

"Tell me about your family, Tom. Kingston-upon-Hull, is it?"

Tom began to cry. "Aye, a good wife and six children. Our eldest, James, very clever, was bound for Cambridge. Four daughters and two sons. I did it for them. Everything for them. Worked hard, Missus Gibbs and I, to make a good life for them. And we did well. Our best dreams were in sight. But–but it all fell apart so quickly. First, the distraint of knighthood penalty–more than we earned in a good year, and that due in full. And then the grain scare. Truth is, I ran from the sheriff. I was bound for debtor's prison. They took our house! We have nothing. How would they repay my debt?"

Robert asked, "Where are they now?"

"My wife's brother has a mill in Cottingham. They work for their keep. But he cannot feed them for long. He, too, is in debt, just hanging on."

Robert replied, "I shall send word to them. Tell me about your plan. Who helped you?"

"Lord Montclair, do you think he, the man behind the pamphlets, may do something for my wife, my family? I tried to do his bidding. If he pays my wife, it will be a strong signal for others to take up his cause."

"Listen to me, Tom. Any money the traitor might send to your wife would only make her a traitor as well. Do you want the same fate for her? Where could she run? For run, she must. The first coin she spends would make her an outlaw. No, Tom, you did the bidding of a coward for no reward. Perhaps I can help you, but you must tell me all you know."

Gibbs buried his face in his hands and sobbed. "There is no hope. Even God has abandoned me."

"No, Tom, God will never leave you or abandon you. You can never lose hope in Him. I said I could help your family. My estate, Montclair, here in Lincolnshire, we have work, and there is a school. If your lad is as clever as you say, he may apprentice with a craftsman or perhaps the Land Steward. I have sent more than one son of a tenant or craftsman to Cambridge."

"You would do that?"

"It is a command to love each other as Christ loves us. Is it not like our Savior to seek and to save the lost?"

Tom sniffled and looked up. "I heard two men talking about the reward at the ferry dock pub. I joined them and read a pamphlet. They said hundreds of pamphlets were left in Kingston. I asked them if they were serious. Both said they would do the job with pleasure but wondered how they could get close to the King. I knew the King was coming. As a member of the Hull Company, I knew he would stay at Burton Constable Hall and then travel to Lincoln on his tax audit. Well, the ferry is the fastest way to Lincoln."

Robert asked, "So the two deckhands arranged for you to be on board when the Royal Coach made the crossing."

"They paid the third deckhand, a young lad, to feign an illness."

Robert asked, "The escape on the dogger?"

Tom sighed. "I dealt with Captain Haakon Anderson before. He smuggles whiskey from Scotland. That's what led to my ruin. I was determined to build a still and make whisky here. Borrowed to build it, then could not afford both the tax and the high grain prices. The little whiskey I made is too young to bring a fair price."

"Tom, did Captain Anderson know of your plan to kill the King?"

Tom looked up. "No. I told him I was running from the sheriff with two other men. I was wantin' to stay out of debtor's prison and was charged with smuggling. I said I had some money hidden, not enough to pay my debts but with money from the three of us, enough for him to make a good profit."

Robert nodded. "And you told him they were deckhands and could best make an escape in a seaway. Tom. For your sake, you better be telling the truth. I will get to the truth. You had no money. What did you plan to tell Captain Anderson when he rescued you?"

"I planned to tell him the truth and offer him an equal share of the reward. The poster said all the successful patriots would be rewarded."

Tom paused. "Lord Montclair, will I hang?"

Robert looked into the frightened man's eyes. "Pray for it. The alternative is far worse."

Robert stood up and looked down at Tom. Robert bowed, placed a hand on Tom's shoulder, and said, "I would like to pray for you."

Tom, sobbing again, nodded. Robert prayed, "Most

Merciful Father grant this repentant sinner peace. Strengthen his hope in the resurrection of life to come. Bless, shield, and protect his family and comfort them in their time of trial. Through Jesus Christ our Lord, who lives and reigns with you, in the unity of the Holy Spirit, one God, forever and ever. Amen."

Robert squeezed Tom's shoulder and silently walked out.

Mister Black was waiting outside the cell. Robert asked, "Who is next?"

"This way. Is it your mission, now, to take in the families of all you arrest for treason? If you provide the lifetime of reward the posters promise, perhaps you will be identified as the traitor."

Robert did not face Black. His eyes looked straight ahead in the dim light of the gaol. "Says the man whose wife turns down no prostitute who comes to the door of their home called 'Gomer's House.' A house named for the prostitute wife of the prophet Haggai."

Black replied, "A woman who found God's love and redemption."

Black sighed and continued. "My friend, I know your heart's desire is to live as a priest and honor the Holy Orders you vowed. But no man can…."

Robert stopped and turned to Black. "We can—we must provide for the widow, the orphan, the prisoner. It is a command of our Lord. Can you and I do it alone? No, of course not. But we can act when we are confronted. The man has repented. Should his family suffer for his sin? I do not absolve him from accounting for his actions, for that is what the law demands. I know neither you nor Lady Justine, your courageous wife, would wish Mister Gibbs' wife or daughters to crawl in disgrace to the door of Gomer's House."

Black gazed into Robert's face for a moment and said, "The deckhands have no families. Simple greed. I doubt you will find repentance from them."

"Even so, after we question them, I will share with them God's love."

Black stopped in front of a cell. "Haakon Anderson, Captain of the escape boat. We found a pamphlet hidden among his belongings."

"Come in with me. We shall hear what he has to say. I will let you begin the questioning."

Haakon Anderson was not shackled to the wall. He was free to pace about in his small three-foot by six-foot cell. Mister Black entered first, and Robert stood by the door. "Tell me, Captain, just when did you and Thomas Gibbs first plan to kill His Majesty, King Charles?"

"I had nothing to do with that. Murder the King? And have half of England chasin' after me? I would have no part of that. Why would I? These are good times for a man in my business."

"And what is your business, Captain Anderson? I know it is not fishing."

Anderson sighed and rubbed his forehead. "I am a fisherman, or was, but I found trading more profitable. At first, I tried selling my fish in other ports–away from the fishing fleets. It's a good little boat. She can get in close most anywhere. Offers came my way. They were good offers too. But I have no reason to harm His Majesty."

Black replied. "You're a smuggler. Tell me about your business with Thomas Gibbs."

Anderson took a deep breath, rolled his head back, and closed his eyes before turning to face Black. "Been doin' business with Tom Gibbs for a couple of years. Traded good Scotch whiskey for cash and his grain."

"You weren't trading Scotch and grain yesterday."

"No. Tom got greedy. 'Wanted to make whiskey here. He came home with me to Islay Island in the Shetlands—wanted to learn whiskey makin' from the Shetlanders. Tom started up all right but went broke. I found another buyer in Kingston. I wasn't about to give up my business there. Tom, knowin' my boat, sent a man sayin' ol' Tom's on the run. He would pay handsomely for passage for him and two others–they bein' escaped prisoners also on the run. Now I wanted to help ol' Tom, he bein' a good customer."

Black continued, "So you agree to pick up Tom from the ferry. You wait at the pier near Hessle. The pier you and Tom used to smuggle."

Anderson nodded. "Seemed strange that Tom said it had to be from the ferry. He couldn't get to the pier. Said they were holed up in a warehouse and could only slip onto the ferry."

Anderson pleaded, "I done nothing against the King. Can I get my boat and go home? I promise I won't be returnin' or dealin' with Tom Gibbs."

Black ignored the question. "There is one problem with your story." Black pulled out a pamphlet from his coat pocket. "This pamphlet was found in your belongings aboard your boat. It calls for the murder of His Majesty. It is the same pamphlet turning up all through Kingston, Barton, and much of England. What was your portion of the reward, Captain Anderson?"

Haakon sat on the crude bed. "That was cargo. True, I kept one; foolish, I know. Curiosity–someone is very determined to see the king murdered and not carin' who does the evil deed or how. Wondered if someone would take the offer. I mean, there are many who would see the king dead. But not me. Sure, I have no love for King Charles. But risk my life to murder him? No."

Black asked, "You say it was cargo. Whose cargo? From where?"

"Where? Cadzand. Who? I don't know. Most don't say, and I don't ask."

Robert stepped into the room. "Cadzand? The Netherlands? Many a French Huguenot made their escape from Cadzand. Did you bring back passengers?"

"Nay, not that time. Cadzanders move goods to and from Antwerp and Bruges. Goods that the Hapsburgs do not permit–without approval and payment–into the Spanish Netherlands. My dogger is a small boat. If I were to pay duties and customs, I would not make a profit. I took my Scotch ashore and expected perhaps passengers, as you mentioned, fine embroidery, tapestries, fabrics, or even porcelain. But pamphlets? A first time for everything, no reason to turn down a good payin' cargo."

Robert replied, "Tell me about this cargo. Who arranged it? Delivered it? I want to know everything you saw or learned."

"Aye. Two men. A local–did all the talking, and another. Never looked me in the eye. Heavy cloak for the weather. Kept his eyes down. But he was an Englishman, no doubt about it. Whispered in English to the local–man I've traded with. He knew what I was sayin' and his boots, English. What the destination bein' in England and the pamphlets and all, no doubt he was an English gentleman."

Robert replied, "Names. The name of your Dutch

contact and his gentleman friend."

"Now, my Lord, I can't be givin' any names. Just not done in my trade."

Robert shook his head. "Captain Anderson, you can answer all that I ask, and perhaps you will be permitted to buy back your ship, or Mister Black will take you to the Tower of London, where the questioning will likely be painful and followed by your hanging."

"Johannes De Vries. Ask for him in Cadzand. Everyone knows him. In truth, I do not know the Englishman. Buyback, my Lord? You aim on keepin' my boat?"

"You are complicit in an attempt on the life of King Charles. Islay is your home. Even if I release you, there is nowhere you can run. I will find you. You will do as I say. Mister Back will explain all that we require. In return, I will overlook your smuggling, and I will report you ignorant of the plot. You will pay a fine to the crown, and the boat will be returned. But you and your dogger will be available to us. Do I have your word?"

"Aye. I give my word."

"Good day, Captain Anderson."

Robert and Black left the cell and closed the door behind them. Anderson shouted, "I'm not being released?"

Black turned and said, "In good time, Captain, all in good time and order."

Outside the goal, Black said, "Better follow the trail before it goes cold."

Robert nodded. "I think Captain Anderson's first duty will be to carry you and three men to Cadzand. Meet this Johannes De Vries. We'll need watchers in Antwerp. Use Karl Schroeder's network to report. I'll send the fine and release order for Anderson and the dogger to you at the inn tomorrow morning. I must travel with the King to Lincoln. No telling what snakes will crawl out from under its old stones."

Black asked, "If Anderson doesn't have the money to buy back the ship?"

"Lend it to him. We can always sell it for repayment."

CHAPTER 3

THE LORD LIEUTENANT
OF LINCOLNSHIRE

Viscount Conway was working alone in a room across from King Charles' apartment. Robert was admitted and waited while the King's Privy Councilor sat writing by the light of a single candle. Without looking up, Lord Conway said softly, "I have much more to do this night, Lord Inquirer, can you be brief?"

"Yes, Lord Conway. I have confessions from the guilty. They will be brought to Lincoln Castle. I ask for mercy regarding their execution–that they are hanged, not hanged, drawn, and quartered. Their leader is most repentant and has cooperated. I ask that it be noted that His Majesty was in no time in actual danger, and I have doubts Mister Gibbs dared to follow through on his plot.

He had the opportunity to take my life, though his life would have been immediately taken. As for the deckhands...."

Lord Conway sighed. "No need to explain. Hanging will send the message. And the fishermen?"

"Mister Gibbs swears, and his word agrees with Captain Anderson, that neither Anderson nor his crew was aware of the plot. They believed they were abetting the escape of Gibbs and two others running from the sheriff and debtor's prison. I believe it is in His Majesty's interest that Captain Anderson be released and required to pay the market value of his boat."

Conway looked up. "Release him? The man was abetting the escape of fugitives."

"Captain Anderson has skills I can use. He shall pay for his mistake–and I have seen no warrant for him or Tom Gibbs for his debt. The full value of his fishing boat will be paid to the King's Treasury. I would like orders for his release and the release of his vessel, by my receipt for the purchase price. I intend to carry them back in the morning."

"Montclair, I have many documents to prepare for His Majesty's signature."

"I intend for Captain Anderson to take my men to Cadzand in Holland in the morning. He has agreed to cooperate–to take us to the man who arranged the shipment of the pamphlets that flood England promising the reward for the King's murder."

Conway put down his quill and straightened up. "Just what has Captain Anderson told you?"

"A Smuggler in Flanders, a Dutchman, Johannes De Vries, and an English gentleman paid for pamphlets to be brought to Kingston-upon-Hull. He will take Mister Black there before the trail grows cold."

Lord Conway stared beyond Robert for a moment, then looked Robert in the eye and said, "I will have the documents you request signed before His Majesty departs in the morning. And Lord Montclair, you will keep me informed. The better informed I am, the more I can support your inquiries and your efforts to protect the King and perhaps persuade him to take caution."

"As you will, Lord Conway." And Robert turned to leave.

"Lord Montclair," Conway called out. "Your report for Lincoln?"

Robert turned. "My watchers have uncovered nothing in Lincoln, but…."

"Yes, caution. Good night, Sir Robert."

Before the sun reached its Zenith, the small dogger was underway carrying Mister Black and three of his best men towards the Netherlands. Robert ordered Thomas Gibbs and the two deckhands transferred to Lincoln castle.

He brought their death warrants in his pouch. As Tom in his cell bound for travel, he asked Robert, "Am I to be hanged?"

Robert nodded. "It will be quick."

"And my family?"

"I have sent word. Do you ask them to witness your death?"

"I beg to see them before I go, but I leave it for my wife to decide if it is at my execution. I am told you were a priest. Will you pray for me, Lord Montclair? And hear my confession? Will you walk me to my execution–as my priest? I am permitted a priest, am I not?"

Robert felt his shoulders slump. His chest fell under a great sigh. *I sought his death warrant, and now I am asked to be his priest and intercessor?* Robert's voice rang in his ears as if from another. "I will make your request known to the bishop. I do not know–I promise nothing. I will do what I can. But pray for you? Oh yes, I shall pray, and I shall honor my promised offer to your wife and children."

Robert joined the lords and holders of royal prerogatives in Lincolnshire gathered at Lincoln Castle to pay homage to the King. They were to answer the king's Treasurer on the collections of royal taxes. The lords of Lincolnshire were led and represented by the Earl of Lindsey, newly appointed Lord Lieutenant of Lincolnshire. Once all the lords and leading men were gathered and stood in order of peerage around the great hall, two royal guards stepped into the room and slammed the staffs of their halberds on the stone floor. A third royal guard announced, "His Majesty, King Charles, King of England, Ireland, and Scotland."

King Charles entered the room, followed by Lord Conway and Lord Weston, Lord High Treasurer. Charles sat in a massive carved wooden chair, his two advisors beside him. The room fell silent. The sound of a single cough echoed through the chamber. At last, Charles said, "Lindsey, when I appointed you Lord Lieutenant, I expected better of you. You did well on the battlefield in service to my sister, Elizabeth of Bohemia. I expected the same resourcefulness, determination, and favorable results in your service to me in Lincolnshire. Do you not know we are in a battle? A battle to rebuild my kingdom after years of war? Do I alone see the need? I am burdened by debt. The treasury, Lindsey, the treasury! Your duty is to fill the treasury. I have lately traveled from Yorkshire, and I was appalled by their parsimonious contribution to the treasury. The misguided, nay, disloyal redirection of royal—of my funds, to their own pursuits. Unnecessary fortifications! Schemes! Yes, schemes to keep what should be mine. And now what do we find in wealthy Lincolnshire, Lord Lieutenant? Lincolnshire, blessed by God above with fertile fields, abundant crops, and prosperous manors? More schemes! A smaller collection! Lord Weston tells me wealthy Lincolnshire's royal tax collections have fallen! Fallen from unacceptable to what can only be theft! Yes, theft, Lord Lieutenant, you abet in the theft from the treasury of your King. What do you say for yourself, man?"

Robert Bertie, Earl of Lindsey, stepped forward and bowed before the King. "Your Majesty, as your loyal Lord Lieutenant, I speak for all the lords and great men of Lincolnshire when I say how honored we are by your visit. As your most loyal subjects, we are wounded, cut to the quick. Let it never be said that the Lords of Lincolnshire would withhold our liege, our wealth, our very lives in service from our King. All owed has been collected, though some has been set aside for...."

King Charles interrupted. "Has all been collected? It is reported some leading men, friends, I am told, of yours, Lord Lieutenant, have not paid the penalty for distraint of knighthood."

"It was thought, your Majesty, the men in question, should be knighted as officers in the regiment of footmen I am raising on your behalf–under my duties as Lord Lieutenant. Rather than a penalty, these officers would provide horses, weapons, and equipment for your regiment as the law intended."

"A regiment? Footmen, you say? I have made peace

with our enemies. I gave no warrant for you to raise a regiment. I require knighthood of every man with forty pounds! They will pay the penalty due. But as for your regiment, Lindsey, I shall grant your warrant. You will recruit and fill it with men of Lincolnshire out of the wealth of your estates. But Lord Weston reports other shortages–from the ship tax."

"Not shortages, your Majesty, just taxes collected but set aside. Majesty, there is the opportunity to increase trade, exports of grain, food, and goods to the continent. Greater exports will mean more revenue for the royal treasury. Grimsby in the north but more urgently, Boston harbor, has silted. And the rivers can be made navigable far inland. Bountiful Lincolnshire can bring wealth to England. Your Majesty, what is good for Lincolnshire is good for England!"

Charles shouted, "No! You have it backward, Lindsey. What is good for England is good for Lincolnshire. I am England–England, Ireland, and Scotland! The taxes are mine. I determine the priorities. You see opportunity. Good. Pursue it on your own. The wealth you foresee could be yours. Let the investment be yours as well."

Lord Lindsey bowed and said, "Yes, my King. It shall be as you say."

The Treasurer, Lord Weston, whispered in the

King's ear. King Charles looked up and said, "Lord Lindsey, I am told your estates are the largest and wealthiest in the shire. You have more tenants, fields, sheep, and cattle than any lord. Yet another lord in Lincolnshire pays the treasury more. Perhaps, I should appoint him my Lord Lieutenant, though he serves me in another office. I speak of Lord Montclair. Should not your great wealth and office bear great expectations?"

"My King, Lord Montclair has established a trading company with ships and barges, wharves, and warehouses in both Berwick and here. He dredged the Lud River and made it his private port. He buys from his own and any other Lord's tenants above the market price in Lincoln. He should pay more! Send your Treasurer to his Land Steward. Surely, he owes even more!"

"Lord Lindsey, you would presume of me, your king, to give you what Lord Montclair has done for himself! And you accuse him of your dereliction?"

Lindsey fought the weakness in his knees and the frog in his throat. "I have executed your orders. All the taxes will be delivered to the treasury. But it is well known that Lord Montclair shows more concern for profitable trade in Amsterdam than in England."

Charles looked around the room. "Montclair. Step forward."

Robert stepped out from where he was standing,

bowed, and said, "At your service, your Majesty."

"You are accused of bringing harm to the tenant farmers of the shire. You do this by paying them more than the traders and dealers in Lincoln. Do you bear ill will towards the merchants of Lincoln and your fellow lords? Do you stand in the way of the Lord Lieutenant's regiment or designs for the improvement of Boston harbor?"

Robert smiled. "If improving the lives of my tenants is a crime, I am guilty. I am guilty of selling grain and food to our protestant brothers in your sister's Palatinate at a lower price by bypassing merchants in Lincoln, Amsterdam, and Heidelberg. But I do not rob my King and do no dishonor to the lords and gentleman of Lincolnshire. They are capable men who can prosper with effort."

The King turned to Lindsey. "There you have it. Before you sit at my table tonight, Lord Lieutenant, all the penalties and held back money will be delivered to the treasury. And I pray no hospitality will be withheld from me or my court at Willoughby House tomorrow night."

Charles stood up, stretched, and said, "Men of Lincolnshire, Lord Weston has further instructions. I will withdraw to the Bishop's Palace, where the lords will join me at the table this evening. Lord Inquirer, walk with me."

Robert followed Lord Conway and King Charles as they left the hall. Robert felt the burning stare of Lord

Lindsey. Outside the great hall, King Charles asked, "Montclair, this business with the assassins, you urge I take caution. You say the plotter is dangerous and cunning–enlisting others to do his evil, yet you ask mercy for the men arrested. A strong example should be made of them."

"I urged mercy, Your Majesty because a confession was freely given with his cooperation which may lead us closer to the plotter himself. And you, my King, are head of the church and Defender of the Faith. The convicted leader is truly repentant. As a priest, I see the church edified by your example of mercy."

Charles mumbled, "Yes. Mercy magnifies my greatness and comforts my people. So, when will they hang?"

"Preparations must be made. Tomorrow, noon."

Charles sighed. "Pity. I must depart early tomorrow morning. Looking forward to a hunt at Willoughby House. Lord Lindsey promised a most excellent hunt. I must not disappoint him; his pride has been wounded. Had to be said–for the others. It is a battle I fight, a battle with Parliament for the rule of England. They forget who is king."

The great hall of Lincoln Castle echoed with sharp voices as the Lincolnshire aristocracy protested and argued with Lord Weston on his expectations of revenue due the crown. Lord Lindsey shouted. "Order! Order! We are men of standing and influence, not a rabble in the streets! Lord Weston has had his say. He has stated his expectations, in truth, his desires. We shall deliver to the royal treasury what is due–what is real and true and what is rightfully the King's under the law, no more and no less."

Lindsey turned to Weston and said, "You have made your wishes known, Lord High Treasurer. You may take your leave, sir. Good day, Lord Weston!"

The room became silent. Weston looked around at the angry lords and gentlemen. Turning his gaze back to Lord Lindsey, Weston feigned a smile, stood up, and said, "You know what His Majesty requires of Lincolnshire. I shall leave you to your deliberations. Good day, lords and gentlemen!"

With Weston gone, Lord Lindsey, standing in the center of the room, spoke. "We gain nothing arguing among ourselves. Go home. Hide nothing and pay what is due and no harm shall overcome you. Weston spreads fear to his advantage. King Charles visits my estate at Willoughby. I shall have his ear at a hunt and what private audience I can arrange."

The murmur of conversation grew into a swell that swept the room and carried its way to the door as the lords of Lincolnshire made their way out. Robert lingered and waited for Lord Lindsey, standing silently in the center of the room, lost in thought. When at last Lindsey started for the door, Robert stopped him. "Lord Lindsey, a word."

"You come to savor your little victory, Montclair?"

"My Lord Lindsey, I salute your leadership. Lincolnshire is blessed with a wise and capable Lord Lieutenant. What you envision, what you laid before the King, is a wise and bold undertaking. I offer my help–what I have learned–and my resources. There is truth in your words. Greater prosperity for the shire is beyond possible. It is assured through better transportation. Ports and rivers–direct access to markets. My tenants invest their profits and increase their fields. They set about draining the marshes at the mouth of the Lud. They find the new fields even richer than the old. It is as if an engine of enterprise has taken hold in Montclair. Your estates could fare just as well. These are hard times for many freemen. Put them to work. They find dignity in work, not the workhouse and not handouts. We can join in ventures– building barges and boats, warehouses, and wharves— mills and looms. You will prosper, as will the tenant farmers, craftsmen, and even merchants. As new money flows into Lincolnshire, trade will increase. And yes, the King will collect his taxes, and he shall see England's wealth increase."

"You would support my plan for Boston and my estates? Why help me? What are you proposing,

Montclair?"

"The whole of England and Europe struggles to eat. Grain prices–the demand. It is our Christian duty to feed and clothe our people. I would be a fool to believe it is my duty alone. I offer you a new system of tenancy–one that encourages growth. Your very words to the King are proven. What is good for Montclair is good for Lincolnshire, and what is good for Lincolnshire may prove to be good for England. Cooperation, Lord Lindsey–a shared approach to commerce. Perhaps shared ventures–for the good of all. My Lord, I have learned a most amazing lesson, as I permitted my tenants to prosper more, my profits increased. It was these profits that bought more fields, more boats, and more profits. The engine, Lord Lindsey, the engine of prosperity."

Lord Lindsey stood silent. "You surprise me, Montclair. There may be wisdom in your words. We shall speak of this again. But now, I must take my leave and return to Willoughby and prepare for His Majesty's visit."

CHAPTER 4

JUSTICE AND MERCY

Only officials were permitted to see a condemned prisoner after a death warrant was signed. Robert interceded and escorted each of Tom Gibbs' children and his wife into Tom's cell, one by one. Robert stood by and watched a broken soul say goodbye to his children. Robert could only close his eyes and hide the tears seeping through his clenched eyelids. Tom's wife, Molly, was the last. Robert stepped out of the cell and turned his face away as Tom's voice carried over Molly's sobs and wailing. "You'll see Molly. It will all work out for good. I did a terrible, evil thing. I meant it for good–for you and the children. And see, my love, it will be well. Lord Montclair is a good and kindly man. He will see you all well. He has shown me that God never abandons us. Lord Montclair, a priest, my love, and a good man, assures me God rewards a broken and contrite heart–a repentant sinner. Your security will be my greatest reward."

Molly sobbed. "Oh, Tom, it is you I want. And the children want their father."

"I know. But our parting must come someday. Why not today when we are rewarded with loving goodbyes and sweet assurances of God's blessing."

"I feel no blessing, Tom. Only loss."

"Will you watch, Molly? And pray for my soul as I drop? I should like my last sight to be your face."

Molly's brow furrowed. *No, please!* She closed her eyes and sobbed. After a sniffle, she said softly, "I will watch, but no child should see their father hanged."

A guard walked in. "The prisoner is permitted his prayers before we execute judgment."

Robert nodded to the guard and said to Molly. "You must leave now while Tom seeks the face of God."

Tom cried out, "A kiss. Please, one kiss!"

Molly sobbed as Tom clutched her in his arms and bent over to kiss his wife.

The guard raised his voice. "The visit is over. Now!"

Tears ran from Tom's eyes as Molly walked out weeping. Robert opened the Book of Common prayer and began, "Remember not, Lord our iniquities, nor the iniquities of our forefathers; neither take thou vengeance of our sins; spare us, good Lord, spare thy people, whom thou hast redeemed with thy most precious blood, and be not angry with us forever."

The parish priest was already into his prayers for the two crew members in the cell beside Tom. Both convicts were silent as the priest read in a lifeless monotone. His voice and every other sound faded as Robert and Tom prepared Tom's soul for his passage beyond the veil.

Tom's voice, shaky at first but growing stronger, joined Robert's in reciting the Lord's prayer. Robert continued, "Grant, we beseech thee, Almighty God, that we, who for our evil deeds do worthily deserve to be punished, by the comfort of Thy grace, may we mercifully be relieved, through our Lord and Savior, Jesus Christ. Amen."

It was Robert's priestly training that spoke. Words separated from his emotions. His mind racing, his voice remained calm as he recited the liturgy, encouraging Tom with God's love. He led Tom through prayers of mercy and David's psalm of confession.

Tom began to sob as Robert read the prayer for 'Persons under sentence of death,' Robert could not mask a crack in his voice. He paused and put an arm around Tom's shoulder and continued. "Dearly beloved, it has pleased Almighty God, in His justice, to bring you under sentence and condemnation of the law. You are shortly to suffer death in such a manner, that others, warned by your example, may be more afraid to offend; and we pray God, that you may make such use of your punishment in this world, that your soul may be saved in the world to come."

Robert looked into Tom's eyes as he read, "It is, therefore, your part and duty, my brother, humbly to confess and bewail your great and manifest offenses, and to repent you truly of your sins, as you tender the eternal salvation of your soul."

Tom sobbed the words, "I repent, oh God, I truly repent. Forgive me, Lord. Have mercy and forgive me."

Again, Robert put an arm around Tom and gently stroked the frightened man's back. He fervently prayed. "Almighty God our heavenly Father, who of His great mercy hath promised forgiveness of sins to all of them with hearty repentance and true faith turn unto him; have mercy upon you, pardon and deliver you from all your sins; confirm and strengthen you in all goodness; bring you to everlasting life; through Jesus Christ our Lord. Amen."

Robert smiled meekly and added. "Father of mercies and God of all comfort; we fly unto thee for succor on behalf of Thomas, thy servant, who is now under sentence of condemnation. The hour of his calamity is at hand, and he is accounted as one of those who go down into the pit. Blessed Lord, remember thy mercies; look upon his infirmities; hear the voice of his complaint… quicken him so much more by thy grace and Holy Spirit; that he, being converted and reconciled unto thee before thy judgments have cut him off from the earth, may at the hour, depart in peace, and be received into Thine everlasting kingdom, through Jesus Christ our Lord. Amen"

Robert read the concluding prayer for Tom. "May God, a most strong tower to all who put their trust in him, be now and evermore thy defense…in the name of our Lord Jesus Christ. Amen."

The prayer and collects finished, Robert stood, stretched out his arm and placed the palm of his hand on Tom's head, and gave the benediction. "Unto God's gracious mercy and protection, we commit thee. The Lord bless thee and keep thee. The Lord make his face shine upon thee, and give thee peace, both now and evermore. Amen."

As soon as Robert finished, two guards pulled Tom to his feet, one on each arm, they marched him from his cell. Robert followed behind. Outside in the sunlight, Tom gazed up into the light. He heard Robert recite the twenty-third psalm and found himself joining him in unison.

Tom looked about and found the face of Molly watching with wet and reddened eyes. They arrived at the foot of the scaffold and began to climb. The two condemned deckhands stood, their hands tied behind their backs, beneath hangman nooses. Robert now began the Lord's prayer. When Robert said. "Amen." The noose was placed around Tom's neck. Robert could not stop himself. "God is love–Jesus loves you, Tom Gibbs. Jesus…"

Tom did not hear the final 'loves you,' as his body dropped and his neck snapped, and he passed from death unto life into the loving arms of his heavenly father.

Robert crossed himself, gave a final silent blessing, and made his way to Molly Gibbs. He said nothing. He hugged her as she cried. When she finally sniffled and wiped the tears from her eyes, Robert said, "Come, let's gather your children. I've arranged for a coach. Tom will be buried at Montclair Church. I know you will mourn some time, but we, Lady Montclair and I, shall do our best to comfort you."

Robert led them to his coach and helped them board. "I have sent a letter to Lady Montclair. She is expecting you. I must attend His Majesty, King Charles at Willoughby House, but I shall return to Montclair Castle to see all is well and introduce you to my estate warden. God bless."

Robert nodded to the driver, tapped the roof of the carriage, and it was off. Robert turned around, stared at the gallows, and watched as Tom and the other two bodies were lowered to the ground. He bit his lip and desperately fought the tears welling up in his eyes. He muffled the cough, which fought its way up from his chest and broke through as a sob. His head bowed, he shook it slowly and purposefully. He needed time to think and to master his emotions. The long ride to Willoughby House was his premeditated flight from accountability. *Eleanor will believe I have abandoned her–leaving her to comfort a grieving family. But I can't do it, not now. I can't face them or answer their questions. I must think–I must sort it out. Lord, help me to sort it out. Judgment in lieu of mercy? Death to a genuinely repentant man? On my account!*

Robert walked to his horse, united the reins from the post, mounted, and rode south in quiet contemplation, meditation, and prayer. Eight hours. Robert had eight hours alone–alone from everyone but God.

I am a priest. I have sworn an oath to God and the King. What if the King does not serve God? Head of the church, yet without love for his subjects, his own countrymen? I know the sacraments–the bread and wine are no less the body and blood of our Savior when offered by an unworthy priest. The presence of the Holy Spirit is not dependent on the righteousness of any man but of Jesus. The blessing is God's, just as submission to the king and bishop is submission to God's ordained authority. And Saint Paul commands us to obey Caesar and obey Jesus.

His head was numb, and his mind conflicted. Robert sighed deeply and shook his head in disgust. *But does King Charles obey? 'This command I give to you—you shall love one another as I love you.' And 'The greatest command is this you shall love God with all your heart and soul and mind. And the second is this; you shall love your neighbor as yourself.' Do I ask too much of my King?*

Robert rode through the streets of Lincoln. He guided his horse through the carts and the many people walking, intent on their business. Robert's eyes saw them. His unconscious brain guided his actions, but his mind was unaware of their presence. *Daniel. Daniel, a man of whom no transgression is recorded—Daniel served not one but three unrighteous kings. And God blessed Daniel—an example to all who serve under a tyrant. But Daniel was able to bring justice and order to the king's subjects. Yes, Daniel was a type—it is Christ who ensures justice, mercy, and order in a fallen world. And the kings Daniel served were not heads of the church. No. I must look elsewhere for answers. Lord, what should I do? Wisdom with mercy, Lord, give me wisdom with mercy!*

Robert rode through the Lincolnshire countryside. He tried to see the beauty of the land and listen to the songs of birds. *A wonder how God speaks through creation.* Robert found beauty in God's creation—beauty and comfort. He tried to clear his mind, but Tom Gibbs' face played in his memory. He saw a good man caught up in the fervor—a dangerous passion spreading across England. Robert's mind went back to Scripture. *David. David served*

King Saul after the Spirit of God left Saul. And this was after Samuel chose David and anointed him king. When pursued, David would not harm Saul, also God's anointed king. David determined that God would deal with Saul, and God did. Yes, David waited and trusted in the LORD. It is true; he trusted in the Lord. And Charles is more than just God's anointed. He has not abandoned God, nor has God abandoned the king! It is well known King Charles is diligent in his prayers and genuine in his defense of the Church of England, though he does not take counsel from Archbishop Abbot and shows no patience for preaching. Even so, Bishop Laud, his chaplain, has his ear and makes good use of prayer. No. Charles may be in error. He may be blind to his subjects' suffering, but he is not outside of God's love. He remains our anointed king. I shall stay the course. I must pray for him and Bishop Laud. Yes Lord, open his Majesty's eyes. Holy Spirit, speak to his heart.

Robert rode on. The sun was low on the western horizon. The air was sweet with the smell of tall, wet grass. *Stay the course? Stay the course and become an instrument of injustice? No! It is a line I must never cross! I shall do my duty to God and king. I shall offer mercy to the widow and orphan. I shall visit the prisoner in distress. I shall protect my king, but I will never— Lord, help me—never become an instrument of the King's injustice!*

Robert sobbed. He self-consciously looked around, but no one saw him. He wiped his tear-soaked eyes with the cuff of his coat sleeve. He lifted his face toward heaven and shouted: "Lord, do you hear me, Lord? Lord, you are sovereign in all the affairs of men. You heard my oath. In your sovereignty, I place my path in your hands. Grant me wisdom with mercy and guard me, O Lord–never, never may I become an instrument of injustice!"

Robert spurred his horse and arrived at Willoughby House just after sunset.

Lady Eleanor, Countess of Montclair, sat in the shade, her infant twins, Edward, and Elizabeth, asleep in a basket beside her. She brushed her red tresses away from her face, tucking her hair back under her bonnet. Beautiful and elegant even in intimate motherhood, she carefully unsealed the envelope in the familiar hand of her husband, Robert, and read. Eleanor sighed deeply and shook her head. "Robbie, my love, what have you done! I told you I never wanted to marry a country vicar! And you send them to me? On but four hours' notice?"

Shaking her head, Eleanor whispered to herself, "It's that big heart of yours and that overbearing search for justice that makes me love you. And these precious babies. The man is worse than a child. But I love him. O Lord, how precious are my husband and children,"

Eleanor paused and stared out across the garden. *The poor woman must be heartbroken. Her husband hanged–and the children—how they must suffer the loss of their father. No, they can be no inconvenience. Robbie was right to send them here."*

Eleanor called to her mother, walking in the garden. "Mother! Come quickly. I need you." Eleanor then called for her servant, Thomas. "Send for Mister Brisby and Reverend Mister Stevens—no, the new priest, the lad, Paul Hawkins. Tell them it is urgent. I will see them in the sitting room."

Thomas replied, "At once, Lady Montclair."

Lady Anne, Dowager Countess of Montclair, read the letter Eleanor handed her. "O my goodness. Six children! Poor dears. What shall we do?"

"Mother, please take the twins to the nursery and then join me in the sitting room. William? Where is William? I thought you were giving him his French lesson?"

Lady Anne looked up from the letter. "He is fine. He is riding. The little man only listens when astride his horse. The Reverend Mister Hawkins is with him. He is an excellent tutor. William adores him like a big brother."

"When Robbie said he would buy Will a fast horse to be his legs, I never thought it would come to pass. Mother, William must be told children are coming, but they will be in no mood for play. Will listens to you. Tell him they are very sad, and he must be kind."

Lady Anne sighed. "Eleanor, you must let go of the guilt you cling to. Will loves you. He is happy you are home. A son's love for his mother is a strong bond not easily broken. Just love him–show him you love him. He is strong and resilient. Much like you, my dear."

The Land Steward, Mister Brisby, was the first to arrive. Lady Eleanor was immediately put at ease by Brisby's calm authority. Brisby was now over sixty years old. He managed the estate since before Eleanor was born. When Robert became Earl, he found Brisby a kindred spirit in innovation, and Montclair estate prospered. "I am at your service Lady Montclair. I was told it is urgent?"

"Yes, thank you for coming so quickly, Mister Brisby—ah! Here is Mister Hawkins with Master William."

William strode confidently up to his mother, his labored breathing lost in his beaming face. "Momma, I jumped a hedge! What great fun! I leaned forward and clung to Thunder's neck, and over we went. I could feel his muscles and his breathing–his power and spirit. Mister Hawkins, is spirit the right word?"

Paul Hawkins smiled and nodded. "It was a low hedge, Lady Eleanor, and an easy lope. He did fine. And his lessons, he is a clever lad and learns quickly."

Lady Eleanor smiled. "I know what joy you find in riding, William, but promise me you will do your lessons."

William replied. "Je promets d'etudier dur, Mere."

Eleanor smiled. "Come, give me a hug. Your French is already better than your father's."

Eleanor knelt before Will. "William, some children are coming today. They will be staying with us. But you must be especially kind. They are very sad and in no mood to play. Do you understand? Kind and quiet."

"Yes, momma. I know what it is like to be sad and lonely. I will be kind to them."

Will's words stabbed through Eleanor's heart, but she smiled and kissed him. "You are my brave little man. No, go along with Nanna. I will call for you when they come."

Lady Anne took Will's hand and led him out of the room. Lady Eleanor straightened up, smiled briefly, and said, "Lord Montclair has arranged for the family of a condemned man to stay here at Montclair Castle. The wife of a grain merchant and their six children. The man, Thomas Gibbs, was hanged for attempting to kill the King. My husband writes that Mister Gibbs repented and was, in truth, a good man driven to evil. His body is to be buried at Montclair Church. A widow and six children—where can we put them?"

Brisby replied, "There are no vacant houses in the villages of Montclair. We have room in the servant quarters here in the castle...."

"No. Putting a grieving family with the servants is

no hospitality. I would rather put them in the house for a time. Though I fear this house would bring only added stress to their grieving."

"The vicarage. The vicarage is large enough for a family. I'm sure the Revered Mister Stevens and I could find lodgings within the village," Hawkins interjected.

"I'm afraid Mister Stevens would be most upset. No, here is what we shall do. The Gibbs family will be my guests until after the funeral. Several days and then they shall move into the vicarage. You and the Reverend Mister Stevens shall move into this house. Heaven knows he has longed to live here for years."

Late in the afternoon, a carriage drove to the front of Montclair Castle. Lady Eleanor, the Reverend Mister Hawkins, and Thomas went out to meet the Gibbs family. James, the eldest son, stepped out first and assisted his mother. His brother and four sisters followed. The children stood in line alongside their mother. Eleanor stepped forward. "I am Lady Eleanor Curtis, Countess of Montclair. I am very sorry for your loss. You have suffered greatly, but Lord Robert and I wish to provide refuge and sanctuary while you grieve."

Eleanor turned to Paul Hawkins. "The Reverend Mister Hawkins, a most kindly priest, is here to comfort and console. He will assist in the funeral arrangements. You have had a long and tortuous day. I will not hold you long. You are welcome to join my table this evening. No need to change, come as you are–simple fare. If you prefer, I can send food to your quarters. My chief servant, Thomas, shall show you to your rooms."

Molly Gibbs stared blankly at Eleanor. She sniffled once and curtsied. "Thank you, Lady Montclair. Yes, my children are hungry. We had neither food nor drink this day. Forgive me, my Lady, where are my manners? I am Molly Gibbs and these my children: my son James, my daughters; Rachel, Leah, Deborah, Sarah, and my son Joseph."

Eleanor smiled. "You are welcome. Shall we say one hour? Thomas, tell the cook supper in one hour. And show my guests to their rooms."

Lady Eleanor turned and went inside. Silently the Gibbs family followed Thomas into the house, and servants came out and carried the few possessions of the distraught family inside. Paul Hawkins stood lost in thought and prayer. Only after the coach drove off did he walk off towards the vicarage.

Molly Gibbs followed each of her children to their rooms. She was pleased that they were paired up. None would spend the night alone. She dusted off their clothes and hugged each one. "My darlings, we will get through this. Be strong, for just a while."

Their bags now delivered, and satisfied her

children were settled, Molly found solace alone in her room. She walked to the window and stared out upon the pastoral view. In the distance, she saw dust rising from the road. She stood and cried as a wagon approached, carrying a lone simple coffin.

CHAPTER 5

WILLOUGHBY HOUSE

James Lynch was seated at a table in the Willoughby Estate Steward's chambers, pouring over lists of servants when Robert arrived. Ignoring any pleasantries, Robert asked, "I'm interested in new men–recruits for Lord Lindsey's regiment as well as servants. Any Irish…"

Lynch looked up. "Just like an Englishman. Always blamin' the Irish devil! Never thankin' the Good Lord for the few good men, the Irish, who keeps his noble arse out of the fire!"

Lynch smiled. "Welcome, Sir Robert! This isn't my first detail."

Robert smiled for the first time in days. "I don't know who frustrates me more, Mister Black who must be entreated to speak his mind or you, James Lynch, who despite all entreaties cannot stay silent!"

Lynch laughed. "Is it true, Black is off to Holland, chasin' after the pamphlets?"

Robert nodded. "Lynch, you are to take the lead in Black's absence. What do you have for me?"

Lynch handed Robert a report. "More Skimmington parades. Whomever is behind these pamphlets, he is getting results. People are angry. The protest parades are spreading and gaining in size. Thankfully, most do not lead to violence. Oh, before I forget, Lord Conway commands your presence first upon your arrival."

"Commands, does he? He can wait."

Lynch continued, "No new men who will have close access to the King. No one in the kitchen or with access to the King's chambers. I know you worry about poison. I was going through the regimental roster."

"Has Lord Lindsey planned a review of his regiment? It is still being formed."

"No, but he intends to employ some as game beaters in the hunt."

Robert sighed. "Would they attempt another Bramshill?"

Lynch nodded. "My thoughts as well. I remembered it was the new gamekeeper's attempt on the life of King James that brought you into this murky business of ours. We don't have enough men to put one with each gamekeeper or beater. I'm working on a priority list. You, Sir Robert, will be with the King and Lord Lindsey. You must make that happen."

"What else do you have? Any pamphlets discovered on the estate?"

"None have been reported, but then Lord Lindsey would not share any damning information. His Land Steward insists all love the King and Lord Lindsey."

Robert quickly scanned the report Lynch gave him, looked up, and said, "I should be finding Lord Conway before the King calls us to his table. I will see you again before retiring."

Lynch nodded. "I'll not be abed this night."

Robert stopped at the door and turned around. "Lynch, you're from one of the founding families of Galway, yet you serve King Charles, hard enough for an Englishman to serve–does his disdain for his subjects ever trouble you?"

Lynch sighed. "You forget, Sir Robert, I am a protestant from a Catholic tribe. An outcast even to my family. My love of Ireland and the Lynch tribe brings me no favor. As for Charles, he is the King. Better men have worn the crown, and he is no friend to the Irish. But he is not ours to choose. I'll give him this. He keeps the Irish from fighting each other–our long and inglorious history. He brings peace, though it comes with hatred. Perhaps that is the price of peace and order–someone else to hate. When he dies, another English king will take his place. So long as he keeps order and a semblance of justice, I will serve him. Not to tell you your priestly business, Sir Robert, but it occurs to me God sets kings over us in our weakness and sin–a punishment for turning our backs on God and our neighbor."

Robert nodded. "You remind me that God gave Israel King Saul in their weakness. But He chose David. Is there no good king?"

"God in His mercy sends one along from time to time. But every king is a burden to his subjects."

"Hmm. The king as our punishment, I never heard that debated at Cambridge. Until tonight then."

The King's courtiers were gathering in the great hall when Robert entered. Lord Conway motioned for Robert and whispered, "Was justice done?"

"Aye, Lord Secretary, all three hanged."

"And your man, Black, sailed to Holland? You are to keep me informed on everything he learns. I expect a report as soon as he returns."

"As you say, Lord Secretary."

"Now, I must tell you his Majesty's schedule. The hunt—after breakfast. Midday meal in the forest. Banquet after sunset, and off to King's Lynn next morning for another ship tax audit."

"I must be close by the King during the hunt."

Lord Conway replied, "Lord Lindsey is the host; he invites...."

"The King was saved from one attempt this week. Lord Lindsey must be persuaded or, if need be, commanded."

The Lord Secretary nodded. "As you wish."

Robert asked, "Will the King continue into Norfolk or travel south to Cambridge?"

"Lord Weston will decide once he has the tax figures. Tonight, the King salves the wounds of the Earl of Lindsey. In truth, he demands both the taxes and Lindsey's regiment. There is talk of renewed interest in the war now that the navy of Sweden's King Gustav Adolphus and the army of Denmark's King Christian IV broke the siege of Wolfgast and have found success in Pomerania. Sadly, too late for the citizens of Wolfgast—men, women, and children, all slaughtered like animals."

Robert's frustration got the better of patience. "Will this bloody war never end? And England, half in and half out. How many years? How many lives lost? With each turn of fortune, our King sends and recalls soldiers. The people and me, yes, me. I have forgotten why this war continues. It began with Frederick claiming the crown of Bohemia, which he quickly lost. Next, it was the King's sister, Elizabeth's holding the Palatinate. Then came the call to protect our protestant brothers. Now the Catholic

Bourbons rattle swords against the Catholic Habsburgs and longtime enemies, the Danes, and Swedes join to recover lost lands in the north. How is this England's fight?"

"Montclair, you would do well to keep your own counsel and mind your duty to protect the King. But I will say this; His Majesty looks to England's interests—trade and a lasting alliance. We are past the follies of Buckingham. England's fortunes cannot be severed from the continent. Consider, if the reformation is extinguished, what would become of the Church of England? Attacked from abroad and a civil war within! Parliament has never had the will to fight, so King Charles will pursue an alliance. Pray he chooses the right one."

King Charles was tired and chose to retire without hosting a drinking party after dinner. Robert caught up with Lord Lindsey before he left the hall. "A word, Lord Lieutenant?"

"It's been a long day, Montclair, and tomorrow even longer. What is it?"

"The Royal visit goes well. The King bestows great honor on you, Lord Lindsey. My request is quite simple. I require to ride beside you and his Majesty in tomorrow's hunt. A simple matter of the King's safety."

"Lord Montclair, I am well on my way to recruiting a full regiment of footmen to serve the King. You insult me to infer I am incapable of protecting his Majesty."

"Lord Lieutenant, Colonel, you have earned your rank in service. If a force of armed men rose against King Charles, I would fall in line behind you and do as you command. But the threat to his Majesty is not an army of insurrection. The threat is from a man or a small group of men acting in secret. Would you have an attempt against the King on your head? It is a responsibility His Majesty has placed on my shoulders. The hunt places the King in the forest where armed men, your gamekeepers perhaps, or trespassers may lurk. It has happened before. These are not men you invite to the King's banquet."

Lindsey sighed. "If you insist, Lord Inquirer."

"Indeed, I must."

"Very well. You say, Montclair, if an army is needed, you would fall in line behind me. You were a Captain of Royal Cuirassiers–I ask you to make them available to my regiment. And your estate tenants, good men of Lincolnshire, allow my recruiters to visit Montclair."

"Lord Barkley, Baron of Cawmills, is Captain of the Royal Cawmills Cuirassiers. You must make your request to him. As for recruiting good men of Lincolnshire, I grant my tenants and servants free will to serve as they please. You may recruit."

"You are a curious fellow, Sir Robert. You treat

your tenants as you would a gentleman. They are farmers and craftsmen, ignorant and crude. It's all in the breeding. I say give them food and shelter. They copulate like animals. That, and plenteous ale is enough pleasure for simple people."

"If you wish to make Willoughby and all of Lincolnshire prosper, you would do well to reconsider. The people on the land, the farmers, and craftsmen– uneducated perhaps, but not ignorant, indeed learned in the skills of trade and survival. Give them respect and opportunity, and they will amaze you with their ability. Surely, you have seen the same from your soldiers? Good soldiers, experienced and capable, have proven themselves superior to incompetent officers. I saw it in the Palatinate. And I saw the best of officers, General, Sir Horace Vere, salute his veterans with pride and affection."

"You tire me all the more, Montclair. I grant that the common soldier can be both brave and industrious. But God, who made us all, has established his order. The common serve the noble, and the noble serve the king. God's order, Montclair. Good night."

As promised, Robert called on James Lynch before retiring for the evening. "Lynch, if all goes well tomorrow, I will return to Montclair Castle tomorrow evening. I will rejoin you in a week or less. Now, who shall we be watching tomorrow?"

Lynch stood up and stretched. He took a deep breath and rubbed sore eyes. "Lord Lindsey may be a good soldier, but his enlistment records are nearly useless. Names, many without ages, city or village, or description of any detail. These men could be anyone. His lordship was satisfied with any name and a signature mark to fill his regiment. As you asked, I listed Irish names and those who identified Irish homes. It saddens me to know that every traitor finds ready recruits–mercenaries–from the Irish. But none were assigned to the hunt. I made a list of the men working the hunt and will concentrate on them. We have enough men to cover most of the beaters and keepers. I've given our men their assignments. How did you fare?"

"I will be at the side of King Charles and Lord Lindsey. He is a man who will not risk his reputation with the King. Where will you be?"

"I will be alongside the gamekeeper. 'Seems a competent man. No one more likely to spot something amiss."

Robert nodded. "Get some sleep. I need you alert in the morning."

After an early night, King Charles was up early in the morning. Following a light breakfast, the hunting party was organized and rode off into the morning mist. King Charles was in a pleasant mood, expectant of a good hunt.

"I need more of this, Lindsey, yes, more fine days hunting. Good to be in thick woods, brings one closer to the game, all the more enjoyable. Your regiment, Lord Lieutenant, you must act with speed. I may soon need them. The war moves to a conclusion. We must join our allies and savor the victory."

Robert listened in silence as Lindsey asked, "I am making great progress in recruiting and training. The regiment shall not disappoint you. Who is the ally we are to join, your Majesty?"

"You surprise me, Lindsey, why King Gustav Adolphus, of course. He will turn the tide. Once the full might of the Swedish army lands, they will not stop until Wallenstein is pushed back to Vienna!"

Lindsey motioned for the hunting party to halt. They were now on a rise in the forest with a small clearing below them. "Majesty, the game should pass from left to right. The opening is small, so your shot must be quick."

King Charles smiled. "Yes. I like a challenge. But you, Lord Lindsey, Colonel of my regiment of footmen, you may have the honor of the first kill."

Each hunter took their crossbow from their saddle, drew back the string, placed a short steel-tipped bolt over the stock, secured the notch on the bowstring, and waited. The beaters could be heard driving the deer toward the clearing. The morning sun was now above the trees and the last of the morning mist burned away. As the beaters came closer, the birds took to wing, raising the tension. No one spoke. All eyes scanned the edges of the clearing. The rustling in the forest underbrush grew louder and louder.

Boom! The loud retort of a musket or arquebus reverberated across the clearing.

CHAPTER 6

INQUIRIES

Robert spun his horse between the King and the clearing. "Lord Lindsey, escort his Majesty to Willoughby House and muster your regiment but wait for my return. Your Majesty, it is best to wait at the house. Remain inside, away from doors and windows. I shall join my watchers and investigate. We shall take no chances. I shall join you soon and report."

Robert's horse pranced nervously in excitement. A light roll with his spurs and his horse galloped down the hill across the clearing into the forest. Robert's eyes searched for powder smoke; his nose was attentive to the telltale odor. Five loud short blasts of a hunting horn pealed from below. As Robert rode, the horn resounded with five more loud short blasts. Now he saw small groups of men running towards a great tree, the tallest in the forest. Robert rode to the tree and soon saw James Lynch alongside the gamekeeper and a trumpeter.

Robert shouted, "Account for all keepers, beaters, and watchers! Lynch, the pistols, make sure we have them all, and none were fired! Then search the woods. We are looking for anyone with a long gun or pistol–anyone at all found in the woods shall be brought bound to Willoughby House!"

Lynch nodded. "Aye, Sir Robert, only our watchers carry pistols. The keepers carry crossbows, and the beaters are unarmed."

Robert was off his horse. "Check all pistols! No one is above suspicion! See if anyone saw or smelled the powder smoke. Take my horse, Lynch. I will be at the house. Circle the woods. Make haste, man! We must not let him escape! I will send Lindsey's regimental volunteers once they have mustered to expand the search."

Robert started down the narrow path that led from the great tree to Willoughby House. Lynch called after him, "The King? How fares the King?"

"The King lives. Do not tarry," Robert replied, not turning, as he ran towards the house.

Lord Lindsey was standing outside as Robert approached. Men were gathering in the coach yard. Lindsey called out, "I have enough men here to start a sweep through the woods."

Robert shook his head no as he gasped for air.

"There will be time for a sweep later. First, we must seal the woods and the village and the roads. No one comes in or goes out. The keepers are already circling the woods. Your muster roll—we begin with a muster and an inventory of arms."

Lindsey shot back, "I must protest. That will take time!"

"Lord Lindsey, the muster and then your armorer's report. You do not know these men."

Lindsey walked to the coach yard and called for his adjutant. "Call the roll."

Robert added, "Those with the beaters are accounted. Any villagers not here will be noted. They can be counted once the village is secured. Call out officers as well. First, the armorer, then send him to inventory weapons."

Fifteen minutes later, the roll call determined twenty men with keepers, thirty men from the village, not present. And one new man, Arthur Pendragon, was unaccounted for. "Pendragon, Arthur Pendragon, does any man know Pendragon? Speak up!"

Robert repeated, "Where's he from?"

The adjutant replied, "Nothing on the roll."

One of the volunteers answered, "Cam, something."

"Cambridge?"

"No, Camel something."

Robert sighed. "Camelot."

The man replied, "Aye! Camelot!"

Robert turned to Lord Lindsey. "You recruited Arthur Pendragon of Camelot, and no one found that suspicious?"

Robert asked, "Please describe Arthur Pendragon of Camelot."

The man replied, "Just a bloke."

"Specific, how old? Tall, short, stout or lean, hair color, scars–think man!"

The witness replied, "My height, brown hair, not so young, thirty maybe. Like every other bloke, really. Wait, there was something, a scar—had a scar across his right ear. Nearly cut in half, it was."

The armorer returned and reported, "One arquebus missing. All other weapons accounted for."

Robert turned to Lord Lindsey. Send a detail to the village. See if any others are missing. We need to know if this Arthur Pendragon has any accomplices. Set up checkpoints on the roads, take custody of any strangers, and bring them here. Send the remainder of your men to support Mister Lynch searching the woods. Pass the description of Pendragon to all searchers. I will report to His Majesty."

King Charles was seated at the table when Robert

came in. The King put down his wine when a platter of roast fowl was set before him. Robert bowed as he entered the room. "If it pleases, your Majesty, I would like to report we are searching the forest for the gunman. We have sealed the wood, blocked the roads, and begun a thorough sweep. We have determined one man and one arquebus missing. His description is being circulated."

"One man and one long gun?"

"Yes, your Majesty, a recent recruit to the regiment."

"I expect better of you, Montclair. This recruit, a member of Lindsey's regiment?"

"Yes, your Majesty. Soldiers–they do not all volunteer with the most honorable intentions. We have a good description. You can travel safely tomorrow to King's Lynn."

"Safely, Lord Montclair? Must I ride between bodyguards? Perhaps you on one side and Lindsey on the other? Lincolnshire disappoints me greatly."

The King went back to his meal. Robert said, "I will keep Lord Conway informed on the progress of my inquiries. Good day, your Majesty." Robert bowed and backed out of the room.

Robert's instinct was to ride off and join Lynch in the search. He sighed in disgust when he remembered Lynch was in pursuit, riding Robert's horse. Lindsey's stable would be empty, every available horse called into service. *Maybe Lynch's horse is still stabled? If I can find a groomsman.*

Lord Conway appeared as Robert hurried towards the door. "Lord Montclair! Your report?"

"Lord Conway, yes, I just informed his Majesty that we closed the roads, are sweeping the woods, and have identified a suspect–a recent recruit to Lord Lindsey's regiment. We have determined one arquebus missing from the armory. I was about to rejoin the search."

"It seems your response is well in hand. Tell me, Lord Montclair, this suspect?"

Robert took a deep breath. "Yes, of course. My man Lynch and Lord Lindsey have the search well in hand. The suspect–yes, most interesting–a recruit by the name of Arthur Pendragon…."

"Arthur Pendragon? Do you jest?"

"No, Lord Secretary, it is worse. He tells his mates he is from Camelot."

"And no one questioned this man's recruitment?"

"Many soldiers are running from someone or something. Recruiters are determined to fill the ranks with able-bodied men and do not ask too many questions. But we have a good description. The man is scarred across his right ear, likely from a sword or pike. We'll find him."

"Must I remind you, Montclair, seek me out before

going to His Majesty?"

"I shall, but the King had just left my company–so much happening so fast…."

Robert paused, then looked into Lord Conway's eyes. "Tell me, Lord Secretary, did you hear the gun here in the house?"

Lord Conway replied, "Yes, quite clearly."

"Did you see or smell the smoke? Where were you when you heard the retort?"

"Well, I was at my writing table, of course. The window was open to the morning air. I looked out after hearing the gun, but I saw nothing. No one came out of the woods until Lord Lindsey and the King rode out."

"Your room faces the woods?"

"Aye, a good view."

"Thank you, Lord Secretary. I shall remember your request."

Robert started again for the door. A servant opened it. As he passed, Robert stopped and asked, "Is there a stairway to the roof?"

"Why yes, my Lord."

"Please, take me to the roof at once."

Robert followed the servant up three flights of stairs. At the far end of the servant's floor, a narrow door was half-open. The servant said, "That door is to the stairway to the roof. It should be closed."

They climbed the narrow stairway, little more than a ladder, and stepped out on the roof. Robert gazed out at the view of the woods before them. He walked to the balustrades lining the edge. Near the center of the roofline lay an arquebus. Robert picked it up and smelled it. It had been recently fired. Robert looked at the thick woods. *He couldn't have seen the King or the hunting party. What game is he playing? Think! He had plenty of time to get it up here undetected, but he could not take it down without the risk of being seen. Why didn't he throw it down? Afraid of being seen or heard? His mistake! It follows that Arthur Pendragon, or whatever his real name, had access to the house and likely, an accomplice. Yes, it is a game. But what kind of game? Well, they are not going to find him in the woods. The stable, he must have ridden off before the search. Or is he hiding in plain sight? But the scar—I must check the stable. And who else? The house servants, yes, and Weston, he wasn't on the hunt. Where is he?*

Robert returned to the staircase and the waiting servant. "Lord Weston, can you lead me to his room?"

"My Lord, I observed Lord Weston entering the library moments before you came to the door. Should I take you there instead?"

"Yes, thank you."

Weston was pacing alongside the windows in the library when Robert entered. "Lord High Treasurer, I suppose you have heard of this morning's events. Tell me, where were you when the shot rang out?"

Lord Weston stared at the arquebus Robert held. "Do you require such a weapon in the house?"

Robert let the stock of the long gun rest on the floor. "Don't be alarmed. It is not ready to fire. Please answer my question."

"Yes. Disturbing. Most disturbing. We must thank God above that our King is safe. Yes, I was in the garden. I heard the shot. I circled to the front of the house in time to see His Majesty and Lord Lindsey return in haste."

"You speak of the garden behind the house. Not in the front facing the woods."

"Yes, I took a walk to clear my mind–so many figures–so many reports."

"You had a clear view of the house. I might imagine one would look up at the sound of gunfire. Did you see anyone on the roof?"

"Why, I did look up. Birds. Yes, birds took to wing. Alas, I was walking away from the house. I then looked about for a path to the front. I don't recall seeing anyone on the roof or scanning the roof, for that matter. I expected the gunshot came from the woods."

"Please try to remember. Did you notice anyone leaving the house?"

"Only a servant. I thought him a servant. Just as I reached the far corner of the house, I heard something scrape the gravel. I turned and saw the back of a man–a servant–right himself and hurry off towards the stable. I thought nothing of it and walked to the front and watched the King approach. Why do you ask about the roof?"

Robert lifted the arquebus. "My inquiries confirm someone was on the roof. If you recall anything which may aid in my inquiry, it is most urgent that you find me. Good day."

Robert left Weston and hurried to the empty stable, where he called for the stable master. A voice called from the tack room. "There are no riding horses left. Go away. Come back after the searchers return."

Robert followed the voice to the tack room and replied, "You speak to the Lord Inquirer, and you would do well not to impede my duties!"

The stable master put down an ale mug and stood up as Robert entered. "My apologies, Lord Inquirer, just a short rest after a busy morning."

Robert ignored the comment. "After the gunshot was heard, did anyone come for a horse?"

"A gunshot, was it? Aye, I heard it. Couldn't say if anyone came for a horse. I was in the inner courtyard washing his Majesty's coach. When I saw the commotion, I told myself, his Majesty may be wantin' to leave. Better get about my business."

"The search party—the men who mounted—were all

of the horses accounted for before they departed?"

"Accounted for? How? Men took horses until none were left. The others left on foot. I didn't–there was no accountin' for horses. Look for yourself; only the coach horses remain."

Robert shook his head and sighed. "Tell me, if I were to ride to the coach road, could I go there without passing in front of the house."

"Well, now, it wouldn't be right disturbin' Lord Lindsey, with travelers passin' by his great house. No, wouldn't be right. It's a short ride through the village behind the stable and the garden. Why a man could walk to the coach road inn in five minutes!"

Robert made his way to the estate steward's chambers. He stood the arquebus in the corner. The land steward was not there. *He must have joined the search. Likely, I won't find the armorer either. The house steward–he should know if any house servant has gone missing.*

The house steward kept a tight rein on the servants. He quickly established they were all present. Robert ran through his questions: "Has anyone seen a servant this morning, other than those here now in the house?"

"No, my Lord."

"Did anyone observe a man leaving the house by the rear door shortly after the gunshot this morning?"

"No, my Lord."

"Has anyone seen a man climbing the stairs to the roof in the last several days?"

"No, my Lord."

"Has anyone noticed anyone or anything unusual just before or during the King's visit?"

"Just the confusion of the King's servants and the Royal Party. But no one that was not introduced as servant or guest."

Robert's sources at Willoughby House were near an end. *It may be hours before Lynch and the others return. I should try my luck at the coach inn and village.*

Robert made the short walk to the village and found the coach inn. The inn was busy with travelers waiting for the road to reopen. Slamming the butt of his pistol drew the innkeeper's attention. The scowling innkeeper made his way through the crowded inn. "A pistol doesn't make you any more important than the next man. I'll be callin' for Lord Lindsey's sheriff."

"I am Lord Inquirer to King Charles. Both you and Lord Lindsey's sheriff would do well to answer my questions. Coaches, when was the last coach?"

The innkeeper swallowed and coughed before answering. "The last coach went through this morning, bound for Cambridge and London."

"What time?"

"Mid-morning. Sometime near ten. Give or take."

"Any passengers board here?"

"Aye, three men."

"Describe them."

"Men. Workin' men. Nothing to notice about them."

"Did one man have a scar across his right ear?"

"Maybe, maybe not. I didn't get a good look. Two sat here waitin'. The third walked up as the coach arrived."

The innkeeper paused. "Some other fellow came by askin' 'bout a man with a scar on his ear. Ain't no one here with a scar. People are gettin' angry, waitin' on the coaches. When you gonna let us get on about our business? Ain't fair to good people–workin' folk."

Robert slowly exhaled. "It may be a while yet. We must wait for the search parties to return. Soon, I hope."

Walking to the door, Robert looked down at a table where three men were hunched over mugs of ale. One man stood up and hit another. "Oaf! Look what ya' done! Spilled ale all over it!"

Robert's eye focused on a wet pamphlet. The headline read: "King Charlie the Devil's King!"

CHAPTER 7
MESSAGE TO THE KING

The Sheriff delivered Robert's note to James Lynch and Lord Lindsey. Lindsey returned to Willoughby House, leaving Lynch to recall the searchers from the woods and return to the estate. The soldiers were ordered to report to the Great House in the morning to resume the sweep and canvas everyone along the roads from Willoughby House. Lynch spent the evening receiving the reports.

Robert had his own report to make before the King called his courtiers to the table. He found Lord Conway studying correspondence at his writing table. Conway did not look up when Robert entered. "You took your bloody time, Montclair. The house is filled with rumors and second-hand reports. Lindsey has returned and shared your note. You believe this imposter, Arthur Pendragon, is gone–likely on the coach? The sheriff has three men in his gaol for your inquiries, another pamphlet. Have you forgotten my instructions?"

Robert replied, "I was constrained without a mount and forced to act directly. I have come to you, as you directed, before going to His Majesty. I cannot speak to what others might have said."

Conway looked up. "The three men and the pamphlet?"

"Indeed. I ordered them held. I did not have time to interrogate. They will be compelled to tell how they came about possession and their intent–strong intent from what I saw, to act upon its call. I have the pamphlet in my possession. It was nearly ruined by spilt ale. It will be carefully dried and studied."

"What can you tell me, now?"

"A new course on sedition. The title is clear, 'King Charlie, the devil's King!' I will provide a transcript, of course, but I intend to send it to our works in London Newgate for evaluation. I want to know if it is from the same printing press–the same paper and ink."

Conway's face betrayed no expression. "You wonder if it is an imitator—if others are joining the seditious campaign? Very well. I will make the report to the King. He may call for you, but as he was in no danger by the gunshot, I think His Majesty will see this episode for what it is—a toothless attempt to keep the King from pursuing his rightful collection of taxes. The King is not so easily frightened. He will travel to King's Lyn in the morning. Your man, Lynch, is it? How you can trust an Irishman strains all credulity. Yes, Lynch can remain here and interrogate the men in custody. You will travel with the court. Lord Cottington is with His Majesty. You have time to make yourself presentable for the King's table."

"Cottington? Back from Spain? Was the ambassador recalled, or did he bring a treaty? Surely, the King would not align with Spain just as Sweden's King Gustav Adolphus at last joins the protestant cause? It is well known the Prince of Orange has rebuffed His Majesty's pleas to join the war against the emperor and fight to regain the Palatinate for Frederick and the King's sister, Elizabeth. The Prince has been careful not to add the Emperor as an enemy as he fights Spain for independence. He regarded King Charles' threats as toothless."

Lord Conway replied, "You are well informed. His Majesty cannot ignore the intentions of King Gustav Adolphus and his new alliance with Christian of Denmark. But I fear Gustav has his own interests, regaining lands in the north. He will negotiate with Emperor Ferdinand. Returning the Palatinate to Frederick and Elizabeth has no importance with Gustav Adolphus."

"But with English troops and money? And King Christian is an uncle to King Charles."

"What money? And trust is lacking."

Robert shook his head. "And King Philip of Spain can be trusted to divide up the Netherlands and convince the Emperor to forgive and restore Frederick? King Philip can make no guarantee, and at what price?"

"A Spanish alliance has strong support in the council."

"What council? The Kings three friends? Not the full Privy Council and certainly not Parliament."

"Philip promises to support the cause of Elizabeth in the Palatinate before both pope and emperor. His Majesty is convinced that upon the defeat of Prince Maurice and the United Netherlands, the Army of Flanders will join the emperor's army and defeat Gustav, Christian, and the German princes. Until the Dutch are defeated, the King is free to support his sister's cause."

Robert replied softly, "As I say, the King listens to his Catholic Lords Cottington and Weston. There is no guarantee of the restitution of Frederick and Elizabeth. And the King overestimates the influence of the English army and navy. It's madness!"

"Others do not see as you. Now, I have work to do."

Robert walked to the door and stopped. Turning to Lord Conway, he said, "Doesn't the King have enough enemies? Word of a Spanish alliance will only add fuel to widespread opposition. He can be confident of one thing; the pamphlets will increase."

The aroma of roast stag led a hungry Robert to the banquet hall. Lord Lindsey was wise enough to have several stags in reserve hanging in his larder before the hunt. King Charles entered alongside Lord Cottington, laughing as he walked. Lord Conway gave his place on the right of King Charles to Lord Cottington, with Lord Weston beside him. A visibly upset Lord Lindsey, the host, sat to the King's left. Robert was surprised when Lord Conway sat beside him.

Conway whispered. "The King's laugh tells the story. Cottington brings good news."

When the stag was served, the King turned to Lindsey, lifted his cup, and roared for all to hear, "Honors to you, Lindsey, your search party found something in the woods to shoot!"

Lindsey grimaced as the room laughed.

The King laughed and added, "Is it true you keep an arquebus on your rooftop as a stag stand? Why not form a regiment of stag hunters? Your regiment may keep me well fed if not well protected!"

Conway whispered in Robert's ear, "The sharpest cut is yet to come."

"Does the King know of the latest pamphlet found in Willoughby village?" Robert replied softly, careful not to be overheard.

Lord Conway smiled. "His Majesty has great ability to hear what he wants to hear."

When the King finished eating, he rose from his seat. "Before we retreat to the drinking room, I must thank my host, Lord Lindsey."

King Charles turned to Lindsey. "You have provided a memorable visit, Lord Lieutenant. I trust you to leave no tax or payment to the crown uncollected. And I heartily commend you on recruiting a regiment for my service. But you may be at ease, Lindsey. I have authorized Marquess Hamilton to raise six thousand volunteers in Scotland to support King Gustav Adolphus. Now, my lords, we shall retire to the drinking hall!"

Conway turned to Robert. "Come with me."

Robert followed Conway to Lord Lindsey. "A word Lord Lindsey," Conway said, interrupting Lindsey's vacant stare. "Tomorrow's schedule. You and Montclair are to ride beside the King's coach to King's Lyn. You, Lindsey on the right and Montclair on the left."

Lindsey stared at Conway for several seconds before replying, "Is this yet another slight?"

Lord Conway sighed. "The King knows you and Montclair are his greatest strength in Lincolnshire. He needs both of you. Do not give worry to his humor. He sees it only as fun. As for his call to Lord Hamilton, be thankful."

Lindsey interrupted, "Thankful? Hamilton has no military experience. The man has never seen a battle, never faced cannon fire. Why he…"

Conway shot back, "He leads for Scotland, and Scotland is not England–a difference perhaps only in the eyes of the King. A difference he hopes Spain will accept. The King's good humor was the news carried by Lord Cottington seated at the place of honor beside the King. Do you know he brought with him a treaty offer from Philip of Spain? Do you, Lord Lindsey, a proven soldier who served alongside the Prince of Orange, wish to be in the field when the King betrays our current allies? When he betrays the Prince of Orange and fights to carve up the United Netherlands? Pray it never comes to pass, but that is his mind tonight."

Robert saw the pain in Lindsey's eyes. "The Marquess of Hamilton has not yet begun to recruit. I know the north and Scotland. Buckingham's disasters linger in the minds of the veteran soldiers–the few that returned alive. He will be hard-pressed to find one thousand, but six thousand? The nobles strain under the taxes, and you have seen the passion of the Skimmington marchers. Time. Time is our ally. Tomorrow, we will ride beside our King in a show of support but also for his protection. He may reward loyalty with an ear to counsel. Perhaps a change in course."

Lindsey sighed. He looked down and nodded. "I am still Lord Lieutenant of Lincolnshire, and Charles is my King."

Lindsey looked Robert in the eye and said, "The noble serves the King. God's order."

The King's baggage was loaded while his Majesty enjoyed his breakfast. Willoughby House courtyard was busy with coachmen, footmen, and household servants preparing for the royal departure. The King's baggage cart was the first to make its way from Willoughby House. Coaches filled with sleepy courtiers began to follow. It was nearly two hours before King Charles climbed into his handsome coach. Sitting on the embroidered seat inside, the King found a bundle of papers bound by a purple ribbon. "What's this? More papers from Conway? Will the man never stop pestering me with petitions from greedy lords?"

King Charles sighed as he picked up the bundle and untied the ribbon. He picked up the sealed letter on top, unfolded it, and read:

"Woe to those who enact unjust statutes and to those who constantly record harmful decisions, so as to deprive the needy of justice and rob the poor among My people of their rights, so that widows may be their spoil and that they may plunder the orphans. Now, what will you do in the day of

punishment and in the devastation which will come from afar? To whom will you flee for help? And where will you leave your wealth? Nothing remains but to crouch among the captives or fall among those killed. In spite of all of this, His anger does not turn away. And His hand is still stretched out."—The Word of the Lord. And I say REPENT! I am coming for you! Repent before you are cut off from the living! Charles Stuart, I leave you with pamphlets for your journey. Read the indictments against you. You have been tried and judged. Only your sentence awaits! One from among your subjects will surely take your life!

Arthur Pendragon, Rex Britannia Emeritus

King Charles crumpled the letter in his hand and tossed it down beside him. He picked up the small bundle of pamphlets, then set them down again. "Summon Lords Lindsey and Montclair! Now! Find them! Tarry and I shall have you flogged!"

Servants and guards scurried off. Both Robert and Lord Lindsey were nearby and heard the King's rant. In moments, the two lords of Lincolnshire were at the royal coach. "Your servants, your Highness," Lindsey said as both men bowed.

"Your damn Arthur Pendragon!" Charles said as he threw the bundles of pamphlets out the window. "More of his seditious, traitorous, and pernicious work! And a letter! He threatens me, his King! Charles threw the letter in Robert's face.

"Lord Lindsey, you brought this man here! Find him! And you, Lord Montclair, my Lord Inquirer, do your job! Capturing bumbling merchants and boatmen is not enough! I want this scoundrel who calls himself Pendragon caught! I want him in the tower on the rack, and I want him hanged, drawn, and quartered!"

Both men bowed and said in unison, "Yes, your Majesty."

Lindsey continued, "I shall double the guard on your journey."

Robert had picked up the crumpled letter and read it. While Charles replied, "I should not have a single member of your regiment near this coach! Is that understood? You, Lindsey, shall ride to my right and Montclair to my left. And may God help you if any harm comes to me!"

King Charles exhaled a deep sigh. "Lord Montclair, what do you make of the letter? A churchman, perhaps?"

Robert replied, "Your Majesty refers to the quotation. It is from the prophet Isaiah...."

"I did not ask for the citation. The traitor–is he a non-conformist? A Puritan, I have heard them called?"

Robert measured his words. "A possibility I will certainly pursue. He quotes the Authorized English Bible, available to any literate subject. But the scripture he quotes also refers to defeat by a foreign power. His complaints are both political and religious. If you have no desire to read the pamphlets, we shall study them...."

"Read them? Are you mad? I will not add to his insult. Take them. See if you find any clue to his identity. Now, I have been delayed long enough."

King Charles tapped the roof of his coach, the coachman released the brake, shook the reins, and was off.

Robert threw the letter and pamphlets to Lynch, who had silently appeared at this side. "Send them to Newgate London, and get me a transcript–and the interrogation of the three men held–where did they get the pamphlet? I'm off." Robert mounted his horse and loped to catch up with the royal coach.

The Royal Coach passed through the South Gate into King's Lynn just before sunset. The King made a brief stop at his apartment at Clifton House before proceeding to Saint George's Guildhall for a banquet. His Majesty was tired and irritable and did not stay long afterward in the drinking hall.

Robert needed to clear his mind and walked along Saint Margaret's Lane to the Hanse Warehouse. The busy grain pier on the Great Ouse River reminded him of Berwick-upon-Tweed and his friends there. *What would Will advise? And Karl, somewhere on the continent. How I miss their company. And Edward, he would certainly have something to say! Religion, foreign alliances, taxes, disputes with*

Parliament—who hasn't King Charles offended?

In his room at the Gryffin Inn, Robert sat down and wrote:

Dearest Eleanor,

It is with great regret that I tell you that I will not return for William's birthday. Events require me to continue with His Majesty to London. A foul plot is afoot-a most dangerous threat to our King.

Please assure William of my love and affection. And the horse—Brisby knows the one-he has outgrown the pony. How I wish I could ride with him! And you, my dear, how I long to ride alongside you once again to the pond below the falls. What sweet memories I have of our recreation there!

Forgive me, my love, for sending you the poor distraught widow and children. I trust your good nature to see they are cared for. I expect that we will travel from King's Lynn to London, but wisely, Lord Conway holds the King's itinerary close. It would be best to send letters to London.

/s/ Robbie

CHAPTER 8
CADZAND CONTACTS

Mister Black did not share Robert's love of the sea. He was glad to hear the lookout shout, "Land ho! Close on the starboard bow!"

Black rushed on deck and ran forward. His eyes could not distinguish between land or water on the gray horizon before him. Captain Haakon Anderson walked beside him and said, "The Westerscheldt opens ahead of us. The United Netherlands is to the left, and the Spanish Netherlands is to the right. Prince Maurice of Orange holds the whole of the Scheldt."

Anderson handed Black a telescope and continued, "Cadzand is just to the right at the river entrance. A small harbor and village at the mouth of little more than a creek, but it is well protected with a stone jetty."

Mister Black stared through the telescope, swinging it to the right and the left. "It's all a gray horizon to me."

Anderson smiled. "Stand still while I swing you towards the church spire. Aye, a good seaman can recognize a harbor by its church spire."

The captain slowly positioned Black, looked from behind him, and reaffirmed, "Surely you see the church and even the jetty. See how it breaks the line of the seashore."

Black looked carefully before handing the telescope back to Captain Anderson. "Is there a land so flat on Earth? Nothing but a thin line of sand meeting the sea. How long?"

Two hours later, Black and his men stood silently behind Captain Haakon Anderson while the customs officer asked his entry questions.

"English, I presume? Last port? Cargo?

"Aye. Out of Barton-upon-Humber." Anderson nodded towards Black and his men, "Passengers–they'll be returnin' with me."

The customs officer looked at Black and said, "They come to inspect their cargo? What cargo will you load?"

"They come to free a relative–believed in Antwerp–a soldier and prisoner of the Army of Flanders. It is a fool's errand, I know. But they are most determined–and pay well."

The customs officer looked at Mister Black and said, "Het Steen, in English 'The Stone.' It is the prison. A castle in the old city. It cannot be taken by storm, and its guards are most diligent. Only parole or a reprieve will see him released."

Mister Black nodded. "Het Steen. We shall begin there. Thank you."

The customs officer shook his head and smiled. "You do not sail into the river Scheldt? You avoid officials in the Spanish Netherlands. You do not believe parole is possible. I wish you well, my friend."

Captain Anderson asked, "If my friends do not return, Cadzand is known for passengers to England, passengers who might want to avoid Antwerp."

The customs officer looked around and replied quietly. "Careful, my friend. There are watchers from the Spanish Netherlands. They linger in the inn and wander the harbor. Go to the church and whisper to the pastor at the communion rail. He will instruct you."

After the customs officer departed, Black said, "You have bought us some time to find our true cargo, and if all goes well, I endeavor to fill this boat with refugees."

Anderson replied, "There is no love lost here for the Spanish Crown or the French. You will never hear a Cadzand official say it, but they know nearly all the boats in the harbor are smugglers. They sympathize with the cause and know it is the livelihood of their citizens."

"Yes, and if all goes as planned, you shall be a

frequent visitor. Now, take me to Johannes De Vries."

For such a small village, the ratskeller was crowded. Anderson whispered, "Welcome to the smuggler's guild of Cadzand. The innkeeper will know De Vries."

The innkeeper greeted them. "Back again, Haakon?"

"Yes. I'm looking for Johannes De Vries."

The innkeeper glanced towards a lone man sitting at the table nearest the bar, then looked up and said, "Johannes De Vries? Haven't seen him."

Haakon replied, "Where can I find him?"

The innkeeper shrugged. "What are you havin'?"

Anderson replied, "Bedankt," and turned for the door.

Black followed the innkeeper's eyes back to the table in earshot of the bar. "Two beers, bread, and cheese." Then made his way to the one open table.

When he and Anderson were deep in the ratskeller, Black whispered. "When looking for someone at an inn or pub, never leave without a drink. It brings suspicion. You heard the customs officer's warning about the Spanish watchers. The innkeeper pointed him out to us–first table. The question is, do we want him to overhear us?"

"Spanish watcher? How did you…."

"You said De Vries is well known, but the

innkeeper wouldn't give you a straight answer. Wait and see what happens. We may soon play both sides. Leave the talking to me."

The innkeeper brought a tray with beer, bread, and cheese. "Johannes has gone. Left last week with an Englishman. The Flemish are asking questions. This may be a United Provinces city, but that doesn't make it safe."

"Did they travel to England?"

"They spoke of a shipment and left together. I do not know the boat or the captain."

Black asked, "The cargo?"

The innkeeper shrugged. "The cheese is excellent—from Gouda."

No sooner had the innkeeper walked off than the man seated at the first table got up and carried his beer over to Black and Anderson. "May I join you, friends? Perhaps another beer?"

Black motioned at an empty chair, and the man sat down. "Ah, English! We share a common interest. I could not help but overhear you asking after Johannes De Vries. I, too, have urgent business with Johannes, but as I am a stranger, no one will tell me where I can find him."

Black took a sip from his beer. "In Cadzand, too many questions will do that. Discretion is required in their business."

"So, I have learned. But you know Johannes. You

have done business with him, perhaps?"

"Perhaps."

"As I say, I have urgent business with Johannes. We are friends. He will reward you–as will I, if you take me to him."

"And what business is that?"

"I am like everyone here. You understand."

Black set down his beer and chuckled. "Yes, I do understand. Johannes has goods to move. Men come here to find cargo, sensitive cargo that cannot be shipped from Antwerp or Bruges, cargo that no English customs officer will ever see. If Johannes is not here, there is always another shipper. You are not here looking for cargo but the man Johannes. I surmise, like everyone in Cadzand, that you come on behalf of the Spanish crown. So, tell me, why does Spain pursue a man who works to restore the Roman Catholic Church in England?"

The man sighed. "So, they all know."

"They are not fools."

"Then tell me, my English friend, why you ask for Johannes."

Black smiled. "His last shipment has proven very popular. The customer has offered a premium for more. But we shall return with a cargo whether from Johannes or someone else."

The stranger tasted his beer. "He goes too far.

Catholic books and pamphlets are one thing, but Johannes now threatens a new English alliance with Spain and the Spanish Netherlands. His pamphlets call for regicide. We cannot have one fanatic bring down this new treaty."

Black nodded. "I have read this pamphlet. It is getting results, though the first attempts failed, and the pamphlets were confiscated."

"Help me find Johannes, and I will give you access to other books. Perhaps not as provocative."

Black lifted his mug and drank. "You say you will reward us if we help. We would want more than just access to contraband Catholic books. You see the risk we take with our friends here in Cadzand."

"Yes, a reward. Gold. We can talk of a reward."

Black looked about the room and whispered, "You can start by telling me where Johannes printed his pamphlets."

Ten minutes later, the Flemish stranger was out the door. Haakon Anderson sat back in his chair and said, "I am going to enjoy working for you, Mister Black. A man in my business can learn a thing or two from you. You are going to pay me the going rate?"

"You have Lord Montclair's word–a fair rate. You will stay here and wait for word. Mister Brown will stay with you and Smith will travel with me. Go to church Sunday and arrange for what protestant refugees may be looking for passage. And, by all means, stay on good terms with the innkeeper. We will need him. Call for more beer now and follow my lead."

When the innkeeper came with two more beers, he said, "A long conversation. A new friend from Flanders?"

Black replied, "He won't be disturbing your customers any longer. It seems Johannes was working for him but shipped something, not on the list. I told him I came to warn Johannes but that he already learned of the danger. Every man has a price; he came cheap. Captain Anderson and I will pick up the slack."

The keeper nodded. "Good riddance to the Flemming. Don't need the likes of him givin' the evil eye to my patrons. Now, will you gents be havin' your supper? A good rabbit stew tonight."

"Aye, bring your stew and more beer. And if there be any cargo for Hull or Barton or any quiet cove on the east coast of England, Captain Anderson has a ship to fill."

"They'll find ye. Always a cargo for that quiet cove."

As the innkeeper walked away, Haakon Anderson asked. "You mean to follow the Fleming?"

Black nodded. "Aye, to a printer in Antwerp."

Anderson replied, "You know that all trade to Antwerp is blockaded–chains across the mouth of the River Scheldt."

Black replied, "And Cadzand prospers because it serves both the United Netherlands and Spanish Netherlands for certain goods and information to cross the frontier. Three days to Antwerp and perhaps a week for my business. Expect to depart in a fortnight. I will send a messenger ahead."

Haakon shook his head. "Smuggling their cargo is one thing, but for an Englishman to enter Spanish Netherlands–risky business. Your story to the customs man–don't you become the man imprisoned in Het Steen! Can you trust this Fleming? They stood by and watched the Spanish army expel their protestant neighbors–looked only to profit on good Christian folks' misfortune."

"Displacements and evil have befallen all of Christendom. We do what we must to survive. But who has been hurt, and who prospers? Antwerp and all of Flanders withers while Amsterdam flourishes with its new citizens from the south. You concentrate on filling the ship. I will worry about our Flemish friend."

Black finished his supper and told Anderson. "I will stay here at the inn. Send my man Jones to see me. Brown is to stay with you aboard the ship for now. You are never to be out of his sight until I return. Is that understood?"

"Aye. I'm glad of the company–glad to be aboard your enterprise, Mister Black."

Black was surprised when the innkeeper came and gave him a room key and a candle. "Figure you'll be wantin' to stay the night in a good bed after your crossing. Room one, top of the stairs."

Opening the palm of his hand, Black bounced the key lightly and stared into the innkeeper's face. "You learn your patrons quickly. Room one top of the stairs. I expect a visitor later. Send him up when he asks for me."

"Knowin' my patrons and their work keeps my inn full. Good night, Mister…."

"Black is the name. I rise early and eat hearty."

"Good night, Mister Black, a hearty breakfast at dawn."

The worn steps creaked as Black climbed. Room one was across the hall at the top of the stairs. Black stood outside the door and listened. He heard voices coming from down the hall but nothing from room one. A single candle at the top of the stairs shed a dim light through the hallway. The darkness at the bottom of the door was unbroken. Mister Black lit the small candle from the one in the hall, slowly slid the key into the lock, and turned it. Standing to one side, he pushed the door open. It swung slowly with only a quiet creak. Black waited ten seconds before stepping into the darkness. He made his way to the candle on the simple table by the window and lit it. Blowing out the small candle, he turned and said, "And who is it I am to thank for arranging my room?"

"Welcome to the United Netherlands, Mister Black. My name is Martens, Henrik Martens. I will provide your contacts in Antwerp and see that your messages are sent to the Lord Inquirer. Forgive the unorthodox welcoming, but we had no advance notice of your visit."

Black smiled. "No, it was all most sudden. The Lord Inquirer saw an opportunity and acted. I shall tell you all, but first, how did you come by this visit?"

Martens replied, "The customs officer and the innkeeper, too. They keep us informed. The customs officer is familiar with Captain Anderson and his smuggling. Wasn't like him to bring passengers here and, well, 'Het Steen,' is our password, as you know. So, I made haste to join you. I know you have met with the watcher sent by her Grace, Isabella Clara Eugenia, King Philip of Spain's governor and Duchess of the Netherlands. A watcher not so well matched to his duties."

"No, clever, he is not. But he is looking for the right man…."

"No doubt you speak of Johannes De Vries. Yes, a smuggler of Catholic books into England. Such smuggling is nothing new. What is the interest in him now?"

"Pamphlets. England is flooded with pamphlets offering a reward for the murder of our King. They came from here, Cadzand, on Haakon Anderson's ship. Lord

Robert foiled an attack not days ago and seized Anderson's ship. De Vries had an English buyer with him here. Like De Vries, he is missing. I have convinced the watcher to take me to the printer in Antwerp. My story is that I seek more pamphlets and Catholic books. Books 'acceptable' to her Grace, Isabella. It seems King Philip has demanded De Vries' pamphlets be stopped as an embarrassment while negotiations continue with England for a new alliance."

Martens stared at the candle and then replied, "The negotiations are privileged. We are told nothing. They could stall or fall apart at any moment. Perhaps they already have. King Charles follows the same ambitions for a Spanish alliance as his father, King James. It would be most unfortunate to be known in Antwerp if they fail once again. How is your Dutch?"

Black shook his head. "French. I will get by on my French. Perhaps I can pass as Walloon."

"I will shadow you to Antwerp. There, go to the tapestry dealer across from Het Stein. He will arrange all."

Black nodded. "Tapestry dealer? One of Karl Schroeder's men? Good. I need to contact Karl. Do you know where he is?"

"Herr Schroeder travels to Saxony. General Wallenstein lays siege to Eilenberg. His man, Werner is trapped in the city. In Antwerp, you will learn more."

"Very well. One of my men travels with me to

Antwerp, another stays here with Haakon Anderson. I have told Anderson we sail in a fortnight with refugees for England. Now tell me about Isabella. I have heard she is called 'the Lady of Netherlands' and that her heir is the King of Spain. Is there opposition to her rule?"

"Any opposition is long past. She is both loved and respected, a most remarkable and capable woman. Lady Isabella has overcome great personal tragedy and brought stability to the southern provinces. As for her heir, her marriage to Archduke Albert of Austria was intended to create a third royal Hapsburg line. She bore three children. All died at a young age. When Albert died, sovereignty returned to King Philip in Spain, but Isabella remains as his governor. She rules in his name but with warm regard for the Netherlands. The Lady champions the arts and commerce. Even now, she works to provide a new port for exports to replace Antwerp and the blocked Scheldt. A pious Catholic, she has restrained the zeal for the persecution of protestants, though they have long ago departed. As long as you present no threat against Lady Isabella or Spain's military campaign, you should be safe to pursue the English connection to these pamphlets–for a time. A time we do not know."

CHAPTER 9

THE PURITAN CONNECTION

The Royal entourage continued its tour of England's eastern seaports, berating and intimidating lords and merchants for an increased ship tax. Yarmouth followed King's Lyn and then on to Ipswich. The King took an apartment at Christchurch Withipol House, home of Viscount Hereford, Leicester Devereux. Lord Devereux's wife Elizabeth inherited the property from her father, the last of the wealthy Withipol master-merchants. The grand house was built near the town center on the grounds of the old Priory of the Holy Trinity. Robert smiled as he read then translated the family motto inscribed from the Latin above the door. "Frugality, so dissipation does not occur." *There is no doubt where the heart of this merchant lay!*

Robert entered lord Weston's chamber, where Lord Conway sat, listening to the King's Treasurer, complain.

"Lord Montclair, good that you are here. A den of thieves, Ipswich. Smugglers, non-conformists, and scoundrels all. They shall not like what their King and his treasurer have to say to them. You will need your wits about you, man. The merchants of Ipswich are no better than the loathsome Irish! Even the Bishop dare not show his face. He fears any interference in their unrestrained religious fanaticism a threat. They grow bold. Wealthy and bold to withhold both respect and tax to their King."

Robert replied, "The letter in the King's coach, you suspect a non-conformist?"

Conway's eyes bore into Robert's. "The King believes it was written by a non-conformist–the clear call for repentance. And Lord Weston has just instructed me in Ipswich's infamous history of smuggling heretical religious pamphlets from the Netherlands. Aye, even the nobles, our host, Lord Devereux, owes his wealth to his wife and has become a master-merchant. The town preacher, Samuel Ward, and his brother, Nathaniel, stir the people with unbridled zeal."

Robert nodded. "I have heard of this preacher. I intend to make inquiries. But I would remind you, Lord Conway, the pamphlets from Kingston-upon-Hull came from Cadzand, no doubt smuggled from the Catholic Spanish Netherlands, not the protestant United Provinces. Hard to believe that Catholics and Puritans, as they call themselves, are working together. Perhaps two plots? And with so much unrest–perhaps many plots. But your warning is taken. My watchers are among the people. We shall be prepared."

Near the ancient Saint Mary's-le-Tower Church, the local inns were filled with puritans waiting for transport to the Massachusetts Bay colony. The common rooms were filled with polite, orderly families taking their meals. While they waited their turn to board the small, cramped ships bound for the wild shores of far-off America, they listened to speeches and sermons of the fervent puritan, Samuel Ward. It was a stark contrast to the inns along the wharves that pulsed with sailors' and drunks' rowdy songs and laughter. Such was the influence of the puritan town preacher that if there were whores in these pier-side inns, neither their names nor faces were known in town.

Robert found a seat among the emigres and listened to the Reverend Samuel Ward as he opened his sermon, shouting, "Woe to that man! Woe to the sinner! Woe to the world for temptations to sin! For it is necessary for temptations to come, but woe to the one by whom the temptation comes! It would be better for him to have a great millstone fastened around his neck and be drowned in the depth of the sea. And if your hand or your foot causes you to sin, cut it off and throw it away. It is better for you to enter life crippled or lame than with two hands or two feet to be thrown into eternal fire. And if your eye causes you to sin, tear it out and throw it away. It is better for you to enter life with one eye than with two to be thrown into the hell of fire."

For two hours, Ward preached. He preached of a world condemned by sin. He preached of men and nations squandering the gifts of God. He condemned the evils of apathy and unfaithfulness for imperiling the Spirit-led reformation. The church was in a war of survival, and the old world, the established order, would be lost. The faithful of England had found refuge in Holland for a time–just as the nation of Israel and the infant Lord Jesus found refuge in Egypt. But the world around them did not see. They were blind to God's truth until, at last, God in His providence provided a new hope–a hope founded on establishing His church in the new world to be the city on the hillside that could not be hidden. The light of this shining city would burn bright before the world. A new Boston, a city where no prince or bishop or power or the anti-Christ pope imperiled the obedient of Christ.

Preacher Ward concluded, "Dearly beloved, you have been called to that great mission of submission to Christ, who said, 'If you love me, obey my commands.' Follow your calling with joy and a fervent heart to be that light of hope to the nations!"

As the faithful quietly filed out, Robert made his

way forward to Samuel Ward. "Reverend Ward, will you be leading your band of pilgrims to Massachusetts?"

Ward looked at Robert. "Do I know you, sir?"

"Lord Robert Curtis, Earl of Montclair and Lord Inquirer to his Majesty, King Charles."

"I have heard of you, Montclair. You are known for your humble works of charity. A priest, I am told. Yet you spy out enemies of the King. No. I will stay here and prepare the path for those who go. John Winthrop leads and governs the faithful in Massachusetts. He is a most capable brother."

"Your sermon, Reverend Ward, 'Woe to the man,' have you preached its brother passage, 'Woe to those who enact unjust statutes and to those who constantly record harmful decisions….'"

Ward interrupted, "So as to deprive the needy of justice and rob the poor among my people of their rights….' I know the passage. It is Chapter 10 of Isaiah. You ask if I preach against the King."

"I ask if you have penned such words as an indictment and a threat against the life of his Majesty King Charles."

"I would be mad to affirm such a thing."

"Or honest to your conviction and fully trusting in your Lord."

Robert paused. His eyes narrowing, he said, "Such

a letter has been delivered to King Charles. It made a direct threat to his Majesty's life and well-being. His majesty believes a non-conformist wrote the letter. This letter was delivered as his Majesty came to Ipswich to address withholding of taxes due him. And you, Reverend Ward, are remembered for your pamphlet condemning your sovereign, King James' prerogative in seeking to match the Prince of Wales and the Spanish Infanta."

"Aye, Lord Inquirer, I spoke against the Spanish match–as did most of the parliament and countless lords. Such a marriage was a threat to our protestant faith. I was tried and exiled for a time. The matter was put to rest. I am licensed by the Church under the supervision of the Bishop. King Charles has granted our Massachusetts Bay Colony a charter. Why would I raise my hand against my King?"

Robert asked. "Then tell me, is his Majesty King Charles' marriage to the Catholic Henrietta Maria any different to his marriage to the Catholic Infanta, Maria Anna?"

"It is different in that Catholic Spain does not rule England. England has not allied with Spain or France against our protestant faith."

"The non-conformist pamphlets speak of the Queen's Catholic influence on King Charles, as head of the Church in England as a threat to our peculiar faith."

Ward cocked his head and replied. "Is he indeed head of the church? Is he not inferior to Christ the King–true head of the holy catholic church? Where does all authority come from, but from God above?"

"The apostles and the fathers have established that we honor and bow to authority granted by God, even if they be in error."

"It is true that God gave us kings to rule over us. It is true Daniel served the idol-worshipping kings of Babylon, Persia, and the Medes. But God acknowledged one king to model kingship. Not the strong warrior Saul. Not the wise Solomon–but David, humble, obedient, and willing to do God's will. A sinner who repented and accepted God's punishment."

"Punishment? Is that what you desire for Charles?"

"Repentance and obedience are what God desires of all His children."

"And lacking repentance, should King Charles be struck down dead? Is that what your Puritan religion teaches?"

No! No, never. Never have I called for the murder of any man. Regicide? No. I leave him to God's judgment."

"And others? Do you stand aside silently, knowing they plan evil? Is that any less damning?"

"I will hear no such talk! It is most un-Christian. You have heard me speak of our vision. But you, Lord

Montclair, send your secret men throughout the kingdom searching, determined to persecute good Christian men whose desire it is to obey our Lord. You must be well pleased that Bishop Laud uses the star-chamber and torture against saints like Alexander Leighton."

"I would correct you in one-point, Reverend Ward. It was not David's obedience that God honored. As you say, he sinned greatly. It was David's heart. He loved God and trusted God, and yes, humbly repented his sin. You question my faithfulness to holy orders. But I, too, have a vision. A vision where all who love God disavow the persecution of followers of our Lord. My vision is of one universal, holy catholic church where the mysteries of God can be explored in humility, recognizing faith is our common bond. Mysteries, Reverend Ward, the whole truth yet unknown this side of the veil. God is our perfect judge. Only He knows our hearts. But I believe this, brother Ward; I believe the church is far wider and larger than the factions created by men will ever acknowledge."

Both men stared at each other in silence. Robert sighed and said, "I trust, sir, that any seditious talk you hear is reported. You would not want the king's blood on your hands or the blood of the innocent who will assuredly pay the price of insurrection. As for Bishop Laud, you rail against him on when to bow or not to bow, on music and liturgy. These are of no account towards faith and our historic creeds. It is your preference, not God's truth, you demand. I see the two of you cut from the same cloth of intolerance. Good night, Reverend Ward."

In the moonlight, Robert walked, reviewing the conversation in mind. He stopped and stared at the stars above. *Why do I let them unnerve me so? Am I wrong to protect the King? Surely, God in his sovereignty, is working His will through his Majesty, King Charles. Do my prayers for Charles' change of heart—his repentance—make me a hypocrite? Am I walking in your will, O Lord?*

Robert laced his fingers behind his neck, stretched, and turned his eyes towards the waterfront. He shook his head and whispered to himself. "Samuel Ward has no motive. The King chartered his colony in America. Any seditious act would see the charter revoked. No, other Puritans, perhaps. Scotland maybe, or Wales but not here. Not Ipswich or Sussex. The man with the scarred ear, calling himself Arthur Pendragon, where is he?"

That night, his watchers reported no sightings of "scarred ear," nor overheard seditious conversations. No new pamphlets were recovered. Thanking them, Robert sent them back out into the darkened city.

In Christchurch Mansion, Robert made his way to Viscount Conway's room. Light crept from beneath the door, prompting Robert to knock lightly. "Yes, I'm awake. Who disturbs me this late hour?"

"Just a brief word, Lord Secretary."

"Montclair. Come through, man. Do you ever sleep?"

Robert entered the chamber and saw Lord Conway at his writing table. "Duty first, as ever, Lord Conway?"

"More pleasure than duty, sir. You have caught me writing to my dear wife." Conway paused then said, "Where would a man be without his wife? I have been twice blessed in marriage, and it pains me to realize I have been absent far more than in the company of one I trust and love. She is the only person I dare trust in these troubled times."

Lord Conway pointed to a chair. Robert sat down as Conway continued. "You are married. Do you find the same?"

"Indeed, it is just as you say. Though I am blessed with friends outside of court and do not share the risks of daily contact with his Majesty."

"Without the many voices of Parliament, one lonely voice dares not to be heard. Now, what is it you have to report?"

"Quiet. No sightings of the mysterious Arthur Pendragon. No new pamphlets and no suspicious talk." Robert sighed deeply before continuing. "I have made inquiries of the town preacher, the Reverend Samuel Ward, a notorious non-conformist. I find him and his flock, no threat. He has too much to risk with his charter for the Massachusetts Bay Colony. In his mind, and in the mind of those waiting to embark on their pilgrimage, they have left England and the King behind. I know His Majesty suspects a Puritan, but not from Ipswich or Sussex. They prepare their families for the promised land in Massachusetts Bay Colony. Perhaps a Puritan from Scotland or Wales, though I will continue my inquiries."

"Aye, Ward is not the threat. No word on the self-ascribed Arthur Pendragon?"

Robert shook his head. "The scar across his ear. A soldier, perhaps. You have spent much time fighting in the Palatinate and the Netherlands. Do our soldiers bear resentment for his Majesty?"

"Most soldiers fight for pay, not cause. But volunteers–officers, gentlemen—they follow their heart. They have watched comrades—brothers fall to save our protestant faith. They have depended on parliament to keep their cause before the King. But now...."

"But now, King Charles has dissolved parliament and pursues a betrayal of our allies. It must pain you, Lord Conway, as a veteran of the wars and once governor of the English occupation of Brim, to hear of Lord Cottington's treaty."

Conway shook his head. "My support for the United Netherlands, the Palatinate, and the protestant cause was well known in parliament. But my work now is to advise the King and see his will is carried out. I am in no position to challenge his decisions. So, I just...."

"You write to your wife. You share with her your concern and say nothing in court."

"Aye, and what about you, Robert? You rescue German Lutherans and Calvinists—and French Huguenot refugees. You send the family of a traitor to your wife. Does she alone know your mind?"

CHAPTER 10

NEWS

The merchants and nobles of Ipswich waited in the great hall of Christchurch House for King Charles to address them. Robert watched as they grew impatient. The soft murmuring grew louder, and voices became agitated as the delay lengthened. An hour passed, and the King's coach rolled to the front of the building. The baggage carts had already left, and courtiers could be seen mounting their horses and riding off. Only after the King's Treasurer, Lord Weston, arrived did the room become silent. Then the King's herald stepped inside, slammed the staff of his halberd on the floor, and announced. "His Majesty King Charles."

The assembled aristocrats and master merchants of Ipswich kneeled and bowed as Charles strode quickly into the room. Without taking his seat, he said, "Good men of Ipswich, you are honored to hear the good news. My

Queen Consort, dear Queen Mary, shall soon deliver an heir to the throne. I must be off to Saint James Palace. Now, as to the collection of taxes, because I am in good humor this day, I shall only say that you must repent of your greed and miserly ways. Thieves and scoundrels offer more to their sovereign than the rich merchants of Ipswich. I leave Lord Weston to instruct you. If he does not bring me a favorable report, I shall send men at arms to collect what fancies them at a percentage to assure an abundance. Now, you may wish me well and pray for the health of Queen Mary and the child."

Before the King finished his announcement, Robert slipped out and found Lord Conway waiting beside the royal coach. "We are off to London, then. Good–I would see his Majesty safe within the palace walls."

Conway nodded. "Tonight, we are at Colchester, then Chelmsford before we arrive at Epping Forest, The hunting lodge. You and your men will take rooms in Chingford. I have arranged The Crown Stag Inn on the green."

"So close to London, why stop at Epping Forest?" Robert asked.

"Not fifteen miles away. His Majesty will spend his waiting time hunting. After the stillbirth of a son but a year ago, he will not see the Queen Consort until he has news."

Robert started to answer but said nothing.

Conway added, "His Majesty worries. He will remain at the hunting lodge until the queen goes into labor. Too many memories of last year pacing the halls of Saint James. The queen is the only soul his Majesty loves."

A single road wound its way from Chingford towards the hunting lodge built by Queen Elizabeth in Epping Forest. The thick canopy of old oaks held back the afternoon sun, and the damp smell of moss and fern hung in the still, cool air. The King's coach rolled to the right as it made its way around a massive tree and across the muddy remains of a spring creek. King Charles loved to hunt, and he gazed from his coach in hopes of sighting a stag as they rounded the turn and approached the lodge bathed in sunlight in an open meadow ahead.

"Stop!" He yelled as he banged his cane against the overhead,

"On the tree. There, on the great oak–something is posted–nailed to the tree! Bring it to me."

A guard quickly pulled the poster from the tree and handed it to King Charles. The King's face burned red with anger as he read.

Woe to Charles, Tyrannus! Woe to him who builds his house by unrighteousness and his rooms by injustice; who uses his neighbor's service without wages and doesn't give him his hire. Shall you reign because you strive to excel in palaces? Your eyes and your heart are for covetousness and for shedding innocent blood and for oppression and violence, I will give you into the hand of those who seek your life. Thus says the LORD, "Write this man childless, for no more shall a man of his seed prosper, sitting on the throne."

The fate of a wicked and unrighteous king!

Arthur Pendragon, Regis Emeritus

Charles called out, "Drive on! And send for my Lord Secretary and the Lord Inquirer. I command they come at once!"

Lord Conway was waiting when Robert approached his chamber. "Another letter from Pendragon. Read it."

Robert took the paper and read, "Handwritten, not printed."

"His Majesty is aggrieved that a threat is made against his child–not yet born. The non-conformists–he is convinced. We are to see him at once. What will you tell him?"

"Again, I will counsel his schedule is not shared. This man, this would be Pendragon, knew the king traveled here. As for the Puritans–perhaps, but not of those seeking passage to the American colonies."

"He will be angry, Lord Montclair, Do not test his patience. We go now."

King Charles glared at Robert as he was announced. "You took your time! Have you captured this

Pendragon? No, of course not. You come late and empty-handed. I want this man's head on a post at the tower and his quartered body nailed to the four gates of London. He threatens my child! The coward! I have said he is a non-conformist. Have you searched them out? Essex is filled with them. He trespasses in my forest and threatens me! And no one stops him? You have men and money, Lord Inquirer. What you have not provided are results! Well, say something! If you want to remain silent, I can have your tongue cut out! Speak!"

"As you say, your Majesty, we search out the non-conformists–Puritans, they call themselves. Indeed, they are many in Essex and Ipswich, but they seek no strife with your Majesty. They set their hearts and hands to build their holy city in America. But you rightly say this so-called Pendragon is filled with religious fervor. He quotes the prophets and pretends at Latin–though he may not be a scholar or a priest. Bibles can be found in every church, and it is from the Authorized Bible he quotes. His letters are penned by hand, not printed like the pamphlets we confiscate. Pamphlets printed in the Netherlands, where men pursue even as we speak."

The King replied, "You suggest there may be two traitors. This Pendragon playing on the pamphleteer?"

"They may be separate, or they may be in a conspiracy. We pursue all possibilities. We search for a man with a scar across his right ear. We follow the trail of every seditious pamphlet. But neither the pamphleteer nor this Pendragon has the courage or the means to act on his own. They look to others to work their evil will. You are well guarded. It is only your travels that are too widely known. The courtiers speak freely in the inns. It would be better if they not now until you have departed. And it would be best if I knew before and sent my men ahead,"

"Trust you, Montclair?"

"I have proven myself in service, your Majesty."

"Perhaps to my father. And if you send your men ahead, what prevents them from being followed."

Robert turned to Lord Conway. "Lord Secretary, do you know my watchers?"

Conway replied, "I know Mister Black...."

"Black is in the Netherlands. He pursues the printer,"

Conway added, "And Mister Lynch."

"Lynch went to London and has not yet returned. You do not know the watchers and the secret men. Nor are they known to the courtiers."

Robert bowed to King Charles, "Your Majesty, the danger is from the outside, but they have eyes and ears in your court."

King Charles sighed. "It is well known I stay here until I return to Saint James Palace. The guard shall be increased. Find this man or men! Go!"

James Lynch was waiting at the Crown Stag Inn when Robert returned. Lynch's Irish got the better of him and venturing the familiar, he said with a smile, "You look tired, my Lord, not getting enough sleep?"

Robert did not laugh. "Tell me you bring good news. There has been another letter posted."

His face now serious, Lynch replied, "I heard, near the Royal Hunting Lodge. Two letters since the last pamphlet. You wonder if they are from the same man. A hand is easier to identify than a printed pamphlet, but there, I do bring news."

Robert waved to the innkeeper and shouted, "Two ales and dinner," before sitting down.

"Go on then. How was your visit to London? More than good sleep in your own bed?"

"Print is much like handwriting. Its maker can be found out. Printers buy their letters, that is, typeset, from makers. The obvious path is to identify the script. But script may be common to many typeset makers who use a similar font when casting hot metal in molds. All casting from a mold will appear the same, and any flaw in a mold will be repeated in the typeset."

Robert interrupted, "You found a flaw which may lead to the typeset maker."

"Even better, we found a match to a known printer.

Here, let me show you."

Lynch opened his pouch and unfolded two pamphlets. "Look, the 's' the break in the crosshatch, and here the 't,' the tail is missing. It is the same in this pamphlet and in every pamphlet we have collected."

Robert studied the script. "You are certain this is unintended?"

"They differ in form from all other letters in the script. Now, look at this." Lynch pulled out a Dutch newspaper with the banner, 'Nieuwe Tijdinghen.' "It's from Antwerp. In English, 'New Tidings.' To the Dutch traders, it's called the Antwerp Gazette. Look at the 's,' and 't.' Same typecast flaw."

Robert studied font. "They're identical. You knew the pamphlets were smuggled from Cadzand, so you began with Dutch documents. You found it aboard a Dutch trading ship, no doubt. Splendid work, Mister Lynch. Brilliant!"

Robert paused. "Black is in the Spanish Netherlands...."

"I have sent word to him."

"While Black makes his inquiries in Antwerp, we have the handwritten letters–and there remains the man with a scar on his right ear, possibly a soldier...."

"The one calling himself Arthur Pendragon."

"Yes. He must be close. Someone in the royal party

is aiding him."

Robert looked down and sighed. "I am glad of your company, Lynch. I need someone I trust, someone with a clever mind and new ideas."

Lynch's eyebrows lifted as he said, "You been missin' me good Irish gift of the tongue. But it is you, Lord Robert, who keeps us on task. Aye, a good night's sleep, and you will be your overbearing self. Oh, I have something else, Letters from Lady Montclair sent to London."

Lynch reached into his pouch and pulled out three letters addressed to Robert in the elegant hand of Eleanor. Robert took them and studied them unopened. Robert looked up at Lynch as his dinner was set before him, smiled, and said, "Overbearing? Your Irish charm will protect you only so far, my friend. Let's eat. Tomorrow, we pursue our regal friend, Pendragon. Overbearing? So says the Irish devil!"

In the privacy of his room, Robert cut the wax seal with his knife, carefully unfolded, and read the first letter.

Dear Robbie

The grieving Gibbs family arrived before supper. Such sorrow! Is it true you accompanied the condemned Mister Gibbs to the gallows and attended his rites? For once, I am proud to be the wife of a humble country priest. I determined not to prevail on them in their grief but let them stay in the house until after the funeral. Young Reverend Hawkins presided. He is such a sweet young man and gifted with a merciful and loving heart. I have offered Mrs. Gibbs the vicarage and asked the Reverend Stevens and young Hawkins to take the rooms in the house. Return soon.

Eleanor

PS: Will asks to add his news.

Pappa,

I jumped the hedge. Well, Thunder jumped the hedge with me on his back! What great fun! You must come home, and we can have a hunt. Thunder is brave. The hounds and the horns will not frighten him. Reverend Hawkins said I am a fine horseman! Nanna and momma say I should be quiet and kind to the new children. They are nice. Come home soon.

William

Robert sat back, smiled, and re-read the letter as thoughts took him back to Montclair Castle. *Why am I here? I have a good life —a wife and children I love—good friends and the means to help many others. Indeed, that is the better calling....*

His thoughts disturbed by a thunderous crash from the inn below, Robert stood up and said to no one listening, "What is going on downstairs?"

The inn became quiet, and Robert opened his second letter.

Dear Robbie,

Paul Hawkins tutors young James Gibbs for placement at Cambridge. Are you confident of this charity, Robbie? Is this done from stewardship and not guilt? I shall trust your heart and will in this matter. The eldest daughter, Rachel, has caught the eye of Paul H. She is not shy in permitting his attention and insists on listening as the smitten Mister Hawkins schools her brother. How can men be so blind to such obvious flirtation?

Will asks to add a few words.

Eleanor

Robert laughed. "So says the greatest flirt in the court of King James! And I loved her all the more."

Robert read Will's note:

Pappa

How are you? I am fine. Mister Hawkins let me ride Zeus today. Ponies like Thunder are too small for a proper hunt. I still like Thunder, and Zeus is so big, but I am getting bigger too and want to ride the hunt. My birthday is soon. Please come home.

William

The noise downstairs grew louder, but Robert's mind was still on his letters. He opened the third.

Robbie,

I know how painful it is to miss Will's birthday. I am certainly not the one to cast blame. Will is resilient, and he loves you so much. Of course, he is pleased with his horse—are you sure he is ready for such a spirited mount? You must take him on a hunt as soon as you return. It is all he talks about. The twins are healthy, and mother is the perfect nanna. We all pray for your safe and soon return.

The Gibbs family has settled into the vicarage. Molly Gibbs shows an interest in our grain enterprise and suggests building a whiskey distillery. It seems that Mrs. Gibbs shows herself in the office of our Land Steward, Mister Brisby, as her daughter, Rachel does with Mister Hawkins. Brisby has never married. The man must be near sixty. Can his head still be turned by a fawning woman?

Will asks me to add: Come, home pappa, I miss you. And so do I, Robbie, come home and embrace me—love me as only you can.

Eleanor

PS: As I close this letter, Katie Hahn sends sobering news. Karl Schroeder has gone to Eilenberg in Saxony. His friend Werner is trapped in the walled city now under siege by the Swedish Army. I am confused. Isn't King Gustav Adolphus a protestant who joined the cause? Why would Gustav Adolphus lay siege to Eilenberg, a city filled with protestant refugees?

Loud cheers rising from the hall below interrupted Robert's thoughts. Three cheers, silence, and now shouts of anger and threats. "What now?" He asked himself as he headed out the door and down the stairs. Entering the common room, Robert saw a young man swaying as he stood holding out a sloshing mug of ale.

"You are all hogs at his Majesty's trough, yet you do not drink to our King's new Spanish alliance–to secure a future for England?"

A man in a rough country coat stepped forward and poured his mug of ale over the young man and said, "You are still young—stupid, but young. It should be my piss I pour over you and the Spanish."

The young man drew a sword, but before he could swing, the old man grabbed his wrist, swung the young man's arm behind him, and threw his attacker down on a table. With one arm, he pinned the young man's head down on the table, and with the other, he took the sword and said, "You are drunk. Time to sleep it off. But remember this, boy, no true Englishman courts an alliance with the Spanish. Charles may be our King, and his papist concubine is despoiling the land with her odious papist mass, but good Englishmen, true Englishmen, will not abide league with the devil.

James Lynch walked over to Robert and whispered, "The lad is Wolsey Percy, aid-decamp to Lord Cottington–well into his cups."

Robert nodded. "And the other, skilled in combat, a soldier perhaps?"

Lynch shrugged. "I don't know."

The young man struggled to get free. "King Charles

is England! No one will deny him his divine right to rule."

Again, the young man's face was slammed into the table. "Divine right? This is England, not Spain or France. We have Parliament, laws–rights for every Englishman. Even the Church Charles claims to head would not crown his French concubine. Aye, he may be King but has no papist divine right. And his French whore is no queen."

Lynch stepped forward. "That's enough friend, As you say, let the man take his leave."

The room was silent. Every eye fixed on the confrontation. The man sighed. "Aye. Lad, take leave of your betters and go to bed."

As soon as the young man was released, he stood and swung his fist at the face of his tormentor. A quick duck and the punch went wide, taking only the man's crude hat, which flew to the floor. Immediately, he had the young man by the collar and lifted him off his feet, head-butted him, and dropped him on the floor.

While young Percy lay on the floor, Robert stared at a scar on the uncovered right ear of the older man.

CHAPTER 11

ANTWERP

Mister Black, Jones, and Martens, sat on horseback and stared across the wide river Scheldt at the center of Antwerp. Het Steen, the fortress castle on the riverfront in the center of the walled city, stood guard over wharves lined with canal boats which moved their cargo between the great cities of Flanders separated by fields and marsh.

Henrik Martens pointed to the north and swung his arm to the south. "You see, Het Steen in the center, but notice the two great fortresses that anchor the city to the north and the south. The city walls are garrisoned all around. A tough nut to crack. It suits Prince Maurice to cut off the city from the German Ocean where the Scheldt turns to the estuary, the Westerscheldt. Lady Isabella has connected the cities in the south by river and canal and will soon open a new port on the coast. But Antwerp remains a strong and wealthy city. We can enter by ferry, but once inside, well, ferries can be stopped."

Black continued to scan the cityscape. "We will listen while we await the ferry. If there is unrest, it will be known at the ferry dock."

Martens asked, "The Fleming–where are you to meet him?"

"I am to ask for him at a canal boat, *The Lady of Netherlands*, moored in front of Het Steen."

Martens nodded. "Might I suggest you come to the tapestry shop first? Better we have some men nearby in case."

"Yes, first the tapestry shop."

The ferry took them to the center of Antwerp just below Het Steen. They mounted their horses and rode across a broad boulevard, careful of the many coaches and carriages making their way onto a market street lined with fine shops. Two doors down, Martens stopped, dismounted, and opened a black service entrance gate between two buildings. Down the narrow alley, they entered a large courtyard in the back. In the center was a stable and carriage house. The perimeter was lined with coal piles alongside cellar chutes and service doors to a dozen shops. After stabling their horses, they walked to the first door on the right. Martens said, "Come inside. You will learn when to use the front door and when to use this door. Antonin is the shopkeeper. He will instruct you."

Black, Martens, and Jones waited silently in a back room while Antonin Van Gaskin could be heard saying, "Yes, I know the house, tomorrow. I can deliver tomorrow. Good day, Heer Van Ooster."

Footsteps followed the sound of the front door closing. Antonin Van Gaskin stepped into the back room. "Henrik, you brought friends from England."

Martens replied, "This is Mister Black and his lieutenant, Mister Jones. They come on short notice, sent by the Lord Inquirer, Sir Robert Curtis."

Black and Jones bowed slightly as Martens added, "Antonin Van Gaskin, our man in Antwerp."

Van Gaskin returned the bow and said, "At last, we meet, Mister Black, or should I say Christian Fauconnier? I have heard of the good work you and the countess do."

Jones was surprised. "Christian Fauconnier? Black?"

Black smiled. "Dowager Countess, a past title. Few people in the trade know my wife or the name she restored for me. You are well informed, Heer Van Gaskin."

"Be certain that Heer Karl Schroeder holds both you and the dowager Countess Bellamy in the highest regard."

Jones shook his head and mumbled, "Your wife, a Countess?"

Black ignored the comment and replied to Van Gaskin, "Indeed, I hoped to see Karl. I am told he is in Saxony, troubles in Eilenberg?"

Van Gaskin pointed to chairs, and they sat down. "Yes, you missed him by but a week. Now, as to your visit to Antwerp. How can we help?"

Black explained, "Pamphlets offering a reward for the assassination of King Charles are flooding England. Already there have been attempts. The pamphlets, we recently learned, were printed here, smuggled by a Johannes De Vries. De Vries and an unnamed Englishman smuggled them through Cadzand. Watchers from the Spanish Netherlands are also looking for De Vries. They fear his actions threaten a new treaty between King Philip of Spain and King Charles. I am to meet the Flemish watcher here, on the canal boat, *The Lady of the Netherlands.*"

Van Gaskin stroked his beard. "Johannes De Vries is a smuggler, not a printer. You say an Englishman? There is a printer here. He came from England, the son of a Flemish father. Devout Catholic, he writes and prints many tracts—pamphlets for Catholics in England. Fluent in both English and Dutch. We watch him. He was known as Richard Rowlands in England, but now he goes by his Dutch family name, Verstegen. He could pass as English. But there are many printers in Antwerp and many sympathetic to their Catholic brothers in England. What else has the Flemish watcher told you?"

"They think me a smuggler. They want the pamphleteer stopped. They have offered a reward for De Vries and substitute goods to smuggle—other Catholic pamphlets that do not directly attack King Charles."

Van Gaskin stood up. "There is an inn on the boulevard along the river near Het Steen. Take a room there and then meet the watcher. Henrik knows the place. I shall send men to follow you and others to learn what we can of De Vries, Verstegen, and other printers. We will talk more tonight."

Martens left Black and Jones at the inn and returned to Van Gaskin's Tapestry Shop. Jones followed Black on foot at a distance and watched as he stepped on board the canal boat. Five minutes later, he followed Black, and the Fleming as they walked to Het Steen. Jones found a shade tree in the square in front of the castle and waited. Fifteen minutes later, the Fleming came out alone, and Jones watched the man return to the canal boat.

Mister Black sat alone in a dimly lit room just off the central cobblestone passageway. It was the last room before the iron-barred gate of the castle prison. The small room contained a table and two chairs. Black noted a second door to the room from the other side of the prison gate. There were no handles or knobs on either door inside the small room. He was at the mercy of unseen guards posted outside each door. Being a patient man, Black waited.

Nearly half an hour passed before a door creaked open, and a middle-aged man wearing the robes of a court clerk stepped inside. "I hope you did not find the wait unpleasant. I had some business to complete before our chat. A most secure prison, you must agree, Mister Black? A few smugglers are here, but you are not a smuggler, Mister Black. No, your trade is more dangerous than that. You trade in secrets for your King Charles. Men like you are why Het Steen is full today. As I say, a secure place from which there is no escape."

The man stopped talking, stared at Black, who replied, "And who is it I am addressing?"

Now smiling, the man said, "But of course you are comfortable. You spend so much time in Newgate prison in London. And how is the Lord Inquirer, Robert Curtis? Shall we expect him as well? Certainly, he cannot manage long without his number one. My name is Meers, Jan Meers. My duty is to protect King Philip and Lady Isabella from men like you. I am the man who decides which door you will pass through when I am finished."

Black nodded. "Heer Meers, it is good we meet as our interests are aligned. You do not want King Philip, or the Lady Isabella connected to an assassin determined to kill King Charles. I can assure you, the pamphlets promising a reward for such regicide have come from Antwerp. I can show you one if you like. Your man, hopefully not your best, has volunteered to help us find a smuggler, Jan De Vries, and lead us to a printer of religious tracts smuggled to England. We also know of another print smuggler here in Antwerp, an Englishman, the son of a Flemish father, Richard Verstegen, who also goes by Rowlands. A timely apprehension of this plotter, and I shall return to my apartment in London Newgate."

"My man has mentioned De Vries. It is true we seek him. Any man apprehended in the Spanish Netherlands will face justice here. We won't send our traitor to England and have Spain, or the Netherlands held to ridicule."

"I have heard King Charles' word on this. The plotter is to be hanged, drawn, and quartered. It is the appropriate sentence for an attack on the crown. But then, you and I can leave the jurisdiction of sentencing to the ambassadors and royal negotiators."

Meers replied, "Your boat captain gathers protestant refugees to sail to England."

Black laughed. "So you have another watcher in Cadzand. One not so clumsy. It is true, why return with an empty ship? They have already made their way from Catholic oppression."

Meers did not laugh but stared into Mister Black's

eyes. "The Dowager Countess Bellamy, your wife, risks her son's career. Do not try the patience of Lady Isabella with this continuing flow of French Huguenots through our land."

Black returned the stare. "Cadzand benefits both sides. When trading routes are cut by war, unofficial routes must be opened. King Philip permits refugees to emigrate, and King Charles allows Catholic books to be imported–along with fine Flemish tapestries and French wine. It will always be the case. As I told your man, the boat that brought me can continue to trade—your trade–with my protection."

Meers sat back in his chair. "Bring me the pamphlet. Tomorrow we will call upon a printer."

Black smiled. "Do we meet here? Or somewhere else more comfortable?"

Meers stood up and rapped on the door Black had entered through. "Breakfast—tomorrow at your inn. Your men Jones and Martens can join us."

Jan Meers and another man were seated at a table when Mister Black went down from his room in the morning. "I trust you slept well, Mister Black. I took the liberty of ordering an English breakfast–or what can pass for an English breakfast in Antwerp. Will you be alone this morning, or shall we wait for Heer Jones and Heer Martens? No? I see they plan to follow at some distance.

Really, my friend, such little trust! Antwerp is my city. They will be of no help if I choose to lock you away in Het Steen."

Black pulled out a chair and sat down. "No need to be blunt, Meers. I know your power. No, I have other matters for Jones and Martens of no threat to your King or the Lady Isabella."

"Yes. News of the war, no doubt. I can help there. The Army of Flanders marches from victory to victory. King Gustavus Adolphus will come too late. Too late for Eilenberg, one of the strongest protestant cities of Saxony, under siege as we speak. You can report to King Charles that the Swedish King is a fool and will fail. King Charles should not tarry if he wishes a share in the spoils. Victory over Prince Maurice and the United Provinces is certain."

The innkeeper arrived with a food tray and set it on the table. Meers smiled. "Eat your breakfast. We start with Richard Verstegen."

Beyond the boulevard lined with ornate merchant warehouses with lavish apartments above, past the market street and the cathedral, towards the city wall, the houses became smaller, and the streets narrower. They stopped in front of a modest home with a guard standing in front.

"Still hasn't returned," the guard reported as Meers approached.

Meers was not happy. "Question the neighbors.

When was he last seen? Who were his visitors? Find out everything they know about him. If they do not cooperate, take them to Het Steen for a more determined interrogation."

Jan Meers spoke to the silent companion with him since breakfast. "Force the door. We shall see what clues he has left us."

Verstegen's tidy, modest home bore the look of an abbot's cell. The main room contained two high back chairs facing a tiled fireplace accented with two fire screens covered by tapestry. Across the room was a writing table with two candlesticks, quill and inkwell, and a journal. Two shelves beside the desk were filled with an extensive library of some three dozen bound books. On the wall above the desk was a finely carved crucifix. "His journal is open. He was about his writing. What is in the other rooms?" Meers asked Black, standing in a doorway.

Black replied, "There is a prayer station with a statue of the Virgin Mother and a smaller crucifix beside his bed–more a cot. Two, perhaps three, changes of clothes. The other is a small kitchen. No fire in the stove. Anything of note in his journal?'

"He reminds himself of tasks–correspondence with Catholics in England, Scotland, and Ireland. Books and pamphlets they seek and the price they pay for them. Nothing of King Charles or pamphlets calling for regicide.

But then, only a fool would record such a thing."

Blacked mumbled, "Only a fool would print pamphlets offering money to kill a King." He walked over to Meers and stared over his shoulder at the journal. "Names. Each name may bring us closer."

"As you say. I will follow each. But I see, he writes, 'Nieuwe Tijding, today.'"

"Say again? Was there a date?"

"A week ago. New Tidings, as you say in English. It is a newspaper. But it has not been published for several weeks."

The guard sent off to question neighbors returned with a shaken middle-aged man in tow. "Heer Meers, this is Heer Vandermolen. He lives next door." The guard pushed the man forward. "Tell Heer Meers all that you told me."

The distraught man fumbled with his hat in his hands and stared at his feet. He slowly began to mumble, "Well, as I told this man, I have not seen...."

"Speak up, man!" Meers scolded. "And look at me. Where is Richard Verstegen? Answer me!"

The man looked up, took a deep breath, and said, "I do not know where Heer Verstegen is. I have not seen him in a week. He is gone."

"I know he is gone. Gone where?"

Regaining his composure, the neighbor said, "I do

not know. A week ago, he came to my door and asked me to look after his house. He said he would be gone for some weeks."

"You did not inquire further? Is this typical? Does Verstegen travel frequently?"

"He was excited. Happy. He said he found the two-edged sword of Saint Peter."

Meers demanded, "What is this 'two-edged sword of Saint Peter?"

The neighbor shook his head. "I don't know. I have never heard of such a sword. But that is what he said. And then he left with a small bag. He was happy. He walked like a child skipping off to play."

Mister Black asked, "Into the city or towards the gate?"

The man stared at Black and answered, "Why, into the city towards the Cathedral."

Meers eyed the man carefully. "Visitors. Did Heer Meers have many visitors?"

The neighbor answered, "Yes, visitors. Doesn't everyone have visitors from time to time?"

"Tell me—who are his friends? Did outsiders visit?"

"Friends? I don't know. But outsiders, yes—like him." The man pointed to Mister Black. "English, I think, and others. They did not speak Dutch. French, yes–and Latin and English. Heer Verstegen is a scholar. He speaks many languages. He writes too. Surely you, Heer Meers, you have read his entreaties in the newspaper, the Nieuwe Tijding."

Meers turned to the guard. "Stay here and get the names of every visitor to Verstegen that this man or other neighbor can recall. I am going to the newspaper print shop."

As Black walked past the desk, shielded from the eyes of Meers or the guard, he deftly picked up the journal and slid it into a pocket in his loose-fitting jacket. Meers turned to him and asked, "The two-edged sword of Saint Peter–have you heard of such a thing?"

"No. Never. But it clearly means something to Verstegen."

Three blocks from Verstegen's house, they came to a small warehouse containing the printing press of the New Tidings newspaper. Meers banged on the door until a voice replied from inside, "We're closed, Next week. Next week we print again."

Meers banged again and shouted, "Open this door, or I will have it broken down, and you shall rot in Het Steen until my anger cools!"

At once, the door was unbarred and swung open. A young man gawked at Meers. "My apologies, sir. But we cannot print until next week, and my father is not here."

"Heer Verhoeven, I presume?" Meers asked. "Your

father is Abraham Verhoeven? Where is your father?"

"He has gone to the Stadhuis as directed by Lady Isabella for news to be printed."

"City Hall," Meers whispered to Black. "As directed by Lady Isabella?" Meers replied to the young man.

"Yes. The Lady of the Netherlands has granted us a stipend and a loan so the newspaper may reopen. It has not been profitable, but with our new press—more copies in less time–all of Antwerp can read the news—the good tidings of our King, our Lady, and our great Army of Flanders. The Holy Church will once again unite all the world."

Meers interrupted, "Richard Verstegen? Do you know the man? You publish his writings. He was here a week ago. What did he want?"

Young Verhoeven asked, "What did he want? I suppose his pay. You must ask my father. But, yes, I know Heer Verstegen, a good Christian, a scholar who writes what priests fail to preach in their homilies–fidelity to the Roman Catholic Church, to the pope, and our Great Lady. He is more than a scholar–a man of passion and persuasion."

Black asked, "You also printed Verstegen's pamphlets and writings."

"Yes, of course. But now he writes only for the

newspaper. It has been some time since we have printed his other works. Though occasionally, he asks for more copies."

Meers followed, "When did you stop printing the newspaper, and what is this new printing press you speak of?"

"More than a month ago, we stopped the newspaper. We could not afford paper or ink. But with the salvation given by Lady Isabella, we now have a new press. Only last week did it arrive. One with a counterweight like the press made by Willem Blaeu in Amsterdam. Such an improvement! A counterweight makes the work fast, requiring little effort–like a counterweight to open a drawbridge–a clever improvement! We still await the new typeset. We sold the old with the old press. That is why we wait."

Meers nodded. "I'm sure it is a splendid press. Tell me, have you seen Heer Verstegen within the last week?"

"No, as I said, if he came, he spoke only to my father."

Meers replied, "Your father is to call on me at Het Steen as soon as he returns. Jan Meers—tell the guard my name. Het Steen–today or he shall not spend another night in freedom."

CHAPTER 12

CELEBRATION UNDER A CLOUD

Thomas announced to Lady Eleanor the imminent arrival of their guests. Her mother, Lady Anne, lifted little Lady Elizabeth onto her shoulder. Eleanor carried baby Edward. Together, they joined Reverend Mister Stevens, the Reverend Mister Paul Hawkins, and the fidgeting seven-year-old, Will Curtis, waiting in front of the gathered household staff. The large black coach bearing the arms of Edward Barkley, Barron of Cawmills, came to a stop at the front door. The baggage coach continued around to the service entrance.

Immediately, the coach door opened, and young Curtis Barkley and his close friend Emil Hahn scrambled out and ran to Will. "Happy Birthday, Will–can we go riding? We want to catch frogs at the pond under the waterfall."

Will looked up at Paul Hawkins. "Can we go?

Please?"

Paul smiled. "I'll ask your mother. And you, Curtis, no hug for your big brother?"

Curtis Barkley, heir to the Baron of Cawmills hugged his older half-brother. "I missed you, Paul. Peter is always so bossy. You're a priest; can't you tell him to be nice?"

Paul knelt down, rubbed Curtis' shoulder then patted his head. "You know how hard Peter must work. Your pappa expects so much of him. And you know Peter loves you very much, just like I do. But everything he does is for mother, your pappa, and you."

Lady Mary Barkley and Katharina Hahn greeted Ladies Eleanor and Anne and smiled at the twins. Katie spoke first. "They are getting so big! Such pink cheeks! Oh, how hale and hearty!"

Then looking up, Katie said, "Wilhelm sends his love–you know him, ever the priest, he will not leave the hospital and poor house to anyone else. How he misses you and Robert. Yes, always he prays for Robert. Often, he will ask what his friend, Robert, would say or do with each new problem that comes his way."

Eleanor smiled. "I'm sure Robert feels the same. Only God above knows the souls of those two like they know each other. And how is Karl?"

Katie's smile drained, and worry creased her brow.

"He is in Saxony. Werner, you remember Werner, Karl's dear friend, and servant? Werner is trapped in Eilenberg–under siege."

Katie turned to Lady Mary, who continued, "Edward has gone with Karl, a shipload of food for the starving refugees and hopes of ransoming or rescuing Werner in Eilenberg. We can talk later. The boys were so excited for this visit, anxious to join Will. I do not wish to spoil young William's birthday with our worries."

Lady Mary made her way to Paul Hawkins. "Paul, aren't you going to hug your mother? Is your grandfather treating you well? You look thin."

Paul embraced his mother and said, "Grandpa treats me better than any other curate! Lady Eleanor has taken us into the Castle and made us at home."

Reverend Stevens smiled and said, "What a blessing, daughter, to find joy so late in life. Paul is a fine priest. I'm certain he will soon be vicar here or at some other fine parish."

Lady Mary smiled at Paul. "Aye, Berwick-upon-Tweed comes to mind."

Paul shook his head. "Mother, we have been through this. Will needs a tutor. and I teach the estate children while I learn my priestly duties. It won't be forever; I promise, but for now...."

"But for now, I give you to my dear friend Lady

Eleanor. And what is this I hear of a young lady that has come to Montclair Castle? Has she caught your eye, Paul? Is that another reason you find such happiness here?"

Paul blushed. "It is not like that at all. She is a friend and a student. I help her brother prepare for Cambridge. You will meet them."

Determined to change the subject, Paul said, "The boys want to go riding to the pond by the falls. There is time before dinner. I was about to ask Lady Eleanor."

Lady Eleanor was standing behind Lady Mary. "Go! There will be no peace until they are off exploring. But I want them back an hour before sunset–no later!"

Paul led the three boys off to the stable, and the women made their way to the house past the bows and curtsies of the servants. Mary asked, "And Robert, it is not like him to miss Will's birthday…."

Eleanor cut her short. "No, troubles–threats against the King. I don't know when I shall see him. I am thinking of returning to London, though I dread the thought of being near the court. Enough of that. You must be parched after your long journey. Drinks await inside."

Paul and the boys stopped in front of a tidy stall. William stroked the well-groomed pony's neck. "This is Thunder, he may look small, but he can jump. Tell them, Mister Hawkins, me and Thunder can jump hedges."

Paul laughed. "Thunder and I can jump hedges. A

gentleman must mind his grammar. But yes, indeed, Master William is a fine horseman. Thunder may seem small, but he has the heart of a charger. You lads wait here while the stable master and I bring out mounts."

Once they were all mounted, Paul Hawkins sternly told the boys, "There will be no jumping today. Not until I see you ride. An easy cantor to the falls pond. As you asked, today we hunt frogs. Master William will lead–remember Will, an easy lope–and I shall follow."

As the young friends rode towards the hidden oasis of Montclair, Reverend Mister Hawkins was convinced the boys were all capable horseman, even young Emil, the Reverend Wilhelm Hahn's city-bred son. "Emil, you ride well. Where did you learn?" Paul shouted.

"Grossvater Schroeder gave me a horse. I ride with him when he visits, and then, of course, I ride often with Curtis."

"Perhaps we shall all jump before you leave. But not today. Your mothers must all agree."

Twenty minutes later, Paul called out, "Master William, a walk now. Better not to tire the horses."

The three young friends now rode abreast. Reverend Hawkins came alongside young Emil and said, "Grossvater? You called your grandfather Karl, Grossvater. You speak German at home?"

All three boys laughed. Curtis said, "Emil, tell my

big brother. He thinks he knows everything!"

Emil smiled. "Yes, at home we speak mostly German. But on Sundays, pappa speaks Latin. He says that when I am older, he will teach me Greek. Grossmutter Hahn speaks no English, only German and French. Her French is the best, so she teaches us all. Grossvater Schroeder always tells me a gentleman must speak many languages, whether a pastor, scholar, or master merchant. He tells me it is sometimes good to listen and hear what others do not expect you to understand. But I help them with English. Mamma and Pappa still confuse their v's and f's. When I grow up, I want to be a master-merchant like grandfather—see, I know the English—and travel to castles all over Europe."

Paul turned to William. "Master Will, you should learn from your friend and become skilled in languages."

"But you say my French is good," Will protested.

The Reverend Mister Hawkins shook his head. "Your mother says it is better than your father's. Your father is a great man–but he would agree his French is barely passable."

Turning to Curtis, Paul said, "And you little brother, does mother school you?"

Curtis said, "It is not French or Latin that frustrates me, brother. It's the Scots who confound me with what they believe to be English!"

They arrived at the woods beside the River Lud, where the trail along the falls began. A pale mare was tied to a tree. "That's our Bessy, Will said. "What is she doing here?"

The boys tied their horses alongside Bessy and scrambled down the path. The river was still running high and sang as it poured over the falls. The rising spray dampened the trail, and they merrily slid down its muddy lane. The Reverend Hawkins carefully made his way down, grabbing branches as he went to maintain his footing. A fall would wound his dignity more than his bottom. Last to arrive alongside the clear pool beneath the falls, Paul was surprised to see the boys sipping cool drinks on a blanket spread in the soft grass. Rachel Gibbs was sitting in the middle.

"Miss Gibbs, I did not expect…." Paul said, his face confirming his surprise.

"How so much like a man–to run off with boys giving no thought to their refreshment after a long journey. And how long until supper? I knew Master William would bring his friends here, so I have prepared a picnic."

Rachel Gibbs looked down at the boys happily snacking on biscuits, and said, "Why not find some frogs and dragonflies, oh yes, large, beautiful dragonflies and then come back for a special treat I have prepared."

"Take off your boots before going into the pond!"

Paul shouted as the boys put down their cups and ran to the pond. "I won't be explaining wet feet and chills to your mothers!"

Rachel patted the blanket beside her. "Sit down, Reverend Hawkins. You can watch them from here."

Paul Hawkins dared a glance at the lovely Rachel Gibbs in her finest riding dress. He glimpsed the string of her sunbonnet rising on her bosom, lifted by a bright white bodice. "Why this is most thoughtful, Miss Gibbs. Thank you–indeed thoughtful and kind."

"Let me pour you a cup of wine to wash the dust away," she purred.

Rachel leaned across the mesmerized Reverend Hawkins. She gently placed her hand on his shoulder as she stretched for the wine. Paul inhaled the sweetness of the nape of her neck. A tuft of light brown hair found its way from under the bonnet and tickled his nose. A tingling sensation coursed from his head to his toes. He could not stop the soft sigh that escaped from his lips. He could not see the smile on Rachel's face.

"Please excuse my reach, Reverend Hawkins. Perhaps I should have asked you to hand me the wine."

"No, no. It's quite all right. A most pleasant respite. The boys are enjoying themselves, and I am most pleased to make better our acquaintance."

Rachel smiled. "Indeed, I feel I know you–I mean,

your love of justice and kindness. It rings through your sermons and shines as you tutor master William and my brother. Reverend Stevens, you grandfather, he gives the pulpit to you. He must be very proud."

"So, he tells me. Though the sermon has never been his passion."

"And what is his passion?"

"My mother would argue that grandfather sought comfort among the privileged, but I believe he has found happiness."

Rachel nodded. "Your mother married a baron. Surely, she understands the comfort of privilege."

"My stepfather is a good man. A man not ashamed of his humble heritage. He found honor from the King and was knighted and made a baron."

Rachel looked into Paul's face and said, "I heard it was on account of Lord Curtis and his father, Viscount Berwick."

"Truly, no men are closer than Lord Montclair and my stepfather, but I must include the third, Father Wilhelm Hahn, for they are three together. Just as they pray that these three lads are as one."

"Is it true they share the fortunes of a trading company? And Lord Montclair has provided both house and stipend to the Reverend Hahn, and your brother is now engaged in their enterprise?"

"Aye, Lord Curtis is a generous man–a great man with a great office from the king."

Rachel smiled at Paul and nodded. "Yes, and he, with your stepfather, will see you well situated. Is it true they are friends of the Archbishop of Canterbury? As a priest, do you see yourself as a bishop someday? Mother told me—is it true, do bishops live in palaces?"

Hawkins blushed. "Bishop? Why I am just a curate finding my way! It is enough for me to learn, to be discipled, and disciple others. Like your brother. He will do well at Cambridge."

Rachel leaned over and kissed Paul's cheek. "That's for helping my brother and for the kind things you said about my father. He was buried as a good Christian. Pappa would have liked you. He would have permitted you to call on me, I'm sure of it."

The Reverend Hawkins was speechless. The awkward silence was broken as the boys returned, each cupping a frog in his hand. "Have you ever held a frog, Mister Hawkins?" William asked.

"Of course!"

"Then let me see your hands," Will entreated.

Paul opened his hands to William. All three boys scrutinized them. "See, no warts! I told you it was only an ole' wives' tale," Will shouted.

"Toads! Not frogs. I said toads cause warts." Emil

exclaimed.

Rachel stood up. "I brought meat pies for everyone. Let those slimy frogs go and wash your hands in the pond while I get our lunch ready."

In the sitting room of Montclair Castle, Lady Mary Barkley confided in her close friend. "I expected Robert would be here. I hoped to hear his opinion—this must be the first time he will miss Will's birthday."

Lady Eleanor replied, "It is the first one he has missed. He is most distressed. You seek my husband's advice? Is something amiss? You are worried about Edward's travel–surely there is no better companion in Germany than Karl?"

Mary shook her head. "No, that is not it. Perhaps, it is better that Edward is with Karl." Mary sighed. It was a sigh that Eleanor knew meant that her closest friend was worried.

"The Marquess of Hamilton visited Cawmills Castle. He came for Edward. He expects Edward to captain the Royal Cawmills Cuirassiers under the Marquess in support of King Gustav Adolphus as he joins the war. King Charles has warranted the Marquess to raise six thousand men from Scotland and the same number from England. It is the talk of Scotland and the north. James Hamilton is even less a soldier than Buckingham was–and look at the men he left dead in France. Our gamekeeper and Edward's lieutenant, Aidan Lilburn, served in France–Aidan counsels against serving vainglorious nobles."

"Vainglorious?" Eleanor asked.

"Lilburn's words. But the Marquess is said in whispers to be a man of no intellect or loyalty. He loves only himself, and his appetite for power cannot be quenched."

Mary leaned down and lowered her voice. "Why, it is said in Edinburgh that Lord Hamilton seeks the return of a true Scot to the throne–he believes he is that Scot!"

Eleanor nodded. "I shall write to Robert. Now, where are those boys? Robert has a gift for William he will want to share with his friends. Sweet man, he has made good on his word to me many years ago."

Mary looked puzzled. Eleanor continued. "I was a terrible mother. When William was born, he was so small, so weak of breath. I was certain he would die. Fearing a broken heart, I pushed him away. Robbie would not hear it. He rebuked me, saying: 'He has no breath and tires when he runs–but the lad will live. I will give him a fast horse to be his legs.' And so, he has chosen a fine and spirited horse. Oh, I do pray he will be safe on such a magnificent animal."

CHAPTER 13

SAXONY

The *Lady Eleanor,* largest ship in the Curtis and Barkley Company fleet, made its way down the broad Elbe River into the maze of canals of Hamburg. Lubeck was the capital of the Hanseatic League, but Hamburg was its crown jewel. Lord Barkley was amazed by the fortifications he saw. The city was founded on the wide Elbe River at the confluence of two large tributaries and surrounded by high stone walls encircled by a great moat. With rivers, canals, channels, and bridges, the city was a giant maze of waterways. Marching an army into the city center was inconceivable. Karl Schroeder instructed the captain on the canal side warehouse he arranged for their berth. Edward Barkley stood attentively and watched Karl wave to his son, Pastor Johann Schroeder, standing on the wharf. "Father, I've arranged three riverboats. It's all I could hire. I hope they will be sufficient," Johann shouted as the crew moored the ship.

"They will have to do. We will sell here what we cannot load, though the buying power in Saxony will be diminished. Have them come alongside at once, no time to waste." Karl shouted back.

Edward cupped his hands and yelled, "And it is good to see you well, Johann. Your sister Katie, her Wilhelm, and your nephews and nieces send their regards. Where is Hulda? Is all well?"

Johann nodded. "Hello, Lord Barkley! Ja, Ja, Hulda is well. You shall see her soon. She is with refugees from Magdeburg, instructing those choosing to return with the ship to England. I see armed men. You wear your sword, and you bring guards. Very good, my friend! It will be a dangerous trip upriver. Saxony is all at war. General Wallenstein marches again, laying siege to cities as he will. Magdeburg is now safe, but people flee, and deserters, bandits, and pirates prowl the river."

No sooner had the *Lady Eleanor* finished securing its last mooring line than two wide riverboats came along the outboard side. A third waited ahead of the ship. Karl instructed the crew. "Grain is the highest priority. Load as much as possible, Then oil, the salt cod, and barrels of salted meat. Distribute equally between the boats. Whiskey we sell here."

Karl turned towards Barkley. "Where's Lilburn? I

want three of his men on each riverboat. You will remain with me on the first boat, and Lieutenant Lilburn will sail on the last. I trust you will arrange communications between them."

Barkley laughed. "Robbie's stories about traveling with you were true! Yes, it's all coming back to me–those days on the Neckar and the Rhine–you were never one to stand on ceremony, Karl. You tend to the cargo–I'll tend to the soldierin'!"

Karl stared at Edward. Slowly his steely gaze turned to a smile, half snorted, shook his head, and said, "Yes, my friend, I am in good company. The good Lord above has sent you and your men with me. My son and his family are safely here. By God's grace, we will deliver this food to the starving and find my friend Werner safe as well."

Johann made his way on board. He strode to his father and hugged him. "Pappa, you have come as you always do, bearing hope and strength. Please, Hulda awaits. The men know what to do."

Johann turned to Edward. "My Lord, very few wish to travel on to England. They know the dangers but wish to stay close to their homes and family or seek refuge with fellow Lutherans in Pomerania or Sweden. Come with us. Hulda would never forgive me if I did not bring you with pappa. You know how she loves you and Lady Mary."

Edward nodded and turned to his friend and gamekeeper, Aidan Lilburn, also his lieutenant of the Royal Cawmills Cuirassiers. "Lilburn, see to the men. Three to a boat. You will man the last boat. Put the sergeant in the middle. I will join Herr Schroeder in the lead boat. Breakout pistols and muskets for each man, powder, and ball. I will return soon. We will depart as soon as the cargo is loaded."

Lilburn touched his hat in salute and replied, "Aye, Captain Sir Barkley. We'll be manned at the ready."

Walking ashore, Edward asked Johann, "Will ten men be enough? They are trained men and marksmen all, but what lies ahead?"

Johann replied, "Ten well-armed men are sufficient against bandits, but you must avoid Wallenstein's men. They are a blood-thirsty lot left to murder, pillage, and defile. General Wallenstein abandoned the protestant faith for Catholicism and preferment from the emperor. He has no regard for Christian mercy or charity. Lord forgive me my judgment, but surely, the man has no conscience."

Karl asked, "Where is Wallenstein now?"

Johann replied, "One of your men, a watcher, is waiting. He tells me only that Wallenstein has marched from Eilenberg. He would say no more. Anymore is for your ears only."

Johann led them to a door between two shops, only

two streets from the harbor. Inside, a staircase led to a second-floor loft filled with people. Hulda Schroeder sat among a small group of refugees at the far end. "Einen moment, bitte." She said when she saw Karl enter with Johann.

"Pappa Schroeder! You are safe, and Lord Barkley, we prayed for your safe travel. Come in, please. Johann, offer them something while I finish here."

Edward bowed, smiling warmly, and said, "Frau Schroeder, dear Hulda, your English is better every time I hear it!"

Karl shook his head. "Already better than that northern brogue of yours, lord Barkley!"

Then turning back to Hulda, he continued, "Come. A hug for the father of your good husband."

As Hulda hugged Karl, he said, "Yes, everyone is safe. All is well with your mother and your brother's family. So, how many will join us in Berwick-upon-Tweed? Will they need work? Yes, I'm sure they will. Food–do you have enough? I can spare some from the relief…."

"Thank you, pappa Schroeder. We are fine. God blesses us, and the need in Saxony is so great. But you shall hear for yourself. Ask them. They will tell you. Still, the famine holds, and the army of General Wallenstein demands everything. Who will rid us of this evil man?"

"Ahem." A man pacing by the window cleared his

throat. "There is news, Herr Schroeder. News from Eilenberg."

Karl kissed Hulda's cheek and released his hug. "We shall talk more, my dear, before I leave. I promise. But let me hear his news and see to my work."

Hulda smiled and nodded. Karl walked to the man at the window. "Come, my friend, we will talk as we walk. I must see to the cargo. Lord Barkley will join us."

"Thirty, pappa. Thirty will go to England. The others will stay here or go on to Pomerania or Sweden." Hulda said as the men left.

Outside, the watcher began, "General Wallenstein has abandoned the siege of Eilenberg, like Magdeburg, he leaves with nothing. Be sure, it was not the walls of the city or their resistance that drove him off. No! King Gustavus Adolphus landed in Stettin."

"Where?" Edward asked.

"Stettin–in Pomerania on the Oder river—across the Baltic from Sweden," Karl replied.

The watcher continued. "As I was saying, the Swedes landed there but did not remain. Gustav Adolphus, a fox, that one, left a garrison at the fortress and sailed on. Two hundred transport ships! Wallenstein does not know where Gustav Adolphus will land his army but heads north towards Berlin–and there to decide where to wait."

Karl nodded his approval. "Gustav Adolphus will choose somewhere in western Pomerania. Now that he has made peace with Poland and Denmark-Norway, and with Stettin securing the east and his supply line, he will land in force and drive south."

Edward cocked his head and thought aloud, "So, Eilenberg is safe. Do they need our relief? Should we wait as well?"

The watcher answered. "General Wallenstein has harassed and pillaged Saxony for over a year. There has been no relief from the famine. A plague of locusts would do no worse. The need remains. As for waiting, how long? Another ship? Another relief?"

Karl replied, "Yes. The need remains. And I must find Werner. I have promised never to abandon him. We go to Eilenberg."

Karl turned to Edward and said, "My friend, I ask you to send the ship back to England with whatever passengers and cargo we can find. There will be another opportunity when more is known."

Edward replied, "Aye. But I shall travel to Eilenberg with you. With Wallenstein gone, Saxony is sure to fall into chaos. Treachery! Aye, treachery at every turn. It is good that I see for myself. I have been away far too long, my friend. I have left this work to you, Johann, and sweet Hulda. You have paid the price."

The work of off-loading the *Lady Eleanor* and stowing its precious cargo on the riverboats moved quickly when Karl and Edward returned. The captain did not take his eyes away from the workers as Edward instructed him. "Our plans are unchanged. Once the riverboats are loaded and the whiskey sold, you will use the proceeds to buy what cargo you can for England. Plan on thirty German refugees. You may carry other paying passengers you find. Don't wait for me to return. Sail when you have cargo and then return here. Tell Mister Hawkins another full load for Hamburg."

"You there!" The captain shouted. "Bring your tally sheets here at once! Mate, count the bags. The bugger is theivin' us!"

Edward stared at the cargo gang.

The captain spoke softly. "Aye. Sell the whiskey. Board thirty German beggars, fill the ship, and return with another load. I hear ye. Will I be waitin' for ye next time?"

Barkley replied, "Aye, we will return on the next voyage."

The mate yelled from the riverboat alongside. "One bag short, Captain–can't have gone far. We'll find it."

"Check for a small raft among the pilings beneath the wharf."

Barkley said, "I'll leave you to your work."

"Aye. Theivin' buggers—the same in every port.

Gotta watch 'em like a hawk. Good day, Lord Barkley."

Early the next morning, the three riverboats set sail and oars for the trip upriver. A favorable wind helped, and in a few hours, the boats passed the burnt-out fortress of Lauenburg and the remnants of the once-proud capital of Saxe-Lauenburg. The days of its profitable salt trade are now a memory. It was after dark when they slowly made their way past Havelberg. Edward, Lilburn, and the volunteers of the Royal Cawmills Cuirassiers stood in silence as the broken city walls and abandoned buildings passed their view. Each charred skeleton of a home or church told them of the cruelty of General Wallenstein's army. The boat crewmen related Wallenstein's orders to destroy anyone who did not yield to his demands. Horror stories were repeated of the brutality inflicted. They spoke of Wallenstein's license to wanton, perverted cruelty. He permitted four days of murder, rape, pillaging, and looting of each vanquished city or village before ordering his army to quarters. A few souls returned in the hope of rebuilding, but most survivors walked north to Hamburg.

Magdeburg fared better. The city walls bore the scars of artillery fire, and it appeared every tree for a mile around the city was felled or burned. There were no crops in the fields. The ground was pockmarked with the remnants of the campfires of the siege army and earthen artillery placements. The wharves and piers had fallen into the river. Only planks served as makeshift piers for the few boats unloading their cargo.

As they passed, a man called out, "If it's food you're carrying, we have money to pay–not forged script or coin, but gold! Only beggars, thieves, and pirates further upriver. Stop and let us see what you have to offer!"

The small fleet sailed on. The boat captain said, "He's right about the company we'll keep from here on. Your men best be watching. After dark, you can be sure we'll have unwelcome guests."

Two hours after passing Magdeburg, the captain pulled the lead boat alongside a small island in the river. The other boats followed and were soon tied alongside. "The river narrows ahead–tricky current for a night passage. All the same, expect visitors."

Edward asked, "Sounds like they expect us to stop here. Are you sure it isn't safer to chance the narrows?"

"I know the river. It is a challenge in the daylight. I'd rather put my faith in your trained men. Aye, pirates may try us, but they won't risk a fire fight if they cannot catch us unaware. And we'll set a few defenses of our own."

The boat crews gathered driftwood and dried grass from the island. They rigged small rafts, little more than floats, and piled the driftwood and grass on each. They soaked the grass with oil and then rowed them out into the river and anchored them around the island. Everyone enjoyed a hot meal on the wet but firm rocky island, and the fire died down to embers. Four men stood watch while the others slept. Each man with his musket at the ready.

A hand over Edward's mouth woke him. He looked up to see the captain kneeling over him, a finger across his lips. Edward sat up and saw another man waking Karl and each soldier. The captain pointed out and said, "Our visitors. At least three boats, maybe more."

Edward heard nothing and then a faint creak of an oar pin and a soft splash. "We'll let them get closer. A good volley of musket fire will convince them."

Waiting is always the hardest part of an engagement. Too many thoughts, too many questions. Thinking but never certain. The boat captain placed the tip of a crossbow shaft in the fire. Six crewmen followed suit. And in a fleeting second, all seven let fly their bolts. First two, then three, and finally four of the rafts lit with flames. More crossbow bolts and all six rafts were aflame. Four small boats with two men each were silhouetted in the light of the floats. Now, with muskets trained on the men. Karl called out in German, "Close enough! Return to your homes if you wish to live." One man began rowing quickly towards them. Two musket shots fell him, and he tumbled into the water, capsizing his boat. His partner flailed his arms and cried out for help struggling to stay afloat as the current swept him away into the blackness of the night and water.

A voice called back, "Friends, we meant no harm. We are just traveling upriver."

The captain shouted, "No one travels these waters at night. Go back, or the same fate awaits you."

Aidan Lilburn fired his musket and holed the bow of the boat of the shouting man. "We've had enough! We're going! Hold your fire."

The three boats spun around and rowed outside the perimeter of the floating torches. Their splashing oars grew quieter as the boats sped back downriver.

The captain said, "Unlikely they'll be back. Be sure, word of our strength will spread. We should be safe to Eilenberg. I'm going to bed. Good night."

Edward nodded. "All the same, we'll keep the watch."

Smoke entrapped in the mist filled the air with an acrid smell. Abandoned firepits, strewn logs, the remnants of the surrounding forest, and the blackened pot-marked walls of the city welcomed them to Eilenberg. They navigated around the hulks of three riverboats, half-submerged and tied to the heavily damaged wharf, and found a relatively safe place to moor. Their arrival was greeted by a crowd gathered at the wharf gate. Karl called out. "My men are armed. We are here with food–relief. But you must stay back. There is a man here, Werner– he…."

Werner stepped forward. "Here I am. Karl. Yes, there must be order. I have sent for the mayor and the pastor. The people have been through much, but they obey their aldermen and pastor. No trouble coming upriver, I hope."

"Nothing, my friend, Lord Barkley and his men were not up to."

The Burgermeister and pastor were led to the boats. Karl said, "We have brought food, grain, flour, oil, salt cod, and salted meat, but I fear I cannot give them to you. I must cover my costs and provide for others as well."

The Burgermeister sighed. "Yes, of course, you must make a profit. We don't have much money, but some. What is your price?"

Karl wrote the prices for a sack of grain, a sack of flour, a barrel of salt cod, and barrel of salt pork, and last, for oil. He handed the paper to the Burgermeister and said, "How much of each can you afford at this price."

The burgermeister turned to Werner. "Does your friend understand our ducats and thalers?"

Werner nodded. "Yes, they look correct to me."

The Burgermeister looked up, amazed. "Herr Schroeder, we cannot buy these items in Hamburg at ten times this amount. Surely, if this is correct, we shall take all you carry. How can you do this for us?"

Karl smiled. "It is a fair price and one to return a small profit for our work. The difference, my friend, is the cost of your war."

Werner smiled. "Now, if that is settled, the Burgermeister will arrange for men to off-load the cargo. Karl, this is my friend, Pastor Rinkart."

Pastor Rinkart nodded and said, "Please. Martin, call me Martin. Welcome to Eilenberg. You are to be my guest during your stay."

Karl bowed. "Tell me, Pastor Rinkart, are there any who wish to travel back with us to Hamburg, perhaps from there to Sweden or England. Some, fleeing Wallenstein, have come to England."

"Yes, some are determined to leave. And the city is filled with refugees from the countryside. It is General Wallenstein's practice to drive peasants to the gate of any city under siege. More mouths to feed shortens the siege. You can see, times here are very hard. The land is in ruins and cannot support the people. Yes, some will travel."

Pastor Rinkart turned to Werner. "And you, my friend, will you be moving on?"

Werner smiled. "Martin, you lead the flock to God. I lead the flock to safety. Yes, I will go. But perhaps we shall meet again. God has blessed the good people of Eilenberg with a faithful servant–a man after God's own heart!"

"Truly, sir, you do me too much honor. I am a simple village pastor. God is our shield and protector.

Aidan Lilburn whispered to Edward, "My Lord, I saw nothing like this with Lord Buckingham at Saint Martin-de-Re. Here I see a cause worthy of the blood of good men."

CHAPTER 14

SCAR EAR

Young Percy lay on the floor of Chingford's Crown Stag Inn, moaning. Lynch stared down anyone looking for further trouble as Robert bent down, picked up the dirty hat, and handed it to the old man with the scar across his ear. "Either a highwayman or a soldier, friend. A highwayman is not worried about England's allies. What regiment?"

The man took his hat and put it back on his head. "Which campaign? But Colonel Vere's volunteers–to the Palatinate–at Heidelberg with Colonel Sir Gerard Herbert, God rest his soul. Aye, he made me a soldier. Men of honor, the three colonels–not their like fighting for England anymore."

Robert's eyes widened. "We were comrades! I was lieutenant to Captain Richard. Sent off by Vere for reconnaissance. Bad business. Left without reinforcements.

Were you there? At the end? Captain Richard, he died–did he die well?"

Robert pointed to a table and called out, "Ale and mugs, innkeeper!"

Lynch sat silently, listening as Robert said, "Tell me all."

The man sat down and said, "Aye, Captain Richard. Got himself arrested. All hush, hush, him bein' an officer and all. But the ol' man let him out to fight. Died well, died well, indeed. Saved my life. We had no shot or powder left. Just swords and knives. Got himself between a thrown pike and me. He took it full-on, and I lived. I held him as he died."

The mugs of ale were set on the table. The old veteran took a long drink, sniffled, and continued. "Captain Richard's last words to me were, 'I gave you your life–promise me, promise me you will live to honor England. Honor England in my stead.'"

Robert leaned back and stared blankly. Lynch was about to speak, but Robert quickly put his hand over Lynch's arm and shook his head. He looked into the old veteran's eyes and said, "You made an oath to Captain Richard. You seek to go back, to fight. You volunteer and go back. Lord Lindsey recruits volunteers. You enlisted with Lindsey's volunteers. Why aren't you at Willoughby House?"

"King Charles chose the Marques Hamilton over Lord Lindsey."

Robert asked, "How do you know this?"

"A friend. A friend told me Lord Lindsey was raising a regiment and that Lord Lindsey has served with distinction, so I enlisted. But, when he told me Lindsey's regiment wasn't chosen, I left."

"But you travel south, towards London. Lord Hamilton raises a regiment in Scotland."

"My friend tells me that English volunteers will be raised soon in London. Scotland is a long journey for a man of modest means."

Robert reached out his hand. "My name is Curtis, Captain Sir Robert Curtis. Did your friend ask you to enlist under the name Pendragon? Arthur Pendragon?"

The old soldier was quiet as he shook Robert's hand.

Robert asked again, "Arthur Pendragon, have you heard that name?"

The veteran began to look around. Lynch had his hand on his pistol under the table. His cold eyes stared back at the old man, who replied. "Pendragon? What kind of a name is that? I don't believe in dragons. Old wives' tales."

"And this friend asked you to place some pamphlets in the King's coach at Willoughby House."

Robert continued. "These pamphlets offer money to the man who kills our King. And a letter, signed by Arthur Pendragon, threatened King Charles and his heir–not yet born. So, Pendragon or whoever you are...."

The old man jumped to his feet, upending the mugs of ale. Lynch was standing across from him, his pistol cocked and aimed. Lynch said coldly. "Sit down. Lord Montclair has more questions."

The man sat down. Robert asked, "Tell me about this friend."

The man stared down at the table and said nothing. Robert nodded. "Then start with your name. Your real name. I know by the scar across your ear you enlisted as Arthur Pendragon. You will answer my questions here or at Newgate prison, where you will be taken."

The man remained silent. Robert said, "You have broken your oath. You are not like Captain Richard. He was my friend. I know his story well. He, too, fell in with plotters against England. But when he was found out, Richard did the honorable thing and told all that he knew. Richard repented his treachery, though his was much less than others. Colonel Sir Gerard permitted Captain Richard an honorable death defending the garrison in the final assault. He died a soldier, fighting for England. You pretend to be Arthur Pendragon. You will not be so fortunate."

Robert turned to Lynch and nodded. "To Newgate."

Lynch pulled the man up by the collar, kneed him in the small of his back, and tied his hands behind him. The counterfeit Pendragon grunted. His face fell to his chest. Then looking up, he said, "I don't know his name. He sends me money and instructions. I swear I don't know his name!"

Three armed men appeared from among the patrons and took custody of the prisoner. Robert instructed them. "Take him to the cage. I want him in Newgate before sunrise."

Turning to Lynch, he said, "Tell them to loosen his tongue. Any means. Tell them I expect every word out of his mouth to be the whole truth."

Then to the prisoner, he said, "Three hours, friend. In three hours, your ordeal begins. I suggest you loosen your tongue. There are men very skilled at loosening it for you."

"Wait! Wait! Let me explain," the man pleaded.

Robert looked at the man and said, "Take him."

After the prisoner was dragged out, Robert said to Lynch. "Go with him. Hear what he says but be back here tomorrow."

Lynch replied. "Your off to Lord Conway. Pendragon captured. The King shall be glad to hear of your progress."

Robert glanced up for a moment and replied, "I don't think Lord Conway will disturb His Majesty with the news of the arrest of a deserter or be too concerned with a drunken assault against young Percy."

"You don't trust the Lord Secretary?"

"I don't trust the court. Someone is leaking the King's schedule. Someone inside the court arranged for those pamphlets to be left in the King's coach. As for our prisoner, he is no man of the church or letters. He did not write the letters ascribed to him. For now, we will keep his connection to the plotters to ourselves. We must find out how this friend of his finds him with letters and money."

The following day Robert arrived at the Royal Hunting Lodge and found servants busy loading baggage carts. Robert made his way to the Lord Secretary's room. Lord Conway placed documents in the red box for the King's immediate attention. Conway noticed Robert entering. "Ah, here you are Montclair. Come through. We return to Saint James today. The queen is in labor. His Majesty chose to enjoy a hunt this morning and will attend the queen after the child is born."

"It won't work."

"What won't work, Lord Robert?"

Robert replied, "The hunt. It will not take his mind off the queen's labor. He has lost his first child, a son. He worries after this child and, dare I say, the health of the queen, the one person he loves."

Conway locked the red document box. Without looking, he replied, "We all deal with worry in our own way. His Majesty is compelled to hide his concern. Appearances. Yes, he must keep up his appearance."

Conway looked up. "I hear you had a spot of trouble last night at the inn."

Robert laughed. "And here I believed I am the Lord Inquirer, charged with keeping you informed. Or perhaps you have another watcher watching me! But you hear correctly, a spot of trouble. Nothing of notice to the King. Young Woolsey Percy, Cottingham's page, was assaulted. An old man, a veteran, and no fan of another Spanish or Catholic alliance, took exception to Percy's boasting. The man was arrested. Can't have old men assaulting gentlemen of a noble family."

Conway nodded. "And the poster, the threat? Anything to report?"

"We continue to pursue several lines of inquiry. We smelled no scent of danger to His Majesty. But it is good that he will be safe at Saint James Palace this very day. I'm sure his mind is occupied, and I do not see purpose in bothering him with this minor event. I shall speak with Percy to see if he wishes to make a charge. Both were well into their cups."

Conway replied, "So nothing new. What are your plans? Where can I find you?"

Robert said, "Our inquires after the man Arthur Pendragon have become more promising. Someone matching his description was reported in the area, but he has moved on. We also pursue the pamphlet printer and the press in Flanders. I return to London. You can find me at Westminster."

That afternoon the church bells of London pealed the good news of the birth of a crown prince and heir to the throne, like his dead brother born a year earlier, he was named Charles, born Duke of Cornwall and Duke of Rothesay. Queen Henrietta Maria was in good health.

Lynch was still questioning the old man with the scarred ear when Robert joined him at Newgate Prison. The old man's face lay down on a table when Robert signaled to Lynch, Lynch said nothing as he left the man and locked the cell behind him. Out of earshot, Lynch said. He has talked, but he holds back. He's protecting someone."

Robert replied, "What have you learned?"

"His name is Forester, Ezra Forester from Lancashire—a small village, Hardshaw, in the Mersey woods. Says he's a veteran, infantry pikeman—fought in the Palatinate and with Buckingham's fiasco. Says he doesn't know who pens the letters or the pamphlets, only does as he is told."

Robert asked, "As who tells him?"

"Says he doesn't know or can't say. Says a soldier always keeps his brother's back. But when I pressed, he added, 'You don't know what he would do. Do with me as you will, but my….' He would say no more. I believe he is protecting someone. He has not been harmed. I don't believe he can be coerced. He will confess to his crimes only."

"He protects his family. He will bear any punishment to save them." Robert paused. Prepare a confession for him to sign. I will question him. I think we will find he can neither read nor write. He receives his instructions by word of mouth. If we act quickly, word of his imprisonment may not be known."

Lynch smiled. "You seek to lay a trap."

Robert's mind was racing. "He was twice seen or recognized at inns–in Chingford and before that, at Willoughby Village. Both times the court was nearby. He meets his contact at the inn. The King has returned to Saint James palace in London. Forester will be expected at a pub nearby. One popular with the court."

Robert slapped Lynch's shoulder. Write the confession. We will press him again within the hour!"

Robert entered Ezra Forester's cell and laid the confession on the table in front of him. "Your confession.

You will sign it."

"Ezra looked up. What will happen to me?"

"Read it."

Ezra stared at the paper and picked up the quill. His hand shook, but he only stared down in silence. "What does it say? What will happen?"

Robert replied, "It is in front of you to read and sign. You accept full responsibility for threatening the life of his Majesty King Charles and his infant son and offering payment for any man or the family of any man who kills our King. Therefore, you are condemned to a traitor's death to be hanged, drawn, and quartered. All your possessions and your family's possessions are forfeited to the King. Your family will be exiled, and your name is forever disgraced."

Ezra could not stop his hand from shaking as he tried to dip the quill in the inkwell. Robert watched and then added softly. "It doesn't have to be this way. There is an alternative."

Ezra looked up. Robert said, "You cannot read or write. How you got caught up in this plot, I do not know. But a plotter and traitor you have become. You have a family–someone you love, and you are willing to die to protect them. There is time to save them. You have an appointment at a pub near Saint James Palace. Agree to help us. Keep your appointment and help us capture the plotter, the educated man you serve. We will protect your loved ones, and perhaps you will live. As a brother in arms, I will make your case before the King."

Ezra Forester broke down and cried. "My daughter. She is in service at Eltonhead House in Lancashire. She is all I have."

He stopped sobbing and wiped his face. The Red Lion. I am to go to the Red Lion Inn and order an ale. I will show the innkeeper my ear. When he brings the ale, I am to give him a bent coin. He will take the coin, tell me what I am to do, and pay me from his change purse. Today. I am to go today."

Lynch's watchers began filling the Red Lion Inn, securing every table. When Ezra Forester entered, a man rose and left the center table empty. Ezra took a seat at the vacant table with his back to Robert. Lynch faced him from the opposite table. Ezra removed his hat and called out to the innkeeper. "Ale." Ezra put his hat back on only after the innkeeper gave the nod. He pulled a bent coin from his pouch and tossed it nervously in his hand.

The innkeeper brought a mug, set it down in front of Ezra, and took the coin out of his hand. "Your change, friend," he said as he passed several coins to Ezra. "Let me tell you about our stew today." The innkeeper moved behind Ezra and bent over near his ear. Robert leaned back, stretching his neck, and listened.

CHAPTER 15

CLOSING IN

Jan Meers left one of his men with Black, who insisted on waiting for Abraham Verhoeven to return to the New Tidings printshop in the warehouse section of Antwerp. Less than fifteen minutes passed when the elderly Verhoeven returned. Abraham Verhoeven read the concern in his son's eyes as he greeted his visitors. "It must be important if it is beyond my son's ability! How can I help you, gentlemen?"

Meer's man asked, "Abraham Verhoeven?"

"Yes. I am Abraham Verhoeven, and you are?"

"Abraham Verhoeven, you are ordered to accompany me for questioning."

The elder Verhoeven smiled. "Then it must be official. Who commands this inquiry?"

"Heer Jan Meers. You will accompany me to Het Steen."

Abraham turned to his son. "I am sure it is a simple matter. I will be back soon. The typeset is at the wharf and will be delivered today. You can start the layout."

As they filed out the door, Black asked, "Heer Verhoeven, do you speak English or prefer French?"

"Yes, English. So, this is a foreign affair?"

Black continued, "Your friend, Richard Verstegen. He is missing. Do you know where he is?"

"Richard missing? I know he went on a journey, but missing?"

Black stared into Verhoeven's eyes. "You must do better if you wish to leave Het Steen alive. You were the last to see Verstegen in Antwerp. It was in his journal, and your son confirms his visit. What was your business with him? Better you tell us. You have a son and hope for your newspaper. Should someone else print of your arrest and punishment?"

"Yes, he came to see me. He and two other men. He heard we sought a new printing press. He wanted to print his books. He proposed buying the old press for unpaid wages and cash."

Black replied, "The other men; were they English?"

Verhoeven nodded. "I believe so. One could not follow our conversation, and Richard would whisper to them in English."

"So, you agreed to sell the press and then?"

"Well, the next day, one of the other men–an Englishman came with Johannes De Vries and two workers. They crated the press, put it in their wagon, and drove off."

"Who paid you?"

"De Vries gave me the agreed amount."

"And the wagon, which way did they drive off. Towards the gate or the river?"

"The city gate. I heard him say something to De Vries about when they get to London."

"When who gets to London? Are you certain he said London?

Verhoeven shrugged his shoulders. "I heard him mention London."

"Describe the Englishmen."

Verhoeven stopped and cocked his head. "Yes. Young men, perhaps twenty or twenty-five. One blonde. Both dressed neatly. One more like a clerk than a merchant. Nervous. Kept passing rosary beads through his fingers as he waited."

Both men saw the scowls of Meers' officer and resumed walking. Black asked, "Richard Verstegen. Did he say when he would return? Did Verstegen go with these men to London?"

"Richard said he would be gone for several weeks. Nothing more."

Black continued, "You print Verstegen's books in English. Books for the English Catholics. Have you met any other of his English customers or friends?"

"Yes, I print his books and pamphlets. But I never met his customers or, as you say, his friends."

Black stopped again. "Pamphlets were printed here, on your press offering a reward for the murder of King Charles. You may think my King is an enemy and has no power in Antwerp. But there is a new treaty between England and Spain–support for the Spanish Netherlands. These pamphlets threaten that treaty. It would be well for you, my friend, to tell all!"

For the first time, fear radiated from Verhoeven's eyes. "I would print no such thing. No, never!"

Verhoeven paused. "But. Perhaps. It is possible. You see, when the newspaper was in hard times and I could not pay–could not print, I allowed Verstegen use of the printing press so long as he bought his paper and ink. I never thought...."

"And you never saw what he printed?"

"No. You must tell Jan Meers. I have done nothing wrong! I support the Lady of the Netherlands! She has bought the new press, and I am to print her news!"

Black turned and looked into Verhoeven's eyes.

"One last question. Verstegen spoke of a two-edged sword of Saint Peter. Does that mean anything to you?"

Verhoeven's blank stare confirmed his answer. "Two-edged sword of Saint Peter? No. But Richard was a scholar and would often say strange things. I think for his amusement."

At Het Steen, Black quickly briefed Jan Meers while Verhoeven waited in the interrogation room. "He sold his printing press to Verstegen and an unknown Englishman. Our friend Johannes De Vries crated it and took it off by wagon. Traveled outside the gate. But likely to London. You can question him yourself. One last thing, he gave Verstegen access to the printing press. Verstegen supplied his own paper and ink. And this, Verstegen was left alone to print. I'm off."

Meers asked, "The two-edged sword?"

Black shrugged and left.

Robert heard the innkeeper say, "Under the London bridge, this side, you will find an overturned boat. Inside the boat, you will find another letter and a pamphlet in a pouch. You are to nail them to the gatehouse near the stable of Saint James Palace. You will do this tomorrow night. You are to watch the light from the gatehouse window. When you see a second swinging light, it is your signal the guard has been called away. Do you understand?"

Ezra Forester nodded and repeated louder than the innkeeper: "Under an overturned boat beneath the London bridge, poster and pamphlet. Nail them to Saint James Palace stable gatehouse tomorrow night. Signal is a swinging lantern."

The innkeeper nodded and said, "Here. Same time next week," and he walked away.

Forester finished his ale, nervously got up, and walked out. Lynch was waiting for him outside. Robert followed a couple of minutes later and found Lynch and Forester waiting in an adjacent alley. Lynch asked, "Should we send watchers ahead? Perhaps the drop has not yet been made."

Robert turned to Ezra. "Have you seen the man who left the other letters for you to post?"

"No, my lord. I have always gone directly as told. The letters were there when I arrived. I saw no one."

"Were you watched?"

"Truly, I do not know. I saw no one. The places were secluded. As I said, I saw no one."

Robert spoke. "Lynch, you will go ahead and observe the bridge. Forester will follow in five minutes. I will follow Forester. Know this, Forester, if you speak to anyone along the way or stray from the path, you will be caught and taken to the tower. The life of your daughter is in your hands."

Forester nodded. "Aye. I am glad to be free of them. Promise me you will protect my daughter."

Lynch arrived at the foot of the London bridge. He found a dark shadow behind a bush to stand and wait. People walked the center lane between houses and shops lining the bridge. Only an occasional coach or wagon crossed. He saw no one near the steps going down to the river. Forester arrived not ten minutes later and went directly down the steps. In less than a minute, he was back up with a crude cloth pouch slung over his shoulder. Lynch met him, and they walked towards Newgate. Robert lingered for five minutes and then caught up with them in the darkened street. At Newgate, Forester was locked in a cell while Robert and Lynch took the pouch and made for the council room.

Climbing the creaking staircase, Lynch said, "We need someone inside the stable when the signal is given."

Robert replied, "My thoughts exactly. I will be inside waiting."

"You, Sir Robert? Isn't that a great risk?"

"Who else can it be but for me? We have no time to arrange a watcher. I have access. Yes, I am known, but my comings and goings are frequent and no cause for alarm. The key is finding someplace to observe after leaving my horse with the groomsman. I have a plan."

Lynch opened the door to the council room and set the pouch on the table, and said, "I shall have men standing by outside to assist in the arrest."

Robert sat in his highbacked chair at the head of the table. "We can't arrest him yet. He may be another courier. The threat is inside the court. We pursue a two-headed snake. I want both heads, the traitor inside the court and the traitor printing the pamphlets and penning the threats. Now, this is the first new pamphlet in weeks. Let's see, yes, the typeset remains the same. But this is new. King Charles as Zedekiah, a reference to Jeremiah thrown down the well, and a demand that the king release the prisoner punished for telling the truth. A religious or political prisoner, but who?"

The sun was setting, and shadows fell across the Saint James Palace gate as Robert announced, "Lord Montclair, His Majesty's Lord Inquirer to see the Lord Secretary." The guard replied, "Pass Lord Montclair."

Robert dismounted and left his horse with a groomsman who handed him a numbered chit. "Only an hour, two at most," Robert said as he walked towards the palace courtier's entrance steps. As he reached the steps, he turned to see a young boy, likely a stableboy, carry a lantern toward the guardhouse. Robert watched as the groomsman raised the lantern towards the guardhouse. The guardhouse door opened, and the guard came out. He stood holding out the lantern, and the guard scolded, "Well, hang it on the hook where it belongs, lad."

The stable boy stood in front of the guardhouse. "Help, sir, I cannot reach the hook."

The guard swore as he walked out of his small shack, took the lantern, and hung it from a post opposite the gatehouse. The stable boy ran back into the stable, and the guard returned to his post.

The courtyard was quiet. No one else was in sight. Robert retreated from the staircase and moved quickly to the kitchen entrance close to the guardhouse in the undercroft. "Lord Montclair! To what do I owe this honor?" Rene, the pastry chef, asked.

"I need use of your window, Rene. For a time. I pray all is well at the French Protestant Church. Please, go about your business, and we shall speak later."

Rene's deep trust and friendship with Robert made no further questions necessary. He went back to work on a piece' montee. Robert watched and waited not ten feet from the foot of the guardhouse. Fifteen minutes later, Robert watched a familiar face lit in the light of a lantern as a trusted man walked to the guardhouse. Through the open window, he could hear, "One of the lads found a wench willing to marry him. He brought a good whiskey to celebrate. Why not go for a nip back of the stable. I'll take your watch for a while."

The guard looked about and replied, "You'll say nothing of me to the sergeant? Well, just a quick one." And he hurried off into the stable.

The baggage master waited until the guard was in the stable before stepping out with the lantern and swinging it in a slow great arc. In seconds, Ezra Forester was at the gate, nailed the poster and pamphlet to the outside, and disappeared into the darkness. Ten minutes later, the guard returned. Robert waited another ten minutes before leaving, promising Rene a visit to his friends at the French Church. The watch changed twice before morning when the poster was noticed by a cook coming to work.

Lynch was waiting in the council chamber of the Newgate works. Robert asked, "Forester safe in his cell, I hope?"

Lynch replied. "Meek as a mouse. Aye, he'll cooperate if we need him again. And your report?"

"The baggage master. I recognized him at once. What better man? He knows the King's schedule well before the King departs."

Lynch nodded. "And the pamphlets found in the King's coach. He certainly has the means and the opportunity. There is no need for another source in the palace. Should we bring him in?"

Robert shook his head. "Not yet. Once the

pamphlet is found, I shall be hard-pressed by his majesty to make an arrest. Lord Conway loses patience as well. The couriers know nothing. The man behind this plot is careful. The baggage master, what is his motive? If only money, then he will know little. Time. I need more time to find the printer and the author of these foul papers."

Robert got up and paced the room. "The prisoner mentioned in the pamphlet...."

Lynch said, "Doctor Alexander Leighton is held the other side of our wall in Newgate. I hear Bishop Laud demands the harshest treatment. Leighton is sick and near death. The man was arrested as a pamphleteer. He used Old Testament references. He called Queen Henrietta Maria a 'daughter of Seth.' Could his supporters be printing his words?"

Robert sighed and rubbed weary eyes before replying. "Bishop Laud's prisoner. Tortured and near death. How could a supporter gain access? Even his family is forbidden to visit. And then there is Sir John Eliot, leader of the House of Commons, imprisoned in the Tower for bringing charges against Buckingham, released only to be arrested for bringing the issue of the Ship tax before parliament, then released and imprisoned again for refusal to pay a forced loan to the crown."

Lynch replied, "Yes, but Sir John remains in the tower out of defiance. He refuses the loan he can afford."

Robert sighed. "The summons to his Majesty, I will wait in my Westminster chambers. I'll take my chances with the King."

Mister Black walked into Robert's Westminster chambers and said, "You're in early this morning, my lord.

Robert looked up. "Ah, Black! Good you're back. I could have saved you the trip. The pamphlets were printed in Antwerp. The typeset matches that of the newspaper, New Tidings."

Black nodded. "Yes, I saw your dispatch before I left. But it said nothing of the Englishman Richard Verstegen, known in London as Richard Rowlands, or his connection to Flemish smuggler Johannes de Vries, the man who arranged the smuggling of the last pamphlets aboard Haakon Anderson's boat. I also know that Verstegen and another man–an Englishman—purchased the press from Abraham Verhoeven and had access to the printing press before they bought it and shipped it here to London."

Robert smiled. "Good work! We have been busy in your absence. Their courier, a man with a scarred ear, enlisted with Lord Lindsey's volunteers as Arthur Pendragon, real name, Ezra Forester cooperates with us in Newgate. Just an illiterate veteran. Last night, I confirmed the king's baggage master as the source in the palace. I expect a summons to his Majesty this morning. Tell me you have the trail of this Englishman in London!"

Black sighed. "I don't know his name. He was with another, both young, 20 to 25 years old. The quiet one with him had a blonde beard. But I also have Verstegen's journal with a list of his English customers."

"So, begin with Verstegen or Rowlands, whatever his name, here in London. While you were drinking wine in Flanders, there were three letters penned threatening the King. One threatened the crown prince. Oh yes. Henrietta Maria has done her duty and borne the King a son, Prince Charles. The King is most impatient for this deadly pamphleteer to be captured. He expects an arrest, but...."

Black noted Robert's pause and said, "But?"

"But the man we seek is clever. The couriers work by word of mouth. We need them to continue. Any word of arrests and our man will fly like a stag from an errant shot."

Black nodded. "There is something else, something Verstegen said. Does the two-edged sword of Saint Peter mean anything to you, Sir Robert? Something you learned in your priestly training?"

A knock at Robert's door was immediately followed by the appearance of a palace guard and a page. The page spoke with an earnest attempt of a voice of authority. "Lord Montclair, his Majesty, King Charles commands you to accompany me at once...."

"Yes, of course. I have been expecting you."

Robert stood up and grabbed his cloak. "Black, I want you and Lynch to find this printer. Names–you have names; hunt them down!"

Robert was led into the King's chambers. The King was alone with Lord Conway. Robert bowed and began, "Your majesty…."

Charles was standing by his desk. He picked up a pamphlet and said, "Lord Inquirer, you have failed me. Do you know what this is?"

Robert saw his opportunity to answer and interrupted, "Yes, majesty, another pamphlet. I have already read it and the note posted with it."

Charles tried to continue. "It is another threat…did you say you read it? And the note as well? It was brought directly to me just this morning."

Lord Conway looked up at Robert. Conway's face was as puzzled as the King's.

King Charles redirected. "When- how is it you— you read it and still allowed it to remain posted? Explain yourself, Montclair."

Robert took a breath and explained, "Yes, Majesty, I read it before it was posted. Your Majesty, if the contents of the Spanish Ambassador's pouch were opened before you, would you tell king Philip of what you read? Would not the information be more useful to you in diplomatic negotiations if kept secret? We have made great progress in uncovering this deadly pamphleteer. Arrests could be made, but, like a patient hunter, we wait for the clean kill. What happens when the bolt shoots through a thicket? The shot is deflected, and the stag is lost in flight."

"I see now Lord Conway's confidence in your ability, Montclair." King Charles replied.

"We have half of a two-headed serpent, but the head with the venom we still pursue."

Charles sat down. "It is a dangerous game you play. Remember, it is the life of your sovereign at stake."

"Majesty, I say venom, for that is what this pamphleteer spits. The others lack the skill or the heart to raise their hand against their king. They are illiterate men of low estate—couriers, servants, and publicans, whose service is bought with coin and not loyalty. I shall keep pulling until I crush the head of this snake."

Robert watched Lord Conway's face as he spoke, now the only man outside of his watchers and the King to know a courier was turned. Conway's expression did not change. His eyes returned Robert's stare.

Robert turned to King Charles. "Your guards are alert. You are safe in this palace. News of the birth of Prince Charles is well received by your subjects. The risk arises when you travel."

King Charles sighed. "Surely, all England rejoices

in the birth of Prince Charles. But I will not be a captive to Saint James Palace. Why next week I must travel to the Forest of Dean. That is all, Lord Montclair. Results. I want results--quickly!"

CHAPTER 16

THE SLIP

Ezra Forester entered the Red Lion Inn, called to the innkeeper, "Ale," doffed his cap, and sat down. Mister Black was sitting behind him and Lynch across. Robert waited outside.

The innkeeper set a mug of ale in front of Forester, leaned low, and whispered, "Same place as last week. The King is off next week to the Forest of Dean. Overnights in Wycombe, Oxford, Burford, and Cheltenham. Repeat it to me."

Forester pulled the mug of ale in front of him and repeated, "Forest of Dean by way of Oxford, Burford, and Cheltenham."

The innkeeper pushed the mug away and slapped Forester across the back of the head. "Were ye not listening? Forest of Dean with overnights in Wycombe, Oxford, Burford, and Cheltenham. Wait here. Drink your ale but wait."

The innkeeper left through a door to a back room only to return a minute later. Walking back to Forester, he said loudly, "Your coin!"

Forester pulled out the small coin, and the innkeeper took it and said, "Your change," and he handed him back the coin and a small slip of paper. He whispered, "Bloody fool. Give the man the paper if you must. No one else is to see it. Eat it if you are followed or arrested. Now go, don't show me you're a drunk as well as a dullard."

Forester finished his ale and left. He walked across the street, around a corner, and past an alley where Robert was waiting. Black was not far behind. Forester did not stop. Without turning his head, Forester told Robert as he passed. "Same place." Both men walked on and stopped to wait for the street to clear of carts and carriages. Still not acknowledging Robert, Forester said, "The King travels to the Forest of Dean next week. Overnight stops at Wycombe, Oxford, Burford, and Cheltenham. Best if you give some space. He'll be waiting for my report. He gave the route it in writing as well."

Robert allowed Forester to walk on and allowed Black to catch up. "Beneath the London bridge. It's where he picked up the pamphlets last week. He passes our story by word of mouth but also has a note. No telling if his contact is waiting. You follow Forester, not too close. I'll watch the bridge from above."

Black said nothing. He knew how to follow and not be seen. When they arrived at the road along the Thames, Black followed behind Forester along the river while Robert walked the other side of the road. Forester walked to the stairs beside the London bridge, walked down to the river, and was soon out of sight. Black made his way slowly, closing on the stairs. Robert watched as wagons, coaches, and a few working-class men crossed the bridge. None stopped near the stairway to the Thames. The river was filled with working boats. Many had their cargoes covered by tarps.

Black reached the bridge, walked out into the first shop, went to a window over the river, and looked down. Seeing nothing, he walked out, back to the stairs, hurried down, and stopped at the abutment. With his back against the wall, Black bent forward and looked under the end of the bridge. In a bound, he was back up and called to Robert, "They're gone! Forester and his contact–the boats, He must be on a boat!"

Robert ran across the street and stood next to Black, scanning the boats below. There was little difference. All, with men at oars, carried some cargo. Black said, "I would have seen if they came downriver. And with the flood tide, the current carries quickly upriver."

Robert stared. "There is one, no, no, there are three

that turn into the Holborn River.….."

Black interrupted, "Others make for the Tyburn and Westbourne or continue up the Thames."

Robert started for the River Road. "The printing press is in London. I'll follow the Holborn. You take the Tyburn. We may yet catch them."

The Holborn river was not far upstream from the London Bridge. It flowed down from the Fleet outside the old London wall. The Tyburn entered the Thames from the north to the east of Saint James above Westminster. It was open along the Royal Park but wound through congested city blocks beyond. Black had a good chance of watching any boats heading up the Tyburn if he could get there before the men rowing.

Robert took the less hopeful Holborn River. He ran up Fleet Street to Black Friars Bridge over the Holborn River. Again, he scanned the river for boats. The Thames boats had already entered the crowded creek and were past the wheat wharf mudbanks. Several boats were moving upstream. Two hooded figures sat in one of the boats, one rowing the other in the stern. The black-robed figure in the back turned for a moment, and Robert saw blonde hair before the figure again turned his back to Robert. Robert's mind raced. *Mister Black's description–a young man early twenties with a blonde beard!*

Adrenalin flowing, Robert made for a cobblestone

road that ran in front of the businesses that backed on the river. Wagons clogged the road, and warehouses, tanneries, coal yards, and chandleries blocked views of the river. He followed the crowded narrow lane stopping at each side alley or street between the buildings. Progress was slow. All the boats looked alike. *A black tarp over the cargo, two black-robed men, one a blonde.* He concentrated on boats moored along the river for any sign of a blonde-haired man disembarking. He scanned the faces of the crowd looking for Forester or the blonde.

Robert was forced to go around a large warehouse. As he looked down an alley towards the river, he saw a boat mooring toward a ship chandler's dock. *Two men—the blonde!* Robert was running down the alley when he saw a young woman lower the hood of her boat cloak, shake out her long blonde hair, and wait for the other man to help her out onto the dock. Robert slowed to a walk and nodded politely to the ship chandler and his daughter. He stepped out onto the pier and scanned the river, still crowded with boats. Robert continued his search street by street and alley by alley, scanning every face and boat.

Nearly an hour later, he came to Newgate Street and stopped. He looked up with eyes closed, ran both hands back over his head, locked his fingers behind his neck, exhaled a deep breath, and thought, *All is not lost. The ruse is believed even if Ezra Forester has escaped with his contact. And where can he go? He fears for his daughter. The pamphleteer and his printing press must be on this river.*

A coach stopped beside Robert. Mister Black opened the door and said, "My lord, get in."

Robert scrambled into the coach and sat opposite Black. "I won't ask how you managed to find a coach, but any luck on our men?"

"Nothing on Forester or his contact. I had clear views of the river past Newgate Street. You don't appear to have fared any better."

Robert stretched his sore body and replied, "No, but I am convinced the printing press may be on the Holborn or Fleet river. Many places to hide a press and move the pamphlets about the city."

Black tapped the top of the coach as they passed the Old Bailey. "Stop here, driver."

Black and Robert stepped out onto the street. Black gave the driver a coin, and both men stood as the coach drove off. They then walked to the alley behind the Old Bailey and continued to the gate at the far end. The door swung open at the ring of the bell. "Lord Inquirer and Mister Black. Good that you are here. The prisoner, Ezra Forester, is waiting for you."

Ezra Forester jumped to his feet when Robert and Black approached his cell. "I recognized him! Yes, I remember now. From Lord Buckingham's failed La

Rochelle campaign!"

Robert opened the cell door and said, "Tell me what happened. He was waiting for you under the bridge."

Forester nodded. "Yes, I went under the bridge, and the boat was in the water. He was wearing a dark cloak with a hood. He said, 'Get in the boat.' I hesitated, and he shouted, 'One, perhaps two men follow behind you. Get in the boat–take an oar. Follow my stroke.' Well, I did as he said. We rowed to the first river. It wasn't far…"

Robert interrupted, "Yes, the Holborn, only a few hundred yards upstream. Did he say anything while you rowed?"

Forester nodded. "Yes, after we rowed under the Fleet Street bridge and came alongside under the far end. He looked at me, laughed, and said, 'The quarry is afield. The sword of Saint Peter will be unsheathed from the Mamertine Jail.' His voice grew serious, and he said, 'Get out. You know the route. The inns will be marked in chalk as before.'

Well, I got out and watched him row up the river, away from the Thames. I thought of returning to London Bridge but decided to follow the boat. I kept him in sight until he passed the Newgate Street bridge. Then I returned here."

Robert asked, "You said you recognized him from

Buckingham's expedition. Tell me more. Was he an officer, a sergeant? Where did you see him?"

"I carried a message to my officer at Buckingham's tent. The man was standing outside, waiting. Yes, same blonde hair. A young man, as I recall, a junior officer, an Ensign or subaltern."

Robert smiled. "You did well to return here. Mister Black will arrange for men to accompany you. You will visit the inns as expected. Black will instruct you along the way."

Forester sighed. "And my daughter?"

"We will see no harm comes to her. Wait here until Black returns."

Black followed Robert up the stairs to Robert's council room. Black asked, "The Mamertine Jail?"

Robert replied, "Go with Forester. Divide the men. Half with you; the others will go with me and the King's coach. The Mamertine jail was in Rome. The final prison of Saints Peter and Paul before their execution."

Black nodded. "You trust Forester?"

"We must keep to our ruse. Now, I must call on the Keeper of Newgate prison."

CHAPTER 17
ENGLISH JUSTICE

Robert walked around the front of the Old Bailey. He shook his head in disgust as he passed three strawmen. The straw in their pockets advertised their availability to testify as told—for a fee. Such men ensured speedy trials in the court, rarely lasting longer than ten minutes. But much greater abuse was reserved for the King's enemies.

Robert continued to the entrance of Newgate Prison, originally part of a Roman London gatehouse. He took no notice of the worn and blackened statue of Richard Whittington, a former Lord Mayor of London, who enlarged the ancient prison nearly two centuries earlier. Robert announced to a guard at the man door in the gate, "The King's Lord Inquirer to see the Keeper of Newgate."

The guard swung the door open and replied, "This way, my Lord." and led Robert to another door, where the guard knocked and announced Robert. The door was immediately opened, and Robert stepped into the sumptuous apartment of the Keeper.

A man at a writing table looked up and said, "Lord Inquirer, don't see you here often. What is it that can't be handled by Mister Black?"

Robert replied, "I'm here to see Doctor Alexander Leighton."

The keeper replied, "Leighton? That's one man you'll not be employing on your side of the wall. No release to him for the army or navy either. The Lord Bishop of London's prisoner– star chamber trial–sent here after sentencing, never to be released."

"I'm not here to buy him out of your gaol. I'm here to question him regarding an ongoing inquiry. Now, if you will, take me to him."

The keeper stood up and interrupted, "You're wasting your time, Lord Inquirer. Doctor Leighton is quite ill, barely conscious. Not fit to answer questions."

Robert's patience wore thin. "Take me to him now, or you'll be on the docket at the Old Bailey yourself!"

The keeper called to the guard. "Escort the Lord Inquirer to the prisoner Leighton."

Robert followed the guard outdoors to a roofless cell. A man lay nearly naked with his arms chained to a post, lying half-buried in a pile of dank straw. Robert told the guard, "Bring him a blanket and two chairs."

"My pardon, sir, but the prisoner is not permitted a blanket. I will look for a chair for you and perhaps a stool for the prisoner."

Robert crouched beside the man and said, "Doctor Leighton? Alexander Leighton?"

Leighton coughed from deep within his lungs and whispered, "Go away. Leave me to die in peace."

Robert put an arm around Leighton's shoulder. "Let me help you sit up."

Robert was careful not to touch Leighton's back which was covered with new, blackened, bloody scars from a recent whipping. Leighton's head fell back as Robert lifted him to a sitting position. Hardened blood not yet fully formed into scabs covered his face. His nostrils had been slit, his ears cropped, and his face branded 'SS.'

"SS?" Robert asked.

"Sower of sedition," Leighton replied. "Who are you? Haven't you done enough? Let me die."

"I am the Lord Inquirer, Robert Curtis. I had heard you were arrested, But this...."

Leighton's voice crackled. "I don't recall you in the Star Chamber. You see my penance as prescribed by Bishop Laud."

"And no roof over your head? No blanket for warmth? It is a death sentence!"

Leighton tried to laugh. "Indeed! And I pray I do die soon. I am sentenced here until death." Leighton began to sob. "Will you carry a message to my family? My wife and children in Scotland? Tell them I hold their memory in my heart. And my love–give them my love."

Robert replied, "Yes, yes of course. And my prayers. I will speak to Bishop Laud! This is most unchristian!"

Leighton was sobbing. Robert asked, "You published a pamphlet in Holland…."

"Yes, it was my undoing. 'Zion's Pleas Against Prelacy: An Appeal to Parliament.'"

Robert crouched down beside Leighton and asked softly, "Where in Holland? Who published and printed your pamphlet?"

Leighton looked up at Robert. "Well, Amsterdam, of course. The city is known for its support of the reformed faith. I am not the first Scottish minister to speak against the Five Articles of Perth! The Kirk must defend the reformation and the Presbyterian church government. Let England have its bishops and all the smells and bells of the high church. Scotland is not England. Our churches call their pastors and handle their own affairs. The presbytery follows the will of good Christian people, lay leaders who seek only to administer the church faithfully."

Robert replied, "You called your queen 'a daughter

of Heth,' a Canaanite, and an idolator."

"And so, Esau's wife was! Esau, son of Isaac, by the promise of God, took a heathen wife! I am not alone in condemning the marriage of King Charles to a Catholic, a threat to all protestants and the very crown of England, Scotland, and Ireland. And what has she done? Taken her papish worship to public places! She honors the murderers of protestant martyrs! Yes, daughter of Heth, worse, a philistine!"

Robert sighed. "You ask me to carry your love to your family. Has anyone visited you since your arrest?"

Leighton began to sob. "No one. Bishop Laud held me in secret for weeks at Fulham Palace without trial. Then I was sent here, chained, and exposed until my recent mutilations. I have seen only guards and my torturers until you came today."

Robert bowed beside Leighton and gently placed a hand on Leighton's head. "Let me pray for you. Heavenly Father, bring healing and peace to this, your servant. Shield him from further harm. Strengthen him to live for you. Protect his family and congregation. And let him live to see justice for the evil poured out against him. Amen."

Leighton did not look up. He said between sobs, "Thank you. Thank you, brother. I have forgotten how to pray."

Robert walked out of Newgate prison. *I will call*

upon Bishop Laud. What kind of beast rules God's shepherds of London? And a letter, I will put it to Edward to find Leighton's family. Perhaps Will can go with him and share the love of God with Leighton's family. Yes, I will write them tonight. But now, I must go to the tower. There is also the prisoner, Sir John Eliot. Am I wrong to put the inquiry before Leighton's demand for justice? O Lord, please don't let me lose my way!

The ride to the tower of London gave Robert time to reflect on what he had learned. *King Charles' cruel treatment of Doctor Alexander Leighton, an opponent of the rigid, top-down Anglicanism the king desires, led his majesty to see all threats as coming from nonconformist Presbyterians or Puritans. Leighton is no threat. He is not allowed visitors, and as he claims, non-conformist pamphlets are printed in Amsterdam by the Dutch, not by Catholics in Antwerp. But there remains the religious nature of the threats and the reference to Saint Peter and perhaps Saint Paul. Our pamphleteer must have a religious education—Oxford or Cambridge?*

At the Tower of London, Robert waited to be escorted to the comfortable apartment of Sir John Eliot, a frequent political guest of King Charles. Robert was surprised to find Parliament's leader of the House of Commons not in his usual penitential apartment but sitting in a small cell furnished with only a cot, two chairs, and a writing table. Mercifully, there was a fireplace and a loaf of bread on the table.

A pacing Sir John smiled when he saw Robert approach. "Montclair! Good to see you! Come, sit down, I have no wine to offer, but the bread is fresh. What brings the Lord Inquirer to my cell? New charges? Please, sit down and join me."

The guard unlocked the cell and let Robert enter. "Now, I would not sit in the speaker's chair. Please, after you, Sir John."

Eliot laughed. "Yes, not quite the halls of Parliament. I begin to think His Majesty tires of me. He no longer affords me an apartment and unlimited visits here by friends and family, as he did after Lord Secretary Calvert freed his friend, John Nutt—the pirate I arrested for the scourge of Cornwall, the south coast, and the colonies. I was returned to office as Lord Admiral of Devon. Nor when he sent me here for the impeachment of his incompetent adventurer, that peacock, the Duke of Buckingham, after his disastrous expedition. Even after I refused his order to adjourn Parliament until after we passed the Petition of Rights when we put an end to his private ship and tonnage taxes—more taxes usurping the rights of all Englishmen–a short visit here. Indeed, we won when we stood up for our established rights. But this time, he seeks to punish me—requiring an apology and consenting to the King's forced loan of two thousand pounds! Can you believe it? Two thousand! No, Lord Montclair, I will not pay, and I will not apologize."

Robert listened and replied, "Sir John, what is your loyalty to King Charles?"

Sir John looked up, surprised by the question. "My loyalty? Who dares question my loyalty? Charles is the rightful King of England, Scotland, and Ireland. I have sworn my fealty–an oath of allegiance. I honor my King, but I hold my liege to his duty to honor the rights of every Englishman. Why, to do otherwise would undermine all that we hold dear—our history, our tradition, our honor, and our rights under God. How can you ask such a question?"

"Have you read or heard of the pamphlets promising reward for the murder of the King? They flood England. There has been one attempt, and we fear another is planned."

Sir John struggled to believe what he heard. "You say someone, some coward, offers a reward for the murder of King Charles? And that our countrymen act on an unproven reward of a cowardly traitor? No. No, I haven't heard this, but then my visitors are severely restricted. Just a priest and my son, my son visited but once."

Eliot shook his head and continued. "Is it true what you say? What has it come to? You do not think I have anything to do with this. Why come to me?"

"Sir John, does the sword of Saint Peter mean anything to you?"

"Saint Peter? Sword? I recall that Saint Peter drew a sword and cut off the ear of a soldier protecting our Lord Jesus in the garden of Gethsemane. But, no, I have never heard of the sword of Saint Peter."

Robert asked, "And the Mamertine prison?"

"Not here in London. 'Can't say I know of a Mamertine prison, but then new prisons are being built all the time."

"Your sons–have you ever had a visitor with a blonde beard?"

"My sons? No. John is at Oxford, little more than a lad. What beard he has is brown. Richard and the others are too young to shave. No. No family with a blonde beard."

"Do you know a man named Richard Verstegen or Richard Rowland?"

"Never heard of either one. Why? What have they said about me? They're lying. I don't know them. Plotters against the king? Murder over a few quid? Preposterous! I am here because I take my stand for the Magna Carta and the Petition of Rights, which constitute the limits of the monarchy. Never have I called for regicide!"

Robert replied, "Two thousand pounds is indeed a large sum. You have written against Arminians in the church, a theological debate beyond most loyal congregants."

Eliot shook his head and replied, "What Oxford or Cambridge man would not know of the debate. Yes, I oppose the attacks against Calvinism in our church, and I oppose Bishop Laud's crusade to force ritualism on all protestants and good Christians, but what has that to do with His Majesty?"

"It is true King Charles, head of the Church, favors Bishop Laud, but Abbot is still Archbishop of Canterbury. His path has been one of moderation and persuasion to find consensus to bring conformity in the practice of our faith. The Archbishop acts on behalf of the king."

Eliot mumbled, "Well, luck be with him on that! He can't convert the Catholics–if they indeed require conversion—the Puritans flee to the American colonies, and the Scots are near rebellion. You sit in the House of Lords, Montclair. You understand that only clear argument and compromise can bring men of principle together. The French Kings and Habsburgs polluted the minds of kings and dukes with their depraved notion of the divine rights of kings! But murder? If I were to murder my opponents, half of the parliament would be dead!"

Eliot paused and looked into Robert's eyes. "And you, Sir Robert, you keep yourself to yourself, a priest, a friend to Catholics, Puritans, and Presbyterians. You are close to Archbishop Abbot, a Calvinist. Where do your loyalties lie? Will you stand against Laud's unholy purge?"

Robert stood up. "Thank you for your time, Sir John. I pray that His Majesty's temper cools and that you are released. I look forward to the day you again lead the House of Commons. I must continue my inquiries."

Robert was out the door when Eliot called out. "My regards to your beautiful wife, Lady Montclair. Assure her that I understand the fate of one found redundant by the royal family."

Robert walked out of the cell towards the Tower gate. *Motive? He's right. Eleanor and I have motives–the whole country is offended–the Catholic threat, the demands for taxes, and the King's disregard of Parliament! Chasing motives will get me nowhere!*

Robert saw the prison keeper approach with a messenger. "Keeper, good that you come. I need to talk to you."

"Yes, Lord Inquirer, but this page has come for you. Lord Conway has an urgent need. You are to accompany the page at once."

"Lord Conway sends a page, yes, I must go–but confirm the testimony of Sir Eliot–he has had no visitors, no blonde bearded man?"

The keeper replied, "Sir Eliot is the king's prisoner. I am to notify His Majesty when Sir Eliot is prepared to apologize and agree to his loan. Until then, he is permitted only official visitors on behalf of the crown. And, of course, a priest. But as you ask, not a chaplain of the Tower, a young man, and yes, he is blonde of hair and beard."

"His name?"

"I don't recall his name; he presented a pass with the royal seal on his first visit."

"When does he come? Does he attend other prisoners?"

"Only Sir Eliot, no others. His visits vary–he once said he has many other calls to make."

CHAPTER 18
NEW TRAILS

Lord Conway was more irritated than most often. "There you are, Lord Inquirer, been chasing after you half the day. His Majesty is most concerned for the young Prince Charles. He commands your immediate attention on security for the prince's baptism at the Chapel Royal, Saint James Palace, on June 27. His decision, not well understood among all his subjects, that King Louis of France and the Dowager Queen of France, Marie de Medici, are to be godparents is cause for precaution. These threats must come to an end! The seditious must be brought to swift justice. What have you to report?"

"There is steady progress, Lord Secretary. We are closing on this deadly pamphleteer."

"Progress, closing, who is he? You don't know yet, do you?"

Robert exhaled deeply. "We are near, very close.

We have turned one of his couriers and identified others. We lay a trap...."

Conway stood up. "You have not arrested them? Why not take who you have to the tower and make them talk!"

Robert shook his head. "No! Our man is too clever by half. The couriers do not know him. They are separate links in his chain. We follow the chain to its ends, both ends."

Conway looked up. "Both ends?"

"Yes, the pamphleteer has eyes and ears here in the court. We have followed it to the Royal baggage, but there may be–there likely are others informing. You have heard me say to withhold his Majesty's schedule. His Majesty's visit to the Forest of Dean tomorrow, who accompanies him?"

Conway sat down and nodded his head. "Yes, It is a brief visit–the private business of the King, back in less than a fortnight. No courtiers will travel with His Majesty. Just myself, several other clerks, and pages, Then, of course, his bed-chamber servants and the French cook...."

"Henri can be trusted. He is a loyal protestant subject, a pillar of the French Protestant Church. The trap I laid–what was the last schedule sent to the baggage master?"

Conway looked puzzled. "Why you gave it to him

yourself not two days ago."

"Very good. Nothing more to him. I gave him false instructions. He will be told once on the road. We have put them on a false trail with my men waiting. I have also identified a man who can lead us to their printing press here in London. You see, Lord Secretary, progress—and safety for his Majesty's travels. Now, tell me of the plans for the prince. Is there to be a governess?"

"Yes, of course. And before you ask, yes, you may make discreet inquiries. Use security for the baptism to your benefit. Lady Mary Sackville, Countess of Dorset, has been chosen. It is not yet determined when the Queen and the infant prince return to Whitehall from Saint James Palace. The Earl of Dorset is Lord Chamberlain to Queen Henrietta Maria. The Earl's London home is on Fleet Street, but the manor house of his wife's family, Croxall Hall, in Derbyshire, has passed to him. The young prince will take country airs there."

Robert nodded. "The King's choice, no doubt. I know of Dorset, a champion of the protestant faith and a strong supporter of the King's sister, Elizabeth of the Palatinate. Popular with Parliament. His voice is heard in the Privy Council. Still, I shall make my discreet inquiries."

Robert paused. "Right! I have much to do before tomorrow morning. You sent a page for me–I need one."

Conway called, "Joseph!" and a young man

appeared. "Joseph, do as the Lord Inquirer asks and return directly."

The young man with blonde hair and beard replied, "Yes, Lord Conway, and then return directly."

Robert eyed the young man and said, "It is quite an honor to be a page to the Lord Secretary—your accent, continental, tell me, who are your people, and where are you from?"

The young man bowed. "Indeed, it is a great honor. I am Joseph Rusdorf, son of Johann Rusdorf, lately Chief Councilor to King Frederick of Bohemia."

Robert smiled. "Elector Frederick is exiled to the Hague in the Netherlands. I believe he would be happy simply to return to Heidelberg in the Palatinate. Who speaks for Frederick and your father in the court of King Charles?"

"My father often visits, as does King Frederick's new Secretary, Wilhelm von Curti. Von Curti is at court as we speak."

Robert smiled. "Very well then, you know of my offices?"

The lad nodded. "Westminster, across from the Chambers of the King's Bench."

"Good. You are to go there and tell Mister Black that the Lord Inquirer is off to Fulham Palace to see Bishop Laud. Mister Black is to wait for me at Westminster Palace.

Tell him we need men tonight."

King Charles favored Bishop Laud's loyal voice in the House of Lords and appointed him to the Privy Council, the Star Chamber, and Royal Chaplain. When Archbishop Abbot's friend, Bishop Andrewes, died, Abbot obediently appointed Laud Bishop of London at King Charles' direction. Bishop Laud was Archbishop Abbot's long-time rival, and soon King Charles found no time to hear from his Archbishop. The Bishop of London's palace was up the Thames in Fulham.

Laud met Robert at the door and did not invite him in. "What is it, Lord Inquirer? I hope you have come with news of this seditious printer of hateful lies."

"I have come here as a priest to intercede for the prisoner, Doctor Alexander Leighton."

"Doctor Leighton? Isn't he dead yet?"

"No, by the grace of God, he lives. What is this penalty? The man has been flogged near death. His face is butchered, chained in an outdoor cell without a roof over his head or a blanket to warm him against the elements. I am told he is your prisoner, that you have passed this sentence. In God's name, how do you abide such cruelty?"

"You will hold your tongue, priest. Leighton was tried in the star chamber. Not only had he defamed her Majesty, Queen Henrietta Maria, but he is seditious–"

"Defamed the queen? Half of England has objected

to the queen's Catholicism!"

"A daughter of Heth? He libels the queen, calling her Esau's wife, a Canaanite despoiler of God's promise!"

Robert replied, "The King himself shipped her French court back to Paris. And Leighton's sedition? Opposition to your heavy-handed imposition of Bishops upon the kirk in Scotland and your preference for liturgical prayer in place of sermons in worship? You declare those views seditious?"

Bishop Laud's face flushed red. "Have you read his words? Come into my chamber, Read his treatise, and then question my actions done to protect God's church in England!"

Laud turned around and stomped off. Stunned, Robert followed behind. Laud walked straight to his writing table, dug through papers, and pulled out a pamphlet. "Read this. Read it and tell me they are not the intemperate writings of a heretic!"

Robert took the pamphlet and read the title: "Zion's Pleas Against Prelacy: An Appeal to the Parliament."

Robert mumbled, "When was this written?"

"1628, yes two years ago. While parliament pursued charging Buckingham before his murder. The King was enraged."

Robert mumbled as he read, "Yes, I remember that Parliament...."

Something about the printing in the pamphlet was familiar; there they were—the missing tails on the t and the other damaged letters–the typeset from the New Tidings–the typeset from the deadly pamphleteer.

Robert looked up. "As you say, quite inflammatory. But the man has been severely punished, and God has chosen to let him live. Perhaps mercy? Allow him to be moved inside, given a blanket, and fare no worse than any other vile offender. Is not his prison sentence until death? How long…"

Laud studied Robert and sighed. "Perhaps living with his punishment will move him to repentance. I will send word to do as you say. Now, what have you to say on your inquiries."

Robert held up the pamphlet. "May I keep this? Perhaps Doctor Alexander has a disciple—as I have just reported to Lord Conway, progress, excellent progress, but I dare say nothing that may put the bird to flight. Good day, your Grace. I journey with the King in the morning and have much to prepare."

Robert did not wait for a reply. He turned and hurried out the door with the pamphlet in hand. He went directly to Westminster Palace. Lynch and Black were waiting as directed, but Robert was surprised to see the Cadzand team: Jones, Brown, and Smith waiting.

The three junior men stood as Robert entered.

Robert bellowed, "Who's watching Captain Anderson?" Before anyone could answer, Robert dropped the pamphlet in front of Mister Black. "Written by Doctor Alexander Leighton, he claims it was printed in Amsterdam. Same typeset as our pamphleteer."

Black looked at the pamphlet, handed it to Lynch, and replied, "Richard Verstegen has been arrested in Antwerp. Jones and Smith attended the questioning at Het Steen. Insists he did not print the threatening pamphlets. Just his Catholic tracts in English. He does admit to helping his English customer buy the printing press from Abraham Verhoeven. Named the buyer, Sir John Wynter, son of Sir Edward Wynter of Lydney."

Lynch put the pamphlet down and looked at Robert. "Same typeset. Could it be a different printing press? How many flawed sets did he make?"

Robert walked to his window and stared into the dusk towards the Thames. "Sir Edward is a recusant Catholic. Served King James. Likely he keeps a priest–perhaps an angry Irishman. His son may have been radicalized. Lydney is in the Forest of Dean. The King journeys there tomorrow. They have taken the bait on the itinerary. Lord Conway assures me that the true itinerary has not been shared. But we cannot ignore Leighton and his pamphlet. The man is near death–perhaps Bishop Laud's hatred and the Star Chambers punishment have given his friends a motive, though he receives no visitors. And there is also Sir John Eliot, speaker of the House of Commons, now the king's prisoner in the tower. A blonde-bearded priest visits him. I want this priest questioned. Find him–take him on his next visit. The blonde beard we chased on the river–the printing press must be in one of the warehouses. Black, you are to search London until it is found! And then there is another blonde beard, a page to Lord Conway. His name is Joseph Rusdorf, son of Prince-Elector Frederick's advisor, Johann Rusdorf. Look into him as well. Discreetly, he is a diplomat."

Black mumbled, "Why not discreetly arrest every man in England with a blonde beard?"

Robert ignored Black and turned to the silent men. "You believe Verstegen?"

Jones replied, "Meers was very persuasive. Verstegen was an intermediator. He found his English friends their printing press. Verstegen's mission is to support the Catholic Church's crusade against all protestants."

Robert nodded. "And Haakon Anderson and his boat?"

"Here in London. We brought word of Verstegen's capture as quickly as possible."

Robert smiled. "You men have done well. It is good you are here. With so many trails, we need every watcher and secret man."

Robert turned to his trusted lieutenants. "Tomorrow, I travel with the king. Lynch, you travel with the empty baggage coach along the false route. Look for the chalk marks. Ezra Forester should meet you at each stop. I want the names of the innkeepers and any pamphlets. If our trap is set, there should be new pamphlets along the leaked route. Send them to me by courier as I travel. Of course, if there is one planning an attack on the King, arrest him. Otherwise, we watch and take names. Only after we reach the head of the snake do we act."

Lynch asked, "No arrests of the pamphleteer's network? It is our best chance to ensure that none escapes. But, as you say, our advantage is lost if we fail to find the pamphleteer."

Robert paced. "The pamphleteer has hidden his identity. His couriers will not know to flee if he is captured—if we keep his capture secret until we sweep them all."

Robert picked up the pamphlet and gave it to Brown. "Sail to Amsterdam with Anderson. Contact Karl Schroeder, and find the printer of Doctor Leighton's tract. Trace the typeset. Leave immediately. Report by fastest means. Go!"

Brown was out the door without further word.

Robert sat down. "There is more. The King named King Louis and the French Queen Mother, Marie de Medici, as godparents to the prince. Catholic godparents will not sit well with the people. The baptism is on June 27 at the Chapel Royal, Saint James Palace. Security. He has named Countess Dorset as the governess. Discreet background. Did I say be discreet? I will interview the Earl and Countess Dorset."

Robert sighed. "That's all. Reserve our fastest horse for a courier between us. I travel with the King to Windsor, then Donnington Castle, Newbury. From there to Chepstow Castle and perhaps Lydiard House. The King's business will be conducted at Saint Braiels Castle in the Forest of Dean. Now, I have one last letter to write."

Black asked, "Lydiard House? Lady Barbara Villiers? A most unpopular woman in the Forest of Dean. Who else does the king visit at Saint Braiels Castle?"

"Sir John Wynter. Yes, son of Sir Edward Wynter. Sir John likely is our recusant Catholic printer. All the more urgent that you find the printing press. And inquire after Rusdorf and the blonde priest. Go! You have your orders!"

After Black and the others filed out, Robert sat down at his writing-table, dipped his quill in the inkwell, and scribbled on rag paper:

Dearest Eleanor

Still, we are apart. How I long to hold you tight and breathe in the sweetness of your soul and the scent of you that brings comfort to my weary spirit. I long to see your smile, gaze upon the sweet twins, Edward and Elizabeth, and feel my pride swell watching William conquer Montclair. It is a hard business I pursue, filled with darkness and cruelty. For certain, God would not call any man to murder his king, and so I pursue a calling. But my heart is torn by the injustice and cruelty meted out in the king's name. To see a man flogged, his face forever disfigured for the offense of worshipping without a bishop—I am appalled and at a loss.

It is with a heavy heart I ask for your help. I need a woman's touch in the court. I remember well the pain you endured in service to Queen Henrietta Maria. Another good woman, I hope a friend from the court, Lady Mary Sackville, the Countess of Dorset, has been chosen to raise the young Prince Charles. There is danger in the court, and questions must be asked. Some things a woman will say only to another woman, one who can be trusted.

I am off to the Forest of Dean with his Majesty but will return within a fortnight. The baptism of Charles will take place at the Chapel Royal on June 27. I ask if you will visit with Lady Mary Sackville soon to congratulate her, of course, and to read the times. My thoughts are for you to accompany me as I make perfunctory inquiries as to the safety of the prince—choosing servants, guards, and procedures. I will excuse myself to inspect for security arrangements and allow you to exchange pleasantries and hear all that is new from the ladies at court—with luck, rumors, ambitions, and influences. I know your talent and ability in these matters. And you have often addressed my social shortcomings. In my position, I rely on Lord Conway's lead at court, a good man in a demanding job also gifted with a wife he loves, but a woman I trust is needed. I need tell you no more, and I know the pain this may bring but has this not been your calling?

Having you and our children in London will bring some comfort until this affair is sorted. Perhaps this responsibility will soon be lifted from my shoulders.

> *Loving you more each day,*
> *Robbie*

CHAPTER 19
ROAD HAZARDS

Lynch and one of Robert's couriers were at Saint James Palace stable when Robert arrived before sunrise. The King's bed and luggage were being loaded into a covered wagon. Robert walked to the baggage master, handed him a sealed order, and said, "Another royal wagon, covered, for my man. Mister Lynch."

The surprised baggage master walked into the carriage house. The king's baggage now loaded; the driver climbed into his seat. Immediately the courier jumped in beside him. Robert presented a letter with the royal seal. "Your new directions. You will do as my man says upon pain of death. Now, off to Windsor!"

Robert rode with a company of King's Guards leading and following the royal coaches. The Lord Secretary and Lord Treasurer rode in the lead coach. The

King and the Lord Chamberlain, Philip Herbert, Fourth Earl of Pembroke, and First Earl of Montgomery followed in a second coach. Lord Herbert was one of Charles' longest and most loyal friends. The second son of the Second Earl of Pembroke and a protégé of the Duke of Buckingham, Herbert had accompanied Queen Henrietta Maria from France. Charles rewarded Herbert with the title of Earl of Montgomery and made him a wealthy man. In addition to Lord Chamberlain, Herbert received lifetime emoluments as Keeper of Westminster Palace, Keeper of Saint James Palace, Lord Lieutenant of Buckinghamshire, Lord Lieutenant of Somerset, and Lord Lieutenant of Cornwall. Herbert inherited the family title and estate, Wilton House, upon the death of his brother, William. Lord Philip Herbert was served by fifty servants at his London house and another one hundred and fifty at Wilton House in Wiltshire.

At Windsor, while the King sat with his three close advisors, Robert left the castle and walked to the village inn. The tables were filled with local tradesmen and travelers. There was not a courtier in sight. Robert breathed a sigh of relief; Lord Conway did his part in convincing the King to withhold the change in itinerary. Only the baggage master and coach driver, standing at the bar with mugs of ale indicated the arrival of a royal party. Once the two royal servants saw Robert, they swallowed the last of their quaffs and left.

Robert recognized the innkeeper from past visits and made his way to him. "A good crowd tonight, none of the misbehaving courtiers, or their unescorted ladies, I presume."

The innkeeper kept busy pouring mugs. "Aye, they pay no more than the good townsfolk and bring their debauchery to my inn. The King's baggage master and coachman just left, complaining they were commandeered by Lord Montclair. Most indignant they were. Worried their friends in the court would demand repayment for his Majesty's changed travel plans, not to mention foregoing any gambling winnings. Weren't too happy to see you come in."

"The King's safety. Nasty business going on. If I had my way, King Charles' schedule would always be guarded. Any pamphlets left about that I should know about?"

"Nay. But then Windsor will always be a safe place for his Majesty. Go sit a table, Lord Montclair, you must be dry and hungry. A fine mutton stew and good ale will put the road behind ye. Will any of your lads be joining ye, tonight?"

"Just me tonight. I plan on making an early night of it."

The following morning, Robert gave directions to

the baggage master and coachman; Donnington Castle, Newbury. The royal party was greeted by Charles Howard, Earl of Nottingham and second son of Lord Howard of Effingham, who led the small English Navy to victory over the Spanish Armada. The ancient Donnington Castle was now restored and filled with memories of England's great triumph over the hated Spanish. Robert was not party to the after-dinner prepared talk that awaited the Earl. "Out of great respect for the contributions of your father, the admiral, you, Nottingham, are exempt from a forced loan, but surely, you see your patriotic duty to support the navy once again with a generous loan."

Robert was greeted by a courier from Lynch with a leather pouch hanging from a shoulder strap. In a small anteroom, the courier said, "Mister Lynch sends his respects and these pamphlets found at the Wycombe inn. The sign was chalk marked as reported. The innkeeper claimed ignorance, a guilty one for certain—easy enough to learn they were left a full day before we arrived. Mister Lynch has moved on to Oxford. I am to wait for your reply before meeting him at Cheltenham."

Robert took one of a pair of identical pamphlets. They bore the same distinctive printer's marks. Robert read the headline: "One thousand Pound Reward for delivering King Ahab, that is, Charles Stuart, to Hell's Fire!"

His eyes focused on the pamphlet, Robert asked, "Our man was there more than a day ahead. He saw nothing?"

"No, Sir Robert. They appeared in the inn a day before the wagon arrived."

Robert snorted. "Must've been the innkeeper. Was he arrested?"

"Mister Lynch said no, not until we see what awaits ahead. We thought…."

Robert looked up. "Yes, that's what we agreed to. Tell Mister Lynch to be prepared to spring the trap. Wait while I finish reading. Robert sat down and read aloud. "What must become of England's Ahab and Jezebel? Their spilt blood should be licked up by dogs and swine, their foul bodies torn apart by beasts and left in the street. For such was ordained by God. Are not Charles and Henrietta Maria the second coming of Ahab and Jezebel? Read on, good Christian, I will show you the truth! Ahab ignored the offerings of his relative by marriage, the good King Jehoshaphat of Judah, and instead married the princess Jezebel of Sidon, the Baal-worshiping daughter of the King of Tyre. Jezebel demanded that the name of Jehovah be forgotten in Israel and Baal be worshipped on every hilltop. King Charles married the papist Henrietta who brings a public mass back to Tyburn Tree. And Charles, gives his word to Parliament that there will be no compromise with our protestant Church but signs such a pledge in secret to ignore our laws against the papists! As Ahab ignored the warnings of the prophet Elijah and pursued and persecuted God's prophets, so Charles shutters Parliament and sends its leaders to the tower! As Ahab pursued an unjust war, so Charles abandons our protestant brothers and allies for a new alliance with Spain against the Dutch. Like Ahab and Jezebel, whose greed could never be sated, Ahab who coveted his neighbor, Naboth's vineyard, so do Charles and Henrietta, his Jezebel, covet the property and incomes, the common rights in the Forest of Dean and the promised rights of the freeminers. Burdensome taxes are not enough for their boundless greed. Good people do not suffer the fate of Naboth! Fight the tyrant! Justice came to Ahab and Jezebel. Bring justice to Charles and his papist whore!"

Robert looked up. "This pamphlet is clearly anti-Catholic, far more than the others. And there is Ezra Forester, a disgruntled soldier. I heard him curse the Queen as a papist. We followed the past pamphlets back to Cadzand, and their Catholic smuggler and their printer in Antwerp. What game does the pamphleteer play?"

Robert turned a page and read more. "But what of the young prince you ask? Prince Charles is yet young and will be raised a good protestant and given his crown when fully prepared, and of age. Good men of England will protect the kingdom and preserve our God-given rights as Englishmen. And God forbid the young prince should die, or the apple has fallen too close to the tree. The King's good sister, Elizabeth of the Palatinate is healthy and has borne strong sons–good men all, and able. Rise up, England! Strike down Ahab and Jezebel!"

His instructions received; the courier rode off to join Lynch. Robert took one of the pamphlets and walked to the great hall of Donnington Castle. A word to the guard and he was allowed to enter. Robert walked behind Lord Conway and whispered the news in his ear. King Charles noticed and spoke out. "Montclair, you bring news of the evil and seditious author of these foul pamphlets that litter my kingdom?"

"Your Majesty do not let me disturb your supper or the evening you have planned with the Earl and his guests. I will leave my findings with Lord Conway. Be assured, the self-named Arthur Pendragon is unaware of your presence here. We make progress in our inquiries."

The king snorted. "The progress I demand is the devil hanged, drawn and quartered!"

Lord Conway answered, "Your Majesty, please excuse me for few minutes while I review the Lord Inquirer's report."

"Go. Both of you. Don't wander off. I will join you within the hour."

Robert had only fifteen minutes alone to brief Lord Conway when King Charles summoned them to his apartment. "Come in, come in. Nottingham has agreed to the loan. Though insufficient to pay the Queen's gambling debts."

King Charles looked at Robert. "Montclair, you look surprised. My dear Mary thinks she can hide her debts from me. But they all come to me. I will not be beholden to these Catholic nobles! As if her insatiable demand for new clothes was not enough, my dear wife has become a most accomplished gambler. Her talent is losing. You are my Lord Inquirer and did not know this?"

Robert answered, "I do not see it my duty or my right to make inquiries after my King and Queen."

Charles smiled. "A wise answer. These loans–money for the Navy, money for the volunteers going to Gustav Adolphus or the Spanish Netherlands, or money for the queen's purchases—it all drains the same treasury. Now, progress, you said. Tell me you are on to this skunking coward."

Lord Conway began, "Montclair has identified several…."

Charles interrupted. "Let the man speak for himself. Cut to the chase Montclair."

Robert bowed. "We have found and turned Lord Lindsey's volunteer, enlisted as Arthur Pendragon. He works for us. The pamphleteer follows a false route to the Forest of Dean, and we note his agents along the route. I hold the proof, another pamphlet found in Wycombe on the false route we passed. We know where the pamphlets were printed, the very press purchased in Antwerp, and how Your Majesty's plans are passed. We are pulling in the line, identifying each collaborator, ensuring not one is left behind."

Charles nodded. "How many are in custody? Show no mercy in interrogating the seditious cowards. You say you have Pendragon; he does not act alone?"

Robert replied, "Lindsey's Pendragon is no more than an illiterate veteran, a courier in the pamphleteer's plot. We hide what we know until we reach the learned man behind this evil. But we shall sweep them all once we know the schemer. He is no fool. The thugs do not know the identity of their employer. But we are closing in on him, and he must not know we are on to him."

King Charles paced the room. "You say this man is given my travel schedule? Someone in the palace…."

"Majesty, we know of one, but there may be others. The traitor will not escape."

Charles nodded' "And another pamphlet. Let me see it."

Robert left the King to read the pamphlet in private. Walking the corridor, Robert thought, *Queen Henrietta*

Maria's debts? That's what this is about? Charles is worse than his father, King James, who never paid Colonel Vere or his men. And Buckingham's soldiers, most dead, nothing paid to their families or the few who survived. Work proceeds on a new palace for the queen and now her gambling debts. Parliament was right to deny him new taxes. Greed and corruption! Charles has no thoughts for his subjects. His realm is only for plunder. Why do I serve him?

Lynch confiscated pamphlets that appeared in Oxford and Bedford. None appeared in Cheltenham, though the inn had been marked by chalk. Word had reached the pamphleteer. The stops on the king's journey at Wilton House, the elegant manor of his friend, Philip Herbert, the fourth Earl of Pembroke, and Chepstow Castle, a residence of Henry Somerset, Earl of Worcester, a recusant Catholic, were without incident. Pembroke was anxious to show Charles the splendid garden designed by Inigo Jones. The King persuaded his friend that such extravagance proved his friend, Pembroke, most capable of a large loan. Lord Worcester was also compelled to lend.

From Chepstow Castle on the River Wye, Charles coached to Saint Briavels Castle in the middle of the Forest of Dean and met with his verderers charged with overseeing the royal forest. King James recognized the mineral and timber wealth of the forest and had authorized enclosures as early as 1624. The partial disafforestation and enclosures displaced many residents, most had lived and worked the forest for generations. The nighttime removal of enclosure fences and other signs of unrest were widespread throughout the forest. The Forest of Dean supplied most of the lumber that built the English Navy. Below ground, rich coal seams supplied fuel for London and iron ore for England's cannons, guns, swords, tools, and nails. The forest of Dean may have been small by royal forest standards, but it was by far the richest.

King Charles was determined to know the price he could demand for rights to royal timber, coal, and iron ore. When questioned, his loyal verderers reminded the king of the common rights of the foresters and the free mining rights of the descendants of local miners who supported King Edward I at the siege of Berwick-upon-Tweed in 1296. Charles argued, "The forest will remain, only smaller." The verderers were told to identify the best coal and iron ore deposits and timber beyond the current needs of the navy. Charles closed the meeting with the admonition. "The American colonies are well wooded. The Navy has ships, let them transport their own lumber."

Outside Charles said to his friend, Lord Pembroke, "Lady Barbara and her agent, Sir Giles Mompresson, are eager to extend their holdings beyond three thousand acres in the forest. But I think another bidder may improve my price."

Pembroke asked "Giles I know by reputation. A notorious cheat. Wasn't he exiled for corruption? But Lady Barbara?"

Charles reminded him, "I pardoned Sir Giles. Took all his estates. He manages Lady Barbara's enclosures in the Forest of Dean. Lady Barbara Villiers, you must know her from court, a relation to my good friend Buckingham, God rest his soul."

Prices set in his mind, Charles clambered into his coach for the seven-mile ride to White Cross Manor in Lydney, the home of John Wynter, England's largest producer of iron. Wynter built upon the near monopoly of iron his father developed through favors and grants in the Royal Forests bought from King James. Sir John knew better than the king's verderers the seams of coal and iron ore in the forest. He knew the timber, the costs of labor and the best routes to his smelters and markets. Sir John knew that Sir Giles was hated by every forester and that vandalism and attacks against his enclosures were increasing. He also knew King Charles was anxious to sell.

CHAPTER 20
LADY SKIMMINGTON

Robert mounted his horse and joined the six palace guards riding in front of the royal coach. Another six followed close behind. As the coach made its way through the castle gate and entered the tall forest of oak and elm, a shot was heard, and a flock of birds rose in response. Robert scanned the forest but saw no sign of powder smoke. The Captain of the Guard called out, "Nothing sire, probably a hunter or farmer shooting at varmint from one of the enclosures."

A half mile into the forest and a loud banging rang through the forest. Metal on metal, not the even strokes of a blacksmith, more rapid, almost urgent. Like the clanging of a pot calling farmers in from the fields for supper. A baker's dozen pair of eyes searched the impenetrable woods but saw nothing amiss. Four more furlongs and another clanging. Robert's mind was drawn to the large boiling pot in his mother's kitchen, the time many years ago as a young boy he banged on the side of the pot with the fire poker to scare off a mouse.

Now there were two sounds. Two different pots, yes, kitchen kettles being struck by pokers. *They're announcing our coming, signaling our progress to Lydney. Why no word from Lynch?*

The captain of the guard came alongside Robert and said, "I'm sending someone ahead. They're telling the foresters and everyone in the woods our progress."

Robert nodded. "My thoughts as well. They know these woods. Likely we'll never see them. It's what awaits us in Lydney that concerns me."

The captain replied, "I could send men to ride our flank through the woods."

Robert scanned the thick forest on both sides of the road. "That would put two men into their hands. Better no further than the edge of the road. If they were going to attack, they would not continue the signaling."

Another mile into the forest and another set of pots and kettles rang on each side as they passed. The coach driver called out to the Captain of the Guard, "Captain, come alongside. His Majesty would have a word. You too, Lord Montclair."

When the men were alongside the coach window, the curtain was pushed to one side. King Charles spoke, "What is that annoying clanging? Can't you do something about it? The Lord Treasurer and I are trying to work figures. A most distracting noise!"

Robert replied, "Your subjects, Majesty, announce your progress to Lydney."

The Guard Captain added, "I've sent a man ahead. He will warn of any danger with a gunshot. We don't believe they mean you danger. Certainly, such noise confirms their presence. The men have weapons at the ready. But any increase in our pace would only make the journey more uncomfortable."

Charles snorted. "Right then. Keep a sharp eye out. I've been warned that certain miscreants, living off the Forest, have arrogantly suggested I owe them a free living from my lands and forest." When Charles finished, the curtain was abruptly pulled closed.

Five miles into the forest, the woods began to thin. Evidence of clearing for firewood and fences for cattle and sheep told them they were nearing Lydney. The guard sent ahead cantered his horse back to his captain. He saluted and reported. "Road clear ahead. It appears the village is preparing for a fair or festival of sorts."

The royal coach continued on. A mile outside of the village, only one row of trees separated the forest road from fenced and well-tended fields. Four drummers were waiting and fell in line behind others coming up the road from the village. The drummers divided in two with lines ahead of and behind the royal coach. The newly formed column paraded towards Lydney. The procession crested a small hill, and the church spire and tidy limestone cottages of the village came into view. At the bottom of the hill a large crowd had gathered. The drummers fell into cadence with a long drum roll and a man stepped forward from the crowd and began to sing:

"O a foolish young Charlie,

married a pretty French thing.

And a wicked papist she,

turned the head of the king,

No love for England—she loves only things French,

For years, alas no child came to he.

But then the queen acquainted Sir Giles, the cheat

and lo the frigid woman went into heat.

Beguiling Mompresson gives her a lesson,

The foolish king—he waits in the wings.

Now London church bells ring,

at last, there's offspring!

Now a smiling Sir Giles is in bed with the king,

but not alone they, the queen a merry tryst brings.

Cheating Sir Giles in bed with the king...."

The Captain of the Guard spurred his horse and

rode towards the singer. The man fell back into the crowd. Immediately five hundred people began to shout and more than one hundred beat pots with heavy spoons or ladles. The others lifted pikes, pitchforks, hoes, shovels, and even a few halberds into the air as they all closed ranks, shoulder to shoulder. The captain's horse reared and spun aside in fright. The captain stood in his stirrup and pulled hard on the reins. The frightened horse backed stepped and stopped. After a few calming strokes along his mount's neck, the Captain's horse and the entire procession came to a quiet stop.

Robert caught sight of Mister Lynch along the front line of the mob. Lynch shook his head and Robert broke eye contact. A dummy in women's clothing was lifted from the center of the crowd. The silence was shattered when a falsetto voice cried out, "Lady Skimmington, your Majesty. I am most pleased you have come to join our special parade! Today Sir Giles receives the justice he deserves!"

A second dummy, an effigy of Sir Giles Mompresson was lifted opposite Lady Skimmington. A winey, shaking voice replied, "Don't be hasty my good lady. All that I do is for the good of our King, England, our beloved forest, and my dear, dear neighbors. Why look, I have brought His Majesty to Lydney! Only good will come from his visit. Money, yes, much money will flow into Lydney. No longer will you scratch the ground in search of what iron ore the Romans left behind. No! work in the village. Good work at the manors and a new smelter and iron works. Yes, the money will find its way to my good neighbors for services rendered!"

Lady Skimmington's falsetto shouted, "Silence, you lying scoundrel! We are not dogs begging for scraps from your table! You steal what has been ours for hundreds of years. A reward from our King, honored by all the kings that followed–until you bent the ear of his Majesty King Charles!"

The Sir Giles effigy voice screamed, "Mercy! I only seek to buy what the King seeks to sell, nothing more!"

"Nothing more? Nothing more? Have the king's men taken measure of the timber you steal? If sold a thousand trees you take ten thousand! And mines, if ten are awarded, do you not open twenty-five? Scoundrel! Liar! Cheat! You are no man! Nay! A green-eyed monster in the skin of a man. Enough whimpering! Come along, your Majesty. The game is afoot!"

The crowd surged forward surrounding the royal coach and the mounted guards seated on nervous prancing horses with their weapons drawn. Once the royal entourage was surrounded the disciplined crowd followed Lady Skimmington to a path off the main road. A furlong down the narrow lane she stopped. "Gather round friends, make room for his Majesty the King!"

The Lady Skimmington voice sang out, "Bring the guilty forward! Let him gaze upon his dig. With the ore now taken there is room for the monster!"

The effigy of Sir Giles was paraded to the edge of a shallow pit. The falsetto of Lady Skimmington sang loudly, "Have you seen one of your digs Sir Giles? Thought not, look closely, bend over and look. No! Better you taste the handiwork of your greed. Throw him in and bury him!"

The effigy was tossed into the center of the hole and men with shovels buried it in minutes. The shrill Lady Skimmington laughed heartily and then cried out. "Why I see a fence! A fence that keeps my cattle from grazing where our ancestors grazed their cattle for centuries. What is this fence?"

Someone shouted, "A new enclosure, Lady Skimmington. One of many."

"Tear it down–and the next. There shall be no enclosures in this forest. Our sheep and cattle shall graze, our freeminers shall mine and our bailiwick to hunt the king's game shall be honored! To the fences! No enclosures!"

Someone shouted, "But the King's men?"

The falsetto laughed and replied, "Let them lead King Ahab from our forest. He will need a change of pants before he bows before his Jezebel!"

The crowd began to chant, "Flee Ahab, run to

Jezebel. Flee Ahab, run to Jezebel."

The strong baritone of the Lord of Misrule, who serenaded the king on the road, sang out:

"Ahab ran to Jezebel when Elijah defeated Baal.

The Lord preserved his prophet

who lived to tell this tale,

England's prophets will soon be

freed from the Tower,

Ahab and Jezebel will swiftly fall from power.

The papist plan to rule England

Will once and for all time fail!"

The hysterical laugh of Lady Skimmington was a falsetto of the Lord of Misrule. It screamed. "To the enclosures!" At once the mob ran into the forest and began tearing down fences, stacking the rails, and setting them on fire. The guards remained mounted around the King's coach. The crowd was gone. The road ahead was clear. The Captain looked back at the coachman. "Drive on to White Cross Manor."

No sooner had the coach resumed its progress down the road than a large, mounted contingent of men rode forward. Their leader called to the Captain of the Guard, "We come from White Cross Manor. Sir John Wynter sends us to escort you safely to the manor. There has been troubling talk of late."

Robert studied the men. *Armed. Probably veterans.*

They ride as trained cavalry. Conveniently late, Sir John. Conveniently late.

Safe inside the gates of White Cross Manor, King Charles called to the Captain of the Guard. "Captain, you and Lord Montclair will attend me in fifteen minutes."

The king then stepped from his coach and was greeted by John Wynter and a phalanx of bowing servants. Charles growled, "You must teach you neighbors their manners, Wynter, or I shall send a garrison to Lydney and quarter them here in White Cross."

Sir John Wynter bowed and said, "My humblest apologies, your majesty. My men are at your service. Rest assured no harm—no further unpleasantness will tarnish your visit to White Cross. A meal awaits after your travels if your appetite is willing."

Charles stared at Wynter, then smiled and said, "Yes, of course. But first show me to my apartment and I must deal with my guard."

Robert followed the captain into the King's chamber. Charles spoke as soon as they crossed the threshold. "We will depart after dark. You will arrange for Wynter's men to join the escort. Everyone is to be armed. And this time anyone approaching my coach will be shot. Captain, prepare your men!"

Turning to Robert, King Charles bellowed, "You have failed me again, Lord Inquirer! No warning? You let me ride into a mob bent on riot! Well, what do you have to say for yourself, man?"

Robert bowed. "I saw my man among the leaders. Permit me to question him. Yes, something went wrong. I will find out. But we know this, Lydney was not written on the false itinerary we passed. There remains another source, a traitor inside the court. The chants of Ahab—the pamphlet has made its way to Lydney. Allow the Captain of the Guard and me to determine a safe route to London. No one else is to know. And permit me to remain behind with my men. I beg leave to join you at Saint James Palace where I can make inquiries within the court."

Confusion widened the king's eyes. "Someone close to me a collaborator? A traitor? Yes. I give you leave. But I want you in Saint James all the sooner. Now go. Both of you. And do not fail me again!"

Outside, a guard approached Robert and said, "Your man, a courier waits at the gate—now that we have the king here safe."

The captain scolded, "Mind your mouth or you'll be mucking out stalls for the remainder of your enlistment!"

The soldier mumbled. "Apologies, Lord Montclair," he saluted and strode off.

Robert found Lynch waiting and did not hold back his anger. "What happened? No word? His majesty is beyond angry, as I am. How could you let him ride into that mob?"

Lynch shook his head. "I sent a courier to Chepstow Castle. Just returned on the same road. Says his horse threw a shoe—went on ahead but arrived after you left. Tried getting back here before you, intent on meeting you on the road. Robert, the unexpected happens. You know this. But I have good news. The rioter, their Lord of Misrule, and the voice of Lady Skimmington, I have identified him. His name is John Eltonhead, a veteran of Buckingham's campaigns."

Robert replied, "Eltonhead? Of Eltonhead Hall where Ezra Forester's daughter is in service?"

"John is the younger brother of Richard Eltonhead, head of the house. Another veteran angered with the king's betrayal of his volunteers."

Robert asked, "And the pamphlets? The rioters knew."

Lynch nodded. "They arrived days ago. Distributed to every house in the village and half the forest. The pamphleteer knew the King would visit White Cross Manor. Proof of another source in the palace."

Robert replied, "The king departs for London tonight. I have his leave to make inquiries and join the king at Saint James Palace in a few days. I want John Eltonhead followed. Your best men. They must never lose sight of him. I need to know if he acts alone, and who his contacts are. At last, someone more than a courier!"

Lynch replied, "We'll stick to him like a leech sucking blood. But you think him more than another Thomas Gibbs? And if he is our man, why no attempt on the king's life? He had the mob worked. Even now they are burning fences from the enclosures."

Robert stroked his chin before he said, "He has come to enjoy the game. He wants the king to squirm. He won't risk being present when the attack comes again. And there is John Wynter—slow to send his men. He must have seen or heard of the pamphlet. Did he see the Skimmington march as a way to discredit Sir Giles? Or is there more?"

Lynch replied, "We'll look for a connection between Eltonhead and Wynter."

"Hmm. Look into Lady Barbara Villiers as well. Sir Giles was her agent. Is she making a change? Perhaps someone less offensive? The nobility and gentry getting wealthy off the royal forests may find dividing the spoils among them more profitable than competing against one another."

"Aye. But what part does religion play? John Wynter and Richard Eltonhead are known Catholic recusants, though John Eltonhead's beliefs are unknown. Lady Villiers by all accounts is faithful to the Church of England–and you heard the mob's papist accusations. Is it only a ruse? If so, a dangerous game for Catholics."

"Indeed. That's why we must make the connections. Right now, John Eltonhead is the link."

CHAPTER 21

WHARF RATS

Mister Black began his search of the Holborn and Fleet riverfronts for the printing press. The sign over every waterfront inn was checked for telltale chalk marks used by the couriers. It was a long shot and indeed fell short. Black posted men in the riverfront inns and taverns and made quiet inquiries on the wharves. Black soon realized this was too dependent on luck and time. Surely, the pamphleteer tightly controlled access to the press. He had proven to be most careful. Black determined his best option was searching all the warehouses within a street or two of the Holborn River and the Fleet River above it. But conducting warehouse searches presented problems. There were too many to search secretly at night, and such searches undertaken without a warrant from the King's Bench would be at the least embarrassing if not illegal, and would surely alert the pamphleteer to move on. Black stroked his chin. *How to search every warehouse in one or two days, sealing the area against moving the printing press?*

The Collector of Customs for London listened as Black shared the urgent news of his inquiries. "You see then, my lord, these smugglers from Cadzand move shiploads of high-cost goods from Antwerp and throughout the Spanish Netherlands. They offload to small boats and move up the Holborn. We followed one of their boats up the Holborn River but lost them among the many warehouses. Years. Yes, years they have smuggled past the King's palaces! You can stop them. Does not His Majesty reward those who add to his coffers? A reward for service and a portion of the prize?"

The official replied, "Up the Holborn, you say. That narrows the search."

Black leaned forward. "It cannot be a routine inspection. The man behind this funds sedition and makes threats against the king. If we do not act against all the Holborn and Fleet warehouses on the same day, he will surely escape."

"Funds sedition, does he? Well, I shall surely put a stop to this, to this treacherous knave!"

"I have a plan. Here is what we should do...."

At dawn, customs boats blocked the lower Holborn River, where it met the Thames and the confluence with the Fleet. Chains were stretched across as an added measure. The streets were closed for two blocks on either side of the river. Chain nets blocked even the sewers running beneath the streets. Soldiers controlled access. Only customs men and the deputized men of the Lord Inquirer's watchers were allowed in or out. The warehouse district was divided into quadrants, and the customs men commenced a search.

Never was the ownership of commodities more disputed as warehousemen pointed to merchants subletting space and merchants questioned how other goods were stowed with theirs. Half the contents of the warehouses were either smuggled or untaxed. Fine brandy and aged port would be in short supply for months. Although only the poor could not afford the tax, and the common freeman engaged in unlawful handling, the wealthy sought out the bargain-priced contraband and encouraged the smuggler's trade.

Black was called to a warehouse on the river just below Newgate Street. He directed two of his watchers to come with him. The messenger led them through a labyrinth of empty casks towards a small door in a false wall beneath the loft in a corner of the warehouse. A voice could be heard shouting. "I tell you, customs has no business here! This is a print shop, as is plainly evident to any reasonably intelligent fellow. There is no smuggled cargo or untaxed product. Now leave the way you came!"

"Well, this is certainly a difficult print shop to find. I must have missed the sign outside, and well, I've found my way through easier mazes in the palace gardens," Black said as he entered the small room. "You mustn't blame the customs officer for being surprised to find you here, Mister…I'm sorry, but what is your name?"

"Yes, well, you see, I am just starting my business and am fortunate to find an inexpensive space to let. As for a sign, it has yet to be delivered, I began with a single commission, so you see, I haven't needed …."

Black had picked up a pamphlet from the stack. "Your name, sir!"

"Yes, as I was about to say, Richard Rowlands, printer."

Black scanned the document, a copy of a Catholic tract written by Verstegen, brought back from Antwerp. Same typeset as the pamphleteer's threats. He spoke as he read. "You've been using a different name, an old family name from the Netherlands—isn't that right, Heer Verstegen" And your commission would appear to come from a papist. This pamphlet has been banned. If possessing one is subject to a fine, what of the penalty for printing? Someone else bought this press with you in Antwerp. You will tell us his name and the names of the others. You will tell us everything."

Black turned and stepped in front of Verstegen, inches from his face, and stared into his eyes. "Be certain of it. You will tell us everything."

Black turned to the customs officer. "Well done!"

Then ordered his watchers, "Take Verstegen to Newgate. He speaks to no one until I return. I want the printing press, the typeset, the pamphlets, everything taken to the works. Send a messenger to Lord Montclair; we have Verstegen and the press—no. First, search the whole warehouse. Who knows if he has hidden anything else—correspondence, personal items, anything that points to an accomplice. A boat—there should be a boat near the wharf. Find it as well. And bring me the owner of this warehouse!"

Turning again to the customs officer, Black said, "No word to anyone of this arrest. You have never heard of the names Verstegen or Rowlands. There is a reward. Do you understand?"

The customs officer nodded. "Empty casks, no one about. On to the next warehouse."

"Aye, Good man!" Black palmed a large silver coin to the man as he shook his hand.

As the warehouse was being searched, a portly man in greasy clothes was shoved in front of Mister Black. "Henry Pitman, owner," the watcher said.

Black studied the man. Pitman's hands were

shaking, his eyes wide with fear. Black asked coldly, "Your protection has come to an end. Such greed. Is there nothing in this warehouse that is not contraband? Ah, the printing press! That was not intended to move. You should have been content with sheltering smuggled spirits. No one will protect you from harboring insurrectionists."

"No. No. I know nothing of insurrection. I am no traitor. The printing press—they pay rent. That is all. I know nothing of what they print."

"Of course not. In your business, it is better not to ask questions. Rent. I'm sure it is a handsome rent the printer pays. Who sought you out? Who pays the rent? It would be better if you told me now. For you will tell me. Perhaps, your cooperation will save your life."

"He said only religious pamphlets—for loyal Catholics. The king has shown tolerance for recusants...."

"Who? I need a name."

Pitman began to sob, "Wynter. Sir John Wynter of Lydney. Came with another man. Never heard his name. Said they would need a boat as well."

Black asked, "Tell me about this other man."

Pitman replied. "Was a gentleman. Young man, ordinary enough. Good clothes, fine boots. Nothing extravagant, but a gentleman. Came by a couple of times at night with another young man, better clothes...."

"Tell me about this third man with better clothes."

"Embroidered coat bore a family crest. Always wore a dark cape, but I saw the coat and crest. Came often. Could handle oars on the boat."

Black asked, "Blonde hair and beard?"

Pitman nodded. "Aye, a handsome young gentleman."

Black ordered, "Take him to Newgate. No visitors. Speaks to no one. I'm off to see the collector of customs. I will return to Newgate shortly."

The collector of customs agreed to continue the sweep of warehouses, the largest London had seen in years. The seized contraband would be sold, taxed, and replenish the king's coffers. The customs sweep would provide cover for the Lord Inquirer's search for conspirators.

Richard Verstegen nervously answered Black's questions. "Yes, Sir John Wynter provided the money to buy the printing press and made the arrangements at the warehouse. Johannes De Vries approached me, offering a stipend to come to London and print my banned Catholic books and pamphlets. I was to teach others and return to Antwerp."

Black asked, "Wynter had a partner here. An English gentleman and another, a young man—with blonde hair and beard. I want their names."

Verstegen nodded. "Wynter had a friend, John

Eltonhead. I was to teach him to use the press. An impatient man. Brought along another—yes, a young man, blonde of hair and beard. Quiet young man. Rarely spoke. An accent—excellent English, but he had an accent. Certainly, unlike any I heard in London."

Black asked, "His name?"

"Peter. Eltonhead called him Saint Peter. The young man did not like Eltonhead calling him Saint Peter. As I say, Eltonhead was brash, even harsh, and laughed when Peter asked him not to call him Saint."

Black continued. "This Peter, what was his surname? Was he with De Vries in Antwerp?"

"I never learned his surname. Just Saint Peter, and No, it was another man, also a blonde. He came once and left immediately. He did not travel with me or the printing press. I did not see him again until the press was set up. He learned very quickly—like one with experience with other printing presses."

Mister Black took a copy of the "Ahab and Jezebel" pamphlet and put it on the table in front of Verstegen. "When did you print this? How many copies, and who were the couriers who took it from the printing room?"

Verstegen stared at the pamphlet. "I have never seen this before. I swear by all that is holy. I did not print...."

"Look closely at the tails of the letters—broken.

Your typeset, your printing press. And there are others."

Black pulled out the other pamphlets and threw them in front of Verstegen. "All of them printed on your press!"

Richard Verstegen was shaking. "No. Never. Never did I—would I print such a thing! No. No!"

Mister Black stood, walked to the cell door, and said, "If your answers do not improve, you shall die a most cruel and painful death."

CHAPTER 22

TWO JOHNS

Lynch was with Robert in Lydney when the messenger arrived from London. "Mister Black sends his regards."

Robert opened the pouch and read. *Under cover of a customs sweep of warehouses, Verstegen captured with printing press. Sir John Wynter and John Eltonhead bought the press and engaged Verstegen. Verstegen admits only to printing Catholic books and pamphlets. Two Blonde-haired suspects, one is known as 'Saint Peter.' Will bring in our suspects for possible identification. Recommend we haul nets.*

Black

Robert asked the courier, "When did you last sleep?"

"Two days, sir," came the reply.

"Get some rest. You will remain with us."

Robert turned to Lynch and said, "Send a courier to

Black. He is not to stop along the way. Tell Black, 'Haul nets.'"

Lynch nodded. "John Wynter and John Eltonhead?"

"We'll bring them in. God forbid we interfere with the king's scheme to pay off his wife's gambling debts. Yes. We ask them to come with us to clear up some scandalous accusations. A small matter of a few days in London. House guests at the palace."

Lynch quizzed, "The palace?"

"William's Norman Thames River Palace—the Tower."

Lynch laughed. "You make it sound almost welcoming. Even so, we are fortunate the King added Wynter's armed men to the royal escort. We should act quickly before they return. All the better, our man reports Eltonhead remains a guest of Wynter at White Cross Manor."

Robert nodded. "Aye, we must make certain not to meet his men on the road as they return."

"And Lady Barbara Villiers? She is connected to Wynter and Eltonhead."

Robert sighed. "We should question her, certainly. There have been no reports of a woman. We are too few here in Lydney. We leave her. We must take the risk she will not run. No. We are off to White Cross Manor now!"

A servant greeted Robert and Lynch at the door. Robert spoke. "Sir Robert Curtis, Earl of Montclair, Lord Inquirer to his Majesty, King Charles. I have urgent business with Sir John."

The servant bowed. "You may wait in the sitting room, my lord. My master is at his table. I shall inform him at once."

Moments later, Sir John Wynter appeared. "My lord, is all well with his Majesty? I sent men along with…."

Robert asked. "Are you John Wynter?"

"Aye. I am Sir John Wynter. What brings the Lord Inquirer to my house?"

Robert smiled. "May we sit?" Robert and Lynch found richly embroidered high-back chairs and sat. Wynter silently followed their lead as Robert continued. "By all accounts, his Majesty travels in safety. I am assured he values the added security you provided. No, it is a different matter that brings me here today."

Robert paused and looked about the room. "You have a fine eye, Sir John. Many imported treasures— Flemish tapestries, French brocades, Spanish chests. The Madonna painting, is it Spanish or Italian?"

Robert didn't wait for an answer. He turned to face Wynter and said coldly, "You let a warehouse in London, filled with smuggled goods and contraband of every sort. There have been accusations. As a man seeking business with the King, I'm sure you wish to sort the matter discreetly."

Wynter turned ashen white. "No, that is yes. Yes, I let a small portion of a warehouse, but I know nothing of contraband! Smuggling, no, never!"

Robert's eyes bore into Wynter's. "Two names were given customs, John Wynter and John Eltonhead. You have business with Mister Eltonhead. We have heard it confirmed in Lydney."

"Eltonhead? Yes, he assists me here in my enclosures in the Forest of Dean. John Eltonhead is my guest. He sits at my table as we speak."

"Well, that is most fortunate. Together, you can help resolve these accusations. Ask him to join us."

A servant escorted John Eltonhead to the sitting room. Eltonhead huffed. "Sir John, this is highly peculiar. Who are these men? What's this all about?"

Wynter turned to the servant and said, "That will be all. Close the door and see we are not disturbed."

The servant bowed and closed the door as he left. Wynter said, "Sit down, John. They come from London. Seems smugglers have employed the warehouse where we retain a small space. Scoundrels seek to lay the guilt upon us. The Lord Inquirer has come to sort it all out."

Eltonhead thundered, "Liars! Well, the King shall hear of this. Indeed! Are we not his trusted agents in the

Forest of Dean? Smugglers! Such a scandalous lie! Tell him, Sir John. Tell him how His Majesty charters us. What need we of smuggling!"

Robert smiled and thought, *Hot-tempered. He shall surely trip up.* "As you say, Mister Eltonhead, this is not the conduct of men honored and chosen by His Majesty. We shall certainly uncover the truth."

Turning to the even-tempered Sir John, Robert said, "That is why I have come—not my man with an arrest warrant. I am here to entreat you to return with me to London and face down your accusers. I thought it best for you and His Majesty's royal forest that we resolve this straight away."

Eltonhead, calmer now, replied. "I have no interest in the warehouse. How am I accused?"

"A small boat. You are said to own a small boat used to smuggle from the ship and to buyers upriver."

"A boat?" Eltonhead replied.

"You deny keeping a small rowboat at the warehouse wharf? A boat that hid its cargo under a black hemp tarp? Your accusers say only you knew what was beneath the tarp. You can imagine what suspicious minds may think with news of smuggling. But, of course, we have not heard your reply. These and many other questions must be answered to put the matter to rest. So, you must agree, the sooner we get to London and uncover the truth, how shall I say it? The sooner Sir John can begin work in his new enclosures."

Robert smiled and sat back in his chair. "If tonight is inconvenient, then first light in the morning. I suggest a coach. A gentleman will require clean clothes at the palace."

Wynter replied, "Palace? Yes, by all means, my coach at first light. You gentlemen shall taste my hospitality this evening."

Robert stood. "That is most kind. Indeed, I shall stay, but my man has business to finish in Lydney."

The next morning Lynch returned with two other men. Wynter's coach was waiting in front of the manor house. Wynter and Eltonhead climbed into the coach. Before following them, Robert said, "My men will ride alongside. With your permission, Sir John, we will travel the road south through Swindon. Only a few miles longer—a letter awaits me there."

Sir John nodded. "As you wish, Lord Montclair."

As the coach made its way towards Swindon, Robert, as a lord of the realm, steered the polite conversation. "Sir John, you must make this visit to London a celebration. Your success in the royal forest— how many acres, four thousand, I hear?"

Sir John smiled. "Aye, for forty years. I shall enclose the richest coal and iron ore deposits. Forty years to mine, and the charter renews again unless the king chooses to buy it back at a fair price. And timber rights as well from the King's lands."

Robert replied, "You plan to open new mines. And then there is the transport. Have you raised sufficient capital? Do you seek partners and backers, or will you seek out bankers in London?"

"Aye, my lord, you see clearly one must spend money to make money. Front money can be repaid quickly if it is spent wisely. As you say, come in fast and strong—like a general against a weak opponent. I will avoid the bankers. Though they do not interfere with the operation, they neither provide the flexibility or the loyalty of partners and shareholders."

Sir John leaned towards Robert and continued, "Tell me, Lord Montclair, do you rely on tenant rents and the small emolument the king provides, or do you find opportunity in trading?"

Robert replied, "My background is far humbler than my title suggests. But I, too, find trading profitable for my purposes. Partners and shareholders, yes. Bankers no, though they provide needed service to commerce."

Wynter replied, "So we are like-minded. You might join my endeavor."

Robert smiled. "And Mister Eltonhead, what is his contribution?"

Wynter slapped Eltonhead's shoulder. "My friend brings skill and energy. Removing obstacles, yes, I count on John to remove obstacles."

The coach arrived after sunset. The Swindon Coaching Inn was busy, but Robert was able to arrange the last two rooms for their party. Sir John spent their time at the table seeking Robert's backing for a new coal mine. "Lord Robert, ten shares I offer you. One thousand will buy ten percent. We can be in full operation within months."

Robert looked up from the tasteless stew and drank from the mug of watered-down ale. *Wretched place! Not sure which is more distasteful, the food or the company.* Robert replied, "An interesting proposition. I shall give it some thought. Though, I must say, my trading company serves me well. It is an enterprise I better understand."

Sir John could not be deterred. "Even better! Your thousand for colliers—barges and ships to deliver coal to London. Yes! A trading company to move and market coal, timber, and iron bars!"

After supper, Sir John Wynter and John Eltonhead retired to their room. Robert met with Lynch and his men. "Have the pamphlets made their way here? Any word of sedition? Messages from London?"

Lynch replied, "No messages. We found nothing posted, but that doesn't mean they haven't made their way. At least nothing new. You seem to have charmed your new friends."

Robert sighed. "Yes, they see me as a backer for their new mine. They believe this is their triumphal entry. I will not press them hard until there is no chance for them to run. They offer me shares."

Robert paused, smiled at Lynch, and said, "Perhaps, Lynch, you have a thousand to buy in?"

"If I had a thousand, I wouldn't be roamin' about Britain and Ireland chasin' rogue lords. Nay, I'd be warming my feet by a peat fire in Ireland with my sweet wife."

Robert laughed. "True words, my friend. You make me the fool I am for parting from the wife I love and sweetest children to pursue a dirty business for a—for a king who—well, for a man rightfully unloved by his subjects."

Lynch shook his head. "Lord Robert, you are not the fool. I thank God above that he sent a good man, a gifted man, to bring integrity and justice with mercy and compassion to a dark business."

On the road the following day, Robert politely asked, "Sir John, the king's tolerance towards Catholics, does it bring division or unity? Loyalty or sedition?"

Wynter was surprised by the question and fumbled to respond. "Why, it's hard to say. One could argue both.

To some, yes, tolerance should unite. Since the death of Queen Mary Tudor, Catholic loyalty has been questioned—unfairly—yes, most unfairly. But then jealousy and suspicion now arise from ardent protestants."

Robert nodded. "I know you follow your father, Sir Edward, as a recusant—Catholics. And yet your family has been awarded lands and enclosures, first from King James and now from Charles. Is it wise to push hard against the acts of Parliament and the crown in warring against the protestant faith and the Church of England?"

Sir John's face flushed red. "We do not war against the Church of England. We pay the tax."

"Yes, I know that you do. But to war against protestants on the continent is to war against the King's sister and protestants everywhere. By war, I also speak of pamphlets, books, and tracts outlawed in England. It could be argued that religious instructions by Catholics, such as leaders of your priestly orders and societies for English Catholics, pose no threat. But then, who determines where a threat lies? Can an oath of loyalty be trusted if the faith is in doubt?"

Robert didn't wait for a reply. Wynter had none. Robert turned to John Eltonhead and said, "Mister Eltonhead, your family has a long history in the Forest of Dean. Wasn't your father keeper at Saint Briavels Castle? You must have a great knowledge of the forest. Your brother, Richard, is head of the house. He does not follow your father's footsteps?"

"My brother is a greater fool than our father. My father was loyal to the king who persecuted our faith—yes, we are Catholic too. My father fought for James and suffered wounds. As you say, he was keeper at St. Briavels, where he served as the King's Verderer. He chose a small emolument over riches to be had—riches taken by Sir Giles and Sir Edward Wynter. Our estate, Eltonhead House at Merseyside, provides a modest income, but Richard chases after Lord Baltimore's dream of a Catholic paradise in America. Am I to starve? I find my own way. I have no ambitions to die of disease or by the hand of some savage in that false Eden across the ocean. I will find my place here. I will find wealth and privilege. Sir John grants me an opportunity, and I will not squander it. I have proven my worth."

Robert stared into Eltonhead's eyes and said, "I am well acquainted with Lord Baltimore, George Calvert. You could learn much from his example. A man of honor and integrity. He served King James well and faithfully and was rightly honored with a peerage. All the more impressive when James named him Lord Baltimore after Lord Calvert declared his Catholic faith. And Baltimore's vision of a land of religious tolerance, Catholics and protestants united as brothers—a vision I find most appealing."

John Wynter coughed politely and asked, Then I can surmise, Lord Montclair, that your inquiries do not pertain to our Catholic faith?"

Robert replied, "I am Lord Inquirer to King Charles, not Bishop Laud."

The morning of the last travel day was wet and cold. Wynter and Eltonhead hurried to clamber into the coach. Neither man looked up to take notice of a new coachman at the driver's bench. As they drove off towards London, three more men followed along on horseback. The curtains were closed against the foul English weather.

Robert removed his cape and said, "Gentlemen, do not allow the rain showers to dampen your spirits. London is before us. Recognition of your deeds and a warm fire await. I thought we might discuss some peculiarities of the accusations against you."

Both men looked up but remained silent. Robert continued, "Sir John, you agree you let space in the Holborn River warehouse but deny accountability for all contraband found inside. Putting aside the owner's sworn statement, a Mister Pitman, there is another testimony, from Richard Verstegen, also called Richard Rowland—a printer only recently arrived from Antwerp. Do you know Heer Verstegen?"

Wynter's face went from surprise to resignation. "I

am acquainted with Richard Verstegen."

Robert continued, "And you purchased the printing press, the paper, the ink, and own the books, pamphlets, and all that is printed in your hidden printshop. Is this not true, Sir John?"

"Instructions in faith for good Catholics. Yes, I acknowledge what you say is true, but...."

Robert interrupted, "You employed the services of a Flemish smuggler, Johannes De Vries, to illegally buy and import a printing press in Antwerp."

Sir John spoke up. "It's not at all like you say! I wanted to end smuggling Verstegen's works. It was slow and expensive. Printing here in England makes sense. The king has made our faith less reprehensible to the crown. Why risk smuggling when it is no longer necessary?"

"You did not know King Charles is negotiating a treaty with Spain—an alliance with the Spanish Netherlands. But there is still more. You printed more than Verstegen's pamphlets. Your man had access to the printing press first in Antwerp and later in London in Verstegen's absence. It was then your man printed the pamphlets that pollute all of England offering a reward for the murder of King Charles and threats against the queen and the infant prince."

Sir John shouted, "No! No, never! A lie, a most foul and treacherous lie!"

Robert bore in. "It is proven. The seditious, malicious pamphlets came off your printing press. The typeset does not lie!"

Turning to John Eltonhead, Robert said, "And you, Mister Eltonhead, you pride yourself as gifted in—what was said? Removing obstacles? You purchased the small rowboat used to move the pamphlets to your couriers. Your boat carried messages and a threat posted on the gate of Saint James Palace. Your accomplice...."

Sir John interrupted, shouting, "Eltonhead! You betrayed me! This is all your doing! You urged me to buy the printing press and bring Verstegen to England. What have you done?"

Eltonhead replied, "You can't lay this on me. There is no witness...."

Robert interrupted, "John Eltonhead, the problem solver. You played the Lord of Misrule and voiced Lady Skimmington at Lydney. You provoked the mob hoping someone would assail his Majesty...."

Eltonhead flushed. "The Skimmington March was meant to dissuade the King from hearing Sir Gile's offer for the king's forest charter...."

Sir John yelled, "You put the King at risk? You set a mob against his Majesty traveling to my house? Scoundrel!"

Eltonhead replied, "Don't feign surprise. I do the

foul work for you, you pious hypocrite!"

Robert continued, "You, Eltonhead, received the false itinerary for the king's visit and arranged for the latest pamphlet to be delivered to the inns along the way. And you distributed the pamphlet to every house in Lydney...."

Sir John Wynter exploded, "You printed the pamphlets? You brought them to Lydney? Every house? And told me nothing? Why?"

John Eltonhead reached into his right boot and began to draw a knife. Robert leaned across and grabbed Eltonhead's hand. The two men struggled for control. A gunshot exploded inside the coach. Acrid smoke filled the confined space. Eltonhead fell over against Robert, dead. Sir John pulled the pistol from beneath his cloak.

Robert and Sir John sat facing each other in silence. The coachman pulled to a stop. The coach door was flung open, and Lynch, pistol drawn, stared inside. "Lord Robert," Lynch asked. "Are you wounded?"

Robert shook his head. "Sir John is going to give me his pistol."

A shaken Sir John began to cry. He lowered the pistol and gave it to Robert.

CHAPTER 23
THE ROYAL RESPONSE

Lord Conway was pacing anxiously when Robert entered the Lord Secretary's chamber. *I can't recall Lord Conway in such a state. I believed him perpetually bent over correspondence on his desk,* Robert thought.

"What kept you, Montclair? His Majesty is waiting. I have passed the cryptic note you sent. The King has questions. I have questions."

"We are still questioning the prisoner. Give me time to…."

"You had time. The King will not wait. Come. He is most insistent."

Lord Conway led Robert across the hall to the King's council chamber in Saint James Palace. The black oak and white plaster of the Tudor palace, adorned in red and gold, showed its age in comparison to the new grand rooms and halls in the refurbished Whitehall Palace.

King Charles was seated. Platters of roast fowl and fruit, a loaf of bread, wine and ale were set before him. The King did not look up, a drumstick in his hand. "Your report, Montclair, do not think you can tease me with a few words on such an urgent matter? Do you have them all? The matter shall not be put to rest until my justice is served."

"Majesty, Sir John Wynter is being questioned in the Tower. His aide, John Eltonhead is dead at the hand of Sir John. Men have been sent to arrest all known confederates, their couriers, and publicans that spread their threats...."

Robert caught the surprise in Lord Conway's eyes at the name of Eltonhead, the King focused on Sir John. "John Wynter? Of Lydney? The man who bought enclosures in the Forest of Dean, a seditious, traitor?" the King asked, looking up in surprise.

"Sir John denies knowledge of the plot. I was questioning them, bringing them here to London. Eltonhead was surely guilty. Eltonhead played the Lord of Misrule and Lady Skimmington against you at Lydney. He arranged for the pamphlets. When I laid the evidence before them, Eltonhead made an attempt on my life. Sir John dispatched him with his pistol. Wynter claims innocence. He bought a printing press to print his Catholic tracts, but Eltonhead put it to his purpose."

"You have them all, Lord Inquirer?" Charles asked.

"Not yet, your Majesty. Another man is known to be Eltonhead's accomplice. Sadly, with Eltonhead dead, we have lost our best source to identify him."

"You leave your King and prince at risk of an assassin? And your bungling denies my justice. The man deserved torture before being hanged, drawn, and quartered."

"The plotter is surely on the run. We shall find him, Majesty."

Charles stared into Robert's face. "A lesson. I will send them a lesson. Every man who aided these plotters—men who carried their seditious pamphlets, publicans that spread them—shall be hanged. Their sentences shall be proclaimed and every man, woman, and child in that village shall be required to witness the fate of those who call for evil against their king!"

Charles paused and bent over his meal before continuing, "And Sir John Wynter?"

"He is being treated well and his story confirmed. He saved my life and had Eltonhead tried to flee, he would have been shot by one of my men. I am not a judge, but I would speak for his release. Then there is the matter of printing Catholic books, perhaps a warning and a pardon?"

King Charles nodded. "Only when you've finished

with him. Then, yes, the Lord Secretary will prepare the pardon."

Robert stood silent for a moment. King Charles said, "There is something else, Lord Inquirer?"

"Yes, your Majesty. This deadly pamphleteer, one or more men, is close or closely connected to the court. He knew your movements and he knew your mind regarding the deforestation in the Royal Forest of Dean. He knew of your Lydney visit—passed to no one else. He gets close to loyal servants and uses them to his deadly advantage. Just as Sir John Wynter was used. I would suggest…I think it prudent…."

Charles was staring at Robert. "Spit it out man!"

"The infant Prince Charles, his chosen governess, Lady Mary, Countess of Dorset. I should like to visit her and insure all is in good order at Croxall Hall."

"You say the scoundrel is on the run. And now you say my son, my heir, is at risk?"

"Desperate men do desperate things, my King. A precaution only."

"See to it. Yes, every precaution! Pursue them vigorously!"

Across the hall, in Conway's chambers, Robert said, "You knew Eltonhead, Lord Secretary?"

"He was my dear wife's younger brother. A troubled man whose abilities never matched his ambitions.

I must write her. She will be heartbroken at such tragic news. She knew his flaws but loved him and did her best to help him. She asked me to find him a position in the court or make introductions to influential men. I told her I would help, but in truth, I would never risk my good office or good name on such a shiftless ne'er do well."

"Your wife an Eltonhead? Any connection to Lady Mary Sackville, Countess of Dorset?"

Conway huffed, "My brothers-in-law would not count John Eltonhead as a member of the family. He was despised. He abandoned the family. Their disdain has only been proven. As for Countess Dorset, none that I have ever heard."

Conway sighed. "Are you going to report this connection to the King?"

Robert lowered his eyes. "My cousin was proven a traitor. No, Lord Conway, I know your loyalty. As it is said, we do not choose our relatives."

In the council room above the 'works' at Newgate Prison, Robert questioned Mister Black. "Two blonde men? Not the same man. What have you learned?"

"Verstegen's testimony. You can question him yourself. But the one called, 'Saint Peter,' the close companion of John Eltonhead, a young man, was not the blonde-haired man who accompanied the smuggler Jan De Vries. So, yes, two different men, the one called 'Saint

Peter'—to his chagrin, and another described only as 'silent' in Antwerp."

Robert asked, "Sir John Eliot's priest?"

"Hasn't returned. No name yet."

"Lord Conway's page?"

Black replied, "Yes, Joseph Rusdorf, son of Johann Rusdorf, Prince-Elector Frederick's Palatinate Administrator. Stayed on in London when his father retired and was replaced by Ludwig Camerarius three years ago. Went off with Buckingham's disastrous expedition to La Rochelle."

Robert's eyes widened. "Another of Buckingham's veterans! An ensign no doubt. What did he have to say for himself?"

Black looked puzzled. "I couldn't question him. He went off with Lord Secretary to the Forest of Dean."

Robert slammed his fist on the table. "No! He was not with the royal party. He must be our man or one of them! And now he has flown! I will question the Lord Secretary, but we have a name and a description. Find him! Question everyone at Whitehall who knew him. Search his room. Send word to our men in Amsterdam, and Frederick's court in exile there. Find his father, all his family. Talk to the veterans angered by Buckingham, and church—where did he worship?"

Black rose to leave. "Where shall I find you?"

Robert sighed. "I wait for my wife to arrive, then we visit Lady Mary Sackville at Croxall Hall."

Black shook his head. "You haven't been home yet? Lady Eleanor arrived two days ago."

Robert's jaw dropped. "I haven't even looked through my letters in days. You say this to my shame. Yes, I should go home and leave the inquiries to you and Lynch."

Black shook his head. "No, my Lord, let it never be said! You bring honor, justice, and mercy along with determination and great skill to this blackest business. But I am glad that Lady Eleanor has come. Her company will do you well. But save some time for rest."

Robert sighed. "Yes. How I missed her and need her. And my children, the greatest blessing in life is a family that loves you without question."

Black nodded. "True words, my friend. We'll find them all. Your will alone will see to it."

Robert rode home to the Montclair townhouse in Whitehall. He didn't take his horse into the stable. Leaving it tied to a post in front of the house, he burst through the door nearly knocking his head servant, Thomas, to the floor. "There you are Thomas. See to my horse. Lady Montclair? The children?" Robert asked.

Thomas never lost composure. He straightened up and dutifully replied, "Lady Montclair is in the sitting room with Lady Justine. The children are not here your Lordship." And stepped outside to take Robert's horse to the stable.

Oblivious to his servant's graceful service, Robert entered the sitting room. "Dowager Countess Bellamy, I just left, Black, that is, your good husband, Christian...."

Lady Justine smiled. "Christian Fauconnier to me but I accept he will be ever Mister Black to you and your inquirers."

Robert smiled and stepped towards Eleanor. "I'm so happy you have come. Forgive me, darling, I missed the note that you have arrived. And without the children? How I have missed you all. Please, a hug and kiss for your love?"

Eleanor stood and accepted Robert's embrace. After they kissed, Robert said, "You're angry. I promise to make it up to you. It's an unholy business and now threatens the young prince. Could I stand by and let evil come to an innocent child?"

"There are others, good men. Why must it always be you? What about your children? Will the twins even recognize you? Poor William: first I abandoned him and now you disappear from his life. How long, Robbie?" Eleanor asked.

Lady Justine said. "You have much to catch up on. I will be going."

Robert replied, "No, it is good that you are here. Please stay and hear why I have called for my wife."

Once everyone was seated, Robert continued. "Lady Mary Sackville, her husband Edward Sackville, Earl of Dorset is Queen Henrietta Maria's Lord Chamberlain. Tell me what you know of them."

Eleanor answered first. "The Earl of Dorset was never among the Queen's court or circle of friends before the King appointed him. And that was after the murder of Buckingham. Before then, I never met or heard Lady Mary's name raised. I know nothing about either of them."

Lady Justine sighed. "You ask me to remember the dark days that I have put behind. Yes, I knew of Edward Sackville, his brother, Richard held the family title then. My French captors knew him as a short-term ambassador to King Louis. A very ambitious young man, former soldier, and investor. I recall hearing him speak of the Virginia Company and Bermuda before the House of Commons. You should remember him Robert, he was a sword bearer at the coronation of Charles."

Robert replied, "You said, 'knew of.'"

Lady Justine replied, "No. He never visited Dickering's pleasure house. His brother, Lord Richard, a notorious gambler, and womanizer, yes. But not Edward."

Robert nodded. "As you say, it was his loyal service to King Charles that led to his appointment. And the

King's affection for his wife appeared after Buckingham's influence died with him. He is no fool if he maintains the trust of both King and Queen."

Robert smiled. "Now I see the King's mind in this! The Countess of Dorset is the perfect choice for a governess. The woman is unknown at court. She shuns the social rituals of courtiers, has made no enemies and is the faithful wife to a loyal servant. And all the better, the last of the Curzon family line, she is the grandniece of Joyce Curzon, a protestant martyr, burned at the stake as a heretic by Queen Mary. What better counterpoint to naming the Catholic King of France and his mother, Marie De Medici, as godparents to the heir of the thrones of England and Scotland? Something for both his Catholic and protestant subjects. No harm in Catholic godparents, good people, the infant Prince of Wales, will be raised by an upstanding protestant country lady!"

Eleanor asked, "Robbie, if you knew this why ask us? Why send for me?"

"Yes, I had her background examined. But sons and daughters, and grand nieces, often go their own way in religion. I want to get a true view of her character and beliefs. I need a woman to befriend her—to see her true self...."

"Robbie, I will not sneak about for you. I will not offer a false friendship—I will not be used or see another good woman needlessly be put to the test."

"No, I do not ask that of you. I must visit her home at Croxall Hall, long the ancestral estate of the Curzon family, now the property of the Earl of Dorset. I go to ensure the safety of the prince. I can question her servants and inquire after her friends and relations. But you have much in common. You are both the last woman of an ancient family. Titles and property falling to your husbands. My suspicion is that she is a godly woman who has no desire for the gossip, backbiting and petty jealousies of court life. I hope you can confirm my favorable disposition, but also see if there exist any connections to families recently proven most intolerant of the king. A good woman can be ignorant of the malevolent intent of someone close to her."

"You wish to remind me of Pierre Brulart? How very unkind." Eleanor snapped.

"No, that is not my intent...."

Lady Justine interrupted, "Eleanor, Robert stood by you. He loves you and would never wish to hurt you. You know this. And you have learned that even the strongest among us can be vulnerable."

Eleanor lowered her head. "I have come all this way. If it will help you return to Montclair—return to me and our children—then I will do as you ask."

CHAPTER 24

RECONNECTING

The coach ride to Croxall Hall would require a three-day journey. The baptism of the young prince would take place in less than a fortnight. Robert was painfully aware of the tight schedule, but more important things were on his mind. *Lord, help me make the best of my time with Eleanor. We are walking apart. Bring us back together. How I love her and need her in my life. She is overwrought with false guilt, pain and hurt. Lord, restore her soul. Make us truly one again.*

Robert and Eleanor sat silent as their coach made its way out of London. As the lovely countryside views opened, Robert asked, "Tell me, dear, is young William happy with Zeus as his mount? And what a good fellow Lady Mary's son, Paul Hawkins, has become. Do they ride often, I remember your concern when I gave Will such a fine stallion."

Eleanor turned from looking out the window and faced Robert. "If you want me to say you were right, yes, William loves the horse. And Zeus has taken to his young owner. Will insists on brushing him himself and never ceases talking to Zeus. Such a large, magnificent horse."

Robert smiled having gained Eleanor's attention. "I hope Paul is firm and doesn't let Will risk jumping and wild chases."

"No. I allow Will no hunts and only slow easy jumps. I ride with Will every day. It is a special time for us. He is good company and very open and talkative when we ride. He misses his father. He asks when you are coming home."

Robert sighed. "Soon. I hope, very soon." Now it was Robert's turn to gaze quietly out the window.

Eleanor chuckled. "I remember what you said when William was a weak and sickly child, always wheezing and struggling for breath. I was so frightened he would die. You never lost hope. You said, 'No matter he is short of wind, I will buy him a fast horse to be his legs!' And so, it has come to pass."

Eleanor's little laugh struck a chord of hope in Robert's heart. He turned again to her smiling. "We have so much to be thankful for. Yes, Montclair is the light I need against the darkness of London and its intrigue. Tell me all. Your mother, Lady Anne, she is well? And the

Gibbs girl, does she still pursue Paul Hawkins?"

"Mother has never been happier! She is never without the twins. You should see them, Robbie. Edward and Elizabeth, both hearty toddlers. They scoot about happily giggling, inseparable. I never had a brother or sister. But Edward and Elizabeth, though different in personality, Edward quiet and curious, Elizabeth bold and daring—it's as if they rely on one another for assurance, they are united in their determination. And Will dotes upon them. He sees they are loved. Family. We are so fortunate that William will put his family before himself."

Robert sat across from Eleanor and beamed with joy.

Eleanor laughed loudly. "You asked about the Gibbs girl. Pursue is not the word! No military campaign has been so carefully and masterfully conducted as that of Rachel Gibbs to win the heart of Paul Hawkins. The poor man is helpless! It is the talk of Montclair. I have never witnessed such obvious intentions, obvious to all but the young Reverend Mister Hawkins. What is it with men? The young woman is shameless!"

Robert smiled. "It is the same with all men. We are incapable of resisting the charms of a determined and beautiful woman. It was you, Eleanor who—do you remember the coach ride to Pembroke Hall? You began your campaign early. And riding the estate together instructing me on what to say and what was really at play in their card games? I was helpless against your wit and charm. Obvious—yes you were most obvious to all, but me."

"Really, Robbie? You think I was obvious?"

Robert moved across and sat next to Eleanor who laid her head on his shoulder. Robert squeezed her hand and said softly, "Thankfully, so obvious that King James, who treated you as his ward and daughter, approved of our marriage. He rewarded me with a title to make me a fit husband for the young noblewoman he so loved."

Eleanor snuggled closer. "I remember the first time I saw you. It was Bramshill House. You and Edward in your shabby uniforms and unpolished boots. You came in with Sir John Doddridge. You strode into the room unphased by Lord Zouche and his wealth. You have never been impressed by wealth or titles. You were so handsome! What steely blue eyes! An unpolished diamond."   Eleanor looked over and ran her fingers through Robert's hair and continued. "Less gray then. Black speckled with gray and ashen gray above your ears."

Robert replied, "You insisted on dressing me before we went to Pembroke Hall. Silver brocade and black trousers—and yes polished high black boots."

"It is still your best color! Your other clothes were…."

Robert completed her sentence. "The humble clothes of a country vicar or minor official."

"Exactly! Not fit for court or the Manors of Lords and Ladies."

Robert said, "Lady Mary never complained about Edward's clothes."

"Edward's clothes fit his personality. He is at his best as a bellowing sergeant! Lots of noise and a great big heart. Lady Mary has no interest in the court or pretention, but I am glad Edward and Mary's nobility of heart has been rewarded."

Robert nodded. "Have you heard from them? What does Lady Mary think of Rachel Gibbs? And Wilhelm and Katie? Any news?"

"What mother is not concerned with her son's future wife? Lady Mary worries Rachel may follow her mother's path of pursuing money. I tell her I think Rachel is not her mother's daughter. There is no longer talk of ambition, of bishop palaces or high appointments. Above all, Rachel Gibbs wants to love and be loved."

"A good vicar needs an understanding and loving wife."

Eleanor smiled. "Yes. As for Lady Mary and Edward, there is news. Edward seeks your advice. The Royal Cawmills Cuirassiers...."

Robert sighed. "The Marques Hamilton requests

their service for his volunteers. He raises troops to fight for King Gustav Augustus' army. It is the promise Edward made Mary, no more soldiering."

"Yes, he does not know what to say to Lady Mary or Lord Hamilton."

Robert exhaled slowly. "Edward has been to Eilenberg with Karl. He is compelled to fight. Tell me, what has Lilburn decided?"

"Lilburn has volunteered as have all or most of the men. They would like Edward to lead them."

"And Edward fears telling Mary of his desire for fear of his pledge to her."

Eleanor replied, "Lady Mary lost one husband she loved. But her children by Tom Hawkins are grown and well established. Edward and Mary's son, Curtis, is strong and healthy, an heir to their family together. She is in a better place now."

Robert said, "Our advice can only be for Edward to lay his heart before Mary who loves him and knows him like no other. They must talk and pray and talk some more. It must be a decision they share."

"Yes. Such decisions must be shared."

Both fell silent. The only sounds were the clopping hoofs, creaking wood against leather straps and the ring of the iron banded wheels over stones in the road. Robert asked. "My good friend Wilhelm, how I admire his heart for God and works of mercy, he is well? And Katie, Karl, Johann and Hulda?"

"Yes, all are well. They serve the people. The hospital and the old people keep them busy. They believe in their work. And Karl, Johann, and Hulda still rescue brothers and sisters from the war. They know their path. They have chosen it and do not turn from it. I thought I knew my path, but I was wrong. I'm not sure where my path lies."

Eleanor lifted her head from Robert's shoulder and looked him in the face. "You no longer have the same passion for your work. You protect a king you do not respect. You cannot live in both darkness and light. Honestly, Robbie, do you know your path? Do you know where we are going?"

Robert lowered his eyes and sighed. "No. No I don't."

Coach road inns are not known for comfort or good food. They offer a meal and a bed for weary travelers worn out by the uncomfortable, bone jarring ride over England's rutted roads. Though tired, Robert and Eleanor were in good spirits when they stopped for the night. They talked warmly throughout dinner before retiring. Their time together was an elixir that swept away tensions that had built over the years.

Confined to the small coach for days of travel, they

talked. Having each other's undivided attention, they rediscovered what attracted them to each other years earlier. Unspoken was the realization that their future would always be together, husband and wife, parents, comforter, critic, friend, lover, and trusted advisor.

On the third day of the journey, Eleanor asked, "What more can you tell me about this inquiry? Just what information am I looking for?"

Robert went through the history of the case, the pamphlets and posters, the many suspects, and remaining lines of inquiry. Her many years at court had sharpened Eleanor's ability to remember names, alliances, and motivations. Rumor and intrigue were the everyday talk of the court.

When Robert mentioned pursuing "the blondes," Eleanor laughed. "Robbie, Queen Henrietta Maria favored blondes, all the courtiers employed blonde pages and protégés in hope of some favor. But tell me more of the man murdered, John Eltonhead, and his relation to the informant, Ezra Forester. You mentioned the army connection and Buckingham's La Rochelle campaign. It changed everything at court. It was more than his fall from favor. It brought together King Charles and Queen Henrietta into a bond—I dare say a deep love. It cemented the Privy Council and Parliament against the King's foreign policy and stirred up resistance throughout the kingdom like no time before."

"Indeed. It was the army connection that brought many but not all the known conspirators together. Forester was the key. He recognized a young officer—a blonde—the courier in the boat. But Forester did not know Eltonhead, only that Forester's daughter is in service to Eltonhead's brother. Very careful, our plotters. And then the Antwerp connections. The pamphlets publish both Catholic and protestant complaints."

Eleanor replied, "Perhaps the conspirator plays his co-conspirators against each other."

Robbie looked up. "The conspirators have different motives, but all want Charles dead. Yet only one man controls the voice and has a very definite end game in mind."

Eleanor nodded. "Sir John Wynter wanted to frighten the King—to discredit his competitor. He was unaware of the broader conspiracy. The Catholic, Richard Verstegen sought only to publish his Catholic texts in England. You have a grandmaster puppeteer pulling many strings. The advantage is following the strings back to the puppeteer."

"But no string is direct. Each is cut and tied to others."

Eleanor asked, "Only someone skilled in intrigue could manage such a plan. A man like Pierre Brulart, skilled in diplomacy, manipulation, and blackmail."

"A diplomat? Steering England's foreign policy, but killing the King? He must be certain of controlling the heir. Brulart has the skill but has proven to be a man of boundaries, of some principle. Pierre Le Garde is a man with no principles, but has he mastered the skills of Brulart? There must be others. Who stands to gain?"

Eleanor replied, "Who wants something from England? The French, the Spanish, the Dutch, the Emperor, Gustavus Adolphus, the Pope, the Scots, the Irish...."

Robert interrupted, "Frederick V of the Palatinate, whose wife and sons are legitimate heirs of the house of Stuart. You see the problem, my dear. There is no end to people with motive. Some might say a former confidante of the queen unceremoniously cast out, and her loyal husband. No, we must focus on the connections we know and determine motives later."

Approaching Lichfield, the coach entered the village of Mancetter. Robert tapped the roof of the coach and called out to the driver. "Stop by the parish church. Please." The stone tower of the old Norman Church rose in the center of Mancetter, fronted by the village green.

"Why are we stopping?" Eleanor asked.

"Family history. The church is often the best source of family history—especially of its noble families. Come with me."

While the coach waited in the shade of a massive oak tree, Robert and Eleanor made their way inside Saint Peter's Parish Church. The floor of the centuries old building was covered with tombstones of past parishioners buried in its vaults below. Stained glass captured pictures of Saint Peter, at the altar, holding a Bible and at the narthex, bearing a sword. The walls round the church bore stone plaques, memorials of departed parishioners.

Eleanor stood and turned around, taking in the sight. "Yes, centuries of memories. Will we be immortalized like this at Montclair? The windows are beautiful. What do they mean?"

Robert spoke as his eyes scanned the plaques. "Saint Peter. The book is the Bible. The sword also a reference to the Word of God, 'sharper than a two-edged sword' and a reference to his martyrdom."

Robert walked to a plaque in a transept. "Here it is. Joyce Curzon Lewis of Mancetter, martyred Lichfield, 18 December 1557. Burned at the stake for spreading copies of the Word of God, the Lord's Prayer, the Apostle's Creed, and the Ten commandments in the English language."

CHAPTER 25
CROXALL HALL

Their coach drove in front of Croxall Hall, the centuries-old home of the Curzon family. The house spoke of age, wealth, and nobility. If there were an *Ancien Regime* in England, the Curzon family would be included. Their titles went back to Norman knights who fought with William the Conqueror. Croxall was the home of the powerful founding family. In the years following, many prominent cadet branches arose and were scattered across the English midlands, unlike the minor baronies of the Curtis family in the wild and lightly populated north.

Lady Mary Curzon Sackville, Countess Dorset, was the last surviving Curzon. The Manor house elegantly combined old Norman with Tudor English updates. Robert recollected the English progeniture laws and considered Curtis Castle now the home of his friend Edward Barkley, holder of the once Curtis title, Baron of Cawmills, but more of Eleanor, the last of the Montclair family, her family titles, and estates now his. What must these women think? The purpose was clear, to preserve property and great estates whole. But at what cost? What injustice? Mary Sackville and Eleanor shared this injustice, raising their young children in houses they grew up in, under new names, titles, and fortunes.

Lady Mary greeted Robert and Eleanor gracefully, introducing her three children. She had received word of the visit by courier little more than a day before. *Three young children of her own, and she is to raise the crown prince?*

"Lord and Lady Montclair. Welcome to Croxall Hall. I am Lady Dorset, Mary Sackville, and these are my children, Mary, Richard, and Edward. Only recently was I informed of your visit, and I have been busy preparing the house for Prince Charles and our visit to Saint James and the Christening. Please accept my apologies if my preparations for your visit fall short of the courts of London."

Eleanor smiled and replied, "Lady Dorset, I find a house blessed by the happy voices of children far more pleasant than any palace! My happiest days are at Montclair Castle with my own three children. It could only be better if I could convince my husband to spend less time in London."

Robert bowed and said, "Indeed, what my dear wife says is true. Any apologies due are mine, and I hope our visit will be short and of little interference to your preparations. I come only because recent events require additional inquiries regarding the safety of the prince."

Lady Mary turned to her daughter and said, "Mary, take your brothers for their lessons. They are not to play in the garden until they have finished. I will send for you later."

Once young Mary escorted her brothers out, Mary Sackville spoke. "Please, sit, and I will do my best to answer."

Robert asked, "Have you added any new staff since their Majesties announced that you would be the governess to the prince? Any new or first-time visitors to Croxall Hall?"

"New staff? No, I have found a nursemaid for the infant. A gentlewoman, a good Christian widowed with a young child. She will accompany me to Saint James Palace and nurse the prince on the return. I have every confidence in her. Very pious in our church, Saint John the Baptist. Recommended by my husband. I met her only after the governess position was offered."

Robert smiled. "Any new help on the estate or among the tenants? And visitors? I am required to make inquiries."

"My estate steward will answer questions of workers outside the house. Visitors? Just the local gentry and close family friends. I have no desire for life at the court, though my husband enjoys sharing in, dare I say, gossip?"

Robert replied, "No visitors then outside of your longtime friends?"

"Just the couriers carrying letters from Lord Dorset. Pages usually. Earnest young men anxious for any opportunity to gain favor with a lord of the court."

Robert smiled. "You mentioned your husband and his interests at court. Does he often entertain guests here at Croxall? Please do not find me rude, but I must ask, when did he last visit home?"

Lady Mary smiled. "Of course, I understand your position Lord Inquirer. My husband enjoys a hunt here once or twice a year with friends from the court. Last fall, his friends enjoyed a stag hunt."

Robert nodded. "Thank you for your kindness. I do wish to be discreet. You mentioned couriers and letters. Do you know these men? Perchance, was one of them bearded blonde?"

"The Earl's courier no, but once another young man accompanied him. Yes, I recall he attended the hunt as well. A page from the court, the son of a diplomat. Hmmm. What was his name?"

Robert asked, "Joseph Rusdorf, perhaps?"

"Yes, I think that is right. And there was another young man with him. Also blonde. Young Rusdorf was ignored, but his friend was treated with respect.

"You do not recall his name or position? Robert asked.

"He spoke very little. Mostly it was young Rusdorf whispering to him."

Robert asked, "Was it on account of his language? German or perhaps Dutch?"

Lady Mary shook her head. "I'm sorry. I don't know. You should ask the Earl. He will know. And as we speak, I recall it was Rusdorf who carried the letter telling me I was chosen as the governess to the prince."

Robert smiled. "Do not be sorry, Lady Dorset. I make only general inquiries for the safety of the prince."

Eleanor spoke. "The queen honors you and must approve of your discretion to have charged you with caring for the heir to the throne."

Lady Mary looked surprised. "I have never met the Queen. My husband sought the position. As Queen Henrietta Maria's secretary, he sees to her correspondence and schedule. It made sense. Croxall Hall is a safe place, and I am content to live here as a mother and now a governess. Why, someone must see to the welfare and upbringing of children. It seems the children of my tenants are better prepared than my nieces and nephews. Their parents spend so little time and effort in their upbringing. I find comfort in the company of children. Their honesty and curiosity, their desire to learn—it is my calling."

Lady Eleanor replied. "Motherhood is indeed a noble calling. And to be honored as governess to our future King…."

Lady Mary looked up, her brow furrowed, and asked Robert. "You mentioned recent events? New concerns for the safety of prince?"

Robert replied, "Yes, pamphlets. Pamphlets are circulating—following the King as he travels, inciting regicide, a reward for taking the King's life. You are not aware of these threats?"

"No. I have seen nothing of the sort. My husband—no one has told me this."

Robert continued, "One vile pamphlet suggested taking the prince or sending him to the same evil fate as the King and Queen. Be assured, the prince will be guarded, but I will make inquiries in the village and the estate. Please introduce me to the estate manager. I will get about my business. I leave my wife, Lady Eleanor, in your good company. Your estate steward?"

"Mister Jones. His house is beyond the stable."

Robert bowed politely and left.

Eleanor smiled warmly. "Your children are so well-behaved. Your daughter, Mary, was it? Such a helpmate to you. Mine are still very young. My son is but eight, and I have twins, a boy, and a girl, little more than one. Like you, I have found the home far more rewarding than the court. I was once—for most of my life—I lived at court. It seems so long ago."

Lady Mary smiled. "Yes, I've heard of you, Lady Montclair. My husband wrote of your dismissal by the queen. It was most uncharitable. Your husband must spend a great deal of time at court. The separation must be difficult."

Eleanor laughed. "Lord Montclair was never one for court life. No, he is at heart a country vicar and farmer, trader, trapped in a world of intrigue. He will never admit it, but he likes what he does and does it well—as a calling, just as the priesthood is a calling. But yes, the separation is hard on both of us. While I served the queen, Robert raised our son. He is a devoted father. I pray for the day he returns to Montclair Castle for good. Like you, I have learned to value friendship. Lady friends with children. But tell me, Lady Mary, the nursemaid—how did you come to find her? Recommended by your husband? Did he see to the arrangement?"

"Yes, Magdalene Fitzhugh came with her brother— her half-brother, Walter Stock, an estate steward for the Percys until he fell on hard times. A wounded veteran of

La Rochelle. But come and meet her. She can answer all your questions."

Eleanor followed Lady Mary as she walked to the servant's bell cord. Eleanor asked, "The brother, Walter Stock, has he stayed on as well?"

"He was to see the estate steward. With an extra six hundred per year, I'm sure there was a place for him."

Lady Mary pulled the cord again. "Where is that girl?"

Turning to Lady Eleanor, she said, "Come with me! We'll go to her room. I will show you the nursery I have prepared for the prince."

"The other servants are quite envious. The nursemaid's room is next to the nursery. A former guest room—quite splendid, with views to the front gardens."

Lady Mary walked Eleanor into the nursery. "The room is large with good light. Guests have always found it cheerful. The heavy curtains are most effective in darkening the room for the prince's naps. It is large enough to grow with the prince and accommodate all the amusements he will be provided."

Eleanor smiled. "Indeed, a splendid nursery. The nursemaid—Miss Fitzhugh?"

"Yes, through here. Her room adjoins. With the door ajar, she will hear if the child awakens."

Lady Mary walked to the far end of the room,

opened a door, and stepped into the nursemaid's room. Eleanor followed. The former guest room was smaller than the new nursery, yet elegant with a high plastered ceiling and two large windows facing the graveled drive to the front of the house. The simple bed, table, and washstand starkly contrasted the room's previous use.

"She's not here," Lady Mary said. "Well, we must find her." She opened the door to the hall and saw the housemaid leaving one of the bedrooms. "Molly, I need Maggie. Have you seen her?"

The servant bowed and said, "Aye, she was in her room reading a letter when the coach drove up. I think she recognized someone. She ran out of her room and down the servant's stairs. She was in a dreadful hurry, my Lady."

"Where did she run to?"

"I don't know, my Lady, she didn't say. May I go now, my lady?"

"Yes, of course."

Lady Mary turned and saw Eleanor reading a letter by the table next to the window.

…Lord Montclair, Sir Robert Curtis will visit Croxall Hall within a fortnight. He is a tall man; some would say handsome with black hair on the crown of his head now silver at the sides—blue eyes, trimmed beard more white than black. He dresses modestly for a man of wealth, usually black with a gray or silver waistcoat. He is given to black riding boots. If he comes

by coach, I have drawn his crest for you. Once his soul is dispatched to hell, you must leave with Walter. His inquirers will surely connect you with your late kin Howard Fitzhugh and brother Donald Stock, called traitors by the heathen English. The Percys will not help you. Make for Liverpool. Friends will see you safely to Ireland.

Erin Go Bragh!

Felim O'Neill

Eleanor turned to the door. "Lady Mary, the way to your estate steward's house—Lord Montclair is in danger!"

"Down the servant's staircase, out the back...."

Eleanor ran down the hall. Lady Mary struggling to follow, shouted, "Next to the carriage house and stables!"

In the rear carriage yard, Eleanor heard the creaking of iron hinges and saw a door swinging open. The sounds of breaking wood and heavy thuds, interrupted by the grunts of men struggling, steered her to the carriage house door. Passing from sunlight through shadow into the darkened room, Eleanor saw Robbie pinned against a thick oak column. She watched the back of a man pressed against him, one arm across her husband's neck, the other outstretched. The attacker's hand clenched a knife. His wrist was held back by Robert's hand in a death grip fighting him off.

As Eleanor rushed in, she saw a pitchfork propped inside the door. Grabbing it as she ran, she lowered it and lunged at the man's back with the pitchfork. She did not see or hear the figure come out from the shadows, but the blow from behind knocked Eleanor off balance, and only the last tine of the pitchfork caught the back of the man's thigh as Eleanor fell to the ground beside the screaming man. Pain and weight told her someone was on her back. Robert's attacker screamed, dropped his arm from Robert's neck and grabbed his gaping wound.

Eleanor roared more than screamed as she tucked her knees, lowered her head, reached over her back, grabbed the collar of her assailant, and pulled with both hands. Now the sound of ripping cloth and another woman's screams filled her ears as a young woman catapulted over Eleanor and landed on her back in front of her. Lady Eleanor clenched her fingers and swung the heel of the palm of her hand as hard as she could into the screaming woman's face. Eleanor pounded her face again, and pinned the woman's shoulders with her knees. The screaming stopped. Eleanor grabbed the torn bodice and pulled the woman up. Her attacker's head fell back. Eleanor grabbed her hair and pulled her face up. The woman's eyes were blank. Eleanor slapped the face, and the head fell back to the ground. "Had enough? No? I'll give you enough!"

Eleanor raised her hand to strike again, but the pain in her hand told her it was enough. She looked over to see

Robert turn the knife towards his attacker as the two men struggled with all their strength. Their tangled bodies shuffled, their grunts the only sound. Both gasped for breath until, at last, she heard one long ghastly gasp. She watched as both men fell to their knees. Blood puddled around them; the head of Robert's attacker turned towards her. Wide, frightened eyes stared at Eleanor, blood trickling from the corner of his mouth.

"Robbie," she cried. "Robbie, are you hurt? Please, tell me you're not cut."

"No, thanks to you, I live and breathe."

Robert saw a traumatized Lady Mary standing at the carriage house door and yelled, "Send for a surgeon. And something to bind his wound. He may yet live."

The wounded man muttered, "No doctor. I would rather bleed out here than hang."

Robert struggled to stand. "Then let me pray for your soul."

"It would do no good, and I am a Catholic."

Robert called out, "A priest. Lady Mary, there must be a Catholic priest nearby. Send for him. Tell him the Lord Inquirer guarantees his safety. I will not deny a Christian his last rites. Go!"

Eleanor, still kneeling on the unconscious woman, said, "You have met Walter Stock. This is his half-sister, Magdalene Fitzhugh. They were waiting for you. She had a letter from Felim O'Neill."

Robert pressed his hand over Walter Stock's wound slowing the bleeding and all to certain death. Stock's breathing was shallow and raspy. Flecks of blood collected on Robert's clothes. "Just revenge, then? Or is there more? There must be cord hanging about, tie her hands before she recovers."

Eleanor moved off of Magdalene's shoulders. The young woman did not move. Eleanor quickly grabbed a leather baggage strap, rolled the unconscious woman over, and bound her hands.

"Robbie, I was so frightened, I could not bear the thought of losing you."

Robert gazed at the only woman he ever loved. "When she knocked you to the ground, my mind went back to the night of the gala opening of the banqueting house, you were lying there disheveled, and...."

"Robbie, you compare this to the night of my greatest embarrassment?"

"No. Let me finish. While I lay dazed and dumbfounded—helpless—the monster, Pierre Brulart smiled at you, licking up your beauty—so unceremoniously exposed before him—he graciously reassured you and helped you up. That moment, I began to fear—fear I would lose you. And I nearly did. I have been about this business too long. I cannot go on risking losing you and all that we love for a king, a mere man, with no heart for his people—for anyone but himself."

Eleanor sighed. She walked over to Robert, wrapped her arms around him, and kissed the top of his head. "My sweet Robbie, I love you and, in my heart, I know we shall love each other until the day we die. There can be no life without risk. We must cling to our love one day at a time. It is all the assurance we have.

Walter Stock gave one last bloody gasp and died in Robert's arms. Robert crossed himself and prayed: "May the Lord in His love and mercy help you with the grace of the Holy Spirit. May the Lord who frees you from sin, save you and raise you up. Amen."

CHAPTER 26

URGENCY

While Magdalene Fitzhugh recovered in a locked room with a guard posted inside and outside, Robert searched and seized all the possessions of Walter Stock and Miss Fitzhugh. Finding nothing more in Stock's bare room, he returned to the stable. "He came with his own horse and wagon," he said to the estate steward. "Show them to me."

"Yes, a fine horse. The red roan at the end."

Robert nodded as he walked towards the horse. "And a wagon?"

"In the carriage house. An estate wagon, not your field wagon of a tenant farmer."

Robert stopped by the horse. "A fine animal indeed! Not a draught horse."

The estate steward asked, "Truly. The estate would gladly purchase him. What is to become of him?"

"Property of the crown. Sold off, likely. I shall put your request in my report."

Robert stepped around the horse and saw a saddle on the stall railing, sitting on its blanket. Something about the way it sat stirred his memory. He lifted the saddle, and the blanket rose with it. *The Reverend Doctor Fitzhugh's couriers. The sewn-on blanket and the hidden compartment.*

"Your knife, please," Robert asked as he carried the saddle to a workbench and turned it upside down.

Robert carefully cut away the crude stitching and removed the blanket. A pouch fell from beneath the panel under the cantle. Robert opened the flattened pouch and retrieved pamphlets. Pamphlets and letters.

A thorough search of the wagon found nothing, and Robert returned to the house. Magdalene was awake, and Robert and Eleanor questioned her. "Magdalene Fitzhugh, daughter of Rose Fitzhugh, no doubt. We have the letter from Felim O'Neil and letters hidden by your half-brother, Walter Stock. He has paid for his treachery, but you can still help yourself if you answer honestly."

Magdalene spat in in Robert's face. Eleanor slapped her, knocking her back onto the bed.

"You are a slow learner! I don't share my husband's patience. Answer the questions!"

Robert asked, "Did you mean to kill the prince or take him alive to Ireland? And who was to provide safe lodging along the way?"

"The prince? I came to kill you. You have taken Howard, Donald, and now Walter. It should be you dead now, not my brother!"

"You name enemies of the crown, not me. And it is King Charles that Walter came against for revenge. He has plotted. I have the proof. Tell all and you may live."

"I know nothing of plots or of hidden letters. I hate you for the misery you brought to my family!"

"John Eltonhead, he arranged for you to come here. The horse and wagon are his."

"He provided employment for Walter and then me. That is all."

"And Joseph Rusdorf, when did you last see him?"

"I never spoke to him. He was a visitor to Mister Eltonhead."

"But Walter did. He was in league with Eltonhead and Rusdorf. They plotted the death of King Charles. Charles who followed the ways of his father, King James in the displacements. Yes, new plantations to plant loyal protestants in Ireland. And now, Charles has an heir and good Catholic Queen Consort, Henrietta Maria, cannot take the crown. Did they plan to kill the young prince or take him to Ireland to be raised a good Catholic."

Magdalene began to think. "Walter told me no such thing. It is true he hates King James and his spiteful spawn,

Charles…but the young prince is a babe, an innocent babe. Does not the church teach us to train up a child in the way that he should go? No, I swear on my mother's grave, I could never take the life of a child. But Walter—Oh Walter, what have you done?"

Outside the room, Robert said, "I must get back to London! There is so little time. Horseback—much faster than the coach."

Eleanor replied, "I'm going with you!"

"Eleanor, you would be much safer in the coach. Send for me when you arrive."

Eleanor turned to one of Robert's men. "Two fast horses. Yes, two of you escort the prisoner. See to it at once. Robbie, give me a few minutes to change clothes."

The watcher looked to Robert.

Robert half-smiled, shook his head, and sighed. "Do as she says. Straight to Newgate Prison."

Eleanor came down in men's breeches, riding boots, a short coat and her hair tucked beneath a hat. Robert shook his head. "I knew you to be a spirited woman, but it appears I married a highwayman!"

Eleanor told Robert's stone-faced watcher, "Don't forget my bags," then turned to Robert and said, "I am not letting you out of my sight."

"You would become my bodyguard?"

Eleanor smirked. "For better or worse, till death do

us part. Now, do try to keep up. I have always been the better rider."

Eleanor and Robert made the best of the early June daylight and stopped only after dusk for a meal and a bed at a coaching inn. Eleanor was seen rubbing her bottom after dismounting. Robert said, "A hot meal and then to bed. We ride at dawn."

While they waited for their supper, Robert stared into his mug of ale. Eleanor said softly, "You're very quiet."

Robert sighed and looked up at his wife. "Until death do us part. What has become of me? My blade took the lives of two men!"

"Two?"

"Before we met. In the Palatinate, a Spanish army major—he forced himself on Katarina. He wounded Karl before—I did not think—I flew at him. My sword pinned him to the wall. Like today, I felt his last breath on my face as he died. Is this the conduct of a priest? I should be serving God and his flock, as Wilhelm and Katharina do. Not risking your future and the future of our children pursuing every man angry with our king. I am angry with the king! He has no concern for his subjects. Selfish, arrogant. He prorogues Parliament, imprisons its speaker, and even ignores his own Privy Council. He demands the loyalty of others but gives none in return. He makes secret pacts with France and Spain against what he promised Parliament, his church, and his people. A wretched man!"

Eleanor nodded. "I know you love Will and Katie, as do I. But works of mercy are their calling, not yours. As for King Charles, I remember some words from your sermons at Montclair Church. Tell me, Robert, is anyone beyond redemption? Beyond forgiveness? Have you forgotten Tom Gibbs and his family?"

"Tom Gibbs was not an evil man. What he did, he did for his family...."

Eleanor spoke louder. "What he did was attempt murder! Has God shown you His plan for King Charles? You preach that God, in his sovereignty, determines the affairs of all men. You have not become Lord Inquirer by your will, or by chance. It is your calling. You must follow it—but follow it with integrity and faith."

Robert sighed. "Have I told you I love you? What a gift you are."

Plates of stew were set before them. Eleanor picked up her knife and spoon and said, "Who is this Rusdorf you ask about, and why are we rushing back to London? The letter from Felim O'Neil—you were her target, not the prince."

Robert swallowed his food. "Aye, her target but not her brother's. Whoever is behind the pamphlets and the attempt against the king uses others, bending their motives to his will and purpose. No, we have captured only puppets. The puppet master pulling the strings eludes us."

"But why the attempt to kill you before the prince arrived?"

"Perhaps I am getting too close, or perhaps a play to misdirect my inquiries. But the prince is still at risk, as is King Charles."

Eleanor asked, "The letter from O'Neil, the time needed to place Magdalene Fitzhugh at Croxall Hall—how could they have known you would visit? It's as if they knew before you did."

Robert replied, "I had time to send a letter to you. And perhaps they didn't know I would visit before the prince's Christening. But the answer is in London, at the court of King Charles."

In London, Eleanor insisted they stop at their Whitehall townhouse before Robert hurried off to report to Lord Conway and meet with Black and Lynch. "Really, Robbie? You need a bath. We can share one if you like, but at least clean clothes."

Thomas met them at the door. "Welcome home, Lord and Lady Montclair. There are letters from Saint James Palace. Yours, Lady Montclair, bears the seal of the Queen."

Eleanor took the letter, broke the seal, and unfolded

it. "I am invited to join the Queen's Ladies in Waiting at the Christening of Prince Charles. I have no desire to see that woman ever again. Robbie, my regard for Henrietta Maria is no higher than your regard for Charles. They deserve each other,"

Robert replied. "You must go. I need you there. This is most fortunate! Yes, I will not need to plead your case with Conway and Sackville!"

Robert went through his letters as they spoke. "Hmm, he murmured as he set down the stack and unsealed a letter. "From Pierre Brulart."

Eleanor replied curtly, "Why would that man dare write to you!"

He's been replaced...."

"Good!" Eleanor shouted. "An animal!"

Robert lowered the letter and looked at Eleanor. "Why indeed write me? Rather cryptic. He writes that Cardinal Richelieu is First Secretary and pursues an undeclared war with Spain. He mentions that Lady Justine's son, Count Bellamy, will attend the Christening with the French delegation along with Pierre Legarde. The count will come early and visit his mother and I—we should attend."

Eleanor cocked her head. "Strange for him to tell us. I've received nothing from Lady Justine. Does he say anything else?"

"I am to give his warmest regards to the lovely and virtuous Lady Montclair. And we are invited to visit his new estate in France. He has been retired from office and made Vicomte and given the estate of an unfortunate Huguenot, betrayed by the Dowager Queen, Marie di Medici. He apologizes, 'It is a sad truth, but the good man was elderly with no heir. If not me, someone else. Count Bellamy is a most capable and godly young man. In many ways you walk in the same shoes.'"

Robert set the letters on the table, and said to the servant. "Prepare a hot bath for Lady Eleanor at once."

The servant bowed and replied. "A hot bath, yes my lord," as he hurried from the room,

Robert turned to Eleanor. "You earned it my dear."

Eleanor smiled. "Don't think you will climb into my bed until after you have bathed as well."

Robbie smiled. "Then we must share the bath for I am rushed both here with you and in the King's service."

Eleanor teased, "And which is the more urgent?"

"We'll entertain the question upstairs." Robert swept Eleanor from her feet and carried her up to their room.

Mister Black assembled Robert's council in the great room above the works at Newgate Prison. Robert addressed his staff. "A new strand to pursue. Walter Stock, brother to

Donald, is dead. He carried letters and pamphlets. His half-sister, Magdalene Fitzhugh, daughter of Rose Fitzhugh and employed as a nursemaid to Lady Dorset, Mary Sackville, is on her way to Newgate. Miss Fitzhugh carried a letter from Felim O'Neil…"

Lynch interrupted. "So, there is an Irish Catholic connection."

Robert ignored him and continued, "She swears I was her only target—revenge for Donald Stock and the Reverend Doctor Fitzhugh. Mister Lynch will lead the inquiry into the O'Neil connection. Miss Fitzhugh's placement was arranged by Eltonhead, and possibly Joseph Rusdorf. Black what have you found of Rusdorf?"

Black replied. "He is in the Hague."

Robert asked, "The court in exile of Frederick V and Elizabeth?"

Black nodded. "He has met with Elector Frederick's mother, Countess Louise Juliana of Nassau, sister to the Prince of Orange. She has returned from Berlin with word from King Gustavus Adolphus of Sweden to the Dutch."

"What do we know of this word?"

"The countess is most influential. She cares for her Palatinate grandchildren in exile and has convinced her son-in-law, the Elector of Brandenburg to negotiate with the Swedish King. She carries terms for an alliance between Sweden, the United Netherlands and the protestant princes against the Emperor and the King of Spain."

Robert asked, "Do they know of King Charles new treaty with Spain against the Dutch?"

Mister Black replied, "The King's secret treaty with Spain is secret only to his English subjects."

Robert sighed. "And the French?"

"The Countess Louise Juliana is the granddaughter of the French Duke of Montpensier and his Huguenot wife the Countess of Bar-Sur-Seine. Her mother, Charlotte of Bourbon raised Louise as protestant. She is an ardent Calvinist, with no love for King Louis and Cardinal Richelieu's new purge of French Huguenots. But I would suspect the French are equally unhappy with King Charles' secret treaty with Spain."

Robert replied, "Perhaps Lady Justine has more to say."

Black looked surprised. "You know of the visit? We received Count Bellamy's note just this morning, He asked after you and Lady Eleanor. Justine was to call on Lady Eleanor today."

Robert nodded. "We must consider a foreign prince or his courtier pulling the strings of English discontent. Someone skilled in intrigue and the ways of court. Someone with eyes and ears in the Court of Saint James."

Black replied, "Every court employs such men. It has ever been so. And every court in Europe has been betrayed by King Charles or would find benefit in the turmoil of a regency or new dynasty. Each willing to place a favorable successor on the throne."

Lynch shook his head. "What a time we live! The whole world at war because royal houses give loyalty first to family and second to religion! Never a thought for those who work the land, produce their merchandise, and fight their battles. God save us all!"

Robert stared at his friend; Lynch answered his stare. "Well, it's true. I know you to be a good man pursuing justice but there comes a point. Where is justice? Forgive me Sir Robert."

"For better or worse, Charles is our King. A strike at Charles is an attack on England. Would you prefer a foreigner rule us? With no concern for our traditions? Our faith? No memory of the rights of an Englishman? Our law or Parliament?"

"Aye, Englishmen not the Irish, the Scots and the Welsh."

Robert glared. "England is not perfect. It is no Eden, but all subjects have rights. You can't believe you would fare better beneath a Divine Right tyrant."

Robert looked at his inner circle, one by one they felt his stare. "The Christening of the prince is one week from today. Lady Eleanor will attend with the Queen's Ladies in Waiting. I will be close to the King. We must inquire after everyone attending. Motives and opportunities must be uncovered."

Robert picked up the report set before him and said, "I must call on Lord Conway. Lord Sackville, and his majesty. You have work to do—and still, no one identifies the blonde friend of Joseph Rusdorf or has found the priest to Sir John Eliot in the tower. Connections, men, connections to foreign powers."

CHAPTER 27

COUNT BELLAMY AND
THE FRENCH CONNECTION

Robert and Eleanor coached to the new Gomer's House not far from the French Protestant Church. As they waited for the bell to be answered and the gate opened, Robert said. "Black has not spoken of the work to this new house. Fresh stone, new rooms, and yet the Norman architecture of the old Benedictine priory is preserved."

Eleanor replied, "You're surprised? Really, Robert? Don't you two talk of anything but plots and intrigue? I thought you considered him a friend as well as co-laborer for the King. Lady Justine cannot turn away any poor woman or child fleeing that wretched profession—women deemed underserving by the parish for food, clothing, or money to escape prostitution. And Christian—do not call him Black in his house—is the best of husbands and helpmate in her work. But as for the new work, her son, Count Bellamy provides generously for his mother."

Robert nodded. "You are right, of course, my love. I count Black, er, Christian, as a true friend. I know his past and I know the redemption he found with Lady Justine. But my friend is not one to dwell on himself."

The gate opened and the coach entered a large courtyard surrounded by a stone quadrangle building. They drove to the far end where Black stood waiting in front of a new façade to the former chapel.

Robert jumped out first and held Eleanor's hand as she stepped out. Black bowed and kissed her hand. "Lord and Lady Montclair, welcome to Gomer's House."

Robert replied, "My friend, please Robbie, and Eleanor."

Black smiled. "Of course, Sir Robert and Lady Eleanor. Lady Justine waits in the house with her son, Count Bellamy."

Robert smiled. "We are most anxious to meet the Count, your stepson, and then you must acquaint me with the progress of the work."

Always elegant, Lady Justine radiated maternal pride as she stood to receive her guests. "Lord Robert, Lady Eleanor, this is my son, Jacques, Count Bellamy."

Turning to the tall young man, still rail thin with

youth, she said, "Jacques, these are our dear friends and saviors, along with your stepfather. I present Robert and Eleanor, Earl and Countess of Montclair."

Jacques bowed and kissed Eleanor's hand. "A privilege to at last meet the lady who has become both friend and supporter of my mother's work. It is my belief that God, who works good in all things, brought you together. Every French refugee in London knows of the good work you both do."

Eleanor blushed. "You do me far too much honor. The praise is your mother's alone."

Turning to Robert, Bellamy said, "I feel I know you after the many stories I have heard from my mother and her good husband, Christian. Thank you for agreeing to see me on such urgent notice. I am told you have just recently returned from a perilous mission. Your service to your king is well known."

Lady Justine interrupted. "Christian, we have time before dinner is served. Why not show Jacques and Sir Robert the new work while I entertain Lady Eleanor?"

Outside, Count Bellamy spoke freely. "Pierre Brulart sends his regards. He insisted I speak with you frankly."

Robert replied, "It was wise not to mention his name to Lady Eleanor."

Bellamy nodded. "He told me she has not forgiven

him. Brulart was as much a captive to the French court as my mother. The House of Bourbon relies on compelled loyalty. They put all who serve them at risk. In truth, Pierre Brulart finds happiness in his new freedom—removed from office by Cardinal Richelieu. I do not know if Brulart is a religious man, but he has a conscience and seeks to make amends for his actions."

"And what compels your loyalty, Count Bellamy?"

The young man smiled. "A weak one indeed. Merely my title and my estate, indebted as I am. So, you see, I feather my mother's nest in England."

Jacques stopped and faced Robert and Black. "I am permitted my title and position as long as I serve the king and practice my protestant faith outside of France. I have no wife or heir to hold hostage."

Robert asked, "Why send for me? Christian has my ear. I trust him with my life, my purse, and my wife. I know his ability and character."

"Brulart insisted you both hear. Time is short. The French royals arrive in two days. The courts of Europe all worry for the English throne. Your King Charles is not safe. Stories of plots and unrest abound. Cardinal Richelieu worries an attempt on King Charles' life during the French royal visit might push your unreliable Parliament to pursue war with France, perhaps, even seize His Majesty King Louis and the Queen Mother. England is the puzzle of Europe. James and now his son, Charles ever seeking new alliances, never trustworthy to their allies, and ever bungling in negotiations."

Black replied, "We have penetrated the plotter's network, broken his chain, and captured many in his employ. Those not yet captured are on the run and the net is closing fast around them."

Jacques nodded. "But you do not know the master behind the plot. Likely, one most clever and capable. The danger remains."

Robert spoke. "The courts, what do you hear?"

Bellamy replied, "The plotters do them a favor. Most princes would prefer Charles gone and a reliable protestant, his sister Elizabeth, or his nephew on the throne. The newborn Prince of Wales complicates the matter, but the removal of Charles would be welcomed."

Black replied, "You speak of the United Netherlands and the protestant princes of Germany."

"I speak of the Swedes, the Danes and the Catholic Kings as well. I come here from Berlin. Countess Louise Juliana of Orange-Nassau, mother-in-law to Elizabeth, King Charles' sister, negotiated the alliance of Sweden and the United Netherlands. A most cunning and ambitious woman, she would do anything to raise the status of Frederick or his son. Charles is abandoning the Dutch, the Swedes, and the protestant cause in favor of a Spanish treaty—with no guarantees for the Palatinate—anathema to her and many others."

Robert replied, "In Berlin, this treaty is known? And you were there, representing France? Is France joining the war? Does France ally itself with Sweden and the Dutch against the Spanish in the Netherlands?"

Jacques took a deep breath and slowly exhaled. "I can say only this. Richelieu advises King Louis. They bide their time to resolve all unrest in France before dealing with the unacceptable Spanish threat to our north and south. The Bourbons, like most of the ruling families, view the Hapsburgs as the true threat to Europe."

Robert nodded. "I remember the Dowager Queen of Denmark-Norway, Sophie of Mecklenburg-Gustrow once saying, 'We must fight, or a Hapsburg boot will be thrust on the neck of every prince in Europe.'"

Jacques replied, "You make my case. Sophie was there. Even with her grandson, Prince Christian of Brunswick killed in battle, she continues her support with money and urges King Christian of Denmark to return to the war. Count Rusdorf attended for Prince-Elector Frederick..."

Robert interrupted, "Rusdorf? What can Frederick offer? His army was defeated, and he was forced into exile in the Hague."

"Count Rusdorf goes where Countess Louise

Julianna directs and advises as she advises. His son serves as secretary to Julianna."

"Joseph Rusdorf is an aide to Julianna?"

"More her protégé."

Black broke his customary silence. "Brulart sends you to tell us a foreign prince or king is behind the plot to remove King Charles. We have followed connections to Catholics in Antwerp, and Joseph Rusdorf has been connected to English and Irish plotters. Our plotter plays both sides with his pamphlets inciting regicide. Does Brulart suspect Louise Julianna?"

Bellamy considered his words. "He does not share his suspicions. Likely, he does not know for certain. But he warns the danger is even greater. Your General Leslie knows of King Charles' 'secret Spanish treaty,' but assures King Gustav Adolphus his army of English and Scottish soldiers will continue their fight for the protestant cause. Once again, an English King would put English soldier against English soldier in this war. Will this not further inflame veterans and all his British subjects? A change in England yes, but not another civil war."

Black replied, "Jacques, you know that King Charles cannot raise an army without taxes, and Parliament will not agree to new taxes to support an English army to fight for Catholic Spain against the Dutch. Our king chases about the countryside forcing loans to repay his wife's gambling debts. It must be understood that a treaty with Spain is toothless."

Jacques smiled. "It is the English Navy he offers. But yes, so Sir John Eliot, Speaker and leader of your Parliament has confirmed. Which shows how reckless Charles is. He cannot be taken seriously as a military threat, yet he risks plunging England into civil war."

Robert listened but considered, *The unnamed priest—the blonde-haired visitor to Sir John in the Tower of London—he is the source of this confirmation. But who sent him?*

Robert asked, "Confirmed to whom? And what was your role in these talks at Berlin?"

Bellamy replied, "I cannot say how this confirmation was obtained—but it was reported. General Leslie agreed to the assessment. As for me—well I brought letters from Richelieu—promises of money. I am pledged not to share the amount, but France is sending substantial support to pay the Swedish army."

Robert tried again. "So, France will remain neutral and not join the war on one side or the other?"

Count Bellamy was young, but skilled. "Cardinal Richelieu finds ways to fight without armies. Do not underestimate him. Spain and the Hapsburg Emperor are the true enemies of France. Any English treaty with Spain will have severe consequences."

Eleanor and Justine stood by a window and watched the men slowly walk the courtyard. Justine smiled and whispered. "The three finest men I know. I do pray Robert warms to Jacques. Robert's heart for compassion is his true gift. Men of state never achieve greatness without compassion and humility."

Eleanor did not break her gaze out the window. "Robert finds the best of men—friends, loyal friends. Will and Edward and yes Christian. He has a gift. He draws men of character to him—men of purpose. How did he find me? How I pursued him and nearly betrayed him, but he would not give up on us—on me. And now, I do not know how I could live without him. At Croxall Hall, when that madwoman went for him—I could not bear to see him die. Justine, I was never a violent person, but I could have—I intended to kill her. Yes, I meant to kill if it would save my Robbie."

Eleanor turned to her friend. And continued "His loyalty—to Will and Edward and yes, your Christian—loyalty to faithful men I understand. But this tyrant of a king? I only want for my husband to live with me and our children safe at Montclair Castle, far away from this wicked city. Why, I would be happy, married to my country priest serving his collection of widows and orphans of the condemned and the good tenants of Montclair. How do I rescue him?"

Justine sighed. "He would not be the same man. You love Robert for who he is—a man of purpose. It is what draws me to Christian as well. We can only trust God to protect them. And thank God, every morning we awake with our husbands to the new day."

As the three men walked the courtyard a young girl approached, bowed, and said in English with a French accent, "My lords, Lady Justine bids you return. Dinner is served."

Black smiled. "Thank you, Gwen, tell her ladyship we are on our way."

As the servant returned, Black said to Jacques, "Most helpful. We should talk more."

Robert added, "Yes, come see me at Westminster tomorrow. And a list—bring a list of all who travel with the French Court."

"The servants as well?"

"Especially the servants. Now Black, er…"

Black laughed. "To you, I am always Black. Yes, let's eat. See how well these French girls can cook!"

At the table, Eleanor asked Justine, "How many are they now?"

Black looked at his wife with a large, seldom-seen smile. Justine replied, "Thirty-seven young women and a dozen children."

Robert put down his knife and spoon. "Thirty-seven? And the children? So many? And you say the parish will not help them?"

"They are doubly undeserving. Prostitutes and French! It is true foreigners may have been welcomed by King's decree but many—and it is the English of privilege who object—will not give them aid. So, here, we are near the French Protestant Church. The pastor and French brothers and sisters work with me to teach the women skills and the children lessons. They soon find employment in the palace. All learn English and even read and write. But we are careful—they must be healed in mind and soul as well, so they never return to prostitution."

Eleanor spoke. "Their French is an advantage in the palace. It is the language of the Queen's court. Why, French-speaking servants should excel in the Queen's closet and chambers as well as at the tables."

"That is what we hope. And some have married. Yes, good men, from the church. They know their wife's past but have hearts of forgiveness."

Robert asked, "Do any hope to return to France and family?"

Jacques sighed. "I pray someday. But for now, it is just a dream. It was the Queen Mother, Marie di Medici, who began the Huguenot rebellion. She used them and betrayed them. She promised them tolerance and autonomy in hopes of power over her own son. But when

Richelieu arranged the reconciliation, she betrayed them—every one of them. Richelieu will do business with protestants, but not in France. Not yet. As for the Queen Mother, the woman is evil."

CHAPTER 28

LOOSE ENDS

Black sat as Robert paced. "Why does Louis bring young inexperienced Count Bellamy to England for the Christening of Prince Charles? And Pierre Brulart insists I meet with him? How did he explain his visit to you and Lady Justine?"

Black sighed. "How sad that our work makes us suspicious of everyone. But I wondered myself. He claims Brulart arranged it before he retired from office—a last request to reward a promising young diplomat, whose mother was wronged in service to the crown. Brulart urged Bellamy be rewarded with a visit to his mother and France would gain access to a valuable contact in the English court—you Sir Robert. Remember, he is knowledgeable of the changing alliances. And I trust him with my life."

Robert stared out the window of his Westminster chambers at the far shore of the Thames River. "Richelieu would want more in return."

Black observed, "You seem more interested in the French delegation than pursuing the trail of Joseph Rusdorf and his ties to Countess Louise Juliana—acting for the Dutch and the King's son-in-law."

Robert spoke under his breath. "I know young Rusdorf's circle in the court. Let me ruffle the feathers in the palace."

A knock on the door and Count Bellamy was announced. Jacques stepped in smiling, "*Bon jour*! I bring the official French delegation list that you requested. Our ambassador the Marquis Chateuneof, assures me it is the final list, received just this morning."

Black looked over Robert's shoulder as he read. Robert said, "A small delegation—that makes our job easier. Black, have five copies made immediately."

Looking up, Robert said to Bellamy, "Do you know these people?"

Bellamy replied, "The nobles are all favorite courtiers. I cannot help you with the serving staff."

Robert said, "Black, give a copy to Lynch, and a copy each to the House Steward and Captain of the Guard at Saint James. Take one to the French Protestant Church.

Ask the pastor to discreetly review it with his members serving in the palace. Find out what they can tell us about any of the staff. I will review a copy with Henri, the King's cook. Discretion, Black! No word should come back to the French. Now, I have a call to make at the tower. It's time Sir John Eliot comes clean on his mysterious priest."

The keeper of the tower answered Robert's question. "The blonde priest that visited Sir John Eliot? No, he hasn't been 'round in weeks. A stubborn one, Sir John, but he'll be singing a new tune once the weather turns. No fine apartment, just a bare cell, and no family visits. Though they do bring by food and drink."

Robert replied, "I need to see him on the King's business, shouldn't be a long visit."

"Aye, the King's Lord Inquirer. Perhaps you can talk sense to the man. A good man too, but stubborn."

When the cell door swung open, Robert saw Sir John lying on a blanket spread in a soft beam of light coming through his window, his eyes focused on the ceiling above. Sir John glanced at Robert and said, "This tower was built by William the Bastard, bastard son of the Duke of Normandy—his name before he conquered England. This cell has been here, what, 450 years? How many men laid here? How many of them never saw their families again?"

Robert smiled. "Sounds like you're ready to give the King his loan."

Sir John sat up, then stood and dusted off his clothes. "Nay, not yet. The king would not send his Lord Inquirer to collect his loan. Why have you come?"

"You lied to me on my last visit. I asked after a visitor with blonde hair and beard…."

"No, you asked if any of my sons were blonde—I answered truthfully."

Robert sat on the one chair in the cell. "Now you are going to tell me about the blonde priest who visited you. The priest is known to be in league with Joseph Rusdorf and with John Eltonhead, would-be assassin to King Charles…"

"I don't know Eltonhead, and I am no plotter against the king."

"Rusdorf has delivered your message to Berlin and the support for a new alliance, in opposition to King Charles' secret alliance with Spain."

Sir John's face contorted. "An English treaty with Spain?"

Robert replied, "Against the Dutch in their endless war."

Sir John shook his head. "Foolishness! An alliance with Catholic Spain? It would never work! England has nothing to gain and little to give. The people would not hear of it. Yes, a blonde priest came to me. He asked if King Charles recalled Parliament to raise new taxes for the navy or to raise an army, how would Parliament decide? I thought the man was just speaking of the politics of the day. I was glad to hear any news from the outside. I knew nothing of a Spanish treaty. I answered as one would answer any man having his cups at an inn. King Charles made a treaty with Spain? Madness! War requires taxes! Is there also talk of a new Parliament?"

Robert said, "What do you remember of this priest?"

"Now that you mention him, he was a bit odd. When the guard came by to check, he recited the liturgy, but he got it wrong—not our Book of Common Prayer liturgy but one mixed with the Roman Catholic response. And his accent—his English betrayed his aristocracy, but the accent—he spent his youth in a foreign land, what was it? Italian. His accent was Italian!"

"Did he say his name?"

"He said call me Father Peter."

Robert asked, "No last name? Nothing else?"

Sir John shook his head. "Lord Robert, I am no traitor. And I never heard of any of the events you spoke of. You must understand."

Robert stood up. "Perhaps it is time you swallow your pride and make the loan. It does you no good to be seen as an enemy of the king in these times. Agree to the loan, then come see me at Westminster. England has need of you."

Henri greeted Robert as he walked into the palace kitchen. "Lord Montclair, I was told to expect your visit. You bring the list. I have already seen it. Come to the counting room, we can speak in private."

Robert smiled at his friend. "I am not two hours behind Mister Black, and you know?"

"We French in London are a close family. Whisper in the ear of Pierre and Henri hears as well. We shall search out every name soon, but one name Henri questions. The man, Claude Passant. Said to be King Louis' cook, has never cooked in the king's kitchen. Be certain we will find him out for his true work."

"Thank you, Henri. Discretion my friend."

"Of course! Always discretion in the palace."

Henri hesitated, looking for the proper words. "Lady Justine, such a good and truly noble woman—she gives so much to our community—her son Count Bellamy visits. He worships with us—seems a good young man— can we trust him? He is in service to Louis. All in service to Louis are, how shall I say, beholden."

"Richelieu's hold on the young count is an illusion. He knows the pain inflicted on his good mother. His heart is with you in worship and service. I find him most trustworthy, though the devil and Cardinal Richelieu can deceive even a good man."

Henri nodded. "Then I am happy for Lady Justine that she finds joy in a good son."

Robert turned to leave. "Always good to see you, my friend. I must be off...."

Henri interrupted, "Have you heard? Queen Henrietta Maria has commanded a feast of new French food the night before the Christening. The food will be prepared under the direction of her Lady in Waiting, said to be a skilled cook, Madame de Vantelet, Marguerite Courtin. The cook Claude Passant will assist."

Robert looked into Henri's eyes. "You must be there and watch them most carefully."

"For certain, but you must insist—for the King's safety."

"Aye, I will see to it."

Henri smiled. "And Lord Montclair, you should worship with us sometime. If not for your soul, then to improve your French—among the worst, I have ever heard."

Believing he had time before the Christening events, Robert went straight to Lord Conway's chambers. He could not hold off any longer in reporting the incident at Croxall Hall. Conway was seated at his writing desk when Robert entered. He did not look up from his work. "Two days. I hear you have been back two days and only now come to see me."

Lord Conway put down his pen and looked at Robert. "I hear rumors all was not well at Croxall Hall. You had time to entertain the French Count Bellamy but no time to report on the security of the Prince of Wales? Unfinished business no doubt. Well tell me or shall I call for Mister Black?"

Robert nodded. "Aye, there was trouble and indeed unfinished business. The prince is safe, no thanks to your brother-in-law, John Eltonhead. He arranged with Lord Sackville, Earl of Dorset...."

"I know the man's title and that he is the Queen's Lord Chamberlain. What arrangements?"

Robert continued, "Your brother-in-law and your page, Joseph Rusdorf, arranged the appointment of a nursemaid—kin to traitors Fitzhugh and friend to the Irish rebel Felim O'Neal. The young woman, Magdalene Fitzhugh, was determined to kill me in revenge. But the real threat was her half-brother, Walter Stock, unfortunately dead, but in possession of the pamphlets and letters from O'Neal. His intent was to kidnap the prince. I delayed my report to put my men on the trail of new evidence. My intent was to delay any hasty action by his Majesty against you and Lord Sackville. Now I ask you to delay your report yet a little while longer. I must make further inquiries of Sackville. As for my meeting with Count Bellamy, it was arranged by the former French Secretary, Pierre Brulart. They report on widespread disdain for the King's Spanish treaty by protestant and Catholic kings alike. He pointed towards Countess Louise Julianna, but I believe there may be a French threat as well."

Conway sighed, then rose in silence. He paced the room slowly, his hands behind his back. He shook his head and sighed once more. "I can't be discovered withholding this news. Tomorrow. I will wait until tomorrow, and then you will report to the king. You suspect a foreign hand guiding this deadly pamphleteer. You must tell him all."

Robert turned to leave before stopping. "Lord Conway, was young Rusdorf acquainted with foreign ambassadors? The Dutch, Palatinate, or French?"

"He carried notes and pouches to all ambassadors. Nothing of importance—invitations and reports. Typical duty for any court page."

"Did he go alone?"

"Well, of course. He carried nothing of state security."

Robert heard Lord Conway mutter, "Oh, my dear, dear, Ellie. What has your brother done?" And Robert was out the door headed for the chambers of the Queen's Lord

Chamberlain, the Earl of Dorset.

Edward Sackville, 4th Earl of Dorset and accomplished soldier, was surprised by Robert's visit. "Lord Montclair, yes, come through. I do have time though your visit is unexpected. I trust you found all is well at Croxall Hall."

Robert nodded. "It is urgent I see you before the news arrives in London. We have little time to prepare, for surely a Star Chamber trial is not out of the question."

"Urgent news? Trial?"

"All was not well at Croxall, though it is now safe for the prince if the King still permits. It seems a nursemaid hired to assist the wetnurse and the young woman's half-brother, a coach driver new to your estate, meant evil against the child and me. The men behind them, John Eltonhead and Joseph Rusdorf—you know these men and accompanied them to Croxall Hall. They plotted against King Charles and meant to kidnap the young Prince of Wales."

Sackville's face drained pale white and his eyes widened. "Young Rusdorf? He is everyone's favorite. Why he is a favorite of the Queen! He introduced Eltonhead. I knew him only as Rusdorf's close friend. Tell me all."

Robert continued. "Eltonhead put forward the maid, Magdalene Fitzhugh, sister and in-law to two convicted traitors. Her desire was to kill me in revenge, having been told in advance of my visit. But her brother, one Walter Stock, carried pamphlets offering a reward for the murder of the King and more to the point, a letter from the Irish rebel, Felim O'Neal, planning the kidnapping of the infant prince to Ireland. Walter Stock is dead, and Miss Fitzhugh is in custody. Rusdorf fled to the continent. But he has another accomplice, a man called 'Peter,' or 'Saint Peter.' A young man, blonde of hair and beard. We seek him and all that can be learned of Joseph Rusdorf."

The Lord Chamberlain composed himself. "Rusdorf is—was Lord Conway's page. He is a most likable young man, quick of wit. He accompanied Prince Henry Frederick, King Charles nephew of the Palatinate on his audience with Queen Henrietta Maria. Rusdorf accounted himself well and was made a welcome favorite of Her Majesty."

Robert nodded. "Rusdorf's father was Secretary to Frederick V of the Palatinate. A likely choice for the young prince."

Sackville continued. "As for the blonde man you seek, Peter or Saint Peter, I can only speculate. The Queen's confessor, Father Robert Philip, is blonde of hair and beard. I have heard Joseph Rusdorf on more than one occasion call him Saint Peter. It was something between them. You could see mischief in Rusdorf's eyes, and it was poorly received by Father Philip."

"What can you tell me of Father Robert Philip?"

"A Scot. Educated in Rome. I met him there in 1624, still a student, one of many British Catholics there. Quiet man, not social. Receives an occasional letter from his family in Scotland. An ardent papist—to him adoration, loyalty, and service to the pope is his service to God. Yes, your question reminds me, Father Philip joined the Queen in arguing for Prince Henry Frederick to convert to Catholicism. King Charles was most indignant when word of the attempted conversion reached him from his sister and brother-in-law in the Hague. Yes, Joseph Rusdorf was with them."

Robert replied, "Yes, most helpful. Tell me, Lord Dorset, what are your leanings? You say you visited Rome."

Dorset replied, "Fair enough question. I am a faithful member of the Church of England. I had just completed my service to King James in the court of King Louis. I asked for time to travel. I went to Rome to visit Marco Antonio de Dominis, one time Archbishop and Primate of Dalmatia and Croatia. A fervent critic of the pope and a dedicated reformer. Sadly, after forfeiting his refuge in England he returned to Rome where he was imprisoned and died."

Robert replied, "I recall the man. Wasn't he tried after death by papal inquisition?"

"Found guilty of heresy. Do not cross the pope. His body was dug up, dragged through the streets of Rome, and burned."

The Earl of Dorset paused for a moment. "Do you intend to arrest the Queen's confessor? And the Star Chamber inquiry—will I or my wife be called to trial?"

Robert shook his head. "It is not in Lord Conway's interest to call for a Star Chamber. As you are embarrassed by Rusdorf's influence, Lord Conway is brother-in-law to the traitor John Eltonhead. You must say nothing on this matter, even as reports come from Croxall Hall. As for the queen's priest. Not a word to anyone."

A new thought came to Robert, and he asked, "You mentioned letters to Father Philip from his family. Does he send letters to his Bishop or others?"

"Yes, His letters go by diplomatic pouch. The French Ambassador picks them up. Yes, both he and Madame de Vantelet are servants of the French crown."

"Who is his bishop?"

"Father Philip is confessor to Queen Henrietta Maria, sister to the King of France. Of course, coming from the French royal family, Father Philip reports to Cardinal Richelieu."

Robert asked, "And Philip and Madame de Ventalet receive letters through the ambassador as well?"

"Of course. Frequently."

"And the queen?"

"The King requires official correspondence through the English ambassador to France. But she has asked a few personal notes to her family be slipped in the French pouch. Her mother, most often. The truth, Montclair. You cannot believe the queen is among the plotters. Madness! She has found happiness with her husband—and now her son."

Robert smiled. "As you say. It would be madness. No, I do not count the queen among the plotters. Now, I will be on my way."

Sackville sighed the relief of a man forgiven. "Before you leave, Montclair, I should tell you that the Queen has changed. Perhaps it is the security of an heir. But she insisted on the invitation of Lady Eleanor for all the festivities. She seeks to make amends to your wife. Perhaps as a new mother, she now understands. You and I have this in common. We have married above our station and perhaps above our deserving. My brother squandered our family fortune. Croxall Hall and all the wealth I enjoy come from my wife. Tell Lady Eleanor she is most welcome at court."

A page, breathing hard after a long run, interrupted. "Pardon, my Lords, but Lord Conway urgently requests Lord Montclair return to him at once."

The sun was low in the sky when Robert returned

to Conway's chamber. A smiling Conway greeted him. "I have bought you time, Montclair. His majesty grants you an audience the morning following the Christening. King Charles received a report from Croxall Hall. I informed him that you were the maid's target—that we have talked, and you are convinced the Manor is safe for the prince. The safety of the prince is his most urgent concern. As for the man killed, Walter Stock, the king is satisfied that you aggressively pursue his fellow conspirators among the Irish."

Robert replied, "Yes, it is good you bought *us* time. Please send your page to Mister Black. Ask him to call on me at my home."

With a glance from Conway's eyes, the page was off.

Lord Conway spoke. "You have time to discuss the schedule. The Royals will stay at the smaller, more intimate Saint James Palace. The courtiers at Whitehall Palace. The French will host a feast the night before the Christening at Saint James. Christening will take place at Saint James Chapel Royal at noon. Following the ceremony, the royals will parade by Thames River to Whitehall Palace. The celebration feast will begin at sunset at the Banqueting House Whitehall. The Royal Guard will accompany the procession with soldiers at arms by barge and at both palaces. Now, are your men prepared? Any word of unrest?"

Robert replied, "Watchers and secret men have uncovered no hint of unrest and they will be watching from positions of concern. By all accounts the King's subjects receive news of the young prince with joy and goodwill."

CHAPTER 29

INVITATION TO DINNER
WITH THE BOURBONS

Thomas greeted Robert at the door of his Whitehall Townhouse. 'Good evening, my lord. Guests tonight. Count Bellamy, the dowager countess and Black, that is Mister Christian Fauconnier. Lady Montclair entertains them in the receiving room."

Eleanor called to Robert as he entered the room. "There you are Robbie! In time for dinner. Lady Justine and Christian are here. I told her they must stay for dinner and then Christian could go through your things…."

Robert turned to the ill-at-ease Black and then back to Eleanor. "What things? Perhaps you should start over."

Lady Justine spoke. "An invitation to the private dinner King Louis and Dowager Queen Marie will host for King Charles and Queen Henrietta Maria—we have been invited. Christian and I and, and Lady Eleanor tells me, you too. Well, Christian's finest may suffice for a funeral, but not for a royal banquet. Lady Eleanor offered your closet."

Robert turned again to Black and began to laugh. "Well, my friend, let's find lipstick for the pig! Forgive me, Lady Justine, I am a great admirer of your husband, and yes, he has a funeral wardrobe. But a royal dinner party? We can dress him, but you must teach him the etiquette and table manners in only two days."

Count Bellamy spoke. "Not to worry Christian. You will not be called upon or noticed. All eyes will be on the royals. Just follow my mother's lead."

Robert said to Black. "Come upstairs. See what we have."

Eleanor called out, "Robbie, you will wear the silver and black, it is my favorite. The royal blue and gold, the Bourbon colors, for Christian."

Robert mumbled softly, "The things we do for love."

Black replied, "Amen."

Out of earshot Robbie said, "It appears the queen's confessor, Father Robert Philip is the third—the blonde 'Saint Peter.' The king's cook, Henri, told me the name for the King Louis' cook is not who he remembers. Queen Henrietta Maria commanded her lady, Madame Vantelet, rule the kitchen as she and Louis' cooks prepare the meal. We must place a good man in the kitchen with Henri."

Black nodded. "Already taken care of. We have put a watch on the Dutch ambassador as well as the ambassador of Frederick V. There are no new visitors to either. You fear the French more than Julianna of Nassau?"

"The French ambassador carries letters weekly to and from her Majesty. Madame Vantelet and Robert Philip send all their letters through the French ambassador's pouch. Queen Henrietta Maria sometimes uses the pouch for letters home."

"We cannot violate diplomatic correspondence."

"No. I only speak of opportunity and connection. You have enough men for the procession?"

Black asked, "Are there ever enough men for security? We have enough for the areas of highest risk and vulnerability."

Robert found the blue coat and gold waistcoat and laid them out on the bed. "The coat hangs loose, open around the waistcoat, which is backless. It should fit. High black boots, polished of course, and you will not need colored stockings. The count should be able to provide a proper hat, gloves, and sword."

Black mumbled, "I'd rather…."

Robert interrupted, "Don't dwell on your unease; rather, consider how stunning the beautiful Lady Justine will be at your side. And I have learned this as well, if you persevere through the night, your wife will reward you afterward beyond imagination. Now, let's go to dinner."

At dinner, Robert asked Count Bellamy, "Is it you we are all to thank for this invitation?"

Jacques smiled at his mother. "I confess to mentioning the Dowager Countess Bellamy would enjoy a good French meal in the company of her countrymen, but you and Lady Montclair, well, her Majesty, Queen Henrietta Marie had included you on her list."

Robert smiled. "Jacques confirms what the Earl of Dorset said to me today. The queen wishes to make amends to you and desires to see you more often at court."

Eleanor began to answer, but only shook her head and tasted her wine.

Robert continued, "I learned today that the Queen's confessor, Father Robert Philip is a Scotsman. What did you make of him, my dear?"

Eleanor looked up. "Father Philip? A strange man. Harsh. I don't mean that he was ever ill-tempered, only that he never smiled, never offered friendship to anyone in the Queen's court. Spoke only French, though I knew he spoke English. I saw letters on his writing table in both English and French."

"Letters?" Robert asked.

"Yes, when he wasn't saying mass or hearing the

confession of the Queen or Madame Ventelet, he was at his table, below the painting of Glastonbury Abbey, writing."

"Glastonbury? Not Rome?"

"He was most proud of Glastonbury Abbey. An ancestor had saved a stained-glass window from the Abbey. A depiction of Saint Peter with his sword. He gave the Queen the window and showed her Majesty what he claimed was the true sword of Saint Peter, saved from the abbey upon King Henry's devolution. Oh, yes, he pointed it out with great pride to all who visited."

Robert asked, "Did you ever hear him called Peter or Saint Peter?"

Eleanor chuckled. "It wouldn't surprise me. He is devoted to the papacy, the seat of Saint Peter. He would nearly rant on that the pope is Saint Peter, that is, the Spirit of Saint Peter fills the pope and gives him all authority in the earthly realm. As I said, not a man given to the simple joys of life. He is strident, a soldier crusading for the pope—whomever he may be."

Robert turned to Black. "I should have inquired of my wife rather than Lord Dorset."

Black laughed. "Please confirm, Lady Eleanor, the good Father is blonde of hair and beard?"

"Yes, why? Is that important?"

Claude Passant stood beside Madame de Vantelet directing

the cooks and kitchen staff in Saint James Palace. He picked up the first of many small leather pouches. "Fresh herbs and spices—new and different than your king has ever tried. And vegetables, sweet and fresh. Filled with flavor."

A cook replied, "King Charles favors meat and sweets. Vegetables are hard to digest and fit only for peasants."

Madame Vantelet interrupted. "The queen commands this feast of the latest French dishes. The best and tastiest vegetables from the gardens of the Louvre in Paris. Not coarse, peasant fare: sweet peas, young asparagus, cauliflower, young carrots, cabbage, radishes, and early vegetables. There will be cheese, crème fraiche, and truffles. And a new succulent beef, slow cooked in the red wine of Burgundy. Simmered with mushrooms. The new fare of the leading court of Europe, the court of Louis XIII!"

An English cook shook his head. "You will serve his Majesty, stew, and vegetables? Cabbages and radishes? Call it new but his Majesty will want his roast venison and game fowl as well."

Passant, the French chef, whispered in Madame Vantelet's ear. She said, "You can prepare the venison and game birds, but even these shall be flavored with herbs and spices not yet found in England. It is Queen Henrietta

Maria's and Queen Mother Marie's gift in honor of the new prince."

Henri stepped outside and found Robert in the courtyard. "Claude Passant does not cook. He does not speak to cooks. Madame Vantelet directs the meal. She appears knowledgeable. Passant brings herbs, spices, and vegetables from France. Also, truffles and common white mushrooms."

Robert replied, "Why bring common mushrooms? England has plenty. And spices? See to it every dish is tasted."

Henri nodded. "My thoughts. There is another small white mushroom, known as the 'death cap.' It looks the same but is deadly. Nightshade and hemlock are but two deadly herbs that have been mixed with spices. Aye, I will watch closely. Passant allows no one to touch his spice bags."

"And my two secret men?"

Henri nodded. "One is assigned as Passant's assistant. He is always at his side. The other will be chief of the bearers from the kitchen to the King's table."

Robert returned to his Whitehall townhouse. Eleanor called down as he entered. "You must dress quickly, Robbie. Christian and Lady Justine will coach with us to Saint James. We must be there by three. Dinner is at four. Come up and help me with my dress."

Robert bound up the stairs. "And Jacques Bellamy?"

"He will arrive with the French delegation. Has my green gown shrunk? Seems tighter than I recall. The bodice is particularly…"

Robert walked behind Eleanor, put his hands on her shoulders, bent over, and kissed the nape of her neck below her red hair worn up and pinned with jewels. He smiled at her image in the mirror. *She bore three children since last wearing this dress. I dare not say she is fuller, for indeed she is more beautiful than ever.*

Robert smiled. "You are beautiful, my love. Emerald green becomes you and adds to the sparkle of your green eyes and the radiance of your beautiful red hair. I am amazed that the Lord above has blessed me with one so, so…."

Eleanor smiled, and struggling with her bodice said, "Robbie, this no time for flattery, though I thank you for it. But my bosom is barely contained. It seems to overflow."

Robbie held back a laugh, kissed her head and said, "And here I thought perfection could not be improved! I know you will work magic with the bodice lace. I'm sure Lady Justine will help."

Eleanor looked up at Robert. "How I enjoyed flirting with you, Robbie. You were so easy, so disarmed by my charms. You still find me pretty?"

"More than pretty, truly beautiful in heart, body, and soul. I will always find you, as you say, disarming."

Eleanor smiled. "They will be here soon. Justine insisted on meeting here, saving us the time to pick them up."

Robert quickly dressed in the clothes Eleanor had laid out. No sooner had he pulled on his polished boots than Christian and Lady Justine were announced. Black was hardly recognizable in Robert's royal blue satin coat and gold waistcoat. A jewel-studded hat sat atop his head.

Justine hurried upstairs to help Eleanor. She knew just how to correct Eleanor's dress. A little lace and diamond ribbon and Eleanor was stunning, indeed daring, but within the bounds of accepted decency.

Eleanor came to the door and happily inspected Robert and Christian before gazing at Justine. Lady Justine was a woman who could never hide her natural elegance, a reflection of her truly noble soul. But a deep blue court gown of diamond studded satin and three layers of fine white lace collar regally supported her finely sculptured head. Her dark hair was coiffed high atop her fair face and her blue eyes which sparkled with warm grace. A lacework of diamonds and pearls fell across the deep decolletage of her bodice.

Smiling broadly Eleanor proclaimed, "Our coach

seems hardly a sufficient transport for such perfection!"

Robert had never seen Black smile so brightly.

Eleanor continued, "Such magnificent jewels!"

Justine nodded. "Jacques brought them from France. Every treasure of the House of Bellamy is now in England. But I want Marie de Medici to see the Huguenot noblewoman she betrayed still flourishes outside France."

Black was silent on the coach ride to Saint James. Known as a man skilled in masking his emotions, Black uncharacteristically fidgeted, his head bobbing as he peered out the window mentally marking the distance to the palace. Robert smiled at his friend. "Won't be long now. You know what is expected of you, I'm sure."

Lady Justine placed her hand on Black's arm. "You'll do fine. Royals are always more interested in themselves than the courtiers that attend them. Just don't pull out that vulgar fork."

Robert's brow lifted. "You brought a fork to a royal dinner?"

Black blurted, "Yes, I eat with a fork! Call me vulgar. I cannot bear greasy fingers. What if I must reach for a weapon? Or touch anything? Napkins? Filthy and never enough—and cuffs that smear everything they touch! It disgusts me!"

Lady Justine said softly. "Just for today, no fork. You may use a knife and a spoon. For me, Please."

Black nodded. "Of course. But tell me, why must we eat with our fingers?"

Lady Justine replied, "The church. I suppose because Jesus ate with fingers…Robert, you are a priest, why does the church say we are to eat with our fingers?"

Robert thought for a moment. "Why indeed? Certainly, it is never commanded in the Bible. The practice acknowledges that our food is a gift from God to be taken up in thanksgiving, much as we receive the blessing with open hands."

Black replied, "We are not asked to remove our gloves before receiving the blessing. And we thank God for the food before we eat. Certainly, I am no less thankful for the meal eating with a fork than with my fingers."

Robert laughed. "You challenge legalism in the church? You have a heart for reformation theology!"

Eleanor changed the subject. "Justine, have you met the Dowager Queen of France, Marie?"

"Many years ago. As a young woman of fifteen, my father brought me to Paris to be introduced at court. I remember her beauty. Oh, yes, a most beautiful woman, and elegant—but cold and aloof. She did not even glance at the nobles she received. They—we, were as invisible as the servants. It was as if no one else was in the room."

The coach passed through the tall, redbrick tower gate of Saint James Palace and stopped at the entrance at the far end of the courtyard. A servant opened the coach door and helped the ladies step down. The grand palace door was opened before them, and the four friends stepped inside and walked to the great staircase that filled the room. Another servant directed them. "Lord and Lady Montclair, Mister Fauconnier and Countess Bellamy, welcome. You will be directed to the Tapestry room at the top of the staircase."

The upstairs servant greeted them. "Lords and Ladies, please follow me." They were led past the Guard Room, through the Armory Room, and into the Tapestry Room, where they were announced. Immediately, Count Bellamy greeted his mother and friends. "Mother, Christian, Lord, and Lady Montclair, come meet the French Ambassador, the Marquis Chateuneof. He has graciously arranged our evening."

The Marquis bowed and kissed the hand of Lady Justine. "The stories of your beauty cannot prepare one for such perfection."

Standing straight and smiling at her face he added, "I have heard of the great sacrifice you made in service to France. It is hoped that this visit reintroduces you to the highest level of court life."

Lady Justine smiled. "It is my son, Count Bellamy, you may reward. What I did, I did for family and faith, not France."

The Marquise Chateuneof winced at the slight to her husband. But the Marquis smiled and replied, "What is France but the Bourbons, Spain and Austria, the Hapsburgs, and England the Tudors? We are all servants of these families."

Turning to Jacques, the Marquis said, "Perhaps Lord Montclair should meet the foreign minister?"

Jacques replied, "Yes, of course."

Jacques waited while the French Foreign Minister spoke with Dudley Carleton, Viscount of Dorchester and Principal Secretary for Foreign Affairs for King Charles. Once he caught the Foreign Minister's eye, he said, Lord Montclair, may I introduce Monsieur Claude Bouthillier, Foreign Minister to King Louis XIII. Foreign Minister, I present Lord Montclair, Lord Inquirer to King Charles."

Bouthillier smiled. "We have heard you are kept busy with a pesky printer. Shall I remove my gloves and show you my fingers are clean of ink? Forgive me, I should not make light of threats against your King. Cardinal Richelieu sends his assurance of the full support of France in the apprehension of any plotter against the throne of King Charles."

Robert smiled. "A pity the Cardinal could not attend himself. As a man of God, I would hear his views on the love of Christ and the brotherhood of believers—everywhere."

"Where I am, the Cardinal is. As for the brotherhood of believers, he would say not all brothers choose to live in the same house."

Robert and Black mixed with the other guests, Dudley Carleton, Viscount Dorchester and Frist Secretary to King Charles, Carleton's friend and fellow councilor, Viscount Thomas Wentworth, their wives, and William Laud, Bishop of London and Dean of the Chapel Royal, who would officiate at the christening.

Rejoining Lady Eleanor, Lady Justine, and Jacques Bellamy, Robert opined, "The guests more resemble two negotiation teams than a family about to celebrate a Christening."

Count Bellamy looked surprised. "But of course, that is why we come to this table. To make peace between France and England, two families and two nations joined in family ties."

Robert nodded. "To put an end to this Spanish treaty madness. But no Richelieu?"

Jacques laughed. "Marie, the Dowager Queen, despises Richelieu and has begged her son to discharge him. King Louis does not like the Cardinal but values his advice. That is why Richelieu sends his loyal Bouthillier, a man on good terms with both the King and Marie de Medici."

A guard entered the room and slammed his halberd

staff into the floor. "Charles, King of England, Ireland and Scotland and Queen Consort Henrietta Maria request you come to the table in the Queen's dining room."

CHAPTER 30

THE ROYAL TABLE

The guests made their way back through the armory and guardroom and into the Queen's apartment through a drawing room, and into her dining room. Jacques cheerfully said, "We are in for a treat! I had the great pleasure of tasting the cook's food."

Robert replied, "You have tasted this secret menu?"

Jacques nodded. "I, well the French delegation, was invited to the kitchen. Madame de Vantelet arranged it."

Robert nodded. "So you are a convert to eating vegetables like a peasant. How noble."

Jacques laughed. "Do you think students at The Sorbonne eat any better than you did at Cambridge? I am no royal. Of course, I eat vegetables. No. It was his roast, crusted in herbs, that delighted me. Seeing my pleasure, the French cook, Passant, gave me a pouch of the herbs. He said not all guests receive a well crusted portion. Take them—enjoy them at the banquet."

Jacques slapped Robert on the back. "A leather pouch full! Not just a sprinkling! Enough for many meals to come. I have it with me. Yes, quite surprising! But then he said—he seemed serious—he said, 'Say nothing. I will deny I ever gave them to you.'"

Robert replied, "I am told he is a new cook. What do you know of him?"

The young count replied, "It is true. The Dowager Queen, Marie, arranged his appointment. After word that the King and Dowager Queen would be Godparents to Prince Charles. This feast is meant as a gift—a taste of home for Queen Henrietta Maria."

A table was set for twenty-four with a card bearing the crests of a guest placed in front of each setting. Black found a beautifully drawn Falcon on a gauntleted arm on the card alongside the coroneted crest of Lady Justine. The guests stood silently at their assigned seats and waited. At last, the brightly uniformed guard stomped his halberd staff and announced, "His Majesty Louis, King of France, and her highness, Queen Marie."

Once Louis and Marie found their places. The halberd was again stomped, and the guard announced, "His Majesty, Charles, King of Great Britain and Ireland, and Her Majesty, Queen Henrietta Maria."

The royals were seated at the center of the table

across from each other. Once the royals were comfortable, Charles smiled and said, "Please, sit."

Queen Henrietta Marie spoke in French. "You are all most welcome at my table. Thank you for sharing this occasion with me. I welcome my dear brother and our mother to England. Thank you for graciously agreeing to be Godparents to our son, Charles, Prince of Wales, and one day King of England, Scotland, and Ireland. My brother has opened his palace garden in France and brought ingredients for the finest meal here. A taste of home for me, no, better—the newest from the leading cuisine of all the world. Enjoy!"

King Louis smiled. "Thank you, dear sister. May we lift our cups to the Prince!"

Charles raised his goblet. "To Prince Charles, rightful heir to the thrones of England, Scotland, and Ireland!"

The guests followed suit and toasted the infant prince.

Bishop Laud spoke. "If I may, your Majesties, give the blessing for the feast."

After grace, waiters stepped from behind the guests and set out crème fraiche with raisins, dried pear, and fresh cherries. Queen Henrietta spoke. "I am delighted to see my friend and one-time lady-in-waiting, Countess Montclair once again at my table. I should like to see you more often in court. Your great service to me, having only recently borne a child, has been an inspiration! I know I must carry on, unburdened by the distractions of motherhood. I will send him off, to a proper governess, away from the foul air of London. Yes, safe in the countryside where his Majesty and I may visit on occasion. You keep your figure well, Lady Montclair. Such beauty would be welcome among the courtiers."

Eleanor whispered, "Fresh air at 600 pounds, more than Robbie's emolument."

The queen asked, "Speak louder, my dear."

Eleanor smiled. "I said you are most gracious, Your Majesty. Indeed, the Montclair Castle countryside is preferable for my three children and most refreshing for Lord Montclair and me."

King Louis put down his spoon. "Brother-in-law, are we not family? This treaty you would have with Philip of Spain is not good for you or me. Yes, Spain dominates the new world and brings war upon all of Europe. King Philip promises you spoils from the Dutch but makes no promises for your sister's return to the Palatinate. King Gustavus Adolphus has the Emperor's army in retreat. Why even your Lords Leslie and Hamilton fight alongside the Swedes. We have made peace between us. We sit here as brothers. Do not join with my enemy."

Charles drank from his wine goblet. "As you say,

we sit here as brothers, at peace. And it is lasting peace that I seek. Yes, even peace with Spain and the safe return of Frederick and Elizabeth to Heidelberg. Cannot I be at peace with Spain and France?"

Charles picked up a cauliflower and bit into it. Turning his head behind the table, he spit it out.

The Dowager Queen Marie said, "It is an acquired taste."

Louis continued. "Spain is my enemy. Philip threatens me from the north and the south. A Spanish victory over the Dutch would free his army."

Louis shook his spoon as he spoke. "Hear me. Philip will not stop with the United Netherlands. No, with his Austrian Hapsburg cousins, he will continue until all of Europe, the new world, Africa, and yes England too, will be under the Hapsburg boot."

Charles looked at the cabbage and asparagus cooked in fat and said, "Bring me meat. I am no peasant!"

Marie de Medici smiled and said. "I must recognize another French noble, missing from the court in Paris. Dowager Countess Bellamy, mother to our diplomat in Berlin. I have heard of your work of mercy with our citizens, unfortunate women, here in London."

Lady Justine blushed. "Unfortunate citizens indeed. Their crime was to be protestant. Their fathers, brothers, and husbands, Huguenot nobles and leading men, the men you promised religious freedom and autonomy in return for supporting you in your feud with your son. You abandoned them to Richelieu's persecution. And what has your alliance with the cardinal given you? Has he proven loyal to you?"

Lady Justine turned to King Louis and said softly. "Forgive my intemperance, Your Majesty, but the turmoil in France was the making of two people, the dowager queen, and the ambitious Richelieu. I was forced—told my own husband held hostage—forced to use young French women to...."

Lady Justine stopped and lowered her eyes to hide the tears she could not stop.

Marie de Medici countered, "I know all about you. Your beauty is your only worth. Yes, you went from countess to courtesan. How many men did you accommodate? Did you leave for the convent? No! You live with your whores, and you married a commoner—a policeman, no doubt most comfortable with thieves and whores!"

Jacques and Black both rose. Lady Justine grabbed an arm of both and shook her head, no. She looked into King Louis' eyes and said, "Only by God's grace was my honor preserved. I have never broken my marriage vows."

King Louis looked at the two men and said. "There you have it, a virtuous woman. I have no quarrel with

Lady Bellamy."

A waiter set a bowl before King Charles. "I asked for meat. What is this? The King asked.

"Beef, your Majesty, slow cooked, tender with wine and mushrooms. The tenderest and most savory of meats."

Charles tried the beef and nodded. "Indeed, most tasty. It is a proper dish for when I am old and lose my teeth. Give me a good roast, well-seasoned that I might tear through it lustily!"

Marie de Medici commanded the head server, "Tell Monsieur Passat to bring the roast venison for his Majesty King Charles. Yes, and a carving table. He shall see that is warm and the best cut made for my son-in-law."

Soon the dining room was filled with the succulent aroma of roast venison. The smell of the fat and rich herb crust was even more enticing than Jacques described to Robert. Two men wheeled the slow-roasted stag on a carving table followed by Marie's new cook, Claude Passant.

The Dowager Queen Marie said, "His Majesty King Charles would taste your roast. The best cut should be his."

Passant bowed. "Oui, your Majesty, the sweet meat, the tenderloin."

As Passant lifted his knife, the King's Chamberlain asked, "Has it been tasted?"

The cook bowed. "I should be honored," and he cut a small portion from the hind quarter and ate it. He then carefully carved the tenderloin from beneath the spine under the chest and set it on a plate for the King.

Marie di Medici said, "The tenderloin is not crusted. Is His Majesty King Charles to be denied the savory spices of the crust?"

Passant shrugged. "It cannot be helped. And the sweet meat is most tender and delightful."

Marie de Medici retorted, "Surely, you have more spice? It is the new spices and new cuisine that I gift to my daughter's husband. Perhaps in the kitchen?"

Robert watched Passant turn to Jacques, raise an eyebrow, and reply to Marie de Medici, "The meat would grow cold. Let His Majesty enjoy the sweet meat and later, if His Majesty has not eaten his fill, a tougher, yet crusted cut."

Jacques interrupted, "I have a pouch of the spices. You may season the sweet meat, the most tender and flavorful."

Bellamy handed the pouch of spices to Passant. "Merci." And Passant wordlessly rubbed them into the tenderloin and placed the plate before King Charles. "Your Majesty, the best in tenderness and new herb spices."

Robert interrupted, "It should be tasted. Monsieur Passant, taste the newly spiced meat."

Passant stiffened and then said. "I will not. I cannot speak for these spices. They are from Count Bellamy or who knows where."

Jacques answered, "But they are yours. You gave them to me!"

Passant shook his head. "No! I deny it! I do not know where…."

Robert demanded, "Passant you will taste the spiced tenderloin. Count Bellamy's spice pouch is from your kitchen."

Passant shook his head. "No. I will not!"

Robert rose and walked around the table to Passant. "You will taste the food, or it will be forced down your throat."

Mister Black and the head server, one of Robert's men, quickly came behind Passant and seized his arms. Then Black pulled Claude Passant's head back and with his right hand squeezed Passant's jaw and opened his mouth.

Passant gurgled loudly. "I will talk! It was the Dowager Queen Marie. She forced me to poison King Charles. Spare me! It is Marie de Medici who acts!"

CHAPTER 31
THE CHRISTENING

The Chapel Royal at Saint James Palace resembled the choir of a large Anglican church or cathedral. Long and narrow, a wall of stained glass above the finely carved paneling surrounding the altar, flooded the room with glorious colored light. Two rows of pew boxes lit by candles faced the center aisle. The royal box was above at the rear of the chapel. The Queen's ladies-in-waiting, the King's Privy Council, and the few privileged guests were seated in the choir.

Robert smiled at Eleanor when their eyes met. He then turned his gaze to the royal box as King Charles, Queen Henrietta Maria, King Louis, and Dowager Queen Marie de Medici entered and took their seats. *She's here. After all that happened last night. Claude Passant is in a Tower dungeon, but she is here.*

Eleanor's eyes followed Roberts, and she, too, watched the royal party. *How haughty Marie appears. And there are no smiles. How strange for me to pity Henrietta Maria; after finding the love of her husband, she is betrayed by her own mother. I wonder what was said after they stomped off last night, and we were all sent home.*

With the royal party seated, Bishop Laud commenced the Daily Morning Prayer. "Grace to you and peace from God our Father and the Lord Jesus Christ." He recited the confession, led the Invitatory, Venite, Jubilate, and Pasha Nostrum before reading a psalm. After the Te Deum Laudamus, the Benedictus Es, and Domine, he led the congregation in the Apostles' Creed and the Lord's Prayer followed by the Collect of the Day and the General Thanksgiving. Bishop Laud was strong on liturgy and prayer but did not favor sermons and gave none. When at last he said, "Let us Thank the Lord," the congregation responded, "Thanks be to God!"

The congregation remained seated as Bishop Laud stepped down and Archbishop Abbot rose from the Bishop's throne and said, "The candidate for Holy Baptism will now be presented."

The royal party stood and made their way down the stairs to the center aisle and walked to the altar. Robert smiled. *Laud is burning inside. He has taken Abbot's seat in the council, installed himself as the King's chaplain, but his enemy, George Abbot, is still the Archbishop, still primate and the only priest worthy to Baptize Prince Charles.*

King Charles took the infant from Henrietta Maria's arms and replied, "I present Charles Tudor, Prince of Wales, to receive the sacrament of Baptism."

It was strange for everyone who attended the previous feast to see and hear Marie de Medici, stand as a god parent and vow to wholeheartedly guide the welfare of the child's soul. Yet she could be heard responding to the liturgy, and the godparents' confession of faith. Archbishop Abbot baptized the young prince and made the sign of the cross on his forehead, proclaiming, "You are sealed by the Holy Ghost in baptism and marked as Christ's own forever."

After a prayer the Archbishop lifted his arms in benediction. "Go forth into the world in peace, be of good courage, and fight the good fight of faith, that you may finish your course with joy; and the blessing of God Almighty, the Father, the Son and the Holy Ghost, be among you, and remain with you, always. Amen."

The congregation waited as the royal party made their exit. Robert felt his heart warm as he waited. *Yes Lord, peace. Give us peace and courage to fight, to finish the course with joy. I pray for them but most of all I pray for the young prince born into a family that knows no peace.*

Robert sighed. *When can I go home, Lord—home to the peace and joy of my family?*

After the service. The young prince was returned to

the care of his wet nurse in the Saint James Palace nursery. Robert had two hours before the royal party would barge down the Tyburn River to the Thames and to the Banqueting house at Whitehall Palace. Black would follow the procession on horseback instructing the watchers and secret men as he went. Robert and Eleanor accompanied Count Bellamy and Lady Justine in Eleanor's coach back to their Whitehall Townhouse.

When they were all seated, Eleanor said, "I'm happy to have this short time together before the celebration this evening. Robbie and I will barge with the royal party, but our coach is yours this evening."

Turning to Robert she continued, "Robbie will see that Christian is there on time as well."

Lady Justine smiled. "You have been most kind. Good friends to Christian and me. Did you see Marie de Medici's face? Oh, to have been a mouse in the room when King Louis and King Charles questioned her! After stirring rebellion against her son, she orders the assassination of her daughter's husband? Treachery to two kings!"

Jacques nodded. "She has done more to unify Charles and Louis than any treaty delegation. King Louis has put her under guard in the palace."

Surprised, Eleanor replied, "King Louis not Charles?"

Robert answered, "Charles does not seek war

against France. He waits for Louis to act."

Jacques nodded. "As you say. And King Louis has instructed the delegation to escort Marie de Medici to the Luxembourg Palace in Paris where she is to wait under house arrest. Transport is being arranged as we speak. King Louis and King Charles have come to an agreement. Charles will withdraw from his secret treaty with Spain and allow more English soldiers to be recruited for service with the Swedish army. France will fund them, and King Louis gifts Charles fifty thousand louis d'or…."

"Louis d'or?" Eleanor asked.

"The same as a Pistole, close to your English Pound Sterling—to honor the birth of his nephew, the Prince of Wales," Jacques answered.

Robert spoke. "King Charles must, at last, be happy. A new and solid alliance that offers hope for his sister's Palatinate prevents a costly Naval war against the Dutch, recruits an army at no cost to him, and fills his coffers. Best of all, it puts to rest the threats against his life and the life of the young prince—no more pamphlets promising a bounty on their lives."

Eleanor replied, "You believe Marie de Medici is behind the pamphleteering?"

Robert explained. "Marie is most skilled in recruiting others to work her will. She convinced the Huguenot nobles to rebel, to support her insatiable desire for power in return for empty promises of toleration and autonomy. You will see that she was behind Eltonhead and Rusdorf, who had fled to the continent. Others were used unknowingly, but used they were. Yes, I am certain I will uncover every detail, but Marie de Medici is the true villain."

Lady Justine asked, "What will become of Claude Passant?"

Robert replied, "We will make inquiries concerning the alleged coercion, though greed appears his true motivation. Perhaps King Charles shall show mercy and allow him to be hanged."

Jacques replied, "Mercy?"

Robert answered, "This is England. The sentence for his crime is to be hanged, drawn and quartered. A most painful and humiliating death."

The coach stopped in front of the Montclair townhouse. Robert put a hand on Jacques' arm. "You should know, my friend, Marie de Medici told Passant to give you the herbs. They planned that the spices would not be on the sweet meat. If you had not offered first, on Marie's insistence, he would have asked you. They meant for you to die as the assassin."

Count Bellamy nodded. "I had considered the same last night. God has saved me for a purpose."

Lady Justine hugged her son. "What will you do?"

He kissed his mother. "Marie de Medici's plan has come to nought. And now with Pierre Brulart retired, I have no friends in court. Do not worry, mother. As it is written, 'Be wise as serpents and innocent as doves.' But my future is not in France."

Robert opened the door and stepped out. Eleanor said, "We leave you here to refresh before the banquet. Thomas will see to your needs."

With the Bellamys inside, Robert told the driver, "Take us to Saint James then return here. You will drive the Count and Dowager Countess Bellamy to the Banqueting house at four."

As the coach made its way slowly through London, Robert suddenly looked up, eyes wide, he banged on the ceiling, stuck his head out the window and shouted, "With all speed, I must get to Saint James at once!"

Eleanor implored, "Robbie, what is it?"

Robert stared in Eleanor's eyes and said. "How could I have missed it? He must act today. The King's life is in danger,"

"Who Robbie? Who will act?"

"Marie's accomplice—the Pamphleteer!"

Eleanor stared back with blank eyes.

Robert continued, "The man who hates Charles more than any other, yet loves Queen Henrietta. The man who wrote the pamphlets, inspired to act with Marie de

Medici. The man with access to the French diplomatic pouch. The man who understands the state of religion in England—who speaks and writes English and French. He has access to the royal schedule. He knew where the king would meet Sir John Wynter and had early knowledge of Prince Charles' governess. He must act today before he is found out—for certainly, neither king will protect him."

The coach came to a stop at Saint James Palace.

As Robert sprang from the coach Eleanor called after Robert, "Not the Earl of Dorset, Edward Sackville?"

Robert was gone, already running into the palace.

Eleanor's head fell back against the cushioned seat back. A slow sigh moved across her lips, followed by the soft words, "Of course. Saint Peter."

CHAPTER 32
THE ROYAL PROCESSION

Robert made his way up the staircase around the corridor towards the Queen's apartments to the chamber of the Queen's Chancellor, Lord Dorset. Not stopping to knock, he entered to find Mister Black standing over Edward Sackville.

"You too, Montclair?" Sackville called out.

Black spoke over him. "You're looking for Saint Peter, the papist priest, Robert Philip. Afraid we're too late. Ran off while the royal party was at the Christening. I've searched his chamber and apartment. A witness saw him leave through a servant's door before noon. Lord Dorset was about to tell me of his habits—friends, relatives, someplace he might go."

Robert shook his head. "No time for that now. He is not going on the run. He intends to act. He knows the royals will barge on the Thames, and parade downriver to

London Bridge in celebration before returning to the Banqueting House at Whitehall Palace. Yes, he will act and gladly accept martyrdom."

Lord Dorset interrupted, "Father Philip is a fanatic. He would willingly die for his Saint Peter, the pope. Though the pope surely would not condone his regicide."

Robert continued, "I will warn the bargemaster and royal watermen. Order the Thames closed to traffic until the royals reach the Banqueting House. Have the watchers secure the river. No boats. Search the shops and houses on London bridge. I will have the bargemaster maintain a safe distance. I want watchers at the mouths of the Tyburn and Holborn. Concentrate on the river. Yes, have the royal watermen put some of our men on the other side. I have requested Lord Conway include me among the Privy Council on the royal barge, but the Royal Bargemaster must approve. You will lead the men on shore."

Black moved to leave. Robert called after him. "When you searched, did you find the sword of Saint Peter?"

Black replied, "A gilded box so marked, was empty. And handwritten letters—drafts of the pamphlets. He no longer hides his intentions."

Before Robert could reply, Black looked up and said, "At the printing press. The boat. The covered rowboat at the Holborn River warehouse. I will start there."

Robert found the bargemaster overseeing his royal watermen preparing the barges. "I am Earl of Montclair, his Majesty's Lord Inquirer…."

"I know ye, your lordship. You interrupt my preparations, my watermen are true men,"

Robert nodded. "Aye, no doubt they are. But a scoundrel is about with evil intent. I must be aboard the royal barge."

The bargemaster straightened up and looked into Robert's eyes. "Evil intent? The watermen would give their lives to protect the King. And there will be guards—armed veterans. The King will be safe."

"They do not know this man. He will not show himself. Should I report that the bargemaster refuses his Majesty's Lord Inquirer?"

The bargemaster sighed. "There are the musicians, nay you would spoil the music. Aye, one more waterman will not be noticed. Come with me. I'll fit you with a proper kit."

"Thank you, but I shall accompany Lord Conway and the Privy Council."

The bargemaster nodded. "We have one hour to the high tide, and we depart."

Robert implored, "You know to stay well off the London Bridge."

The bargemaster replied. "His Majesty parades to

be seen by his subjects. The river is the best and safest route in London. We will stay near the center of the river, passing close only to Westminster. The King wishes to honor his officials and gentry who could not be accommodated at the Banqueting House. The Tyburn is narrow in its approach to the Thames at Westminster. In any regard, we must pass in a single line as we round Westminster. It is the normal practice to control who views from there."

Robert nodded. "Aye, I know Westminster was once nothing more than a gravel island in the delta of the Tyburn where it enters the Thames. A wonder that it has not sunk for the weight of the stone and brick! Yet, despite the stone walls, a villain with knowledge of the court could enter. Precisely why I must be aboard the royal barge. After Westminster?"

"After rowing past the lesser nobles and gentry we parade the center of the river, but will not go under London bridge. We shall come about and row directly to the privy landing at Whitehall Palace. Many more will view from Whitehall. An hour, no more than two, on the river. The King commands when he tires of the water music."

While Robert waited with Lord Conway and the Privy Council, Black rode to the Holborn River warehouse where his fears were realized. The small rowboat used to smuggle the pamphlets was gone. No one took notice of the man who rowed downriver. Hurrying through the busy warehouse road, Black found his watcher standing in the middle of the Fleet Street bridge over the Holborn before it flowed into the Thames.

"A small boat, one man at the oars—did it pass under the bridge?" He asked impatiently.

The watcher replied, "No boats have passed since the Thames was closed an hour ago."

Blacked asked, "Before the river closed, a man at oars, blonde of hair and beard? Perhaps a man hooded?"

"I have been here since noon. Many boats passed before the closure. No one blonde as the suspect we seek, nor a lone man robed and hooded—I surely would have uncovered him. No, Mister Black, he has not passed since I arrived."

Black showed rare emotion, swearing under his breath. "He is hours ahead of us. He could be anywhere on the river. Stay here until dusk. If we fail, he may return this way."

Black crossed over the bridge and rode to Westminster Palace.

At Saint James Palace, the musicians boarded the royal barge. At seventy-five feet long, the clinker-built boat, with narrow overlapped planking, resembled a Viking longship. The hull and interior were brightly painted in Tudor red and white, with gilded gunwales running from the low spindled bow to the high narrow stern where a short mast carried a large silk flag bearing the royal coat of arms. The Bargemaster steered from a sweep oar abaft the stern canopied royal cabin. Five massive oars on each side were drawn by twenty royal watermen. The musicians took their places between the watermen. The Privy Council and ladies-in-waiting took their places between the royal canopy and the watermen. The sight of Eleanor radiant in her gown brought a smile to Robert's face and, for a few happy moments, took his mind off the danger that lay ahead. Three more barges filled with favored courtiers.

Two barges filled with palace guards departed when the royal party appeared at the landing. Noticeably absent was Marie de Medici. Queen Henrietta Maria was helped aboard first, followed by King Louis and King Charles. The band began to play as the royal barge pushed off from the landing and the watermen silently pulled water.

Robert listened past the music for any sound ashore on either side of the boat. They passed under bridges that crisscrossed the royal park. The narrow river made its way towards Whitehall where it turned and passed behind the Palace of Westminster, the towering roof of the abbey recognizable to all who visit London. The music echoed as the royal barge passed under two more bridges accessing the back gates of the Palace of Westminster's walls. Everything appeared just as it should. The barge made the last turn in the river, and passed under the last bridge and entered the wide Thames.

Black had made his way to Westminster, stopping at the watermen's stairs at the lower corner of the palace yard before making his way to the center courtyard and the edge of the peers' stairway to the river. Everything seemed to be in order. His watchers and the royal guards reported, "All's well."

The royal watermen pulled harder on their oars and the Bargemaster took large bites of brown water as he pushed lustily on the steering oar, turning the barge to port, close in front of Westminster Palace. The barge moved past the old King's apartments, now the chambers of the King's Bench. As they passed beneath the window of Robert's Westminster chamber, the Bargemaster called "Oars!" The oars at once were lifted parallel to the water and the boat glided in front of the large courtyard in the center of the palace grounds. A thousand voices shouted "Huzzah, Huzzah!" as the royals appeared. King Charles, King Louis and Queen Henrietta Maria acknowledged the crown officials with softly waving hands. The cheers warmed King Charles' heart.

Just as the Bargemaster called out, "Pull water,"

and the oars fell back into the river, a figure in a black robe and hood ran out from the crowd, onto the landing at the top of the peers' stairs. Black was on him in an instant. A watcher and a guard quickly followed. Landing hard on the stone, a young voice screamed, "Stop! I meant no harm! Please don't hurt me! I just wanted to see them up close. Queen Henrietta Maria—she is pretty, not the witch I heard her called."

Black turned the young man over and pulled open his robe and pulled off his hood. "Who are ye, lad? How did you get in the palace?"

"I'm Peter, Peter Bates. I sing in the choir at Saint Margaret's here in the palace. I meant no harm."

A priest came up from behind. "Aye, he is Peter Bates. One of the choirboys."

Black let go of the boy and hurried off to his horse.

The royal barge was moving towards the middle of the river, the musicians playing jubilantly. Robert took his gaze from the commotion on Westminster's Thames River stairs and caught the worried eyes of Eleanor seated near the Queen. He sighed and shook his head before turning to Lord Conway. "Not to worry, My Lord. My men are at the ready."

Lord Conway replied, "For your sake, I pray it is as you say."

The two guard barges took up stations on each side

of the royal barge. The other barges, filled with favorite courtiers, followed along behind. The music carried over the water and announced the coming of the royal barge parade. King Louis took in the sights. Paris had the Seine, but it was nothing like the Thames in London, the main thoroughfare of English royalty. Soon London Bridge was in sight. No traffic was visible, the road down the center was obscured by houses and shops built three and four stories high. Every window in every house was open, and people crowded to get a glimpse of the royals. Huzzahs and whistles drowned out the royal musicians as the royal barge neared the ancient span and then swung around and headed back upriver towards Whitehall Palace.

Robert strained to see beneath the many arches that supported the bridge, looking for any sign of a boat or movement that implied a threat. He saw nothing. *Where is he? Perhaps he did run. A coward in fear of his life. There is yet the Banqueting House, but that is most secure.*

Robert scanned the shoreline, the river and even the other barges in the parade. Nothing appeared out of place. The royal barge neared Whitehall Palace and the King nodded to the Bargemaster who immediately steered a course for the palace stairs. It would be an easy landing as the high tide was just beginning to ebb. The royal barge could come alongside the top of the landing built out into the river.

Black stood on the landing, waiting. The barges ferrying Saint James Palace guards moved offshore of the royal barge protecting against any threat from the river while Whitehall Palace guards formed a corridor from the landing to the palace entrance. The order was given, "Raise oars!" Well drilled watermen pointed ten heavy oars vertical in unison. Immediately docking lines were passed fore and aft. As the barge was brought tight against the palace stairs, a small boat silently slipped from beneath the arched abutment and pilings of the landing. A hand reached from the small boat and grasped the gunwale of the royal barge pulling the small boat alongside. Royals and courtiers alike watched in horror as a man swung over the gunwale and jumped aboard the barge alongside the canopied royal cabin. Surprised guards dare not shoot for fear of killing a king.

It's him. The priest, our mysterious Saint Peter! Robert scrambled towards the intruder but Black, jumping from the dock, was there first. A pistol shot rang out and Black fell to one knee. The priest, his blonde hair and beard bright in the afternoon sun, dropped his pistol and drew a sword from his belt. As Black struggled to stand, he parried the sword stroke at the hilt with his bare hand. But the frenzied priest would not yield and pushed hard against Black. Bleeding from his side and his wrist, Black began to fall back towards the landing. Robert was now on them. He grabbed the sword hand of the priest as he kneed him in the groin and forced the man down.

In a clear Scottish Brogue, Father Robert Philip called out, "Why God, why won't this apostate king die? I did it for you Lord and for Henrietta Maria."

Robert turned the sword on the priest, kicking and forcing him down on his back. With the point of the sword at the crying priest's throat, Robert called out, "Your Majesty…."

King Charles did not wait. "I want him alive. I will invite the pope himself to see this priest hanged, drawn, and quartered!"

King Louis turned Henrietta Maria and said, "Sister, do you desire mercy on your priest? He is yours by wedding contract."

Robert stood watching the royals. The sword's point still at the assassin's throat. The queen stared at her confessor. "There are other priests."

Father Philip let out a loud scream, grabbed Robert's hands and with all his strength pulled the sword down into his neck. The scream became a gurgle as blood gushed from his mouth and sword-pierced throat.

CHAPTER 33
THE PAPERWORK

For once, Robert had Lord Conway's undivided attention. Conway sat behind his desk with Robert's report before him. "All of this came from Queen Marie de Medici's manipulation? I see how the renegade priest, Father Robert Philip, could be manipulated, and he had access to closely held information as the Queen's confessor, but did he recruit the others, Eltonhead, Rusdorf, Wynter, and even Felim O'Neil? And when did it start? What made her plot against her daughter's husband? Queen Henrietta Maria had won both the King's heart and his ear. Oppression against Catholics had ceased. Catholic nobles are accepted as loyal to the crown."

Robert replied, "What is Marie de Medici's relationship with Cardinal Richelieu? You have told me their cooperation has come to an end—again they feud.

Richelieu has chosen a different path for France, the alliance with Sweden, the Dutch, and the protestant Electors, against the Hapsburgs. As Louis' chief minister, he has no need for Marie and her desire for a de Medici French empire. I shall tell you why this plot has ended, but you must know, there are others that I have not recorded, unintended, but collaborators, nonetheless. Chief among them, you Lord Conway—you shared secrets with your wife, and she with her brother, Eltonhead."

Conway sighed. "Yes, I feared as much when Eltonhead was named. I must resign."

Robert replied, "There is no need to name her. So many in court are careless with secrets, The queen herself, in confession—Lord Dorset, her chancellor. Good people, serving with honor. No. We shall lay the connections through Marie and the priest."

Conway smiled meekly. "Rusdorf remains free and Felim O'Neil?"

Robert spoke. "Rusdorf knows the plot has failed. It is known that the queen and the priest tried to convert young Rusdorf to Catholicism—failing his conversion they saw his dedication to Louise Julianna of Nassau. He was led to believe and act for the mother of Prince Elector Frederick. He was dedicated to elevating her daughter-in-law, Elizabeth, and her grandchildren, the young princes of the Palatinate. But that opportunity became more desperate when the Prince of Wales was born. Marie de Medici and Father Philip could not countenance murdering the prince. That is when they compelled Eltonhead to arrange a kidnapping instead. Marie de Medici saw her daughter in Marie's own experience—Queen, and regent until her son, raised Catholic in Ireland, returned. But O'Neil's only hope was to hide the child in Ireland with the Queen's help. That will not happen. O'Neil is in hiding. His capture will come."

Conway responded, "And Verstegen and Wynter served their purpose in printing and distributing the pamphlets—they knew only that they served English Catholics with books and pamphlets, totally unaware that their printing press was being used by Rusdorf and Eltonhead. And the content, penned by Father Robert Philip—first appealing to protestants and non-conformists, then Catholics, meant to compel any discontented Englishman to regicide, but also to distract from the source. So many people deceived."

"Marie de Medici is a master of deceit. Were she not the Dowager Queen of France she would surely pay with her life. It is sure to catch up to her one day."

Conway smiled. "You have not heard? Marie de Medici has been exiled to the Chateau de Compiegne. She is under house arrest—never to leave. Richelieu has defeated her. He won both the trust of King Louis and the

French alliance with England and with all protestant Europe."

Robert replied, "I believe Richelieu was on to Marie's plan all along. He arranged for Count Bellamy's visit and Pierre Brulart's letter. He intended for me to see a French connection to Rusdorf and the Loise Julianna. He trusted we would uncover Father Philip. Cardinal Richelieu is the true grandmaster manipulator. He allowed Marie de Medici to do his will and seal her own fate."

Robert paused. "My Lord, the King is safe. England is on a course agreeable to parliament and loyal subjects. Perhaps it is time I go home and…."

"I shall hear no more now. I tell you this. The King has commanded that you appear before him for recognition…."

"Not unless Mister Black is recognized as well."

"Yes, Black as well. He is recovered, is he not?"

"Aye, though he is well bandaged upon wrist and torso. The ball passed through his side; the wound cauterized by a skilled surgeon. Fit enough for honors."

"Good. Sunday next. Whitehall Palace. The Countess Montclair and the Dowager Countess Bellamy as well. See that your Master Inquirer is properly dressed. Afterward, we shall speak again."

Robert asked, "And my watchers and secret men? The recognition is theirs as well."

"Aye, they may attend. But not as beggars and vagabonds—presentable and quiet."

Robert laughed. "They are skilled at remaining unnoticed."

Sunday morning, Robert, Eleanor, Black, and Lady Justine made the short coach ride to Whitehall Palace. Along the way, a grimacing Mister Black, clutched his side and said, "Not my place, Sir Robert. I'm no noble…"

Lady Justine interrupted, "Never say such a thing! True nobility lies within the heart and soul! A heart with love for justice and righteousness and the soul of a servant. It is pity aristocrats do not honor the truly noble."

Black squeezed his wife's hand. "They recognize it in you, my dear."

Then turning to Robert, he asked, "Did you recover the sword? Is it truly the sword of Saint Peter?"

Robert smiled. "Indeed. I sent it to Cambridge, to an expert in antiquities. Seems the steel is wrong. Not Damascus, or Roman—inferior steel of old Viking origin. As fraudulent as his faith."

At the palace, they were escorted to the King's box at the Chapel Royal for worship. Only following worship did the Catholic Queen Henrietta Maria enter. With the Queen at his side, King Charles walked forward, stopping in front of the altar rail. A page slipped a robe of ermine over his shoulders, gave him his scepter, and stood behind him holding a sword. Robert and Black were led to the center of the chapel. Ladies Eleanor and Justine followed behind.

The herald called out, "Master Inquirer Christian Fauconnier come forward and be recognized."

Why must I be first? I will surely make a fool of myself, Black thought as he nervously stepped forward and kneeled before the King.

King Charles took the sword from the Lord Conway, touched the blade to Black's shoulder, and said. "I dub you Sir Christian Fauconnier. I grant you the title, Baron Fauconnier. Rise, Sir Christian."

Black stood up on trembling feet. King Charles continued, "You have proven your loyalty and your skill. Today I name you Lord Inquirer."

Black managed to say, "I am honored, your Majesty." He bowed and slowly backed away. He could not see the smile and tears of Lady Justine and his dear friends.

The herald called out. "Lord Inquirer Montclair, step forward to be recognized."

Robert made his way forward and knelt before the King.

"Lord Montclair, you have proven your loyalty and invaluable service to me and my son, the Prince of Wales. I appoint you Lord Inquirer General, and Lord Lieutenant of the Star Chamber. You will preside over Star Chamber Inquiries and ensure the Lord Inquirer is resourced to safeguard England. Well done, Montclair!"

Robert replied, "I am honored, Majesty. I live to serve."

After the King and Queen exited the chapel, Lord Conway, president of the Privy Council introduced Lord Montclair and Lord Fauconnier to the other Lords of the Privy Council. Conway smiled and said, "Robert, I could not—the Privy Council could not—lose you. Your service is reserved for the highest inquiries in the realm. And with Lord Fauconnier as Lord Inquirer, a most deserving and capable man, your load is lessened. You can take your leave at Montclair Castle until called upon, assured Lord Fauconnier guards the state."

Lord Conway laughed. "Take cheer my friend, his Majesty considered you for the Privy Council itself. It would have meant a rare event to see Montclair Castle again. And you, Lord Fauconnier, no more Mister Black, and have Lady Fauconnier, a woman of impeccable taste, choose your clothes."

Sir Christian shook his head. "Never, never in my dreams did I think...."

Lord Conway interrupted. "It is the best thing his Majesty has done. High reward for the right man—Oh, let me not forget, this."

Conway pulled a document with a royal seal from his coat. "Your title, your warrant, and emolument, six hundred a year, as Lord Inquirer and the estate he grants you with the title, Grayling Priory in London. A small estate, little more than ruins, but with it, fine lands in the Lesnes Forest. Queen Henrietta Maria insisted on another priory for Lady Justine's work."

Lady Justine stepped up and Kissed Black's cheek, She put her arm around him and said, "You may escort Baroness Fauconnier to her coach."

Christian replied, "Baroness Fauconnier? Not the Dowager Countess Bellamy?"

She smiled. "To Jacques, I will always be his Dowager Countess, but in England, I am a Baroness Fauconnier."

Eleanor chuckled. "To your friends you are always Lady Justine."

Robert was about to speak, but Christian cut him off. "At least you, Sir Robert can still call me Black."

Robert nodded. "When you call me Robbie."

Then turning to the guests, all watchers and secret men, Robert called out, "Where is Lynch? My red pennant!"

Lynch walked forward. Robert looked at Sir Christian. "Lord Inquirer instruct your new Master Inquirer—charge him to lead our way to drink!"

Lynch hugged first Black and then Robert before quipping, "Aye, remember the Irishman only when it comes time to drink!"

As the rejoicing watchers and secret men escorted Lord Fauconnier and Master Inquirer Lynch out of the Chapel Royal, Lord Conway took Robert's arm and said softly. "A word, my friend, before you join your men."

Robert smiled at Eleanor. "Please go ahead. I will join you outside."

Eleanor walked ahead with Lady Justine.

Alone with Robert, Conway reached inside his coat and pulled out a letter with the royal seal. Lord Conway handed it to Robert saying, "His Majesty agreed to 2500 pounds for the Abbey and Lesness estate. Lord Fauconnier's title is well earned; the King deems this a loan, the treasury being what it is."

Robert smiled. "Lord Fauconnier is not to know. Tell me, has King Charles ever repaid a loan? Has he ever granted a title not paid for by others?"

Conway shook his head and laughed. "There is the Lord Treasurer, but then Weston uncovered the King's ancient prerogative for the distraint of knighthood, not used in centuries. And his successful defense of expanding the ship tax brought the King wealth far in excess of the Treasurer's emolument. His Majesty would find rewarding others from the treasury a novel idea."

Robert nodded. "I thank God, not King Charles, that through this ordeal, England is steered back on a safe course. As the Bible teaches, 'Be sure your sin will find you out.' So, I fear one day King Charles will be called to account for stopping his ears to the cries of his people, the widows and orphans, the displaced, the wounded and the families of the dead, and the just men imprisoned unfairly."

CHAPTER 34
MONTCLAIR CELEBRATION

The morning sun highlighted Robert's silver hair as he stood before the altar of Montclair Church. *What a joy, Lord, it is to be here today! My soul is filled with joy and peace. Happy faces, and two people so very much in love! Thank you, Lord!*

Robert looked down at the bride and groom standing before him and began. "Dearly beloved: We are gathered together in the presence of God to witness and bless the joining together of this man and this woman in holy matrimony."

Eleanor was seated beside her mother, Lady Anne, behind the beaming Edward and Mary Barkley, Lord, and Lady Cawmills. Across the aisle sat Molly Gibbs and her children. A rotund middle-aged gentleman snuggled close beside her.

Father Robert Curtis recited from the Book of

Common Prayer, his eyes moving from the nervous couple to his dear Eleanor. "The union of husband and wife in heart, body, and mind was ordained by God: for the procreation of children and their nurture in the knowledge and love of the Lord; for mutual joy, and for help and comfort given one another in prosperity and adversity, to maintain purity, so that husbands and wives, with all the household of God, might serve as holy and undefiled members of the Body of Christ; and for the upbuilding of Christ's kingdom in family, church, and society, to the praise of His holy Name."

The two young lovers straightened, gazing into each other's eyes when Robert asked, "Do you, Paul Hawkins have this woman, Rachel Gibbs to be your wife? Will you love her, honor her, comfort her, and keep her, in sickness and health; and forsaking all others, be faithful to her as long as you both shall live?"

The Reverend Paul Hawkins, vicar of Montclair Church looked into Rachel Gibbs beautiful brown eyes and answered, "I will."

"Will you, Rachel Gibbs, have this man, Paul Hawkins...."

The congregation clapped when they heard Molly's strong, "I will."

Robert's eyes caught Eleanor, smiling lovingly, not at the happy newlyweds, but at the man she adored officiating this holy and joyous event. As she swept away a tear, she thought, *I'm hopelessly in love with a country vicar. I do not want to share him with a vainglorious king anymore.*

Eleanor and Robert hosted a reception in Montclair Castle. Robert was at peace, catching up with friends and family. James Gibbs shared his joy at being accepted to study at Cambridge University. Molly Gibbs introduced Robert to the Lord Mayor of Lincoln who was becoming more than a business partner with Molly in a whiskey distillery, to the great relief of Brisby.

As the bride and groom beamed, Eleanor commented to Robert. "A good marriage. Rachel has chosen love and a good man over wealth and privilege. And James, too, a fine lad. I am happy to see Molly Gibbs has moved to Lincoln."

Lady Anne whispered, "Missus Gibbs has found a like-minded partner in the Lord Mayor for her enterprise. Not a young woman either. Not one to gossip, but a partnership with benefits. She has other skills from what I hear."

Eleanor scolded, "Mother! I'll hear no more of that!"

Wilhelm and Katharina Hahn approached with their son Emil. Will hugged Robert. "It has been too long my friend. Come, visit us, see the work the Lord blesses. The hospital, orphanage, and home for the elderly—we're expanding as is the junior guild…"

"Junior guild?" Robert asked.

"I will not call it a workhouse! No! We added more crafts. Yes, with the help of our brothers and sisters, refugees from Germany, we teach nearly every trade and craft. Ja! It is a junior guild! Robert, you must visit Berwick-upon-Tweed and convince the guildhall to support us. You are Viscount Berwick, and Baron of Tweedbridge, and a guild member. They will listen to you!"

Robert smiled. "Aye, my friend, I have longed to visit you, Katie and our friends in Berwick-upon-Tweed and Cawmills too."

The three young friends, Will Curtis, Emil Hahn, and Curtis Barkley, interrupted their parents. Will shouted, "We want to ride to the pond below the falls."

Robert glanced at Eleanor. "Two hours, no more. Return in time for supper. Change your clothes. And no swimming!"

Will pleaded, "We will be back in time. And not muddy. More of a bath than a swim."

Eleanor laughed. "Go then. No hedge jumping without an adult."

The boys were out the door. Robert asked, "What word from Karl and Johann?"

Katie replied, "There is hope. The Swedish Army has turned the tide. But our brothers and sisters are still in peril. Food is scarce, plague is widespread, and soldiers rob everyone. But God is good; praise His Name. He gives strength and comfort. It is well said, 'A mighty fortress is our God—and He shall win the battle!'"

Peter Hawkins came over, bowed, and said, "All is well with the trading company Lord Montclair, but a visit to Berwick-upon-Tweed would be well received by your many friends."

Robert gave a pat on the back of his young business protégé and replied, "And so I am being reminded. What a fine day this is for your mother and your family. I think your father, in heaven, looks down in joy and pride."

Edward Barkley, with Aidan Lilburn trailing, came over. "Robbie, a word with you. Aidan has a request."

Aidan looked down and stammered. "The lads have asked me to speak with…."

"Lads?" Robert asked.

He lifted his head and looked Robert in the eyes. "The Royal Cawmills Cuirassiers, we've joined up, as a company, with Colonel Hamilton's Regiment. We're going to join the fight. And the lads ask, with the full support of Lord Barkley, well, my Lord, we want you to lead us. You and Lord Barkley."

Robert turned to Eleanor….

ABOUT THE AUTHOR

David Martyn retired from a career in the Maritime industry and lives in Gig Harbor, Washington (nicknamed *The Maritime City*) with his wife Karen. David writes Christian fiction.

David's historical fiction series, *The Robert Curtis Mysteries*, take place during the 17th Century Thirty Years War (when the Church was at war with itself) and the lead up to English Civil War. These mysteries include: *Called Into Service, Soldiers of the King: the Bramshill Affair,* and *Lords and Ladies: the Banqueting House Plot.*

His Biblical series of novels, the 'Hall of Faith' series, include: *The Praise Singer: a Disciple of Melchizedek, The Oak of Weeping: the Story of Isaac, Deborah, and Rebekah, and The Epistle: a Story of the Early Church..* David also wrote a pocket novel, *Huldah and the Last Righteous King,* and a collection of short stories, *A Light in the Darkest Night.*

David's short stories can be found in Blue Forge Press anthologies: *Unconditional: Ten Stories of Enduring Love, Unnerving: Volume 2,* and *Unnerving: Volume 3.* A complete listing of David's works can be found on the website: blueforgepress.com